KÖNIGIN'S SOLUTION

KEITH SHERRY

Cover design by Ana Voicu
www.books-design.com

Book design by Maureen Cutajar
www.gopublished.com

ISBN: 978-1-7355088-0-1 (print)
ISBN: 978-1-7355088-1-8 (mobi)
ISBN: 978-1-7355088-2-5 (epub)

For Evette, Elexa and Mikaela

AUTHOR'S NOTE

My earliest notes for the development of *Königin's Solution* date back to the fall of 2011.

Between that time and the publication of this book, the world has changed in profound ways. And even as I write this Author's Note in August of 2020, I look at a rapidly changing world that is all at once struggling to cope with a pandemic and its economic and social consequences, along with civil unrest.

As you read *Königin's Solution*, you will see similarities to the life that we are now living, but what may seem like an intended coincidence, or even a blatant borrowing of a headline, are really nothing more than my telling of a future, in a conceptual sense, that I felt was inevitable. But even I am surprised by the extent to which reality has already caught up with certain aspects of my story. Thankfully, much of this tale remains wildly fantastical – at least for now.

In our current existence, most of us find it difficult to "catch our breath" emotionally, intellectually, and for some, spiritually. And for many, financially. But while the story that you are about to read contemplates those life challenges, *Königin's Solution* is not intended to be a cautionary story of impending doom, rather, it somewhat playfully (except in the darkest of scenes) questions our supposed "understanding" of authority and its legitimacy, our freedom, and our lack of self-responsibility and personal empowerment.

– Keith Sherry

1

Young David Clairet watched as the police interviewed his father at the family kitchen table. Königin, his older sister, gently stroked his hair with trembling hands as they looked onto the scene from the family room.

"Why are you wasting time interrogating *me* – you should be out there looking for *her*," Dr. Clairet shouted as he pointed out the window above the sink.

A detective sat across from the doctor while another stood with his arms crossed, the butt of his revolver poking out of the top of his pants.

"You can be sure everybody's looking for her, Dr. Clairet," the standing detective said. Then he lifted the blinds that hung above the kitchen sink window and looked out. "There's a dozen news trucks out there right now and about thirty reporters. When Pearl McCloud disappears, you can be sure the whole world is looking for her."

"Pearl McCloud-Clairet, detective," Dr. Clairet said, carefully enunciating the "t" in "Clairet."

"I don't get it, isn't the *t* silent in *Clairet?*" the sitting detective asked.

"No, it's not," Dr. Clairet answered. "And who cares, just find my wife."

"How come she never took your name when she was in the movies?" the same man asked.

"Who knows. I don't know. Why does any of this matter?" the doctor asked, putting his head in his hands.

"How come your eight-year-old daughter called the police about her going missing, instead of you?"

Dr. Clairet shook his head and said, "Well, Königin noticed her mother's absence before I did. I was very busy in my workshop all afternoon."

"She told the officer that took the call that she was banging on the door of your workshop, but you didn't open up," the standing detective said. "Your little girl thought you were both missing."

"I didn't hear her knocking. I was in the middle of testing a new device. I lose all sense of time and the existence of the rest of the world when I'm in there."

"A man should never let the thought of his family's well-being escape his mind, not even for a second. And especially on a day like today, with that strange phenomenon of silence occurring – the first thing I did was call my wife," the detective said, his arms still crossed.

David shivered at the mention of the silent moments that had enveloped the world earlier in the day. Königin hugged him and rubbed his arms.

"You're a science guy, right?" the sitting detective asked. "Isn't that what kind of doctor you are? Why do you think the whole world went silent for a few seconds today? What do you think that's all about?"

"Don't ask me that, detective. I just want my wife back. And their mother," he said, looking over at David and Königin. "The three of them are very close. Very close."

The detective leaned forward in his chair, his face only inches from Dr. Clairet's. "So you're pretty sure that she didn't make a lifestyle change?" he asked, using his fingers as quotation marks for the last two words of his sentence.

"What do you mean by that?" Dr. Clairet responded, wrinkling his forehead.

"You know, run off with some hot young actor. Or actress."

"Positively not, detective," Dr. Clairet shouted. "I'll ask you to stop that line of questioning immediately. Pearl is an incredibly fine woman."

"Must be the reason she got out of the movie business, right?" the detective asked, now sitting back in his chair.

"Yes, at least that was one of the reasons," Dr. Clairet answered.

"She took a lot of heat for her last picture, I remember," the standing detective said. "Pissed off a lot of powerful people. But that was a great movie – she deserved that Addorra. Didn't she also write and direct that one?"

Dr. Clairet nodded. "Yes, she did."

"I always forget the names of movies, what was that one called?" the sitting detective asked.

"*Critical Heart*," Königin answered, looking up at the crystal statuette stuffed on a crowded bookshelf next to many lesser film awards.

The detectives and Dr. Clairet looked over at her and David.

"Thank you, young lady," one of the detectives said, smiling.

"Look, this is going to be very tough for your kids, doctor," the standing detective said.

"Well, of course it's going to be very difficult for them. They've lost their mother," Dr. Clairet responded.

"No, I'm talking about them watching you go through what you're about to go through."

"What? You're arresting me? Based on what?" Dr. Clairet asked, now raising his voice.

David started to cry and Königin squeezed him tight to her keep herself from crying. "Take it easy, Dr. Clairet – I'm not accusing you of anything."

"Then what are you talking about, detective?"

The detective pointed at the window. "I don't need to see one second of the news tonight or one word in tomorrow's newspaper to know that you stand accused of your wife's demise. And I don't need to tell you that the press is going to set up two sides, both starring you – the gentle, heartbroken husband versus Pearl McCloud's wicked spouse who got rid of her. They'll be on both sides of the bet, and they don't care which side anyone takes, so long as they take a side. The truth and the outcome won't even matter."

Dr. Clairet slumped in his chair and lowered his head.

Königin ignored the lump in her throat. Somewhere, in her little heart, she knew to stay away from those feelings that were trying to creep up. And she told herself that her father needed her to be strong.

2

London is cold and rainy in the springtime. But like every general rule, exceptions surprise, and the sun unnaturally warmed the air on that Sunday.

"Am I God? Are you God? Perhaps we are all God," said a man standing on a rusted little stepladder, challenging the two people that stood in front of him.

"But would we even know it if we were God?" he continued. "How can we know, how can we be sure? We can't know," he shouted.

The speaker was just one of a dozen speakers in Hyde Park that day, all pitching and preaching something. Like everyone else in London, he hadn't expected the sun, and sweat stains pressed through the armpits of his oversized tweed jacket.

The Crown owned the park. Hundreds of years earlier, near the very spot where the speaker now stood, thousands of people had been hung at the end of a rope from the Tyburn Tree – one of London's busiest gallows.

"You can't prove that I'm not Lucifer!" the speaker shouted, pointing at the man and woman standing only a few feet from him. "You can't prove that you're not Lucifer. You can't. You can't prove anything, anything at all."

Königin rolled her eyes and smiled.

"Oh, I saw that. I saw it," the speaker shouted. "You're a know-it-all, are you? Hear me – you're the worst kind there is."

Königin turned to her friend, Jess, and squinted at him.

Now the speaker pointed at Königin and shouted, "You people never look and you never see. You're blinded by your own stubborn delusion. Did you ever stop and think? Ever stop and question, my smug friends? Oh, how you stand there, mocking me – looking at me like I'm a lunatic. You're the lunatics, you sprinting runners. Running, running, always running to this and running away from that."

Anyone with a voice could preach to the people and admonish them at Speakers' Corner. Many of the speakers shouted about politics, human rights, and governments. Some were just mad but treated to a willing audience, nonetheless. Before the condemned were hanged from the Tyburn Tree, they were permitted to speak their last truths – and Speakers' Corner was the descendent of that right.

"What's wrong my pretty twentysomething, have I made you uncomfortable?" the speaker asked Königin in a taunting voice.

Königin forced her hands as far into the front pockets of her jeans as they would go, her arms now straight and her shoulders raised. She looked down at her boots.

"Good, that's my job. I have succeeded." The speaker jumped up and down on the top of his little ladder, wringing his hands. He smiled widely. "Don't be afraid of that feeling, my girl, embrace it – it's the only way to get there."

"Let's go, I can't listen to this," Königin said to Jess.

"Why? He's just getting started," Jess answered.

She started to walk away, her arms crossed and her head low.

"The truth will follow you," the speaker called after her. "And soon you'll think my scolding is a delight compared to what's coming."

Königin kept walking, not looking back.

"Good day, Mr. Speaker," Jess said as he began to follow Königin.

The speaker shouted, "Good day? What's a good day? What's good? Tell me, my little prophet, what is good? And what is bad? Answer me those questions and I'll abdicate my throne forever."

Jess stopped and turned around. "Abdicate your throne?" He smiled and connected with the speaker's eyes. "You'll abdicate the throne that you seated yourself on? Is that a legitimate throne, sir? What is a legitimate throne, I ask you?"

The speaker's smile faded, and he looked at the young man with a glassy stare.

"Very good. Very good, my boy," the speaker said, slowly.

Königin tugged at Jess's hand. "Come on, let's get out of here, I want to get to the Water Pavilion – and I don't want to argue with this loon – he scares me."

Jess turned back to Königin and they began to walk.

"He should scare you," Jess said. "Don't dismiss his words so quickly – he's not necessarily a loon. It's dangerous to classify people as crazy just to make yourself feel better. You don't have to agree with what you're hearing, but don't miss the messages in those words. Canary in a coal mine, you know what I mean?"

Königin just shook her head and said nothing.

3

The speaker continued to call out to Königin and Jess as they walked away, but his scratchy voice evaporated behind them. They walked the edge of the Serpentine, a bent pond in Hyde Park named for its snakelike shape.

Königin listened to the faint murmur of life in the park, punctuated with bursts of laughter and the playful shrieks of children.

As they approached the old brick art gallery sitting near the Serpentine and sharing its name, Königin and Jess stopped abruptly when the Water Pavilion came into view. Throughout the previous century, temporary buildings constructed of metals and woods, plastics and ceramics, and fabrics and glass had stood next to and in the shadow of the gallery, built to host exhibits of that day's thinkers. But now the gallery stood in the shadow of a creation towering high above the park, far taller than any other before it. Banners of different colors flew from the top of the thing.

"It's even scarier looking than I thought it would be," Königin said, unable to unfix her eyes from the structure standing in front of her.

Keeping her feet planted, she leaned in toward the ninety-foot tall building as if she were studying it with her body.

Jess shook his head and smiled. He turned to Königin and put his hand on her shoulder. "Look at you, look what you did," he said.

"What are you talking about, Jess? I didn't do this."

"Okay, whatever. Let's go check this out," he said, starting to walk without her. Annoyed, Königin walked quickly to catch up with him.

Hundreds of visitors surrounded the Water Pavilion. Columns of people walking in single file entered and exited the pavilion to and from immediately forming openings of parted water in the sides of the structure, which then vanished in an instant to become a solid sheet of water again. But the pulsating water had a solid quality to it – not a drop was dripped, and each corner and bend of the pavilion was hard and decisive like steel.

From far above Hyde Park, looking down, a celestial observer would witness humanity clamoring to see what should be seen – a liquid marvel as the epicenter of intense interest, a radiating march of those coming and going in and out of the Water Pavilion.

The building was surrounded by a moat of flowing water, with foot bridges made of firm water that spontaneously formed over the moat when an opening in the wall of the pavilion appeared. When the last foot of a group of people stepped off a bridge, the smacking of falling sheets of water echoed the abrupt disappearance of the bridge. Orderly movement of visitors in and out of the pavilion over the bridges suggested careful orchestration and most certain timing. What initially seemed chaotic quickly took on a rhythm of timed, fluid discipline very sure of itself.

"Wow," Jess said. "Now I see why you love playing with water so much. Quite cool."

"I don't play with water, Jess. I just try to make it cooperate so we can easily get it to people who need it," Königin said.

As the two approached the moat, a small covered bridge instantly formed over it, connecting the pavilion to a platform next to them. Wide and tall, a rounded double door formed in the wall of the pavilion at the other end of the bridge.

Königin squinted and peered, trying to see through the somewhat translucent doors made of water.

When the doors did finally open after a few moments, a gangly fellow filling out a well-tailored dark suit started over the bridge. He walked slowly and deliberately, settling his eyes on Königin. She quickly looked away and crossed her arms as this man and his small entourage approached her and Jess.

"Take a look at this suave guy," Jess said in a low voice while he still could.

"Oh, shut up. Please don't be a jerk. Why did I bring you?" she whispered back.

"Hello, hello, hello – welcome," Tad Corliss shouted, both arms opened in greeting but obviously devoid of any intention to hug.

"Jess Frank," Jess announced, reaching for Corliss's hand. Corliss heartily returned the handshake but kept his eyes fixed on Königin.

"And this," Jess motioned with his free hand, "is Ms. Königin Clairet."

"Yes, of course, I know that Mr. Frank, but I appreciate your kind introduction."

Corliss's narrow face filled her vision, his smile beamed.

"Königin, Königin, it's so wonderful to meet you and to have you here," Tad Corliss said in a quiet voice, only inches from her face. He was holding both of her hands down near her waist.

"You'll be so delighted with what we've done with your ideas," he said, motioning across the moat. "I'm so pleased to share it all with you today. We'll chat after the tour of the Water Pavilion, but first, I want you to address the press and the public visiting the exhibit."

Königin's eyes widened and the color left her red lips. Corliss put his arm around her shoulder and began to lead her to the corner of the moat. Looking back, she searched for Jess who was walking right behind her. He shrugged his shoulders and smiled at her. When she looked ahead, Königin saw six broad columns of water rising and then swirling and then forming a platform, and on that, a pulpit decorated with filigree of coursing water.

"I really don't want to say anything. I have nothing to say, please don't make me speak, Mr. Corliss," Königin said in a high pitch. She tried to gently pull away from him, but he held her tight around the shoulder.

"Mr. Corliss, perhaps Königin should just tour the pavilion now," Jess said. Königin looked at Corliss for his reaction.

"Nonsense, nonsense. She missed her moment this morning with the prime minister but she's not going to miss her moment now," Corliss said.

Corliss faced Königin and again took her hands in his, saying, "It's all about getting to the people, Königin. Get them to love you. Even better, get them to need you – then they'll be yours." Corliss took a deep breath and prepared to address the crowd of people waiting in line to cross the moat and enter the pavilion through the visitor's entrance.

"As chairman of the Association of Comprehensive Solutions, I ask you all if you wish to hear from Ms. Königin Clairet, the genius whose ideas brought you this exhibition hall made of controllable water, the woman whose command of science over nature will change your lives. A blossoming goddess providing answers to the most pressing problems of the day."

Königin saw Jess roll his eyes. She answered the erupting cheers with her head hung, looking at the ground, dreading what was to come.

"Listen Königin, you don't need to do anything you don't want to do. Don't speak if you don't want to," Jess said.

Still looking down, Königin said, "You know, Mr. Corliss, I think I'll tour the pavilion first and then maybe address the crowd."

"Oh, of course, no problem, Ms. Clairet," Corliss said.

"Thank you for understanding, Mr. Corliss. I really don't know what to say to these people. I'll just ramble on and they'll know what a fraud I am," she said laughing, now relieved.

"Yes, of course," Corliss said, then adding, "It was a wonderful scene this morning, I'm sorry you weren't able to join us."

"Yes, me too. I saw it on television, it looked quite amazing," Königin said, immediately wishing she hadn't said that. She saw in Corliss's face that he decided to ignore the comment that suggested her deliberate truancy.

"It was great to meet your father this morning," Corliss said to Königin. "He's a brilliant man and a wonderful speaker."

"Hopefully he was able to please the crowd," Königin said, feeling Corliss's little pinch.

"Oh, yes, he did. He was splendid, so magnetic."

Königin smiled at Corliss but said nothing. Jess looked straight up at the sky.

Corliss shrugged his shoulders and said, "Well, I guess we'll just go into the Water Pavilion now. The global solution technology being exhibited by the participating innovators will make you feel like an underachiever. You'll enjoy your father's contribution."

"I'm sure I will," she said. Jess nodded in agreement but rolled his eyes at the same time.

Königin began to walk in the direction of the bridge that Corliss had walked over, but Corliss did not follow. Instead, he called after Königin, "Ms. Clairet, Ms. Clairet." She stopped, turned around and slowly walked back toward him.

"You know, I'm just thinking, it would be helpful to get your comments out of the way now," Corliss said. "I'd like to just check the box and have it off my list, you understand, right?"

Königin didn't respond. She wanted to run.

"Look, whatever's best for you, Ms. Clairet, really, it's no problem – whatever you want to do," Corliss said.

Königin watched Corliss's eyes shift from her face to something beyond her. "Ah, it looks like the press is packing up," he said, his raised eyebrows betraying a hint of defeat. "Oh well, no matter," he said.

"Mr. Corliss, I'm so sorry, but I don't like talking about my ideas or me or my unqualified opinion. I don't like hearing myself through the loudspeaker – I can't even stand the sound of my own voice," Königin said.

"Yes, of course, of course, I really understand, Ms. Clairet." Corliss sounded sad. "Forgive me for even bringing it up again," he continued. "I owe you an apology for that. It's just that so many people worked so hard for this day, me included, and all of the other exhibitors spoke, you know, kind of feeling like it was their responsibility." Corliss spoke slowly and quietly, looking down at his shoes. "And to have your father and you publicly endorse the exhibit and the Association and its work would have just meant so much after how much of my life this has consumed." He then looked up at Königin and said, "Just ask my poor wife."

"Oh, Mr. Corliss," Königin said. "I really don't want to disappoint you. If it's really that important, I guess I can say just a couple of words."

Before she could even finish her sentence, Corliss had ascended the stairs to the platform and was now standing at the pulpit. Immediately, the crowd quieted down. In the press area, the cameras took aim.

"Ladies and gentlemen, members of the press, and citizens of the world around, I want to thank you all for your interest in our Comprehensive Solutions Exposition as well as this beautifully designed pavilion of water which houses some of the most important technological innovations of our time. This exposition will have an everlasting impact on humanity in only the best of ways. You have all patiently waited and watched today as various exhibitors have come and spoken, and now I have the privilege of introducing the woman whose ideas led to the harnessing of water – ideas that have allowed us to make water into structures which would otherwise be built from solid materials, now opening the door to endless possibilities. I'm confident that her many creations in the years to come will delight and inspire the world and help all of humanity. And in these difficult times, when a beacon of light is hard to find, let it be found in technology. With the world's problems seeming insurmountable, and the unrest and unhappiness and strife of humanity greater than ever before, we must demand contributions from minds like Ms. Clairet's, for the betterment of all. Having said that, I am honored to introduce the young and talented, and as of yet, unsung hero of modern science, Ms. Königin Clairet."

Again, Königin wanted to run. The applause just made it worse. She looked up at Corliss as he descended from the platform, nodding to her. Königin now looked up at the beautiful water pulpit, and then at her feet, and then she looked at Jess. He motioned to her to go up the pulsating stairs of water, as if to say, "Go ahead, you agreed."

Königin slowly put her right foot on the first step. She pulled her head up and slowly climbed the stairs, forcing a smile when she reached the top. She looked down at the people before her, a sea of heads waiting for her words. She didn't know what to say. She wasn't even sure of what she was thinking at that very moment.

Pulling the microphone close to her mouth, Königin anticipated her own words, not knowing what was going to come out.

"Thank you all so much for coming," she said in a quiet voice that echoed throughout Hyde Park. She looked at the Water Pavilion and said, "It's beautiful. I never imagined that something like that would be built from what I envisioned, although it's really not a use that I had ever thought of for my technology." Her eyes shifted and squinted and her mouth tightened at the corners. "In fact – and it's okay – but I'm a little surprised by the creative liberties taken with my technology."

Before Königin could speak another word, a collective gasp rose up from the crowd. In the thinnest slice of time, Königin realized that she was the focus of that gasp, and she was now looking straight up at the sky, lying on her back in a shallow pool of water. The pulpit and stairs were gone – dissolved.

Then Königin's view of the sky was blocked by Jess's face looking down at her, his eyes wide.

"Königin, are you okay, can you hear me? Königin," he yelled.

She felt Jess try to cradle the back of her head, but he jerked his hand back, looking at the blood dripping from his fingers. "Oh, Königin, no," he said.

4

Königin lay in her hospital bed, her head aching. Her father had not yet come to visit her since the accident the day before, but she knew that he was busy entertaining a group of inventors in from the United States. She figured he would show up sooner or later, when he could.

She fidgeted in her bed like a restless child. The thought of not getting any work done tormented Königin.

Even under her covers, she was cold in her hospital gown. The room was bright, but all color was washed from the walls, leaving only variations of gray.

Königin briefly thought about getting up and leaving – just getting dressed and walking out of the hospital. She figured that she was fine, but she wasn't sure, and she knew that she wasn't supposed to walk out. Königin didn't want to break any of the hospital's rules.

After eating breakfast and turning the television on and off a few times, she was defeated by boredom. She surrendered by giving herself over to *The Whole Truth Trustee* newspaper sitting at the foot of her bed, still neatly folded and untouched. Königin leaned forward and pulled it toward her with her fingertips.

It was printed in nearly 100 different languages around the planet. The readers of *The Whole Truth Trustee* paid nothing for the newspaper, other than with their time and attention and trust. In cities around the world, the publication could be found sitting in stacks at bus stops, outside of office buildings and in the lobbies of apartment buildings. Deliveries of the paper were made to soup kitchens and the growing encampments of homeless families under bridges and inside of abandoned buildings.

Königin didn't care for *The Trustee*, but she knew that most people liked it, appreciating that it gave two sides of most stories. Depending on the reader's viewpoint, the paper would be read from one side or the other – it had two first pages and no last page and it just needed to be closed and flipped around to get to the side that the reader wanted.

Within five years of the newspaper's appearance, the circulation was well over one billion. Countless printing plants produced the newspaper and efficiently spread the paper out around the planet every single morning, without fail.

Königin was aware of a general sense of annoyance that she felt whenever she saw the paper, since it seemed to fall into her field of vision so many times during the day. And her favorite newspaper, *The International Informer*, had been acquired by *The Trustee*'s parent, The Whole Truth Information Trust, and then quietly liquidated.

The Trustee was printed on paper that was practically transparent, like tracing paper, and it had a coarse matte finish. Königin briefly shivered as she began unfolding the newspaper.

For the first time, Königin gave her full attention to the newspaper. She studied the masthead across the top, noticing the globe to the right of the newspaper's name. The globe was tilted on its side with longitudinal lines running up and down the continents, and Europe was highlighted on the globe, as this was the English language European Edition.

Looking closely, Königin saw a very thin ring of text surrounding the equator of the tilted world. It read, "For a World That's Split in Two, We Bring You Both Sides."

Still studying the masthead, she could just barely make out the Great Lakes of North America since she had the European Edition and the North American continent was mostly faced away from her. But seeing those lakes, those huge freshwater bodies, reminded her of her water project and her technology and what she hoped to accomplish with it. Königin gently touched Lake Huron with the tip of her left index finger, and with her right index finger, she tapped on sub-Saharan Africa. "I'll get you there," she said quietly to herself.

Without warning, the thought of what had transpired the day before crept into Königin's mind. Her head pounded again. Trying to distract herself, she quickly scanned the top half of the front page for anything that would catch her interest, but nothing did. She flipped a few pages, only to be met by a picture of herself staring back at her. It took Königin a second or two before she could understand that she was looking at herself in the newspaper.

The article was titled, *Young Hydro-physicist Injured By Her Own Invention.* Instantly she felt her face heat up. "My invention?" she thought.

"I hate that picture," Königin said out loud. For a moment, she actually considered not reading the short article, but she knew that she had to.

LONDON, ENGLAND

The Comprehensive Solutions Exposition, which opened yesterday in London's Hyde Park, welcomed Ms. Königin Clairet, 27, the creator of the exposition's temporary home known as the Water Pavilion. Ms. Clairet suffered a concussion when the controlled liquid platform on which he was perched during a presentation to the press and public abruptly collapsed.

The technology, developed by Ms. Clairet, allows the control of water as a solid without changing its physical liquid qualities.

The young hydro-physicist could not be reached for comment, but Tad Corliss, the chairman of the Association of Comprehensive Solutions, explained that Ms. Clairet's technology was deployed according to her exact plans and specifications. He further expressed regret that "She was injured by the failure of her own work."

Königin flung the newspaper against the wall and pulled her covers over her head.

She dozed off half an hour later, but not before thinking about how many times she had seen her father's picture in the newspapers and on television after her mother disappeared.

5

Jess rented a small room in a row house in Brixton, south of the River Thames. His cold little cell with its complaining floorboards had briefly served as the offices of the European Bureau of *Indie Voices Weekly*, a magazine dedicated to musical freedom.

Jess's tired suede western-style jacket, complete with dangling fringe, rested on a hanger suspended by a make-shift broomstick clothes rack. Below, on the floor, a pair of saddle brown squared-toed boots waited. Next to them were neatly folded jeans and then two stacks of plain t-shirts, black and white.

Then there was the wooden desk, etched with many sets of initials, darkened by time. It was too big for a child yet too small for an adult. A matt-black spiral notebook sat next to a sharpened pencil and a ball point pen. The desk was otherwise empty.

Jess carefully tucked his bed sheet under the corner of his mattress. Then he did the same with the other three corners. He looked at the flat white sheet on the bed with its straight sides and its four corners – it reminded him of a fresh piece of unlined paper.

After methodically placing his notebook and pencil and pen in his canvass messenger bag, Jess threw his jacket on like a cape and buckled up his boots.

As he stepped out into the upstairs hallway of the narrow old house, the sound of the television rushed at him with sirens and shouting. The commotion grew louder as he banged down the wooden stairs.

"Now what's happening in this crazy world?" Jess asked his landlord, a wrinkled little man sitting only two feet from the television.

"Smoke bomb on the trading floor of the New York Stock Exchange. Look – they've all emptied out onto Wall and Broad."

Jess watched but said nothing.

"Apparently, somebody called in a bomb threat. The exchange shut down and all the traders went running for their lives."

"At least no one was killed," Jess said, staring at the images on the television.

"I wouldn't say *that*," the old man said. "The market dropped several thousand points before they could halt trading – all on account of some smoke."

6

"They took my work and used it to make a parlor trick," Königin said, shaking her head.

Jess didn't respond. The sounds of central London echoed between the floor and high ceilings of Dr. Clairet's flat.

"I developed my technology so we could move massive amounts of water from one place to another, to help people." Königin said. "I was never interested in constructing buildings out of water or bridges out of water or doors out of water. I go and lend the Association my technology to include in their exposition and they build a monstrosity with it. People appearing and disappearing through doors that appear and disappear – the whole thing looks like a contraption that eats people and spits them out."

Jess sat down next to Königin on her bed but still didn't say anything.

"And what a waste of money," she continued. "We funded most of the Comprehensive Solutions Exposition and we can't even afford to rebuild Miami."

"We?" Jess asked.

"Yes, *we*, Jess – the United States. You know what I meant – our home across the Atlantic that doesn't even have enough money for hurricane disaster relief."

They sat in silence for a couple of minutes.

"I know," Königin said, not looking at Jess. "You warned me not to get involved with that whole thing, but I'm trying to get things going again and I figured that being involved in the exposition couldn't hurt."

"All I said was that you're flailing and that being part of the exposition wasn't going to change that," Jess said.

"Jess, I'm stalled, and I need to do something – anything. If I can't defend my dissertation, I'm dead in the water. My doctoral committee is set on denying me my title, and they're probably right to – I'm sure they know better than me."

"No, they don't," Jess said, laughing. "They're just a bunch of jealous assholes that are pissed off that you have more great ideas in a lock of your hair than they'll ever have amongst their entire cabal. Forget about titles and stop asking for permission to be great."

Königin looked up at the ceiling. "You just don't get it, Jess."

Jess stood up off the bed and faced her. "You're the one that doesn't get it, Königin. Let me give you a quick history lesson and explain how you fit in. The stories of most civilizations that have existed and perished on this planet are fairly similar. You want to know why? Because the personalities and infirmities of the characters are all the same – like a disease that can't be cured. The insecure and the petty would rather sink their own societies than see the brilliant minds flourish. From era to era, people don't change – and our punishment is that we suffer the same fate over and over again. Jealous mediocrity works hard to discredit and hold down those that would actually help us, while raising up false saviors instead. Königin, for those people that seek to erect barriers in your path, their biggest fear is that you'll succeed – even though your success would benefit them. You're letting them stifle you, Königin. Just do what you need to do in this life. And start by getting the water to where it's needed, one way or another."

Königin jumped off the other side of the bed and faced Jess. He could see a light sheen of sweat forming on her face.

"You make it sound so easy, but even if I wanted to, how could I? Who would listen to me? I looked like a fool lying on my ass in a pool of water at the exposition," Königin said, her voice cracking a little.

Jess flopped himself back on the bed and said, "Don't dwell on that. Who cares? I wouldn't let it bother me a bit."

"Then there's something wrong with you," Königin said. "I don't enjoy looking like a fool. It's hard enough to get people's respect in the world and an episode like that doesn't help."

Jess leaned back and put his arms behind his head. "I play the fool often, and it's a role I relish. You should try it sometime." Then, in the voice of a southern minister, he said, "Release yourself from the bondage of public opinion."

"Well, isn't that convenient for you? Everybody expects you to be the fool. Face it Jess, you're not the most popular guy. If your philosophy is to not care about what people think of you, I applaud you, you are unshackled." And then Königin's face relieved into a big smile and she laughed at her own words.

Jess sat up and said, "Wow, who knew you had it in you to be such a hard-ass."

"I surprise *myself* sometimes," she said, still laughing.

The dull sunshine creeping in through the windows suddenly dimmed as the clouds took over. The room darkened.

"I'm glad you're in London," Königin said. "At least for a little while, until I get sick of you."

"Please, don't try to flatter me. You just needed a fool in your life."

Königin rolled her eyes. "No, I already have plenty of them."

Jess stood up and took his coat from the chair. "I'm taking off. I'm going to Otto Veltraria's concert tonight."

"Nice, those press credentials pay off, don't they? That's an impossible ticket to get," Königin said.

"My press credentials were revoked. Someone in the press suite is sneaking me in."

"That doesn't sound good," Königin said. What happened?"

"Apparently you need to be a working journalist to keep your credentials."

Königin looked at Jess, her forehead wrinkled in confusion. "I thought everyone from *Indie Voices* was getting rolled into *The Whole Truth Trustee* – what happened?"

"They said that my writing was dry – all facts and no spin – my articles wouldn't have a place on either side of the newspaper."

Königin's face blushed and Jess could see that she didn't know what to say.

"So they fired me. Who cares? I wouldn't even light a bonfire with *The Trustee*," Jess said loudly.

"But what are you going to do? You're a reporter and there's nowhere else for you to go," Königin said with her hands on her hips.

"I'll figure it out. Don't worry about me."

Königin took a deep breath and shook her head slowly.

"Hey listen, do you want to go to the show with me? I'm sure we can both get in."

She nodded quickly and told Jess that she had to first take a shower.

Jess slung his bag over his shoulder and spoke as he walked out of her bedroom. "Make it quick, Königin, I don't want to miss the opening number. Besides, no amount of showering will get you clean." He heard a sarcastic "Ha, ha," as he walked down the hall to the living room.

The huge old flat was still. Jess stretched out on the hard leather sofa, his boots resting on the arm.

The photographs hanging on the walls were painted in the red of the sinking sun coming through the tall picture windows.

Jess lay there, thinking how empty and lifeless the flat was. It was a big place for just one man to live by himself. Jess wondered whether the doctor was happy when his daughter showed up and took the guest room for her own.

After a few minutes, he stood up and slowly walked around the living room, as if he were in a museum. Jess looked Dr. Clairet's grandfather clock up and down. Then he turned his attention to the photographs of the people in the doctor's life. He found only one picture of Königin and her brother – it was from when they were kids. They weren't smiling. Then he looked for pictures of Pearl McCloud. There were none.

Jess jumped when the first chime of the grandfather clock rang out. Then he stood still and calmly listened to each inevitable toll, one after another. Looking at his wristwatch, he observed that the clock was running nearly eight minutes fast. In the silence that followed, Jess pondered how a man who was considered a technological genius could tolerate such inaccuracy.

7

The press suite was packed. There wasn't a single reviewer or entertainment reporter from *The Trustee* absent.

"Jess, hello, hello, lovely to be with you at this wonderful event. How've you been? Who's your gorgeous girl? Hadn't heard you had such a girlfriend," the jolly fellow said, looking Königin up and down quite obviously.

"Take it easy," Jess said. "This is my friend Königin. Her good taste in men precludes me from consideration."

"Oh stop it Jess, you're a beautiful boy and your friend shouldn't hesitate to consider you–"

Königin interrupted. "John Candle, right? Author of *The Fourteenth Tail?*"

"The same, my exquisite lady," Candle said, bowing slightly in a yellow outfit that resembled a kimono.

"Well, I enjoyed your book," she said, hesitating somewhat. "I really liked it."

"You've no doubt read it, Jess, haven't you?" John Candle asked.

"No. Not my thing," Jess answered.

"Not your thing? The most beautiful love story ever written is not your thing?" Candle wafted his arms in the air, his many rings glowing.

"I'm confident that your self-critique is a bit of a stretch – no – actually a huge stretch," Jess said.

John stared hard at Jess, but Jess returned the look, holding his ground. Königin looked away.

"I say you're just a rude boy, aren't you?" John Candle mock-scolded, having dismissed his initial anger. "Don't you know you're not supposed to say things like that, Jess Frank? It makes you ugly. And no one wants that." Then John walked off and found someone else to talk to.

"What was that, Jess?" Königin asked.

"What?" Jess responded, his eyes wide.

"Attacking John Candle like that."

"Lay off, Königin, that's who I am."

Suddenly the crowd in the Royal Albert Hall roared as a few organ keys clinked.

"Besides, *The Fourteenth Tail* is nothing but sugary garbage consumed by people with a sweet tooth," Jess said.

"So? Despite how you feel about his book you should've been polite and found something complimentary to say – even if you had to lie," Königin said. "He's an important guy and you shouldn't piss him off. Maybe he can get you a job." Her demeanor had calmed to one of concern.

Jess shook his head and laughed. "I don't waste words saying what isn't true."

The lights of the hall went down and the thick sound of a bass, the steely pop of electric guitars and the deep notes of the hall's tall organ pipes rose above the din of cheers.

Königin and Jess walked out onto the press suite's balcony, pushing their way to the railing.

"I've never seen so many journalists out here," Jess said. "They usually hang out inside and eat and drink and drink."

"It's understandable," Königin said, "Nobody wants to miss this guy."

"I know, that's what worries me," Jess said.

In the center of the stage, Otto Veltraria sat behind a keyboard and pumped a rock-gospel rhythm through the nearly 10,000 pipes of the organ that were perched above and to the sides of him. He sang in a deep, calm voice:

There's a rumble in this world
And a dark that's come unfurled
That thunder shaking beneath our feet
It knows nothing of a steady beat

Raise your fists to the sky
Raise your fists so high

You try to live with a little grace
That icy wind blowing in your face
Why should it all be so hard?
For what sin were we dealt this card?

Raise 'em up, raise 'em up to the sky
Raise 'em up so damn high

The audience's obedient silence was snapped with the first praise of a whistle, followed by an explosion of loud gratitude. Otto took a sip from his water bottle and nodded in acknowledgement.

"Are you kidding me? Königin, do you believe this? What a load of shit," Jess said, shaking his head and laughing.

"Come on Jess, shut up, what's your problem? Everybody loves him," Königin said. "You're so dramatic," she continued, before quickly motioning to Jess to stop talking by covering her mouth with the tips of two slender fingers. But the two soon realized that they were being watched by those journalists and guests who did not share Jess's critique of Veltraria's song.

"Now you've done it! I won't take it. I haven't a care if you wish to scurrilously attack my work, but attack Otto Veltraria? No, no," John Candle said. He was on a roll and he had an audience. The group surrounding them applauded him. "I suggest that you and your too-pretty-for-you friend watch the show from another locale, perhaps with the good people in steerage," John said. Before Jess could protest, Königin had begun to pull him out of the press suite to the sound of more applause for John Candle's brave stand. They exited the suite amid spitting insults, but no one confronted Jess or Königin directly – the words were tossed at them like little grenades by people that distanced themselves from the words as soon as possible.

"That worked out great, Jess. Where to now, genius?" Königin asked.

"Sorry. We'll find seats somewhere," Jess said.

But after half an hour of repeatedly being denied seats, they walked the ramps and climbed the stairs that took them to the topmost level of the hall. Königin used the railings and moved a little slow.

"Are you hurting from your fall?" Jess asked.

"Yeah, a little. Just so you know, if we were on a first date, I would never go out with you again," Königin said.

"Then lucky for me this isn't a date," Jess said.

"Tickets. I'll need to check your tickets," an usher said.

Jess shook his head. "Are you kidding me? These are the worst seats in the place," Jess said, motioning down at the steeply sloped seats. But as he did, he noticed that every single seat was filled.

"I'm sorry, sir, but you can't sit up here without a ticket." There wasn't a hint of tone in her voice.

Jess hesitated and then said, "Okay, I understand, thank you."

"Come on, Jess, let's just get out of here," Königin said.

"No, no, I have another idea."

Jess led Königin down a couple of hallways which were successively narrower than the preceding hallway, until they came to a short service ladder. Königin looked up.

"Oh no, Jess. This isn't for me. My head still hurts from my last adventure."

Jess smiled, "But that was your fault, wasn't it? That defective technology of yours."

Königin crossed her arms and looked down.

"Oh lighten up. Just follow me." Jess climbed up the short ladder and went through the opening in the ceiling. He poked his head back down and extended his hand to Königin. After a moment, she quickly climbed up the ladder and slapped his hand away as soon as it was in reach.

"Ow. I think you broke a nail," Jess said, smiling at her.

"Shut up, Jess. What are we going to do now, smoke cigarettes?"

"Good idea, but no. Follow."

Jess led Königin on a catwalk high above the stage of the great oval hall.

The two sat next to each other on the steel walkway, their legs dangling. They looked down at Otto singing to a praying crowd, on the very same stage that Winston Churchill had rallied an audience during the Second World War.

The music quieted down and Otto paced the edge of the stage with a microphone in his hand.

"So, who needs a hand?" he said to the crowd in a low voice.

A blend of shouted responses filled the place. "Me! I do!" and "Over here, I need a hand!"

Otto waved his hand high above his head. A collective cry of joy answered.

"Oh, no. Not again," Jess said, now covering his eyes.

"I can see the Water Pavilion from here," Königin said, craning her neck to see through the glass roof of the hall. Jess dropped his hand and looked too.

"Come on, Königin." Jess jumped up. "Let's go see your monstrosity."

She shook her head back and forth. "No, no, don't make me." She closed her eyes and smiled.

"Let's go, you'll get us in. Hey, if they're going to blame you for that thing, they should at least let you in."

8

"We're honored to open the Water Pavilion for you, Mr. Veltraria," Tad Corliss said.

"Please, call me Otto – or Mr. Veltraria, if you're more comfortable with that."

"Yes, of course," Corliss responded.

The water hissed as they crossed over a suddenly appearing bridge across the moat. Otto walked slowly, testing his footing as he took each step. By the time Otto's entourage reached the open doors to the pavilion, which were now in the shape of two huge musical notes, Otto's steps were sure, and his back was stiff and straight and his strides reaching.

The main hall had been configured for the visit of a dignitary. Gone were the flowing and lighted apparatus to move the people around.

Otto stood the collar up on his black polo shirt and handed his jean jacket to one of his attendants. This was the outfit he had closed the concert with.

A blue line appeared in the dry water floor – it was an arrow indicating the proper direction to move in. Otto giggled, and then Corliss gently took him by the arm and the two proceeded down the line with Otto's people following.

"This place is remarkable," Otto said in a quiet voice, looking up and surveying the temporary cathedral-like ceiling. "I've never seen anything like this. How can water be solid without being ice? The possibilities are limitless."

"Indeed, they are," Corliss agreed.

"So, how does it work?" Otto asked.

"What?"

"You know, making the water solid and then liquid again – and then solid again?"

"It's very complicated," Corliss answered. "Lots of physics and molecular engineering."

Otto stopped walking. He turned to Corliss and smiled. "You don't know, do you?"

"Pardon me, sir?" A little sweat perched on Corliss's upper lip.

"You don't know how it works, do you, Mr. Corliss? You have no idea how this technology works, do you?"

"You know, I'm not a scientist, Mr. Veltraria. I just have a basic understanding of the concepts at work here."

"Very well then," Otto said. "If you don't know the answer to my question, just tell me. Don't try to talk over me. It won't work, I promise you. Understand?"

"Yes, yes, of course. My apologies, Mr. Veltraria." Again, Corliss lowered his head. But his apology was devoid of remorse and he carried an air of confidence even when wrong.

A throbbing blue light projecting from the liquid ceiling hanging high above the group made the great room feel icy. Otto reached out to touch a liquid wall next to him, but he hesitated and kept his index finger half an inch from the pulsating but solid water wall.

"Go ahead, Mr. Veltraria. It won't hurt you," Corliss said, smiling.

Otto looked at Corliss and frowned. He dropped his arm to his side. "And even if it did hurt, who cares? I'm not afraid of pain, Mr. Corliss. At least not physical pain," Otto said.

"Then, sir, you are braver than me. I'm afraid of pain. Any kind of pain," Corliss said, smiling.

The configuration of the room shifted and the cathedral ceiling quickly fell lower and now flattened out. Otto and his people ducked, but Corliss didn't move. Clearly, he'd seen this trick before.

"Son-of-a-bitch. I thought that ceiling was coming right down on us," Otto said.

"I know, it's quite an illusion, is it not?" Corliss said.

Otto ran his hand through his long hair and then looked at his hand. A slight sheen of water reflected off of his fingertips.

"Don't be alarmed, Mr. Veltraria, the technology does yield small amounts of liquid from time to time," Corliss said.

Otto looked up at the newly formed ceiling now suspended not too far above his head. "I see."

In front of the group, a round concrete pedestal quickly pushed through the floor and came to rest. A long, thin, rust brown rod came through an opening in the ceiling and balanced on its end on the pedestal. The hole in the ceiling disappeared.

Otto looked at Corliss.

"Doesn't look like much, does it, Mr. Veltraria?" Corliss asked.

"It looks like crappy, expensive art. I should know – I've got seven homes filled with garbage that looks like this." Otto's people chuckled, but not too much.

"I don't doubt it, Mr. Veltraria," Corliss said, smiling. Otto ignored him.

Otto noticed that the narrow end of the rod floated just half an inch above pedestal.

"Clever. The rod levitates," Otto said, rolling his eyes. "You must have better than that."

"Oh, we do. That's just an old steel rod. Probably would look great in your living room," Corliss said. "The trick here is in the pedestal. It modulates gravity."

Corliss's human shadow, a barrel-like man with meaty fingers, adjusted a hand-held control unit. The rod went up and wobbled, suspended a few feet above the pedestal. Up and down the thing went as the man turned the control unit's dial.

"Neat-o. Does it work on a larger scale?" Otto asked.

"Not yet. There are some significant limiting factors," Corliss answered.

Otto stepped close to the floating rod. He watched it slowly twirling. Without warning, he reached out and grabbed the rod, pulling it from its reduced gravity environment.

"Mr. Veltraria, please, you must not touch the exhibits," Corliss said, trying to keep his voice down.

Otto laughed and twirled the rod like the baton of a parade marshal. "I've got a trick for you," Otto said. Then he tossed the rod high into the air, where it seemed to hang for a minute, and then he caught it on its way down after a half a dozen revolutions. "That's a more useful trick – it actually entertains people," Otto said, still laughing.

"My goodness, Mr. Veltraria, I beg you – please put that down," Corliss said.

Corliss's man began to walk quickly toward Otto.

"Malcolm, no!" Corliss shouted. The man abruptly halted his approach.

"Relax, Corliss, I wasn't going to drop your precious piece of metal." Otto's smile faded as he returned the rod to its place above the pedestal where it again floated.

Over the next forty-five minutes, the group toured the Water Pavilion without incident. Otto kept his hands off of the exhibits, even though he really wanted to play with all of the toys.

Other than Otto's tour, the pavilion was empty at that late hour. But every light and pump system and invention was running. Changing colors and constant motion filled the multi-story structure. The interior walls morphed from display shelving for inventions to screens with pictures and video of the inventors and their creations and the communities that could be served by them.

"Very good, very impressive – what a young man," Otto said as a short video clip ended featuring one of the inventors.

"Yes, yes, he is. I can't imagine how a mind like that works," Corliss said.

"Probably totally foreign to you, Mr. Corliss," Otto said, smiling.

Corliss let out a fake little laugh and said, "Actually, this was kind of an interesting situation with this young man. Barely out of high-school and somehow he developed technology to grow fully-formed fruits and vegetables in just minutes. He was about to enter into a very lucrative deal to sell his rapid-grow patents when we met him. Thankfully, for all of us, we were able to prevent him from signing a contract that was going to make him millions. He was literally dangling his pen over the contract when we successfully stepped in and scuttled his deal."

"Scuttled?" Otto asked.

"Well, *scuttled* is probably the wrong word. He was chasing profit and we helped him see the light, if you follow me."

Otto tapped his chin in thought. "Yes, yes, I think I get your drift, Mr. Corliss." Otto's exaggerated wink turned into a pretend twitch over a raised eyebrow. Corliss immediately turned red.

"Please forgive my attempt at subtlety, Mr. Veltraria, but this whole subject can be touchy."

"How so?" Otto asked.

"You know, some people forget that we're all in this together – everything that's plaguing the world today. And they just forget about helping out. It's kind of disgusting and selfish, but in the case of this young man, you really can't fault him, he just didn't know any better. Don't get me wrong, he did create his technology to help people, but he also wanted to make money doing it, and I think that by removing the profit motive altogether, the Association will be more effective in implementing his technology – once we can procure the proper funding. Look, I admit, I'm particularly sensitive to all of this given the mission of our organization. We're all about helping the world through technology, even if that means putting one's own interests aside."

"Back up a bit – what do you mean once you can procure funding?" Otto asked. "Aren't a handful of nations pitching in to fund all of the Association's endeavors?"

"They were, but they're not willing to extend their commitments. Or should I say, they aren't in a position to continue funding us – at least on their own."

"So what's the game plan then?"

"Happily, an immense new financial partnership is in the process of being established. It's really quite exciting, but somewhat unpublicized for now."

"And they've agreed to fund the Association?"

Corliss leaned into Otto and said in a hushed voice, "They may be funding more than just the Association. Very exciting. It's just what the world needs."

Otto shook his head, puzzled. "Who are the partners of this partnership?"

"I can't say," Corliss answered. "It's not a done deal yet – negotiations are ongoing. I trust you'll hold this information in confidence."

Otto tilted his head and smiled at Corliss. "Of course, Mr. Corliss. I really hope that you receive the funding you seek."

"Thank you, Mr. Veltraria, thank you so much. You have no idea how important your words are to me."

Otto laughed. "I'm all about words, Mr. Corliss."

By now, the group was on a low-ceilinged mezzanine level just beneath the top floor of the Water Pavilion. Otto's tall head of hair was dangerously close to the harsh, bright flood lights above him.

"What is this place?" Otto asked. His voice echoed against the water walls that were now textured like glazed subway tiles. He crossed his arms.

"This, Mr. Veltraria, is one of the most remarkable pieces of equipment in this entire exposition."

Otto looked around the tight, square room and saw only a white, round disc sitting atop a heavy steel platform.

"This thing?" Otto asked, pointing at the disk.

"Yes, I know it doesn't look like much," Corliss said. "Just wait."

Corliss nodded to Malcolm who then walked out of the room and quickly returned with a garbage can. Malcolm labored as he carried the can to the edge of the disk. Corliss again nodded to Malcolm, who responded by dumping a small mound of garbage on the clean disk. Malcolm produced a handkerchief from his suit jacket and wiped his forehead.

"Thank you, Malcolm," Corliss said.

"Yuck. Do you really need cigarette butts and soiled baby diapers to demonstrate this thing?" Otto asked, his brow furled and his face tight.

"It all really helps to make the point, Mr. Veltraria," Corliss responded. "Sure, we can recycle our refuse, right? But not all of it. Not all of our garbage has residual value, does it? Some of it just needs to disappear. If it doesn't add value in some way to the greater good of the planet and is just standing in the way of attaining that perfect existence that man strives for, then it must be addressed in the most efficient way possible."

"Yeah, okay. So let's see the fancy trash compactor work," Otto said through a slight laugh.

Corliss worked the remote control carefully as he spoke. "Allow me to present – the *Plate*."

The disk began to slowly turn. The lights in the room dimmed slightly as the mound of garbage gradually disappeared over the next five seconds. Then the lights returned to their original intensity.

Otto turned to Corliss and said, "Wow. That's impressive." His voice was hollow. "And very scary."

"Scary? How so, Mr. Veltraria?" Corliss asked.

Otto didn't answer. He walked to the edge of the machine and saw just a tiny mound of ashes and a faint outline of the garbage that had just been there. Even the smell was gone.

"You've just witnessed *Plating*, Mr. Veltraria," Corliss said. "This machine has given us a new verb, and I know you're a man who can appreciate the birth of a word." Corliss laughed – alone.

Still looking at the device, Otto said, "It's not an entirely new word. Ever worked in a restaurant, Mr. Corliss? Plating the food before it goes to the diner is an important part of the presentation. The food must be appealing. It's all about presentation, isn't it? I have to *plate* myself for the people when I go out onto the stage, don't I?"

Otto snapped out of his babbling fit and looked up at Corliss. "Perhaps you could use some good plating, Mr. Corliss."

Corliss forced a smile, but for the first time in the evening, Otto saw that he had finally reached Corliss – he had finally pinched him and Corliss had grimaced. Otto felt both good and bad about it.

"Mr. Corliss, I thank you for this wonderful and enlightening tour, but I think I must lay my head down. I've done a lot today," Otto said as he led the way out of the room, not looking back at Corliss.

"I understand entirely, Mr. Veltraria, I understand. But you really shouldn't leave before you've seen Dr. Clairet's exhibit. Please, just another fifteen minutes."

"Let me guess, Dr. Clairet has fashioned a machine to turn water into wine," Otto said. Everyone laughed.

"Yes, a hearty red. I could go for a glass," Corliss said through the fading of his laugh.

In that moment, Otto caught a glimpse of Corliss as a person. A feeling of pity and guilt welled up inside of Otto.

"Yes, of course, Mr. Corliss, let's go see Dr. Clairet's exhibit." Otto gently patted Corliss on the back as Corliss led the way, smiling.

The group now stood in the lobby of the uppermost floor of the pavilion, and the colors and sounds that dominated the other areas of the exposition were gone. Respectful silence reminiscent of a funeral parlor filled the lobby.

They stood in front of two huge closed doors. But these doors weren't made of water. Corliss led the group right up to the doors – they were pewter, etched with a complex geometric pattern that resembled strands of DNA.

"You've surely noticed that these doors don't fit in with the rest of the water theme of the Water Pavilion," Corliss said, watching Otto study the doors. "But they hold a significance to the man who developed the technology that sits behind these beautiful barriers."

Suddenly, the heavy doors, fifteen feet tall and ten inches thick, began to slowly creek open toward the group.

Corliss's eyes grew wide as he cautiously peered into the space created by the opening doors.

"Ms. Clairet, Ms. Clairet, my goodness – you gave us such a startle." Corliss said.

Königin and Jess now stood in front of the group.

"I'm sorry, Mr. Corliss, I didn't mean to surprise you," Königin said. "The security people downstairs said that we could walk through the pavilion."

"Mr. Corliss, would you like to introduce me to this young lady with the name of Clairet?" Otto asked, sounding annoyed.

"Yes, of course, my apologies for being so rude, Mr. Veltraria. This is Königin Clairet, the daughter of Dr. Clairet." Corliss bowed slightly as he waved the two together.

Before Otto or Königin could say anything, Corliss quickly inserted, "Ms. Clairet is a brilliant hydro-physicist – she developed the technology used to build this exposition pavilion."

"No kidding, Corliss," Otto said. Then Otto smiled at Königin and shook her hand. "How are you feeling? You took a nasty fall, didn't you?" He gently put his hands on her shoulders.

"Oh, I'm all right. I just have a lingering headache," Königin said, before turning to Jess and motioning him over with her head. "This is my friend, Jess Frank."

Jess approached Otto and extended his hand like a young child being instructed to do so. Otto's smile evaporated as he firmly took Jess's hand and engaged in the obligatory ritual.

After a moment, Otto tilted his head and asked, "You write for *Indie Voices*, don't you? Or used to, I should say."

Jess nodded.

"I've read your articles – you're a talented writer. It's too bad that magazine is gone. Just like the rest of them, I guess," Otto said.

Jess nodded again.

"I assume you're with *The Trustee* now – in their little entertainment section. What's it like writing for them?" Otto asked.

"I wouldn't know, I don't write for them," Jess answered.

"Mr. Veltraria, please, this way," Corliss said, interrupting the conversation. "We'd like to close the Water Pavilion for the night and I'd like you to see Dr. Clairet's work before you depart."

Otto looked away from Jess, and after a moment's hesitation, he proceeded through the open doors. Königin and Jess followed the rest of the small group back into the tomb housing Dr. Clairet's apparatus.

The room was long and the ceiling was high. Elevated arches of static water pulsated with a golden light. For a moment, Otto thought that he might actually be underground, in some carved-out cavern. His brief disorientation was hidden by his gazing up at the elegant buttresses above him.

"How on earth did you figure out how to build such a place, Ms. Clairet?" Otto asked, still looking up.

Jess smiled at her, mockingly. Corliss raised his eyebrows.

"Well, Mr. Veltraria, this wasn't really what I had in mind when–"

"She didn't," Jess said.

Otto abruptly leveled his head and looked at Jess. "I beg your pardon?"

"She didn't. She didn't figure out how to build this place."

Otto looked over at Königin, who lowered her head.

"Oh, I see. No matter young lady, whatever your contribution was I'm quite impressed." Otto said.

"She did something much more important than design this amusement park attraction." Jess said.

Otto became aware of a low hum, charged with electricity. The floor vibrated with the heavy sound. He refocused on the conversation. "Tell me, what was your role in this?"

Königin lifted her head and looked at him directly. "I developed a process to control water while preserving its liquid state. Then someone figured out how to build a structure like this using my process."

"Why so unhappy about that, Ms. Clairet?" Otto asked. "Mr. Corliss and his group made good use of your technology, didn't they?"

Jess leaked a sound in protest. Otto ignored him.

"I suppose so, but I had a different purpose in mind," Königin said. "People are dying for lack of clean water around the world. But there's plenty of it – it's just not everywhere that it needs to be. As a force, water has been harnessed in so many ways, but I came up with a way to control its very form, not just control its movement. I'm developing a few different concepts to move water around the globe in efficient ways to get it to the places where it's desperately needed."

Otto stared at Königin and burst into a broad smile and said, "That is just so good, I love what you're trying to accomplish. The world is starving for people like you, now more than ever. And I feel like I've been carrying that burden on my shoulders for my whole life. But none of us can save the world all by ourselves – and that's a hard truth for me to swallow." Königin smiled at Otto. Then Otto said, "Just look at some of the technologies showcased in your Water Pavilion." But then Otto saw Königin wince, and he added, "I mean, their Water Pavilion, well, you know what I mean."

"Yes, of course, Mr. Veltraria, I do." Königin said.

Corliss piped up. "Yes, Ms. Clairet's technology is truly amazing, and I think we've done a wonderful job showcasing it here. Perhaps you can be more successful than me, Mr. Veltraria, in persuading Ms. Clairet to work with the Association on the next phase of her development of this remarkable technology."

Jess pointed his head toward the cathedral ceiling and said, "Don't you ever stop?" Everyone looked at Jess who was just shaking his head and laughing. "Where's your *off* switch, Corliss?" Jess asked.

Otto looked at Jess and broke into a little giggle. "Ms. Clairet, your friend is quite a rude young man, isn't he?" Otto said, devoid of any anger.

"Yes, sorry."

"He clearly doesn't know a thing about being polite. I'm shocked by his behavior." Corliss said.

"Okay, we all agree, I'm a rude boy. But I'm not sorry. As much fun as it is to beat up the guy who says what everyone else is thinking but won't say it, why don't we get off of me for the moment. Corliss, show Otto this contraption that Königin's dad built."

"It's Mr. Veltraria, address him as Mr. Veltraria." Corliss corrected.

"Okay, then show Mr. Veltraria this thing," Jess said.

Corliss's long fingers tapped on a command module. Instantly, a rectangular opening began to form in the roof high above the group. The still water parted, permitting a long thin opening about forty feet long and five feet wide. The bright light of London's night sky revealed only a few stars through the lit haze.

A smooth metal block, in the same shape as the opening in the roof, vibrated as it sat on steel legs. By the time the opening had finished forming above, the huge chunk of metal, supported by its telescoping legs, had been elevated to within a few feet of the hole in the roof.

Otto rested his hands on his hips and looked up at the apparatus that had climbed nearly twenty-five feet.

"Ms. Clairet, are you sure that father of yours is an inventor and not a sculptor? If this machine did nothing other than just stand here, I would still think it's beautiful," Otto said. "The elegance of its lines and the color and texture of its surfaces are bold and strong."

"My father does have a thing for aesthetics. Everything must be pretty, at all costs," Königin said.

"Corliss, your setup is totally wrong, and as the chief salesman of this exposition, I would have expected a much better sell from you." Jess said. Corliss turned his head to face Jess in a way that said, "I had forgotten you were even here."

"Pardon me." Corliss said. "I'm no salesman and I'm not selling anything. Besides, what am I not doing that you think I should be doing, Mr. Frank?" Corliss asked.

"You've got a big glass tank full of dead fruit flies over there – aren't they the star of this show?"

Everyone looked in the direction that Jess was pointing.

Built into one of the walls of the great room was a large glass tank that seemed empty. Only a dim green light filled the tank. Otto approached it, and being rather tall, he leaned down and examined the contents of the tank closely. His eyes narrowed.

"That's nauseating," Otto said. "That's even more disgusting than the pile of garbage we just watched disappear." Otto's eyes were fixed on the hundreds of lifeless creatures lying on the floor of the tank. He thought to himself that years ago such a repulsive sight would have made a great album cover, just for the shock value. But not today. Otto now found such images grotesque and troubling and preferred to avoid them altogether.

"Ms. Clairet, since your friend doesn't like the way I explain things, or as he says, *sell* this exhibit, perhaps you should explain your father's work here." Corliss said.

"I've never seen it demonstrated, Mr. Corliss. I only know about it conceptually," Königin said.

"Oh, so you just looked at it when you were in here?" Corliss asked.

"Yes. Since I was a kid, my dad conditioned me not to touch his toys."

"Then you should really enjoy this. And you'll see, this is no toy, Ms. Clairet," Corliss said.

Corliss again played with the control unit. The metal block held high to the sky began to moan and hum and the vibration could be felt through the floor of the room. The lights of the room dimmed as the machine sucked power from everything around it. Otto looked up at the monolith above. He thought he saw it glow, ever so slightly. The humming and vibration became louder and heavier. Königin moved closer to Jess and stood right next to him. Jess smiled at Corliss who then looked away.

The long piece of metal now glowed red and then slowly transitioned to yellow and then to blue and finally to black. By that time, the whole floor shook and the hum was close to deafening. Königin grabbed Jess's hand. Abruptly, the sound died and the vibration died and the room was silent.

Slowly, the hole in the roof began to close as the metal block returned to its steel color. The telescoping legs carefully collapsed with the goal of returning the apparatus to its resting place.

Suddenly, Corliss lifted his hand and pointed at the glass tank. Everyone looked in its direction. They all moved closer to the tank. Otto once again leaned down to look in, but only saw the mound of dead flies.

"What am I looking for, Mr. Corliss?" Otto asked, his eyes searching the inside of the tank.

"Please, Mr. Veltraria, be patient. The machine is processing the waves it's harvested from space." Corliss said.

Jess stood closely behind Königin as they both surveyed the lifeless bugs.

The group stood in silence. The Water Pavilion sat in silence. No movement, anywhere.

"Let me guess, it's a flea circus," Jess said. "A flea circus on strike."

Otto burst into laughter.

"Jess, that's not funny. Or nice," Königin said, stepping a foot away from Jess.

Otto couldn't hide his smile.

"You really don't know when to stop, do you, Mr. Frank?" Corliss said. "You seem to have some kind of disorder – you say anything that comes to your mind. You have no control. You seem to be impervious to the damage that you cause with your words. You have no sense of responsibility for your words." Malcom began to move in Jess's direction.

Otto stomped hard on the floor. The group abruptly turned toward him. He stared into the tank and touched it with his right index finger.

"Look, one of those little guys is flying," Otto said. No one made a sound. "Look, there goes another one. Up and away," Otto said. He paused and touched the glass as a few more of the tiny black specks buzzed their wings and began to fly.

Otto stood up straight, and in his full singing voice said, "He's reanimated life." Otto then lowered his head and looked at his shoes. "Who has ever done that?" he asked himself out loud.

"No one, Mr. Veltraria. No one," Corliss said. "And that's why Dr. Clairet has named his creation the *Animator*."

"So, Dr. Clairet is collecting some type of energy with this apparatus of his to bring these disgusting little creatures back to life?" Otto asked.

Corliss smiled and answered, "Yes, you've described it quite well."

Königin stood silently with her hand over her mouth, staring at the hundreds of little flies now moving around in the tank. Otto tapped his square chin, his eyes shifting from left to right and back again, not looking at anything in particular.

"How do we know that the little flying dots were actually dead?" Otto asked. "Maybe they were just immobilized, drugged." Otto turned to Königin and said, "Forgive me for asking this, Ms. Clairet, but could this just be a performance? I mean, really, the theatrics of it all are passable as theater, even if not good theater."

Königin shrugged her shoulders, as if to communicate that she wasn't offended and had no intention of defending her father.

Corliss spoke up. "Mr. Veltraria, I assure you, Dr. Clairet's widely held reputation as a world-renowned scientist should resolve any skepticism that you may have."

Otto looked into the tank again and watched the little flies buzz around. Then he shook his head and said, "It's nothing short of a miracle."

9

Kimberly Long had not taken her husband's name, "Corliss." But it had never been a point of contention between the two. Her husband appeared to be passive about those matters that he didn't care much about. In his eyes, he was routinely magnanimous toward her and her needs and wants. In her eyes, he was dispassionate and accommodating. He gave in anywhere he could, as long as it didn't matter to him. She knew that he loved to give away that which he did not care about. And it annoyed her to watch the spectacle of his empty generosity, with that smugness of his self-appreciation that elicited her praise out of guilt and placation and to avoid an odd silence that would otherwise result. But this dynamic did create an absence of conflict in her life and in her home, and for that, she was both appreciative and resentful. He was methodical, and delicate, and well scripted, and he knew how to avoid a fight.

But none of this meant that her life was easy. Moving five times in the past three years had drained her. And their child, not yet a year old, had been on more airplanes than most adults ever had throughout their entire lives. But that was the deal. Or at least, that was her husband's deal. Pursuing a career would be worth it, she thought. But to chase work, to chase a title – that was unsettling. To find a cause and then manufacture a passion for that cause in order to make a living could confuse a man to the point where he no longer knows where his true passion lies – if he had ever been lucky enough to have had any passion.

Kim heard a key make its way into the lock of the door to the flat. She took a deep breath. Moaning, the heavy door slowly opened. Kim heard him hang up his coat and put his briefcase down on the wooden floor. His height and his stride and his dress shoes made his approaching steps sound official. She could feel him standing behind her in the doorway of the bathroom and she could smell the dampness of London on him.

Kim kept her eyes fixed on her baby in the tub as she washed his hair gently.

"Hello, hello. What luck, my beautiful wife and my handsome son have stayed up to see me," Tad Corliss said.

She laughed without turning toward him. The baby squinted and tried to grab her hand as she rinsed the shampoo from his head, water pouring over his eyes. He squeaked out a futile protest.

"How could we rest knowing that you were out there working so hard?" Kim said.

He crossed his arms. "We all do what we need to. I'd love to see your pretty eyes."

She turned her head toward him. "Sorry, I was just keeping my eyes on him."

"What's for dinner?" Tad asked.

"Dinner? It's nearly midnight. Didn't you eat already?" Kim asked.

"No, I'm starved."

"Sorry, dear. I'm sure you can find something."

A gentle gust of night air blew in through the open french doors in the adjacent bedroom. The lace curtains glowed with the city's light.

"No problem. If we're both doing our jobs, there'll be something for me," Tad said.

Again looking at the baby, she rolled her eyes.

"Remarkable what an appetite one develops trying to help the world," Tad said. "You only have to take care of one person, or two if you count me."

She turned to him and said, "Or three, if you count me."

"Oh, well, I had already factored you into that equation."

Yelling, and then a handful of voices erupted from the street below. The baby and his parents looked toward the window.

"Down with the king and off with his rings, down with the king and off with his rings," the crowd below chanted as they made their way down the street.

"Now they're going after the king," Kim said. "What do they want from him? He didn't cause any of this madness."

"No one is exempt from this madness," Tad said, retreating from the doorway of the bathroom.

"Good thing the Tower of London is a museum now," she said to the baby in a playful voice.

Tad called from the kitchen. "There's really not much here. But no problem, I'll just go to bed hungry. Millions do it every night, anyhow. Of course, many of them starve to death."

"I'm sure you'll survive," she said.

"Yes, probably, but maybe you could look yourself. You'll see something obvious that I don't, staring me right in the face. And I hate to admit it, but I don't think I'll make it through the night. I'm not used to sleeping on an empty stomach like all those poor saps."

"Tad!" Kim shouted.

"Just kidding, dear. Just kidding."

She let out a deep breath. "Let me see what I can find."

Kim propped the baby up on a makeshift seat of towels as he splashed his hands in the water. She walked quickly to the kitchen.

"Nothing here," Tad said, leaning against the open door of the pantry.

She looked hurriedly in the pantry, kneeling down and then standing on her socked toes. "How about I make you some rice and beans?"

He crossed his arms. "Really, that's the best you can do?"

"Look, I can't leave the baby in the tub. You go in and look after him and I'll come up with something and bring it in."

"He'll be fine for another minute. I know I'm not going to like whatever you make, you've got nothing here."

She faced him. "I hate when you're hungry, you can't control your nastiness."

"Well, I'm upset. I work really hard, trying to do the right thing for everyone. And not just for you and the baby, but for humanity in general – and then I'm not even fed dinner."

"Humanity?" she laughed. "Maybe if by *humanity* you mean one particular human."

"Kimberly, don't be mean," he said in a calm voice.

She felt her insides start to burn. This time she wanted a fight. "You know what, I'm so sick of following you around while you chase a paycheck – a paycheck barely big enough to cover the monthly payment on our Full-Life Loan. And it isn't just about the money for you, but it's definitely not about humanity. It's about seeing your name and picture in *The Whole Truth Trustee*, it's about sitting on speaking panels, and about people lauding you with hollow respect – they're all chasing after an influence that they think you have, that they hope you have. An influence that you dream you have." Kim's lips twitched as she stared into Tad's tight face.

He glared back at her, but said nothing.

"If you're going to make yourself into the man that you think you are, you'd better do it already. Stop pretending, don't just go through the motions – actually be that person, if you're even capable of it."

Tad closed his eyes and was silent for a moment. Then he slowly inhaled a deep breath and reopened his eyes.

"Oh dear, listen to us," Tad said. "I'm so sorry. It's terrible of me to allow you to become so upset." He hung his head.

When there was an altercation, which was rare, this is how it ended. Peace keeping. Nothing resolved. Condescension. Kim was peacefully furious, but relieved the fight was over.

The mother and father stood facing each other, not making

eye contact, not speaking. Their little flat let in every sound of the street below, which had steadily become louder with the night's growing trouble.

"My God, listen to it out there," Kim said. "It's every night now – always protesting about something. In the morning they're yelling that there's not enough food, or it's too expensive, and by teatime, they're bitching out loud that there's no tea."

Kim's head jerked in response to a shrill yell from a drinker leaving the pub across the street. Then a bolt of fear went through her as the silence from the bathroom struck her.

She ran past Tad who watched her with raised eyebrows, and then understanding, he followed her.

The baby was face down in the tub, having slipped off the mound of towels.

Kim let out a guttural yell – she scooped the child out of the tub. He gasped and coughed for a moment, and then released a long, loud wail. She held the child closely. "I'm sorry, baby boy, I'm so sorry. I'll never leave you again." The baby's chin quivered as he screamed, his eyes clamped shut.

She quickly turned to her husband. "You'd better get this figured out Tad or we're going back to the States."

"Now you're just getting hysterical, Kim, calm down. This could have happened anywhere."

"No, no, don't say that, you know that's not true," Kim said. "If you could hold down a steady job things would be stable in our life – no surprises, no sudden moves, no packing, no strange looks from neighbors we never get to know, no old bathtubs sitting on four legs, no creaky old wooden floors and ceilings so high that the rooms feel lonely and cold. I don't know what to expect any more when I wake up."

Tad answered with silence. The baby continued to grind out his hoarse cries.

Kim and Tad listened to the sounds of an irritable London but didn't speak. Kim closed the French doors, and eventually, the baby fell asleep.

"I haven't even told you about the private tour I gave Otto Veltraria tonight."

After a moment, Kim asked, "What's he like?"

Tad paused, looking up to think. "Fine, just fine. Says what's on his mind. I think he was tired."

"Did he like the Water Pavilion?"

Tad's voice rose. "Oh, yes, he loved it. Loved the exhibits. You know he's all about helping people and saving the world. He said that his *Take My Hand* tour kind of ties into what we're doing at the Association."

"Wow," Kim said blankly.

Tad started unknotting his tie. "Do you remember meeting Dr. Clairet, the scientist that developed that huge machine on the top floor that reanimates–"

"The one with the dead flies? That was so gross," Kim said.

"Yes, that's the one. Anyhow, his daughter was there, touring with her obnoxious friend."

"Königin Clairet was there?" Kim asked, now engaged.

"Yes, that's her – she was there. I can't imagine why she'd be seen with that Jess Frank fellow."

"She must be brilliant," Kim said, smiling.

"He was just so antagonistic and mocking," Tad said, undressing.

"How is she feeling, Tad?" Kim asked.

"Who?"

"Ms. Clairet – you know, has she recovered from her fall?"

Tad shrugged his shoulders. "She's fine, I guess. I didn't ask her."

Then Tad went into the bathroom for a couple of minutes before climbing into bed next to Kim.

"Want to hear the punch-line?" Tad asked.

Kim didn't respond. She had already turned away from her husband.

"Mr. Veltraria made Jess Frank his biographer for his world tour. How's that for a crazy world?"

Kim was asleep.

10

Sheldon McCloud napped in the sun while his grapes grew. He slept through the rustling of the oaks pushed around by a steady wind blowing through the valley.

A car turned onto the gravel road leading up to his winery. Sheldon began to wake up as the sound of the tires spitting out gravel grew louder.

He slowly stood up from his wooden chair on the porch as the car pulled up. He twirled the thin end of his mustache without even thinking about.

The car's tinted passenger window rolled half-way down.

"Where's Magnum Peak Winery?" the voice behind the window asked.

Sheldon took a breath and looked in, but he couldn't see past the big sunglasses on the woman's face. "This is the valley of the little wineries," he said. "I'm sorry but you're way off course."

A little chatter took place in the car before the window rolled back up.

Sheldon looked the vehicle over. It was a new sports car, complete with newly issued paper license plates. He recalled reading that only several thousand new cars of any kind had been made that year and only a few hundred of them were sports cars.

The window rolled back down several inches.

"How much for directions to Magnum Peak?" the woman asked.

"Nothing," Sheldon answered.

More chatter in the car.

"But how will we know you're telling us the truth?" the woman asked.

"What would paying me for directions have anything to do with whether I'm giving you proper directions?" Sheldon asked.

Leaning toward the barely opened window, the driver, a man, spoke up. "Nobody does anything out of the kindness of their heart, fella. It's all about price."

Sheldon laughed to himself before turning around and walking into the little farmhouse. The screen door slammed shut behind him.

"Who's that out there?" Sheldon's wife asked, motioning her head toward the window.

"Lost people," Sheldon answered, sitting down at the simple wooden table.

"Did you point them in the right direction?" she asked.

"Liv, street directions are not what those people need," Sheldon answered, sipping a cup of coffee that she had put down in front of him.

One of the car's doors opened and then closed hard. In just a few strides, the approaching shoes made it to the screen door after quickly taking every other step up to the porch.

"Where'd you go?" the man in his short leather jacket asked through the screen door. His sunglasses were even bigger and darker than the woman's. Sheldon turned around in his chair to face him.

"Come in, please," Liv said without hesitation as she opened the door. The man didn't enter, or even look at her.

"I'm in a hurry," the man said, retrieving some cash from his wallet. "So, if you could just tell me how to get to Magnum I'll get out of here."

Sheldon stood up and slowly walked to a counter at the far end of the kitchen. Above the counter were dozens of awards from around the world, and on the counter were four bottles of open wine, their labels stained different shades of red.

Sheldon twirled the end of his mustache as he looked at his bottles. He then carefully lifted one of them and slowly poured his blood colored creation into a small round glass. Moving heavily toward the man who still hid behind his sunglasses, Sheldon held the glass of wine out to his guest.

"I don't think you understand," the man said, smiling and shaking his head. "I want wine from the Magnum Peak winery. I mean, your little winery is very quaint, but I need the real deal."

Sheldon retracted his arm and took a sip of the wine.

"Can I get you some water?" Liv asked the man, who ignored her again.

"All right, I'll tell you what," the man said. "Sell me two bottles of wine and throw in the directions, okay? I get it."

Sheldon shook his head and said, "No, you're not ready for it."

"What? What does that mean?" the man asked.

"I think I was pretty clear," Sheldon answered, taking another sip of wine. Liv started washing dishes in the sink.

"This wine," Sheldon said, holding the glass up, "is made neither by science nor God alone, but is made by both together."

"God? What if I don't believe in God?" the man asked, chuckling and shaking his head.

"God has all kinds of names and even more forms, but I assume that you're quite sure that no life-giving energy moves through this universe in whatever form," Sheldon said.

"You assume quite correctly, fella, and I assure you that your wine is nothing more than fermented grape juice," the man said, smiling widely.

Sheldon nodded. "Then I was right, you're not ready. In fact, you're not ready for anything that's beyond your senses."

The woman with the big sunglasses trotted up the steps of the porch. "What's up? Can we get out of here now?" she asked.

"Yes, he's ready to go," Sheldon answered for the man.

"This guy's just an old nut, baby," the man said to the woman, laughing. "He thinks wine is the marriage of –" The man finished his sentence, but no sound came out of his mouth.

No sound came out of anyone's mouth. The protest of the oak trees against the hard wind couldn't be heard. Not even the sound of a distant tractor hummed.

Liv turned from the sink and looked at Sheldon, her eyes wide. Behind her, the water poured from the faucet, silently.

The silence was big and loud.

The woman pulled her sunglasses off and yelled and yelled, pulling at the man's arms, tears rolling down her cheeks. Sheldon could feel the breath of her yells, but he couldn't hear her.

The man stood where he was, not moving, his mouth slightly opened.

And then, like a switch had been flipped, the woman's shrieks ricocheted inside the kitchen of the little farmhouse. Sheldon jumped when his ears were suddenly assaulted by the sound coming out of her mouth.

As soon as the woman realized that she could be heard – that everything could be heard again, she shut her mouth and ran back to the car, crying.

The man swallowed, and without saying anything, he rigidly turned himself around and stumbled back to his car.

The gravel crunched as the car slowly found its way back down the driveway. It was the kind of careful departure usually executed by a driver pulling back onto the road after receiving a speeding ticket.

11

"What do you think caused it, Königin?" Jess asked.
"I just don't know. I mean, I have a couple of weak theories – but they're a bit convoluted. You'll need some time to listen."

Jess cracked his gum on the other end of the phone line. "Not now."

"Then why did you ask me?"

"Just confirming how smart I think you are."

Königin laughed. "Okay, later then, if you're actually interested."

"I might be," Jess said. "But you know how I loathe speculation, so let's just see if this little episode of world silence eventually gets explained without me having to think about it too much."

"Fine, let's not tax your mind unnecessarily," Königin said, laughing.

"Thank you, dear Königin."

Königin stretched out on the sofa in her father's living room, but her feet didn't reach the end like Jess's did. Looking up at the crown molding in the ceiling above, she felt like she was in a dollhouse.

"So, how's it going with Veltraria?" Königin asked. "I'm surprised he hasn't electrocuted you with his electric guitar yet."

"He plays keyboard, not guitar, genius," Jess said.

"Right, I forgot. Well, either way, I'm surprised he hasn't had his roadies work you over."

"I think it's coming. I'm constantly pissing him off."

"Can't you manage to keep your mouth shut, Jess?"

"Why ask me a question you already know the answer to?"

"That was more of a statement than a question. Tell me about him – is he arrogant as hell?"

Jess paused. "Not in the way you would expect. It's not so much that he thinks he's better than everyone else, it's more that he's sure he's right about everything. And of course, everyone has to agree with him." Jess cracked his gum again. "And that's why he's already sick of me."

"What's with the gum? It's getting on my nerves," Königin said.

Jess laughed. "What, all the way from Paris?"

"You know what I mean. You hate when people fill your ears with garbage – and that noise is garbage."

Königin heard Jess spit the gum out of his mouth. "Making any progress on the supreme water cannon?" Jess asked.

Königin laughed. "I love that name, that's great. I might need to use that, if I ever get it working. It's difficult though. I'm able to form the water into whatever shape I want, and I've just about perfected how to launch such an immense amount of water – it's just the landing that's causing me trouble. It's breaking apart in flight. I drowned an entire town in the simulator."

"You're such a bitch," Jess said.

"That's not funny – don't joke about this. There's a profound scarcity of clean water for drinking and cooking – and people get sick from using pond and stream water that's full of dangerous bacteria. And a lot of young girls can't go to school because they spend most of their time fetching water from miles away. The lack of clean water is a barrier to achieving the most basic standard of living, so the longer I take getting the water launcher to work, the more suffering there will be – they need the water right now."

And after pausing a moment, she added, "I feel so guilty for not being able to help yet."

"Stop self-indulging yourself with guilt, Königin," Jess said. "That's not going to motivate you. That's just going to bog you down in emotional quicksand, gum up the gears of your brain."

"I disagree, guilt is a good motivator. At least for me."

"Come on," Jess said. "You're telling me that you're motivated to figure out how to get water to the driest parts of the earth because you feel bad about it? Bad in the sense that somehow you contributed to that condition, that you bear some responsibility for it?"

"I'm sure in some indirect way I do bear some responsibility, and so do you. I'm not telling you anything new, Jess."

"Okay, sure, I concede that everyone and everything is connected in a sense, but there isn't a sufficient nexus between your mere existence and the horrible suffering of those people to justify guilt on your part. I mean real guilt, where you know you've acted against your principles."

"Okay, counselor." Königin said. "Don't forget, you never passed the bar. Finishing law school doesn't make you a lawyer."

"That's mean. I bet you won't feel guilty about saying that."

"Probably not," Königin said, laughing. Then, after a moment, she went silent.

"Königin? You there?"

No response.

Königin sat up and crossed her legs underneath her. She turned the chrome deco lamp on, but the light was so dim and yellow and weak that she turned it off right away. She preferred the darkness.

"Hey, you there?" Jess asked again.

"I'm here," Königin said, quietly.

"What's going on?" Jess asked.

After a moment, Königin said, "With all that talk about guilt, some of my mom's words came back to me. She's been gone for so many years, but I just started hearing her say things."

"Like what?" Jess asked, his voice serious but soft.

Königin talked slowly. "Well, a few times she brought me with her to this community of little cabins that she helped build for homeless people who were trying get back on their feet. And I remember seeing those people there, young and old, even little kids living with their parents, and I told my mom that I felt guilty that those people had nothing."

Jess just listened as she looked into her past out loud.

"When I said that, my mom said something about guilt being a selfish feeling." Königin paused. "Yeah, guilt was a selfish thing, and that I should show my care for people through deeds, not with feelings of guilt. And she said that words and actions that came from guilt were just medicine or pain killers or something like that for the people who said or did things out of guilt."

"Wow," Jess said. "Your mom sounds like the kind of woman who could just cut through the confusion of emotion. A woman who could see things clearly."

Königin nodded, even though Jess couldn't see her.

"She actually helped build that community?" Jess asked.

Königin's voice brightened up. "Totally. She was amazing. Great with a circular saw. She loved to build those cabins. Each one was unique, and the people that lived in them felt special and right at home. The residents would leave the community capable of taking care of themselves. Looking back, I see that they were empowered."

"I think you may have learned more from her in eight years than most people ever learn from anyone," Jess said. "Keep thinking, Königin. Keep remembering."

"Okay," Königin said, quietly. Then, after a moment, she spoke up and said, "How can such an outspoken fellow be so sweet?"

"I'm programmed to fool about everything," Jess said, "but not your visions of clarity. You may be on your way."

"On my way?" Königin asked.

But before Jess could answer, Königin heard the lock in the door being worked. She knew the door would open only ever so slightly, just enough for her little father to slip through the crack.

"Hey, listen Jess, my dad's home. I'm going to hang up, okay?"

"Sure, but what's the hurry?"

"He wants to take me to dinner and he won't have the patience to wait. I've got to go."

"Dinner with your dad, that's nice. Where are you guys going?"

"Chinatown. We're going to Chinatown. Let me go, okay?"

"That sounds really good. Hey, you know that place we loved on Wardour Street? It burnt down. Probably a duck fat fire. Maybe you could overnight me a couple of egg rolls—"

"He's coming. I'm going. I'll call you later."

Königin didn't wait for Jess to say "goodbye," she just hung the phone up and got it back on the end table before her dad reached the room. She sat in the dark and waited.

12

The president addressed the nation from the Oval Office about what was now being referred to as "the Silence."

"Whatever the cause of the Silence, we'll hopefully figure it out soon," the president said into the camera. "But we should assume that its cause is a damaging, destructive force, which if unchecked and uncontrolled, will likely lead to catastrophic consequences."

In family rooms around the country, children turned to see their parents' mouths opened in shock. Cars lined the shoulders of roads, pulled over to listen to the president's address. Radios delivered the message to anyone not in front of a television.

"Congress is wasting no time. First thing tomorrow morning, hearings will be convened on Capitol Hill to investigate the Silence," the president said.

People covered their mouths and their eyes grew wide.

"I have conferred with other world leaders," the president said, "and we have agreed to work together in whatever way possible to understand and combat this phenomenon."

The president signed off and the people resumed their lives – they had become accustomed to accepting a reality of deteriorating conditions.

13

"Once again, another excellent performance, Mr. Veltraria," Corliss said.

Otto flexed his fingers and then stuck them in a bucket of ice water held by a woman in a dark flowered dress.

"Really? Well, thank you," Otto said, looking at his hands in the bucket. He held them in the ice water so long that Corliss shivered.

"Oh, yes, of course. What a showman you are. Quite impressive," Corliss said.

Otto quickly pulled his hands out of the bucket and laughed to himself, his eyes closed. "A showman. That's amusing. I've never really thought of myself as a showman."

"Please, take no offense, I meant it purely as a compliment, Mr. Veltraria," Corliss said.

Otto opened his eyes and looked directly into Corliss's eyes. "Yes, I know you did. We all look at the world differently, don't we?"

The crowd continued in its deafening praise of Otto Veltraria, refusing to go home, even though the show was over.

Otto's assistant of many years set the bucket down and took his hands in hers. "Come on Otto, you've got one more in you, don't you dear? They need it," she said in her soft British way.

"Victoria, Victoria, I'm so tired, please let me retire."

"No, no, Otto. The hour is late and they need you more than ever. Answer their prayers, please. They need you to lead them to their salvation," Victoria said.

Otto looked at the ground and let her hands go. "Oh, please, stop with that salvation business or I'll begin to believe it myself – and then we'll all be in trouble." Otto looked up and smiled at Corliss, who was already fixed on Otto's eyes and smiling at him.

"What do you think, Mr. Corliss? Should I give them one more? Just to make them happy?"

Corliss quickly nodded his head, but then stepped toward Otto and put his hand on Otto's shoulder.

"Listen, Mr. Veltraria, I have an important matter to discuss with you at once."

Otto looked startled. "Really? Right now? Can't it wait?" Otto asked.

"I have to be up early tomorrow morning and I'd appreciate it if we could discuss it now, so I can leave before you finish your show."

Otto frowned. "It will have to wait, Mr. Corliss. There's forty thousand people waiting for me out there and I'm guessing they'd like to go to bed as well."

Corliss chuckled. "Oh, I understand, but I'll make it quick, let me explain. So here's the situation–"

Otto's feet pivoted 180 degrees in an instant and he walked back onto the stage to yells and whistles and chants. Corliss watched Otto walk toward his keyboard. Each step was deliberate and meant something. It was clear to Corliss that Otto was in no rush for any of it to be over.

As he made his way across the stage, Otto blew a kiss to his band leader, Althea, a woman with a trumpet in her hand. Then he bowed to Shiloh, his drummer, who in exaggerated cliché stood and saluted Otto with a drum stick.

Otto pulled his big wooden bench in under him and touched the keys of his old Hammond. Otto's every move earned him louder praise.

"All right my children, quiet down. We've got some more work to do," Otto said.

From where he stood on the side of the stage, Corliss saw that everyone was on their feet, hands clapping, all swaying to music that hadn't yet begun.

Otto smiled and took a deep breath. "I'm going to treat you to something from the old days." Then he tapped on a few keys, feeling his way, trying to get comfortable. He and Althea made eye contact and Otto nodded to her.

"This one's called *Four Walls* – I'm sure you've heard of it," Otto said, his lips just half an inch from the microphone perched in front of him above his keyboard. After a short burst of excitement, the big cave fell silent.

Otto started out softly, and then Althea's trumpet gently played along-side his deep voice.

> *I hear you now*
> *Your wall of faith doesn't move me*
> *You fear me now*
> *Your wall of hate doesn't scare me*
> *Run with me now*
> *Your wall is only what you see*
> *Take my hand now*
> *Your wall will fall and set you free*

Once Otto finished his song, the sound was deafening as he took a long, single bow. He walked toward Corliss who was still waiting in the wings.

"Amazing. Really top-notch stuff," Corliss said to Otto, slowly banging his hands together.

"Thank you, Mr. Corliss. Was it worth waiting for?"

"And how, sir," Corliss said.

Otto shook his head and smiled at Corliss. "Let's have that chat. What's on your mind? It must be important to keep you from your sleep," Otto said.

Corliss looked down and smiled, choosing to ignore the comment. He was there on a mission.

"I need your help, Mr. Veltraria."

"Oh?"

Finally, the house lights came up and the steady din of cheers subsided.

"Yes. As you know from your tour of the Water Pavilion, the Association is doing some wonderful things, but I need an alliance, a partner, a patron – someone like you."

Otto looked at Corliss in silence, and then said, "You said you needed my help. Is it you or the Association that needs my help?"

Corliss let some air escape from his mouth, making a noise. He shook his head. "Please, please, Mr. Veltraria, of course, you know that I meant the Association."

"Did I?" Otto asked.

"If you didn't, then you should have. I come in the name of official business and not on my own behalf. Besides, does it really matter – what difference does it make?" Corliss asked.

Otto stared at Corliss. "Just tell me what you want, Mr. Corliss, my bed is calling me too."

"We want you to associate yourself with the Association. You've no doubt heard of the newly formed Guiding Institutions Collaborative – every organization on the planet is going to be looking for money from it, not to mention our own government seeking help to fund its revenue shortfall."

"Revenue shortfall? That's the understatement of the night. The government doesn't even have enough revenue to print its useless funny-money. And yes, I've heard of the newly formed collaborative – I read *The Trustee* like everyone else."

"Then surely you've read that the Guiding Institutions Collaborative has established the *Fund*. With your endorsement and involvement with the Association, I'm confident that we'll receive a generous disbursement from the Fund," Corliss said.

Otto looked at Corliss for a moment without responding. Then he said, "I was under the impression from our little chat at the Water Pavilion that you pretty much had the money in the bag from this new partnership."

"Oh, no, no – I didn't mean to give that impression. We very much need your help."

Otto waited a moment for Corliss to continue, but Corliss just looked at him, waiting for a response.

"Go on, Corliss – speak," Otto said, now raising his voice.

"I ask you to lend your persona and your charisma to a worthy endeavor that will help the citizens of the world. I assure you, there will be very little burden on you. We just need that wonderful smile."

"So you need me as a figurehead? The face of the Association. But you'll still be running things, right?" Otto asked.

"Exactly," Corliss said, smiling widely.

"Forget it. Not interested," Otto said as he walked past Corliss, whose smile hadn't yet faded.

Corliss spun around and stretched his long legs to catch up with Otto who was on his way to his dressing room, dispensing smiles and nods to his roadies backstage.

"Mr. Veltraria, please, you mustn't dismiss my request so hastily."

"Mustn't I? I think I must." Otto kept walking.

Corliss kept pace behind Otto and spoke to his back. "The world is in shambles, it's on the brink, things are a mess more than ever before. And now, with the Silence, people are desperate for any kind of help – it creates a perfect opportunity for the Association. But we need a boost. With the energy of your *Take My Hand Tour* and the financial backing of the Guiding Institutions Collaborative, the Association can accomplish anything. We'll be partners, you and I."

Otto stopped walking and turned around to face Corliss.

"I'm a soloist with a back-up band of my choosing. I got rid of my partners a long time ago. Besides, you're not even talking about a partnership. Who knows what you'll drag me into, Mr. Corliss. I'll continue to control my own destiny, thank you."

Otto turned around and immediately resumed his march. Corliss didn't even bother going after him.

14

With his messenger bag banging against his waist, Jess double-stepped up the little staircase to the door of the jet. He walked in, but hesitated upon seeing Otto pointing at the seat facing him.

Jess sat.

A minute later the engines pushed hard, and the two men looked at Paris from above as the plane left the ground.

Once the nearly empty plane broke through the clean white clouds, Jess looked at Otto, who was already looking at him. The engines relaxed to a hum.

"What's your story, Mr. Frank?"

Jess scratched the side of his head, contemplating, not wanting to waste the wide invitation.

"Come on trouble-maker, don't think so hard," Otto said.

Jess smiled. "Please narrow your question, Mr. Veltraria."

Otto laughed. "Okay. Where were you born?"

Jess pulled his head back. "Oh, you really want my story, don't you?"

"You're my official biographer for this tour, aren't you? I admit, I find myself trying to avoid you, but I think we should get to know each other a little better," Otto said in a serious tone.

"Washington, D.C." Jess promptly answered.

"Washington? I would never have guessed. You have the delivery of a New Yorker – without the accent," Otto said.

"That's funny, Königin insists that I'm actually from New York."

Otto looked blank for a moment.

"Königin Clairet, you know, Dr. Clairet's daughter," Jess said.

Otto furled his eyebrows. "I know who Königin Clairet is, Mr. Frank. In fact, I knew her mother before you ever graced this planet."

"You knew Pearl McCloud?"

"Are you kidding me? She was a friend of mine," Otto said. "We moved in the same circles when I was with Knew Society. Lee Earlman secretly dated her just before she got together with Königin's father."

Jess's eyes widened. "Königin's going to freak when she hears that her mom dated Knew Society's triple-neck guitar playing Lee Earlman." Then Jess shook his head and added, "I'm sure she doesn't know that – and I doubt she's even aware that you knew Pearl."

"You're probably right," Otto said. "I had never met Königin until the other night at the Water Pavilion – and I barely know Dr. Clairet. Once Pearl started dating Clairet she kind of dropped out of the social scene. I don't think he liked her hanging out with the other movie stars and us filthy musicians. She ended her acting career long before she disappeared."

Jess nodded and then asked, "Do you think Dr. Clairet had anything to do with Pearl's disappearance?"

Otto laughed and said, "You certainly know nothing of subtlety, do you?"

Jess remained silent, waiting for an answer.

Otto stopped smiling and said, "No, no I don't." Jess said nothing.

After a moment, Otto added, "I remember feeling bad for him. The world loved her and he was an easy target – the weird little scientist that looked like the stereotypical villain in a lab coat. But no evidence, never charged – guilty nonetheless to so many. And as with every situation like that, there are two corners of the boxing ring – and I was in Clairet's. They tore him apart and I thought it was terribly unfair. But, like most of the world, I watched it all unfold from a safe distance."

After a moment, Jess said, "Tell me about Pearl."

Otto smiled and said, "In a sea of celebrity mediocrity, she stood above most – in every way. Talent, looks and heart. Real heart. While everyone else in the entertainment business was running around pretending to care about the world and going to black-tie fundraisers with red carpets, she was developing calluses on her hands helping people."

Jess sat back and listened.

"But back then, most of us thought she was going a little nuts because she was literally helping one person at a time. And I still think in that sense she was wrong, even though she was so well intentioned. She was a genuinely caring person, but her acts were just too small in scale to make much of a change."

"Unless you were one of the people helped by her," Jess said.

"No, no, don't get me wrong, Jess – I actually want to be more like Pearl. I'm ready to really help now, but on a grand scale – and I've been trying. Back then, I was so consumed by the Knew Society phenomenon. But I guess that's understandable. We were the biggest rock group ever, and–"

"*Arguably*, the biggest rock group ever," Jess said. "Or, better put, one of the biggest rock groups ever."

Otto stared at Jess silently, his mouth opened slightly.

Jess continued. "I mean, we could get into a whole discussion about who sold more albums, who topped the charts more often and who grossed the most from tours as between Knew Society and those skinny Brits that stayed together long after Knew Society had packed–"

"Don't interrupt me, Mr. Frank," Otto said firmly.

Jess looked at Otto but said nothing.

Otto took a deep breath and settled back into his seat. "Okay, so you're from D.C. Your parents still there?"

"They are."

"Still together?"

"They are."

"Impressive. It's rare to meet anyone anymore who's not from a broken home."

"How true."

"Like Washington, Jess?"

"Like Washington? Yes and no. Love the movement and energy of that city – it's as if something good's going to happen. I used to get a thrill every time I saw a motorcade go by. It looked like people who were chosen to do things were rushing to meet other people who were chosen to do things, and everyone needed to get out of their way, and that was okay, because it seemed like something good was just on the horizon. But the only thing on the horizon was a setting sun and more darkness. I've come to accept that everyone in that town is just a salesman, like all of us. It's just one big brothel, everyone's available. But I have an undying respect and awe for the stagecraft."

Otto laughed a little and asked, "What did you do for fun there?"

Jess thought for a moment, and then said, "I snuck into the National Press Club every chance I had. I saw everyone speak there. Every criminal and every saint. It's funny, you really can't tell them apart. And I spent hours reading and researching at the National Archives and the Library of Congress."

"Really? What were you researching?"

Jess thought to change the subject, now wanting to turn the interview around.

"Come on Mr. Frank, I see your hesitation. Tell me, what was so interesting? At that age I was probably signing my first recording contract and getting into fun trouble."

"I had lots of interests," Jess said.

"Okay, name one."

"Governments. Revolutions," Jess said.

"That was two. But, no matter. Governments are boring. Like you said, just a bunch of whores."

"No, what I said was that Washington was a brothel."

"Whatever. Revolutions – now you're talking. That's interesting stuff. But usually too much blood and rape for my taste," Otto said, moving his mouth as if he'd just eaten a lemon.

"Well, yes, violence is often a part of revolution," Jess said.

Otto shook his head. "I couldn't stomach it. The things that people do to one another, it's haunting. I couldn't get through that fellow Carlyle's first volume of his account of the French Revolution. Don't get me wrong, I totally saw where the people were coming from – revolution was necessary. It all had to happen and I would have probably been involved myself for that cause. But the blood, yuck."

Jess smiled and said, "I can just picture you entertaining an adoring crowd from an executioner's scaffolding before a dozen heads are lopped off."

"Anything for a good cause – I guess," Otto said, sticking his tongue out in disgust.

"Don't forget, that big blade dropped more than 200,000 times for that *good* cause," Jess said. "I can't imagine that so much death was necessary."

"Probably right," Otto said. "It does sound excessive. But listen, we weren't there, so who knows what was necessary to get the job done."

"There were relatively peaceful revolutions, too, you know," Jess said. "But those kinds of revolutions were led by individuals who cared more about people than doctrine or self-fulfillment. Their love of humanity was greater than their love of party or themselves. And those leaders knew how to bring out the very best in people and foster what was good in them. They knew how to nurture and govern long after the revolution was over. But leaders like that are practically extinct now."

Otto quickly sat up straight in his seat and loudly said, "But let's get serious here. Who cares about that intellectual garbage? The people in this world need food, shelter, clothes, peace and a piece of mind. Too many people complicate the solutions – they say, *don't treat the symptoms, get to the root of the problem.* Wrong. Let's just treat the symptoms. Kids need to eat and so on. All of this human need is killing our morale and our desire to live – it's just killing us." Otto paused and smiled, looking straight into Jess's eyes. "And that's what pulled me out of retirement to give birth to the *Take My Hand Tour.*"

15

Corliss sat, one leg folded over the other, reading *The Trustee.* He stuck his long arms straight out in front of him and delicately pinched the newspaper with his index fingers and thumbs.

A sweet little bell jingled as Königin let the door of her usual coffee house close behind her. Without even looking directly in Corliss's direction, she saw a misplaced suited fellow hiding behind a newspaper.

"Good morning, Finley," Königin said to the young man working the espresso machine.

"What's good it about then?" he replied with his steep Cockney tongue.

"I'm not sure, really," Königin said.

"Then let's stop pretending, shall we?" Finley replied.

"Okay."

"Fine. Now that we got that out of the way, is it the regular for you, my lady?"

"Please," she answered.

Königin stood in silence, waiting for her coffee. After a minute, Finley put her drink on the counter in front of her.

"Where's the steamed milk, Fin?" Königin asked, looking down into her cup of coffee.

"There's none," he replied.

"You guys are out of milk?" she asked, laughing a little.

"That's right, us *guys* are fresh out of milk. We've run dry on milk here in London. How does that grab you?"

Königin didn't respond.

"Still a good morning, is it?" Finley asked, looking into Königin's eyes.

Königin quickly turned away and looked for a place to sit, wanting to disappear into the crowd of people there. But there wasn't an empty table in the place. She walked toward the door.

"Ms. Clairet, Ms. Clairet," a voice called after her. She turned around to see Tad Corliss, who was folding his newspaper as he smiled at her.

"Figures," Königin whispered to herself.

Corliss waived his hand over the empty chair next to him. "Please, come join me. I've never seen such a crowded coffee house – you'll never find a seat. What luck that you found me."

"Yes, what luck, but I was actually on my way out, Mr. Corliss. Good to see you." She turned and began to walk toward the door.

"Wait, wait, please sit for a few minutes so we can catch up. How is your father?"

Königin stopped and slowly turned around. Corliss rose and pulled the chair out for her. She hesitated, and then sat.

"He's fine, thank you. In the States right now."

"I see. What a brilliant man," Corliss said.

"Yes," she said. "Do you like the coffee here?" She saw that he had nothing in front of him, except his newspaper.

"Oh, yes, splendid. Some of the best."

Königin shook her head and smiled. "Just hanging out at the coffee shop, are you?"

"I love it," Corliss answered. "The smell of coffee, the young people. Even looking at all of the tattoos is fascinating."

Königin laughed.

Corliss's face turned serious. "What, what's so funny?"

"Oh, nothing, Mr. Corliss, you just seem a little out of place here."

"Don't be silly. I'm a man of the people. A man for the people and of the people. Right?" Corliss left no room for disagreement in the matter and smiled smugly. "Before I forget, how is that precious head of yours? What a nasty fall."

"I'm fine. The headaches went away."

"How frightening," Corliss said. "It could have been so much worse."

"Yes, that's true. I'm just thankful that it was me who got hurt and not some visitor to the pavilion. After my fall, I really thought about pulling the plug on the whole thing – I was so afraid someone else was going to get hurt. That incident made me question whether my technology was ready."

"It's a good thing that you didn't try to *pull the plug* on the whole thing – because you don't control the plug. I do." Corliss forced a little laugh.

Königin shifted in her chair. "Yes, I understand your position with the Association and your authority over the Water Pavilion, but it's my technology. I granted the Association a license which I can revoke if I want to."

Corliss looked straight up at the ceiling and slowly rocked his head from side to side as if he was contemplating Königin's statement. "Well, yes and no. I mean, it's really not that simple. You're kind of along for the ride, aren't you?"

Königin set her black coffee down. "I don't like the sound of that at all. Look, my father's lawyer reviewed the licensing agreement. I'll ask him to take another look at it. I'm sure that he wouldn't–"

Corliss raised his hand in front of Königin's face. "Come now, Ms. Clairet, we've totally gone off in the wrong direction. This isn't what I had in mind at all. Please, we're friends and colleagues. Let's talk about something else."

Königin stared at him.

"Okay?" Corliss asked in a conciliatory tone.

"Fine," Königin said, crossing her arms as she sat back in her chair.

He put his hand down and said, "Let's stay on the topic of water and your technology." Then he picked up his folded newspaper and raised it above his head. "This newspaper is full of stories about water and people who need it, right?"

Königin nodded.

"Okay, so what are you doing about that, Ms. Clairet?"

Königin looked around as if someone might validate her confusion. "You know what I'm doing about it. What's your point?" She asked.

"Oh, sure you're developing your global water cannon technology, but by the time you're done farting around with it, millions more will be dead, won't they?"

"I should hope not. I'm trying to help, but it takes a lot of time to develop properly. It's just not ready yet."

"Please, Ms. Clairet, I've seen the results of your trial runs – what are you waiting for? It's time to aim that cannon and fire." Corliss smacked the table.

"Mr. Corliss, it's just not that simple."

"Yes, yes, it is that simple. You're just making it difficult because you're scared. And because you don't have the guts to pull the trigger. People are dying, or at very least, living in deplorable conditions. It's just unconscionable." Corliss shook his head.

"The global water cannon is a complicated and dangerous apparatus – I would just prefer to wait a little longer as we run some more tests."

"How many tests do you need? The thing works. I think you're stalling, and I'd like to know why."

"What are you talking about? Why would I stall?"

"Because you're afraid. And I guess there's the problem – you're just not an experienced scientist like your father, a man who has conviction and who can execute. I think you're much more of a theoretician. It's really too bad."

Königin looked down at the table. Then she looked up to find Corliss looking directly at her.

"Ms. Clairet, I have the benefit of life experience which you simply don't have, but take it from me, you're standing at an intersection right now, a crossroads in your life, and you need to make a decision about which direction you'll take. Trust me, you don't want to make a mistake here."

"I know, I understand, but what if it doesn't work properly? What if there's a problem and something goes wrong? I think I just need a little more time to perfect the technology."

"I think you're asking the wrong questions. You should be asking *what if it works*? What if millions of people are given the water that they need – and you made it happen? You'll be set, won't you? You'll be a hero. You'll dwarf any achievement of your father's, won't you?"

"I'm not in competition with my father, Mr. Corliss," Königin said, and then laughing, she added, "I think you must be reading too much science fiction."

Corliss shook his head and didn't smile. "No, that's not me, Ms. Clairet – I don't read fiction at all. In fact, I only read the newspaper."

"Oh."

"Let's stay focused here," Corliss said. "Your global water cannon – it must become a reality, and we're going to help you achieve that."

"But I'm not sure I want help, Mr. Corliss," Königin said, shrugging her shoulders. "Look, I'm not going to agree to anything right now."

"Oh yes you are," Corliss said, firmly. "Because you know it's the right thing to do. So do us all a favor and stop fighting the inevitable, okay?" Corliss was leaning across the table, staring hard into Königin's eyes.

Königin slumped back into her chair and asked, "How can you help?"

Corliss smiled and said, "It's simple, the Association will fund the entire project."

"But you don't have your grant from the Fund yet, do you?" Königin asked.

Corliss's eyes shot wide open and he suddenly had the expression of a man who's just walked into a sliding glass door. "I beg your pardon? That's – that's totally irrelevant to our discussion, Ms. Clairet. And where we obtain our funding from is none of your concern – do you understand?"

Königin nodded in silence.

Corliss took a deep breath and closed his eyes for a moment. Then he calmly said, "The Association presently has enough money in its coffers to fund the water cannon, so you needn't worry. With what's going on in the world, the Association is likely the only immediate source of funding that you'll find. And this will be a high-profile project, bringing you and the Association enormous exposure."

Königin remained silent.

"You must do this, Ms. Clairet. Any other course of action would be totally irresponsible. Don't miss this opportunity – the time is right," Corliss said.

At that moment, Finley reached over Königin's shoulder and set down a plate with a few chocolate covered graham crackers carefully arranged on it. Königin turned and smiled at him.

"Sorry for being such bruiser," Finley said. "I'll see if I can beat some milk out of somebody for your coffee tomorrow."

Corliss frowned and said, "Excuse me, but we were having a conversation here, about something very important – do you mind?" Finley stared at Corliss for a moment, but then laughed and walked away.

Königin shook her head and said, "Okay, Mr. Corliss, you made your point – I won't blow it – we'll work together on the cannon." Then she leaned toward Corliss and said, "But if you're going to be a man of the people, at least try to be a little nicer to the people."

16

Königin heard her father's voice coming from the end of the long hallway. Maybe even from inside the elevator. It always amazed Königin that such a little man could make so much noise talking to people.

From her office she heard his voice coming closer. Then his voice stopped approaching – he was talking to someone he ran into. Königin hoped that he would be detained for a while. And he was, and she was temporarily relieved. But after a few moments passed, she was annoyed that he would rather talk to a stranger than rush to his daughter who he hadn't seen in some time.

Finally, Dr. Clairet made it to the doorway of Königin's office, leaning in and smiling.

Before he could say anything, her dread turned into excitement. She jumped up and hugged her father. "Thanks for coming."

"Of course," Dr. Clairet said. "The flat is so quiet without you. But I've barely been home."

Dr. Clairet sat in one of the mismatched chairs resting in front of Königin's dented metal desk. He surveyed the office without saying anything.

"Michigan's beautiful, isn't it?" Königin asked her father.

He nodded, and then asked, "How far are we from the water launch site?"

"About four miles – straight east into Lake Huron. Just on the other side of Mackinac Island," Königin answered.

"So, tell me, how is it going here? Are you ready to shoot your big water gun?"

Königin laughed. "It's not really a water gun, but *it will* launch hundreds of thousands of gallons of clean water in minutes." Then she added, "Hopefully landing where it's supposed to."

"Still worried, Königin?" Dr. Clairet asked.

"Yes, it's still too soon, but–"

"It's time to take some risks, Königin," Dr. Clairet interrupted. "It will work, you're a smart girl."

"I know, but I feel like we're rushing everything. And Corliss keeps telling me that the budget is stretched." She shook her head. "But I can't walk away now because–"

"Walk away? What are you talking about, Königin? You've just got the jitters. Just let the thing fly already. It will work fine. You're probably driving Tad Corliss crazy."

"Yes, I guess."

"You should just be happy that they invited you here and set you up. Not a bad gig. And the press you're getting is amazing. I'm jealous."

"True, the exposure has been very good," Königin said, sitting back in her chair.

"When that water hits the ground in Africa, you're going to give Mr. Corliss's organization quite a boost – the Association's coffers will be replenished by the Fund a thousand-fold. The Collaborative will be eager, even thankful to back the Association."

"Yes, I suppose," Königin said. "But I'm doing it so people have ready access to a basic necessity – at least for a few months."

"And after that?" Dr. Clairet asked.

"We'll shoot them as much water as they need, whenever the need it, from anywhere there's an abundance of it. The setup is totally portable."

At that moment, Corliss leaned into the doorway of Königin's office. "Dr. Clairet, so good to see you, sir. It's so wonderful to have you here."

Dr. Clairet stood to shake Corliss's hand. Königin watched them standing together, talking about nothing. And then talking about something.

"The Animator on display at the Pavilion is a fine crowning achievement for you, Dr. Clairet, and we are just so pleased to be a part of that endeavor," Corliss said.

"Listen to you, Mr. Corliss, you would think that the Animator is my swan song," Dr. Clairet said, smiling.

"Oh, please forgive me, I really didn't mean anything by it, why, in fact–"

Dr. Clairet cut Corliss off. "The ĒMAD, Mr. Corliss, that will be my greatest accomplishment."

Corliss stopped talking and looked confused. It was clear from his wide eyes that he didn't know how to respond. "The ĒMAD, Dr. Clairet?"

Königin was shocked. Dr. Clairet rarely spoke about his most important project.

"Yes, Mr. Corliss, the Essential Material Acquisition Device," Dr. Clairet answered.

"The Essential Material Acquisition Device?" Corliss repeated with some difficulty.

Dr. Clairet looked over at Königin and said, "See, I told you, it's a stupid name. It's a mouthful."

Königin didn't respond.

"No, no, hardly, Dr. Clairet, I'm sure it's a fine name. Please tell me what the device does."

Dr. Clairet pursed his lips and looked at Corliss who was waiting for an explanation. Königin knew that her father was now regretting opening his mouth to Corliss. This was nothing new, though.

"Dad, weren't you going to take me to lunch? I'm hungry." Königin said.

"Oh no, Dr. Clairet, you're not getting off that easy. Come now, you must have mentioned it to me for a reason," Corliss said.

Dr. Clairet looked at Königin. The man who was always talking was now not talking.

"Fair enough, Dr. Clairet," Corliss said. "I respect your unwillingness to disclose more, but sharing information about your project with me, in total confidence, could only be helpful – for both of us."

Dr. Clairet forced a hollow laugh. "Yes, Mr. Corliss, I would love to tell you about my new machine, but Königin's hungry and I've promised to take her for sushi. We'll get together soon and chat about it."

Königin quickly stood up and took her worn denim jacket off the back of her chair.

"I completely understand, Dr. Clairet, absolutely, only when you're ready."

Dr. Clairet breathed deeply and then smiled. The three of them walked out of Königin's office and into the hallway, sheeted in dim fluorescent light.

Corliss followed them to the elevator.

"Ah, sushi, I love sushi. It's been ages," Corliss said. "I didn't know you could get sushi here in St. Ignace."

"You can't," Königin said. "We're driving down to Petoskey."

"Oh, are you? I've been meaning to get there, I hear it's a very pretty town," Corliss said.

"It is," Königin said.

"Look at the three of us, here in upper Michigan together," Corliss said, smiling so wide that Königin could see his fillings. "It's really so nice to be together. You don't mind if I join you, do you?" he said, not really asking. "We'll have Königin update us on the upcoming water launch," he said to Dr. Clairet.

As the elevator door opened, Corliss said, "We'll have Malcolm drive us." And there, in the elevator waiting for the three of them, was Malcolm. His eyes hid behind narrow slits of fat and he raised the corners of his closed mouth in the shape of a smile.

They all stood in silence as the noisy box made the three-story descent. Corliss's black limousine parked in front of the little office building looked out of place. Malcolm opened the door of the long car, and with his melonlike head, motioned to Dr. Clairet and Königin to get in. Corliss let himself in on the other side of the car.

After a few minutes of thick quiet, Dr. Clairet said, "This bridge is magnificent." They were crossing the Mighty Mac, one of the longest suspension bridges in the western hemisphere.

"It's just a miniature version of the Golden Gate Bridge – it's really nothing special," Corliss said.

"Hardly," Königin said. "Look at the metalwork, it's beautiful."

"Yes, indeed. Which firm built it, Königin?" Dr. Clairet asked, his eyes fixed on the long suspension cables climbing into the blue sky.

"U.S. Steel. In the mid-1950s."

Corliss sat back in his seat and crossed his arms.

"What's the main span length?" Dr. Clairet asked.

"Thirty-eight hundred feet," Königin answered without hesitating.

"Height of the main towers?"

"Five hundred fifty-two feet," Königin answered, smiling.

"So, this bridge essentially passes over the straits where Lake Michigan and Lake Huron meet, right?" Dr. Clairet asked.

"Yes, exactly," Königin answered.

"Come, Mr. Corliss, you can't deny that this bridge is a metal marvel," Dr. Clairet said.

Corliss smiled and said, "It's just a bridge to me, Dr. Clairet."

And then, from the front of the car, Malcolm blurted out, "A right lousy bridge that costs twenty dollars to cross – and that's why it's bloody empty." Königin exchanged glances with her father.

The group rode in silence until they reached the restaurant.

Malcolm waited in the car as the three sat cross-legged on pillows. Corliss's legs looked like matchsticks in suit pants. His hairless rods connected pant cuffs to perfectly shined dress shoes, which he had refused to remove. Königin's boots and Dr. Clairet's brown suede loafers were neatly placed on a mat at the front door of the restaurant.

"Mr. Corliss, what would you like to start with?" Dr. Clairet asked.

"Totally up to you," Corliss said.

Dr. Clairet ordered edamame and seaweed salad to start with.

"Wait, miss, one moment," Corliss said before the waitress in the kimono left. "We are celebrating today, what kind of champagne do you have?"

"Celebrating? What are we celebrating?" Dr. Clairet asked.

"Don't be silly, we're celebrating Königin's success – the *Global Water Launcher.*"

"Mr. Corliss, I think it may be a bit premature to celebrate," Königin said. "Besides, I doubt they have champagne here."

"It's going to be a success – it has to be," Corliss said.

"Saké or beer, Mr. Corliss?" Dr. Clairet asked.

"Dad, you don't want to start drinking now, do you? In the middle of the day? I've got a lot of work to do."

"Take it easy, Königin. Mr. Corliss just wants to unwind and have some fun. I'm sure we could all use a drink. Besides, saké is child's play," Dr. Clairet said, smiling at Corliss, who smiled back. Königin crossed her arms.

A small white bottle of saké and three little white cups were delivered almost instantly. Königin tried to protest when her father filled one of the cups for her, but he quieted her by holding his index finger to his lips.

"Mr. Corliss, the floor is yours," Dr. Clairet said.

"Oh, for what?" Corliss asked.

Dr. Clairet tilted his head just barely and said, "For the toast, you know, toasting Königin and her achievement."

"Oh yes, of course, how stupid of me." Corliss raised his cup and faced Königin. "To a great girl who is doing great things for everyone." And with that, Corliss shut his eyes hard and gulped down the saké.

Dr. Clairet and Königin laughed a little at Corliss's show.

"Miss, miss, I need a glass of water, right away, please, right now," Corliss said to a woman who wasn't their waitress.

Königin smiled. "Well, thanks Mr. Corliss."

Corliss's much needed water was supplied, and the food order was given, entirely by Dr. Clairet. A variety of rolls and sashimi, lots of tuna and salmon. But Corliss stopped the waitress before she could leave.

"What he ordered sounds lovely, but can I get just a plain piece of chicken? Maybe with some rice. White rice, not fried rice or anything like that," Corliss said.

Königin smiled at her father and finished her cup of saké. She then filled Corliss's empty cup.

"Oh, I'm not sure Königin, I really shouldn't," Corliss said.

"Just in case, Mr. Corliss," Königin said.

Dr. Clairet was on his fourth cup by the time the food showed up.

"So, tell me Corliss, what are your thoughts on the Silence?" Dr. Clairet asked.

Corliss sat silent for a moment. Then he sat up straight in his crossed-legged position and took a breath as he prepared to speak.

"Okay, so here's what I think. Ready? The Silence is nothing more than a cosmic hiccup. Just a bunch of nothing. And of course, people are overreacting. It's nonsense."

Dr. Clairet finished a fifth cup of saké before Königin rebuked the waitress's attempt to bring more. He wiped his lips with his napkin.

"Here's what you're missing, Corliss – people are scared," Dr. Clairet said, raising his voice a little. "They're living in fear. Fear of what's coming next. They have no idea what's around the corner. Whether the Silence is something or nothing is irrelevant, isn't it? Every person creates their own reality from their own perspective with the limited information they have to work with. It's not just a matter of whether someone sees the world from a mountaintop or a valley, no. For most, it's a matter of hoping to see some light through the blinding darkness of uncertainty, trying to understand their world and themselves through the constant screaming interference that prevents that understanding. And that's where the fear comes in. People have a hard-enough time understanding what's right in front of them – but subject them to something that's perceived as hidden, well, then you'll have pandemonium, won't you? And yes, it is silly." Dr. Clairet threw his napkin down on the table. "In fact, it's just downright annoying. We live amongst thousands of unexplainable mysteries every day, but people keep themselves sane with little explanations that they tell themselves. And here comes along just another mystery and people are ready to slit their wrists in panic."

"Dad, take it easy."

"No, Königin – this happened years ago and no one thought the world was coming to end."

"But that was a very different time, Dad. You have to put the Silence in today's context. People are losing their jobs and the businesses that they've built. The gears of our economy – of the world's economy – are turning slower every day now. And life's become just too expensive and the living loans are drying up." Königin looked down and shook her head. "Throw in political and civil unrest and people feel like the whole world is unraveling. The Silence just ignited that fear into an inferno of dread."

Dr. Clairet shook his head angrily. "They're all just a bunch of scared children. Right now the collective fear of this planet is like a dynamo of energy. If the power of that fear could be harnessed, anything could be accomplished. Just point the flock in the right direction and tie ropes to their tails and tell them to *pull, pull*," Dr. Clairet said loudly, shaking both fists above his head.

Königin and Corliss sat silent. Dr. Clairet tilted his empty saké cup into his mouth and shook it dry. Then he held the cup up to make a toast. "Here's to uniting the frightened children because their little world went silent for forty-eight seconds."

Corliss shrugged his shoulders and said, "Well, the people are primed for a solution."

"And guess what?" Dr. Clairet said. "That solution is the ĒMAD. The Essential Material Acquisition Device. It's a game changer."

Königin looked at her father but didn't say anything. Corliss remained silent and didn't move a muscle. He didn't even breathe.

"Don't you want to know what it is, Corliss?" Dr. Clairet asked.

"Only if you feel comfortable talking about it, Dr. Clairet. It's not my way to pressure people, in fact–"

"The ĒMAD is a machine that will open a hole into the next dimension and harvest a fundamental building block element in the form of a hot gas. That element will be a raw resource to create food, water, clean air, and every other material and thing that the world will ever need. The ĒMAD will give us access to the universe's endless gift of this substance. We'll have the ability to create anything from practically nothing. It will be the end of shortages and the beginning of a new society where peace is made possible because no one will go hungry or want for anything."

Corliss's and Dr. Clairet's eyes were locked. Königin looked down into her lap.

"Can you actually do it, Dr. Clairet? Is this just a theory? You know, I've heard an idea like this before."

"Not just a theory, Mr. Corliss. I've actually done it. I've been working on this project for years – since Königin was a little girl. Now she's grown up and so is the ĒMAD."

Corliss blinked and shook his head. Speaking very slowly, he said, "If that's so, then we're about to enter a whole new reality."

Dr. Clairet smiled at Corliss and nodded.

17

"Shouldn't you be somewhere in Europe following Otto Veltraria around?" Königin asked Jess when he unexpectedly showed up at her hotel room door.

Through Königin's tight hug, Jess said, "I think he was glad to get rid of me for a couple of days." She laughed. "I'm sure."

Königin went back into her room and grabbed her shiny metal briefcase and a little brown leather purse. "Let's head downstairs, I need some iced coffee before the test."

As they took the stairs down to the lobby, Jess asked, "So, how's it going here?"

"Fine, I guess."

"Fine? Just fine? What's the problem?"

Königin knew that talking about the project was going to make her even more anxious than she already was, but she couldn't avoid his questioning. "Look, I'm really worried about the water launch. There's so much more that should have been done, but the Association's just about out of money for this project, so I think it's tomorrow or never," she said.

"That doesn't sound promising," Jess said. "What's the magic of tomorrow? Can't you postpone the launch?"

"No, no, it will be fine," Königin answered. "I shouldn't have said anything. I'm just afraid of failure, I guess."

When they reached the bottom of the stairs at the lobby, Jess turned to Königin and said, "Actually, I think you're afraid of success, not failure."

"What does that mean? Who's afraid of success?" Königin asked.

"Someone who thinks they're not worthy of it, someone who thinks that they don't deserve it, no matter how hard they've worked."

"That's just stupid. That's not me."

"Okay, whatever you say," Jess said.

"Maybe you should have stayed with the *Take My Hand Tour* instead of coming here to bother me," Königin said.

"Oh, come on. Don't be mad at me. Listen, that warm anger you're feeling right now means that my arrow hit close to the mark. Maybe even a perfect bullseye."

"Will you shut up already?"

"Sure, I'll stop talking. Besides, my words will eventually sink into your head."

"You better have your own room, Frank, or you'll be sleeping on a chaise lounge at the pool."

Jess and Königin sat in silence on the veranda of the Grand Hotel on Mackinac Island, drinking their coffee.

The old hotel was an immense, five-story white wooden structure with square columns framing out the expansive wooden planked veranda. People sat on rockers that were lined up for 200 feet. In front of the hotel, horse drawn carriages picked up passengers and dropped them off. There were no motorized vehicles allowed on the island, so everyone traveled by foot, bicycle or horse.

"Isn't it a little ridiculous to have your high-tech operation just off an island that's stuck in the 19th Century?" Jess asked.

At first, Königin didn't answer him. Then she said, "Mackinac is perfect. Lake Huron's freshwater is excellent, and the island and St. Ignace have the resources we need. We wanted to stay away from heavily populated areas."

The Association took three entire floors of the Grand to house the water launch's crew.

"When is Corliss coming in?" Jess asked.

"He's already here."

"And your dad?"

"He's already here too," Königin answered. Then she said, "Corliss is all over my dad about this technology my dad's been developing. Corliss is obsessed with it. He thinks it's the panacea the world's been waiting for. I think Corliss must have some kind of attention deficit disorder because it seems like he's already losing interest in the water launch technology before we've even had our first launch."

"How sweet, Corliss is courting your dad," Jess said.

Königin laughed. "Totally."

"I'm looking forward to dinner tonight. It should be interesting," Jess said.

Königin leaned into Jess, who sat still on his rocker. "Look, you'd better not start trouble tonight, okay?"

"Start trouble? I never start trouble. All I do is tell the truth. It's not my fault that trouble often organically evolves from telling the truth."

Königin shook her head. "You know what I mean, Jess."

Jess took another sip of his coffee. "You know, I actually retract my last statement."

Königin looked at Jess and tilted her head in question.

"Or at least the use of the word *trouble*," Jess said. "Trouble is relative. Trouble for a liar is not trouble for the innocent. You know what I mean?"

"No," Königin said.

"Calling me a trouble-maker when all I do is call things as they are is not correct. Untruth is trouble, and so I try to stop trouble and end trouble by reminding people about what the truth is. But, you know, it's a funny thing, people don't like to hear the truth. Not about their friends or their family, and least of all, not about themselves."

Königin looked into the sky. "Got it, Jess. Just don't make trouble today at the test or tonight at dinner – or at any time, okay?"

"Harsh," Jess said. "I fly in from Rome to join you in your moment of glory and I'm scolded before I've even misbehaved."

"Yes," Königin said.

"Well, then I'd better earn that scolding," Jess said.

Before Königin could answer, she was called over by a group of Association officials. She and Jess joined the group and they all made their way along a narrow-paved path that ran around the entire perimeter of the island.

Several minutes later, they arrived at a small concrete dock. A couple of thousand feet into the water sat two huge barges, and in the distance loomed four warships of the newly formed Great Lakes Fleet.

The group was ushered onto a small military motorboat moored at the dock. The boat quickly departed and Jess tried to yell over the sound of the motor and wind to Königin, but she just smiled and shook her head. Jess gave up and tilted his face toward the sun.

As the motor quieted down, the short ride to the main barge neared its end. Standing forty feet tall, the Global Water Launcher had square lines and was very broad at its base, tapering as it pointed to the sky. The machine's wide muzzle aimed southeast at fifty-five degrees. The whole contraption sat atop a series of widely spaced horizontal steel grids built over a twenty-five-foot square opening in the barge that provided access to the lake water below.

Königin climbed down between the grids to inspect the underbelly of the stainless steel launcher, assisted by two technicians in Association uniforms. Jess followed them, effortlessly balancing on one of the grids.

"Which foundry did the metal work?" Jess asked.

Königin and the technicians stopped talking and turned their heads toward him.

"He shouldn't be here. This is a restricted area," one of them said to Königin.

"Why not? This is my project," Königin said.

"No, Ms. Clairet, this isn't your project – it's the Association's."

"You know what I mean," Königin said.

"I'm not sure I do," the woman responded.

"Look, he's a journalist, and he's–"

"A journalist? Really? Where's his press badge?" the woman asked.

"I am not here in that capacity, miss," Jess said.

"Ms. Clairet, you know that only *Trustee* journalists approved by the Association are permitted to report on Association activities," the woman said.

"But I'm not reporting," Jess said. "In fact–"

The woman pulled her radio up to her mouth. "I need security. Now."

"Are you kidding me?" Königin said. "Do you believe this, Jess?"

"Yes, I do, Königin. I really don't disagree with her. I don't have any clearance to be here."

Königin shook her head. "Shut up, Jess."

"Meet me at the pool when you're done here," Jess said.

Within five minutes Jess was on the loud motorboat headed back to the island. He tilted his face up to the sun.

18

In the late afternoon, Jess succeeded in talking Königin into going down to the hotel's pool. She had spent over eight hours on the barge preparing for the following day's launch.

The hotel was built at the top of a hill with a large garden of well-tended flowers terracing down from the busy entrance where guests climbed in and out of covered carriages drawn by well adorned and perfectly manicured horses. On a broad plateau midway down the hill, a huge lawn hosted sunbathers of every age and type of swimsuit. Servers dressed in black pants and buttoned white shirts shuttled drinks and food around on little round trays. And further down the hill was the pool. It was long and wide with a couple of awkward bends, surrounded by a wooden deck.

"I don't think I've ever seen you in shorts," Königin said to Jess as he put a towel down on a chaise lounge.

"I didn't own a pair of shorts until this afternoon. And of course, these were all they had at the gift shop." Jess held his hands up so as not to block Königin's view of the seersucker shorts with a large "G" embroidered on them. Königin laughed. "Very sharp, Mr. Frank."

Jess settled in and propped himself up, pulling his notebook and pen out.

"You going to take your shirt off?" Königin asked, still standing. "Maybe your shoes, too?"

"No, why?"

"You just look so uncomfortable. It's hot out here," Königin said.

"If I'm uncomfortable, I'll tell you."

"Okay," Königin said. He was still looking at her and she became aware that he was going to watch her get comfortable. She wished that she hadn't drawn attention to the removal of clothes. She stood there for a moment waiting for Jess to turn his attention back to his notebook, but he didn't.

"Do you mind?" Königin said.

"Mind what?" Jess asked.

"You know," she said as she wobbled her head.

"No, I don't know."

Königin could see that he was genuinely puzzled.

"Do you have to watch me? I mean, do you have to be so obvious about it?" she asked.

Jess smiled widely. "That's funny. You could be totally without clothes and I wouldn't care."

"Well, I would," she said.

Jess looked down, opened his notebook, and pulled the cap off of his pen.

Turning around, Königin faced in the opposite direction. She unbuttoned her white shorts and let them drop to the ground. Then she pulled her blue tank top off and tossed it on her lounge.

In her hotel room, Königin had already approved of the way she looked in her white one-piece swimsuit.

Before she turned back around to face Jess, Königin saw a man lying on his lounge looking at her, clearly not caring if she noticed. She quickly turned around, only to find Jess looking at her too.

"That wasn't so bad, was it?" Jess asked.

She quickly sat on the lounge in an attempt to hide from the man's eyes.

"You know, your ass looks pretty good in that swimsuit, Königin. I don't know why you're so self-conscious."

Ignoring his comment, she said, "That guy over there was staring at me. Is he still looking over here?"

Jess looked around Königin to see. "Yes, he's still looking in this direction."

Königin quickly put her sunglasses on and picked up a magazine.

"You know who that is, don't you?" Jess asked.

"No, do you?"

"Yes – Admiral Lansing. He's the commander of the Great Lakes Fleet. You should probably thank him for providing the military support for your little operation. I'm sure that's why he's here."

"Oh," she said, before turning in his direction again. He smiled at her but she didn't smile back.

"He's quite a handsome man, isn't he?" Jess said.

"I'm not looking at him in that way, Jess."

Königin looked down at her magazine, but she couldn't concentrate. She felt like he was watching her every move. And she pictured his symmetrical face and she wondered what the tattoo on his thick arm was. She had only taken a quick glance before, but the snapshot in her mind showed a herculean chest and tailored stomach, and muscular legs, separated by short red swim trunks. She just knew that he was still looking at her, and then she thought that it might be rude if she didn't acknowledge him. So, she slowly turned again toward him, ready to make eye contact. But his eyes weren't there. None of him was there. And then she heard the collective cheering of a handful of sailors as Lansing sunk himself deep into the pool in the form of a cannonball.

"What a child," Königin said to Jess, shaking her head.

"He's just having some fun, tight-ass," he replied.

"You be quiet. You're supposed to agree with me, but you never do. I don't know why I bring you along," Königin said.

"I'll agree with you when you say something agreeable," Jess said, without looking up.

She ignored Jess and leaned back and closed her eyes. In less than a minute, she was asleep.

—◦◦◦—

When Königin awoke an hour later, most of the guests had left the pool, including Admiral Lansing.

She turned on her side toward Jess. "Still writing?"

"Yes."

"What are you working on?"

"I'm just journaling about this place. I hope it's still in business a year from now," Jess said, with no trace of a smile.

Königin nodded.

After a few minutes she asked, "Things better between you and Otto?"

"Not at all. I think he's almost at the point of hating me."

Königin sat up on her elbow and looked at Jess. "You're quite a well-liked guy, aren't you, Mr. Frank?"

"If you want people to like you, Ms. Clairet, only tell them what they want to hear." Jess didn't look up from his notebook.

Königin leaned back, closing her eyes again. "I'll try to remember that," she said, smiling.

19

"I'm sorry, sir, you can't enter the hotel dining room without a jacket," the host said to Jess.

"But I am wearing a jacket," Jess said, raising his arms so that the leather fringe of his jacket hung straight down. Königin giggled.

"A dinner jacket, sir. I'm sorry, but we can't make any exceptions," the host said from his tuxedo.

"But I don't have a dinner jacket," Jess said.

"No problem, sir, I'll have one brought up for you. What size do you wear?"

Just then, Tad Corliss and Dr. Clairet exited the tiny elevator in the lobby and approached them.

"Königin, hello dear," Dr. Clairet said, giving his daughter an awkward hug. Then Dr. Clairet turned to Jess. "Hello, Jess. Very kind of you to come in for the launch."

"Yes, Mr. Frank, how delightful to see you," Corliss said, slowly tilting his head up and down, surveying Jess. "I'm surprised that your exquisite cowboy jacket meets the dining room dress code."

"Oh, yes. In fact, I think they're making suede mandatory in the dining room," Jess said.

Dr. Clairet and Königin laughed.

"I'll be in nothing but chaps tomorrow night," Jess said to Corliss.

"There won't be a tomorrow night, Mr. Frank," Corliss said.

Jess hesitated, and then said, "That doesn't sound good, Mr. Corliss. Hopefully that won't be your doing."

At that moment an attendant arrived with a dinner jacket. He held it open for Jess. It was bright green with a gold embroidered "G" on the chest pocket. Jess smiled at Königin and allowed himself to be jacketed.

"Mr. Frank, you look somewhat respectable in that garment. Perhaps you should retire that old thing that you wear around," Corliss said as they all walked single file to their private dining room. Jess didn't respond.

There were several round tables set up for the group. The china, crystal and neatly folded linen napkins matched the royal looking furniture of the room. Some of the water launch party had already arrived and were snacking on nuts and chocolates.

At a table near the center of the room, Admiral Lansing sat between two of his officers, talking to one of them. As soon as Königin saw Lansing, she quickly turned away and headed for an empty table in the corner.

"Königin, where are you going?" Dr. Clairet asked.

Lansing looked up at Dr. Clairet and then Königin. He quickly stood up and his two wingmen followed a half a moment later.

"Ms. Clairet, it's very good to meet you," Lansing said, smiling. "The Great Lakes Fleet is pleased to be a part of your historic project."

Before Königin could respond, Corliss said, "You mean the Association's project, Admiral Lansing. The launch is an Association project."

Lansing's smile faded. "Yes, of course, Mr. Corliss," he said.

Jess, who had dropped his head when Corliss made his comment, now looked at Lansing. "Forgive him, Admiral Lansing. Mr. Corliss has a habit of correcting everyone and stating the obvious in the process," Jess said.

"Please, Jess, stop," Königin said quietly.

Corliss raised his hand to dismiss the comment. "I'm not going to ruin the evening by even responding."

Dr. Clairet glared at Jess as he and Corliss took a seat at Lansing's table.

Lansing and his two men remained standing, and upon Lansing's subtle nod, one of the men moved over to make room for Königin. She stood still, not moving toward the empty seat – until Jess gave her a little shove, for which she returned a mean pinch to his leg that no one saw. Jess sat on the other side of the relocated officer.

"Thank you for your help with our project, admiral," Königin said, aware that her hands were entertaining each other.

"We're very glad to do it," Lansing said. "You're using your technology in the right way – it will feel good to get that water where it's needed. And like you, I enjoy helping people, or in some cases, saving them."

Königin looked at Lansing and smiled in response.

"Hopefully you won't need to save anyone tomorrow, admiral," Königin said.

"Not to worry, I'm sure everything will go fine. But we are going to surround the perimeter of the launch site with some of our best assets, and we'll clear a broad no-fly zone," Lansing said. "There are just too many destructive forces working now to take any chances." Then Lansing reached for a roll and the plate of butter pads, each arranged perfectly and branded with a miniature "G."

Königin looked over and saw Jess animated in a conversation with one of Lansing's men. Then she turned to Lansing to see that he was watching the same conversation as he ate his roll.

"Sorry for my friend's outburst before. He has a habit of being rude and not caring about it," Königin said.

"Don't apologize for him, Ms. Clairet," Lansing said. "You're not responsible for his actions. Besides, he just spoke his mind, and that's not such a bad thing – at least we know what he's thinking."

Königin nodded. "Yes, that's Jess."

After sitting in silence for a few minutes, Königin became aware that her muscles were tired, but not from the work she had done earlier in the day at the launch site, but rather from the tenseness she felt in every part of her body – she had tightened herself up, and it hurt. She looked around at the tables, all filled with people talking, and she tried to relax.

Lansing leaned across her for a dish of toffee that was on the other side of her. She immediately tightened up again. His scent touched her. It was a mix between the starch of his blue uniform and some mild wintergreen aftershave finished with a deep gentle wood.

"Oh, sorry, I could have gotten that for you," she said, fumbling her words.

"I didn't want to interrupt you," Lansing said as he handed the dish over to Dr. Clairet who had asked for it.

"Interrupt me?"

"Yes, you were thinking. That's the worst time to interrupt someone," Lansing said.

"I guess you're right, so thanks," she said. He smiled at her, but not for a moment too long.

The tables weren't too large, seating only six or seven people, so Königin was able to talk to everyone and listen in on conversations she wasn't a part of. She noticed that Lansing was doing the same thing, sometimes for long periods keeping quiet and observing. At moments she felt as if she and the admiral were hosting a dinner party.

"Can't we build the ĒMAD in a more scaled-down fashion? It's simply too expensive," Corliss said to Dr. Clairet.

"If the Association can't get the Collaborative to finance the project, I'll find another way to get the money from the Fund," Dr. Clairet answered.

"No, we'll make it happen," Corliss said. "But we'll need exclusivity on the project while we figure it out – you'll have to agree to not discuss doing it with anyone else."

Dr. Clairet took a sip of his red wine and shook his head. "I don't know, Tad, I'm not sure that I want to limit myself. If you don't have the firepower to make it happen, it's really all right –

there are other things we'll find to work on together. Besides, it's not just the funds required to complete the project – I'm concerned that the Association is such a new organization with not much of a track record or any kind of cache in the international community."

"Oh, so it's good enough for your daughter's project but not yours?" Corliss said, not wasting a moment.

"That's ridiculous, Tad. Don't be so argumentative. The ĒMAD is unlike any apparatus ever built. It's going to be an extremely demanding project. Not just to build it, but to start it and operate it. Frankly, I'm not even sure it can be done with our current resources. It's incredibly demanding. It probably needs all of the energy output of the entire planet – and then some." Dr. Clairet finished the wine in his glass and tapped the top, prompting an immediate refill.

Corliss sat up straight in his chair and said, "Let's get past the water launch tomorrow and then I'm going to figure this out. It'll be great for you and the Association. How do you think international cache is developed? Through successful projects. And I'd also like to think that the Exposition has been very effective in bringing great exposure to the Association."

Dr. Clairet took a sip of his wine. "I suppose."

Königin turned to see that Lansing was watching Jess and the officer discuss Jess's chronicling of the *Take My Hand Tour*. Jess kept stretching his arms straight out in front of him attempting to loosen his green jacket.

"The tour's been like a drum roll, starting out low and steady and growing in tempo and volume," Jess explained. "I'm just waiting for the pop of the kick drum and the smack of the symbol."

The officer laughed. "What's he like?"

"Fabulously talented and convinced that he was born to help. But sadly out of touch from his perch of thirty thousand feet," Jess said, his mouth full of London broil. "Have you ever seen him in concert?"

"Oh, yes," the officer answered. "I've been to nine of his shows over the years. I must say, though, I miss the Knew Society days. Does he ever talk about Lee Earlman?"

"Never. And I've broached nearly every subject with him, but that one I stay away from," Jess said. "At least until the end of the tour."

"I can understand that. What a nasty business," the officer said, shaking his head. "I can't believe that Earlman is spending his life going from town to town playing small gigs."

"That's his choice. He's been invited to play lead guitar for the world's best bands, but he'd rather do his own thing," Jess said.

"I guess, but it's got to be tough watching Veltraria's success through the years," the officer said. "I mean, even when Otto took years off from recording and touring, he was still insanely popular. Earlman can't enjoy watching that."

"Maybe he doesn't care," Jess said.

"Well, if he doesn't, then there's something wrong with him."

Then Lansing spoke up. "So you assume that money and adulation are the most important things to everyone?"

"No, sir, no I don't," the officer said. "But I think it's only human nature for Lee Earlman to look at his old bandmate and be envious of the fame and fortune that he built for himself."

Now Dr. Clairet and Corliss were also listening to the conversation.

"I've never met Veltraria," Lansing said. "But if I were to guess, I'd say that fame and fortune weren't his primary incentives. Look at his body of work and you'll find a pretty consistent theme of activism. He's part folk singer, part humanitarian, part rock and roll idol, part motivational speaker and part choir organist. And who knows, maybe one day part politician. His ability to move people with his music is quite extraordinary. I've followed his work for years and I don't think he embarked on the *Take My Hand Tour* for money or worship – he has enough of both. He saw the world falling apart and he probably thought that this was how he could help. Wouldn't you agree, Mr. Frank?"

"Not totally, Admiral Lansing," Jess said. "I think playing the role of savior has always been a selfish indulgence for Otto. It gets him off. But he'd deny it because he isn't aware of it – if he was aware of it, he couldn't pull the whole thing off so well. He really thinks he cares. And maybe to a certain extent he does. I just don't know yet."

Before Lansing could respond, Corliss spoke up. "What nonsense, Frank. I find it pretty lousy that Otto is kind enough to take you along on his tour and you would even dream of saying something that wasn't one hundred percent favorable toward him. What kind of man does that?"

Just then, the sound of jet engines rumbled overhead, and the entire dining room looked up. Lansing put his hand on Königin's shoulder.

"Just policing the no-fly zone," Lansing said to the table. In a moment his words spread to the next table, and in a few minutes, the tables at the far end of the main dining room knew that navy jets had flown over as part of an operation that was taking place in the lake.

"I must say, Admiral Lansing, I'm very impressed with the security measures you've put in place. I didn't expect so many ships and planes," Corliss said.

"A necessity, Mr. Corliss. We had to take each threat seriously," Lansing said.

"Each threat? How many were there?" Königin asked.

"Half a dozen or so," Corliss answered.

Königin looked at Corliss, her eyes wide. "Half a dozen? Why didn't I know anything about this?"

"What was the point? What would you have done? There was no need to trouble you with any of that," Corliss said.

"I guess, but it's a little unsettling," Königin said.

"Don't worry about it, young lady, it's not a concern of yours," Corliss said.

"Who were the threats from?" Königin asked Lansing.

"All of the groups that you would expect – Light of Freedom, World Fatigue, the Crushed – and others. No one surprising," Lansing answered.

The table sat silent for a moment.

"But oddly absent from the list was Inevitable. Can't think why they wouldn't want to ruin our fun," Lansing added.

"Who knows," the officer said. "They're the worst of the griping groups – by far the most extreme. Rather than remake civilization, they'd prefer to burn it to the ground."

A server put a small piece of chocolate cheesecake on Königin's plate. It was covered in strawberry sauce. She felt sick.

"Are you all right, Ms. Clairet?" Admiral Lansing asked.

"Yes, thanks, I'm just tired." Königin looked at her father and Corliss and then to Jess and the officer. Finally, she turned to Lansing and said, "Please excuse me, I'm going to turn in. We have a big day tomorrow."

Lansing and his two men quickly stood as she rose from her seat. The rest of the men at the table remained seated.

"Königin, do you want me to walk you to your room?" Jess asked. Königin shook her head and Jess went back to chatting with the officer.

No one saw Lansing's subtle nod to a man sitting by himself at a small table in the shadow of the constantly opening and closing door to the kitchen. The man stood up, straightened his necktie, and dropped twenty feet behind Königin as she left the dining room.

20

The early red sun reflected off the smooth metal surface of the water launcher. Königin stared at the machine from the central control barge a hundred yards away. She listened to the chatter of the technicians as they prepared to initiate the launch sequence.

Another pass of the jets confirmed the skies were clear. Admiral Lansing's fleet surrounded the barges.

The fact that she built what she had imagined in her mind, and was now looking at, gave Königin a feeling of complete satisfaction, which had only been an abstract concept until now. For that very moment, she felt a sense of peace, even though she was anxious about the launch. That familiar feeling of confusion and questioning and searching had dissolved for the moment. She had never been sure if there was any such thing as a divine purpose, and she still wasn't sure, but she was pleased that she had given herself this purpose. She finally felt in control of her life.

"For your sake, I hope it works," Corliss said over Königin's shoulder.

"If it was built correctly it will work, Mr. Corliss," She answered.

Observing the launch preparations, Dr. Clairet calmly walked behind the row of technicians working at the long control panel covered with round dials and digital numbers. Thick power cables covered the floor of the control barge like spaghetti and then made their way to the launcher over narrow pontoon platforms.

"Ms. Clairet, we're ready. We're commencing the water intake process," one of the technicians said.

"Good. Don't rush the cleansing process. Just take your time," Königin said.

A low loud hum filled the air as the launcher gathered the water to fire. For the first time that morning, Königin became aware of the dozens of automated *Trustee* television cameras set-up on a nearby barge.

Königin thought of Admiral Lansing. He seemed kind, or at least courteous. And strong, maybe too strong. She didn't like how he never flinched, even in the most awkward situations. For a second, she hated him, thinking that he was smug. But then she thought that maybe he was just confident. Königin wasn't sure how she felt about him.

"They're ready in Saba Saba to receive the water. We have clearance to launch," one of the technicians announced to the small group gathered near the control panel.

"Well, Ms. Clairet?" Corliss asked.

"Confirm that the airspace is clear," she said.

"All clear," a technician answered.

Königin put her hands together and began to play with her fingers.

"Is the area secure? Do we have clearance from the fleet? Is Admiral Lansing clear to go?" she asked.

"All clear," said a mechanical voice through a radio speaker.

Königin pulled her long hair up above her head and began to stroke it quickly. She looked at her father, who was scribbling in his notebook, and then at Corliss, who was staring at her.

"Maybe we should run through another test, Mr. Corliss, I don't want to take any chances," Königin said.

"Nonsense, Ms. Clairet. If you won't give the order to launch, I will. You have ten seconds," Corliss said.

"Okay, Mr. Corliss, okay."

Königin twisted her hair and left the mess sitting on top of her head.

"Fire. Initiate the launch," she said quickly.

With that order, a woman sitting at the control panel pressed a flashing button without even turning around to acknowledge Königin's words.

A perfectly tailored segment of water sixteen feet in diameter and fifty feet long erupted from the muzzle of the stainless steel launcher. The self-contained capsule of water shot into the sky, cracking the sound barrier as it launched. Then another water missile was fired, and then another, until thirty-five of them had been sent high into the atmosphere, only to turn back toward earth at the right moment and land nearly eight thousand miles away in a massive water collecting receptacle designed by Königin. Each water segment was like the car of a bullet train pulling into a station at great speed and abruptly coming to rest.

Königin looked into the sky as the last delivery of water disappeared into the clouds.

21

The Whole Truth Trustee ran the headline, "Association's Water Launcher Hits Its Mark." The story ran on the first page of both sides of the newspaper of every edition around the globe.

SABA SABA, KENYA

Hundreds of villagers danced in this African town as they greeted a most unusual delivery of water. Not by truck or train, but by air – without a plane. Flying through the air faster than the speed of sound after being fired from a massive cannon-type device, the water made an arch from its launch point in Lake Huron, located in the American state of Michigan, to the village of Saba Saba, north of Nairobi.

In the time span of approximately ten minutes, over 350,000 gallons of clean water traveled thousands of miles to massive stainless steel receiving and holding tanks. Almost immediately, the water began to flow through a distribution system designed and built in anticipation of its delivery.

The water launch project was sponsored by the Association of Comprehensive Solutions, which is also the purveyor of the now renowned Comprehensive Solutions Exposition housed in the Water Pavilion. The Pavilion, located in London's historic Hyde Park, showcases newly developed technologies focused on world preservation. In an interview this morning, Association chairman Tad Corliss told *The Trustee* that the water launch project is just one of the world changing technologies that the Association has developed. "We're on a march, a march toward providing for all of the needs of humanity. And as conditions worsen, as they surely will, the Association will be there to help," Mr. Corliss said.

The Association funded its global water launch project from its existing monies, but according to Mr. Corliss, the Association only has the financial resources to fund one more launch. However, Mr. Corliss has disclosed to *The Trustee* that as a result of the successful water launch, the Guiding Institutions Collaborative is considering sponsoring future Association projects through the Collaborative's ambitiously capitalized Fund. "We have a major new project that we're about to embark upon, one that will demand far more than the Association's remaining resources, and we're hopeful that the Collaborative will make a generous grant from the Fund to support that project as well as the global water launch project," Mr. Corliss said, declining to disclose any further details.

The Guiding Institutions Collaborative is an enterprise established by select companies, lenders, organizations, institutions of higher learning, and high net-worth individuals who are committed to achieving the best results in light of current and anticipated conditions (this newspaper's parent, Whole Truth Information Trust, is a proud member of the Collaborative). The Collaborative formed the Fund to provide financial resources to governments and struggling organizations to allow them to continue their operations as revenues have fallen and public and private debt have ballooned to unmanageable limits.

Several nations and their militaries cooperated in clearing air traffic along the water's route from the United States to Kenya as well as providing security at both the launch and landings sites. Admiral Lansing, commander of the United States Great Lakes Fleet, assumed the lead role of coordinating the joint military effort, which saw no incidents during the operation. Although several threats were made against the launch by a variety of subversive groups, none of the threats materialized.

The next water launch is scheduled to take place two weeks from today.

22

Sitting cross-legged on the metal floor of the outdoor observation deck, Ann Raye looked down at the city streets more than a hundred stories below. The people on the streets looking up at her and her fellow captives blended into one faceless mass.

The wind slapped Ann's face, and she was reminded that there was little mercy – and certainly none from nature. She held on tight to her daughter who sat on her lap and said something every few minutes. "Mommy, I'm cold," and "When can we go home?"

They had all been ordered to look down, which was easier for her than looking up at the people that were now in control of her life. Only a few of them had their rifles pointed at the group. The rest were working together to hang banners over the side of the observation deck. Her captors spoke to each other from behind canvass shrouds.

One of them, a short one, quickly approached her. Ann pulled her daughter close to her, eliciting a complaint from the child. Little holes in the black shroud revealed bright hazel eyes. "Please, look down, please – it's for your own good," the female voice said before quickly walking away.

Police helicopters circled the observation deck that sat on top of the most iconic midtown Manhattan office building. The noise of the flying machines was deafening, and the mother covered the ears of her child.

Spotlights mounted on the helicopters took turns blinding the dozen captives and their handful of captors. One of the lights flashed on a banner before it went over the side of the deck – it read "THE BEAST CRUSHES."

Ann heard orders being given behind her and she turned her head quickly, trying not to alarm her daughter with the sudden movement. Three members of the group were preparing to lower more banners over the side. One read "CRUSHED BUT ALIVE." and the others were long, narrow red banners, each with a city's name on it – Chicago, Moscow, Lagos, Paris, Madrid, Rome, London, Mexico City, Los Angeles and Tokyo.

That morning, the Statue of Liberty was Ann's intended destination. Then Times Square and Central Park. But her six-year-old woke up with a fever, so they spent the day in the hotel room watching movies and eating what snacks they could find. In the evening her fever broke, and they went to see the city lights from that high place.

Ann thought about how the smallest decisions in life can have such profound consequences. Then she thought about the banners and assumed that this was the group that called itself the *Crushed*. There were so many voices clamoring to be heard in the world now – so many that she found it difficult to hear what they were saying and what they stood for – each one with its cause and its flag. These groups were more than just disgruntled revolutionaries – each one moved in a specific direction, employing whatever means it deemed appropriate to advance its agenda. But Ann understood why these groups had formed. As the flow of money narrowed to a trickle, the quality of life deteriorated rapidly, and it seemed as if nothing could be fixed through conventional means. She too felt crushed – she had exhausted all of her options to pay for life. But still, Ann couldn't bear to deny her daughter the trip to New York that she had promised.

Suddenly, a cheer rose up from the three shrouded group members who had lowered the "CRUSHED BUT ALIVE" banner. One of them held a small radio to his ear and reported to the other two. Then one of them yelled to the rest of the group, "*The Trustee* radio station is covering us – and our campaigns in London and Chicago. Mexico City too."

Ann exchanged questioning glances with the other captives. No one knew what the celebrated victory meant. The group's members hugged one another and laughed and whistled from behind their shrouds.

"And now Tokyo, they're talking about us in Tokyo," one of them reported. He was the biggest of them all, a man with a big deep voice. "Now let us be heard here in New York," he shouted to his group.

This man was no shorter than six and a half feet and was built like two stacked oil drums. His blue jeans, tennis shoes and ski jacket would have been a perfectly ordinary outfit on a man without a canvass shroud pulled over his head. He surveyed his group of captives. Now, no one even made an attempt to look down – wide eyes looked at each other.

The helicopters continued to swirl around the building with their lights trained on the observation deck. But the wind had picked up and Ann could see that the choppers were being pushed around by the gusts.

The man stood tall, and with a megaphone in his hand, he addressed one of the beams of light focused on him.

"Why has it come to this?" he shouted. "Why must we take these drastic measures to wake everyone up? Why are we broken?" He then shook his head before continuing. "We have been taken advantage of in every way. And we have allowed this to happen, time and time again. But who is more guilty – those that crush us or us who allow ourselves to be crushed?" He placed his free hand on his heart and said, "For most of us, it's too late. We will never know a different world."

Then he quickly approached Ann and her daughter and extended his hand to the young girl. "No!" Ann yelled as she held her daughter tightly to her.

"Come now, you have no choice," the man said as he pulled the girl from her mother's grasp. One of the other captors pointed his rifle at Ann's face and she sat in her place, watching as her little girl was hoisted on the shoulders of the man. The child screamed as he walked to the edge of the deck nearest to the helicopter that had been providing his spotlight.

"Quiet, quiet," the man said. The girl controlled her screams to sobbing as she tried to turn around to see her mother. The man held her in place.

"This girl, she is the reason we do this tonight. She and all of the generations, born and unborn, who suffer and will suffer for our collective failures. No more empty promises of a decent life, no more paying for the past with our future, and no more taking everything from us one dollar at a time. We demand–"

A bright light momentarily flashed from the helicopter and a short crack rang out above all of the other noises in the sky that night. A bullet passed straight through the man's chest and bounced off the floor of the observation deck, making a whizzing sound. He staggered toward the short railing as the girl screamed. As his legs buckled beneath him, Ann jumped up and grabbed her daughter's ponytail from behind and pulled her backward onto her. Before they could try to sit up, gunfire and shouting erupted as a SWAT team stormed the deck. Ann rolled over on her daughter, covering every bit of her.

Within five seconds the gunfire was over. Ann slowly picked her head up and looked around, still lying on top of her daughter. Her captors were motionless, their bodies lying and sitting in awkward positions taken as they fell. The tall man's body was slumped over the railing, facing down toward the pavement far below.

Ann sat up and put her daughter on her lap. Putting her cheek next to her little girl's cheek, she looked over the child's shoulder and saw two of the SWAT officers talking over the body of the hazel-eyed girl who had told her to look down. Her shroud lay on the deck, and now revealed was the delicate face of a woman in her mid-twenties, pretty, with long hair. She lay motionless with her eyes open and a thin stream of bright red blood dripping down her cheek.

One of the officers shook the dead woman's weapon in the air and shouted, "These rifles are empty – all of them – they never even planned on returning fire!"

For the first time since the ordeal began, Ann cried.

23

Halfway through his show, Otto paced the stage and spoke to his silent audience. "And that business last night in New York and Tokyo and London – what was the Crushed trying to accomplish?" Otto let out a little laugh and said, "Sounds like the name of a garage band – and a lousy one at that." Some laughter broke the silence of the audience. "What are any of these angry groups trying to accomplish?" Otto asked.

The crowd's answer was a mud of yells and cheers.

"Well, it seems that we agree, don't we?" Otto said, smiling. The crowd now exploded into laughter.

Otto looked down at the floor for a moment, and then he squinted into the stage lights above as if looking for something. "Like it or not, something's happening here," he said. "And when I say here, I mean everywhere." Then he quickly walked to the center of the stage and pointed at the people. "It's you and it's me," and then swinging around he motioned toward his band, "and it's them – even Shiloh."

Shiloh broke into a short drum solo bringing the crowd to another cheer.

"It's a feeling we're all having," Otto continued. "And it's not just the money thing – I mean, let's be honest – I'm a bit immune to that problem. But dammit, I've been feeling something for years. Just listen to my earliest records and you'll hear it, you know, me complaining about that feeling. It's an angst, an ache – this underlying feeling of dread that something is fundamentally wrong in our world. It feels like we're being chased by a pack of dogs trained to keep us running, but we can never quite see the faces of those that set them upon us. It's this pressure to move faster, to move better, to play the game – and most of all, to win the game. The steps and stations of our lives are determined by those that need to use us to accomplish their varied objectives – some political, some sadistic, but almost always financial. The course of our existence is invisibly put into motion in a way that seems like there's simply no other way to live. It's a feeling of helplessness – and it grows by the day."

The entire concert hall was quiet.

"And the Silence certainly hasn't helped. Who caused it and why can't we get a straight answer about it from our worthless governments?" Otto shouted. After a few moments, voices from the crowd spoke up and shouted "why" and "tell us."

Otto shook his head and smiled. "Oh no, don't go there. Don't go dragging me into that." The crowd cheered and the band started laughing. "Look, one side of *The Whole Truth Trustee* reports that World Fatigue is responsible for the Silence while the other side of the newspaper says it was Inevitable – but your guess is as good as mine, my friends. But I'm not here to speculate, I'm here to offer you my hand," Otto said, extending his right hand out to the crowd. "My hand to you in strength, to lift you up by your heart, that's why we're together tonight here in beautiful Berlin." The crowd erupted as Otto ran to his old Hammond organ and sat behind it, giving a cue to Althea.

Sitting there in his black jeans and charcoal frock coat that hung over the back of his bench and touched the stage, Otto's hands glided over the instrument's two keyboards. He never looked down and he never looked like he was working at it. The entire band was onstage now – voices, brass, strings and drums. Althea played her trumpet with one hand while throwing cues to the band with the other. Their huge sound filled the indoor venue, which was sold to capacity. Otto's voice was clear as he enunciated every word.

Otto had always been very careful to make the lyrics of his songs understandable. He didn't want a word to be missed. As early as Knew Society's first album, he included a separate sheet of lyrics along with the vinyl, maintaining that the tiny liner notes were insufficient afterthoughts of album design. When asked about that by Jess, Otto had answered, "Every word which is uttered and written is so important because it has an impact of one sort or another. People throw words around without realizing they're like little darts. Some people shouldn't be allowed to speak. And some people should have a lifetime limit on how many words they speak, you know, when they hit their allocation they can't speak any more. Maybe this way they'll actually think before they talk, or at least they'll mean what they say and make every word count."

Not all of Otto's former bandmates shared his passion, or near obsession, with lyrical integrity. During the same conversation that Otto had explained his position on words to Jess, Otto recounted a fight with lead guitarist Lee Earlman that contributed to Knew Society's breakup.

"It was a lifetime ago," Otto told Jess. "We were preparing for our big show in Black Rock. You were too young to be there, but I'm sure you've seen all of the video – we had an elaborate light and stage show. For the time, it was quite advanced. But today, it would be laughable."

Jess jotted quickly to keep up.

"The trouble started on a bouncy minibus ride after a sound check," Otto said, starting his story.

"All right, tell me what you think of this," Otto said to Earlman, reading out of his spiral notebook:

Who put you in charge?
You're so illegit, I needn't even quit
A farce of a crown, really no more than a clown

Lee was lying across the short seat of the minibus with his eyes closed. Otto could only see his bare legs and sandals.

"That works, right?" Otto asked.

The bus bumped and everyone jilted up and then down as if in slow-motion. Then the ride smoothed out a little. No response.

"Lee?" Otto said in a loud voice.

The legs spoke. "Yeah, it's fine, Otto."

Otto shook his head. "Fine, what do you mean it's fine, Lee?"

"I mean it's fine, Otto. What more do you want?"

"I'd like a little feedback, Lee."

The bus was hot and sandy. Otto wiped his face with a handkerchief.

"I think your lines are fine, Otto, they're getting your general point across, I think."

"My general point? What's my general point, Lee?"

Keeping his eyes closed, Lee sat up in his seat, slumped. His white t-shirt was light beige from the sand of the day.

Speaking in monotone, Lee said, "That you're pissed because you don't believe in the legitimacy of any government." Lee then slid back down onto the seat.

"Not bad for a guy who's half asleep. Listen, I'm really kicking the word *farce* around in my head. Not sure that it really hits the mark," Otto said, tapping his fingers on his knee. "You see, the crown itself isn't a farce, it's just an expensive hat acting as a symbol of government, of leadership. And even though that kind of symbol itself isn't a farce, the government that it represents is just a fiction created by people who agree to be led and get along. But what about the people that didn't sign up to be led? Those that are forced to be good little citizens? What if they won't recognize the king or president or prime minister as a legitimate leader? I mean, if the people can't choose to opt in or out of their chosen government, their government isn't legit. Forced governmental legitimacy is inherently illegitimate, is it not?"

"They're not all expensive," Lee said from his reclined position.

Otto tilted his head sideways. "What?"

"They're not all expensive."

"What are you talking about, Lee?" Otto asked.

"Crowns. Some are made out of twigs and leaves. Look at Julius Caesar. The man ruled an empire with a laurel wreath on his head," Lee said.

Otto shook his head and said, "I feel like I'm writing this album by myself, Lee."

"You just now figured that out, Otto?"

"What's wrong with you?" Otto asked.

"I think you're asking the wrong question," Lee said.

Otto shook his head again. He wasn't smiling. "Okay, I'll play, Lee. What question should I be asking?"

"Thank you, Mr. Veltraria. The question you should be asking is, *What is wrong with me?*"

"What is wrong with me?" Otto said. "Nothing. Nothing is wrong with me, Lee."

Lee sat up and looked at Otto. "And that's your problem, Otto. It's the world that has to be fixed, but never Otto. Always start the failure analysis from within, old friend." Lee laid back down. "And I really don't give a shit whether you use *farce* or *clown* or *wench* so long as it sounds good and makes some sense. You're killing me with your endless wordsmithing against every common, popular enemy that you can point a finger at. Go find the real enemy and then write a song about that. Maybe a whole goddamned album."

Otto lowered his head and turned around in his seat.

Other than looking at each other across the stage for cues during shows, Otto and Lee ignored each other for the rest of what became Knew Society's last tour.

From the wings of the stage in Berlin, Jess saw Otto shoot a look to the guitarist that replaced Lee years ago, and the song took a turn toward its crescendo with that cue. The crowd cheered and chanted in German and English, and soon the strings and horns fell back, yielding to Otto's keyboard, which now sounded like a church organ.

Jess watched Otto's feet dance on the long wooden foot pedals while his arms, seemingly disconnected from his body, punished the keyboard. The back of Otto's coat was soaked with sweat.

Within ten minutes, the show was over, and the people slowly made their way to the exits. Tour shirts had been dropped to half price and the vendors couldn't sell them fast enough.

✑⟶ 24 ⟵✑

All three of the *Take My Hand Tour* shows in Madrid were sold
out. Otto's face looked down at the Spaniards from huge
concert posters dotting the city.

In the oldest bullring in Spain, Jess sat a few rows behind Otto
in a circular crowd of 25,000 people. Otto made Jess sit with *The
Trustee* reporters.

Jess could see the back of Otto's head, his long black and gray hair
neatly tied up and his neck partially covered by the short collar of a
red Nehru jacket. Otto was the guest of Spain's prime minister and
Señor Tuerto, a media magnate, and he sat between them in the ring's
premier box. From Jess's vantage point, Otto's big white teeth flashed
every time that he turned to one of his hosts. He seemed to be smiling.

Red and yellow banners flew high above the bullring. A fast
paced, two-step rhythm played as the first fight's matador prepared for the bull's entry into the ring. The sun was bright and it
illuminated the matador's blue and gold outfit.

A massive black bull was let into the ring, its white horns
pointed toward sky.

The matador watched the bull closely, studying his movements,
carefully noting his behavior. After a few minutes, the matador tested
the creature's charge with a wave of a cape. The bull was easily bated
by the taunting.

Jess figured that Otto was enjoying the pageantry of the event. Watching Otto's head rotate, Jess could see that Otto was following every move.

Two heavily padded horses entered the ring. On each was a man with a sharp lance. These men, picadors, took turns sticking the bull in the neck, drawing blood and weakening the creature. The bull angered and charged its tormentors but they skillfully avoided his attacks.

Otto shook his head slowly, almost imperceptibly.

Then, the matador coaxed the bull to charge again, and as the bull passed, the matador planted a colorful barbed lance, a banderilla, in the bull's shoulder. With each pass, the matador planted another banderilla, drawing more blood. The bull charged, angered but weakening.

Five banderillas now hung from the bull's shoulders. The animal's head and horns hung low.

After a few minutes, trumpets announced the final stage of the fight. The prime minister pointed to the ring. The crowd cheered as the officially designated embodiment of evil, the accused enemy of the people, the troublemaker, futilely charged the matador in angered confusion.

Otto's back and neck stiffened straight up.

The bull was nearly spent after his charge.

The matador displayed his sword to the crowd and the people approved with a unified cheer. Then he waved a small cape, enticing the animal to make another pass. And then another.

Jess moved his eyes between Otto and the action in the ring.

The bull and the matador stood silently, facing each other.

The matador waved the small cape and the bull grunted.

After running in a small circle, the bull made its final charge and the matador drew his sword back. As the bull made his pass, the matador swiftly drove the sword between the bull's shoulder blades and right into its heart. The people erupted in celebration.

Otto locked his fingers and put his hands on the top of his head.

The bull faltered, and gasped, and then laid down to die.

The first kill of the day was complete and the crowd approved. The smiling prime minister turned to Otto, who returned a forced smile. Jess could see that the corners of Otto's mouth were pulled too low for a real smile.

"Come now, Señor Veltraria, don't tell me you are sad," the prime minister said laughing. Otto didn't respond.

The crowd quieted down and the dead bull was dragged from the ring by mules.

Tuerto turned to Otto and said, "What can be done, my musical friend? I think it will take more than singing, right?"

Otto shrugged his shoulders and answered, "What do you mean?"

"Control. How do we get the world under control? Too much troublemaking," Tuerto said. "I think the time may be nearing for something serious. You know, a drop of the fist."

Otto was silent.

"I so appreciate that you accepted my invitation to join us today," Tuerto said. "I want you to know that I have always enjoyed your music, but I did want to tell you personally that you may be stoking some fires that should be extinguished instead."

Otto looked at Tuerto without responding.

Tuerto smiled and said, "I just ask you to consider my words. Remember, no one likes the bull – he's against all of us."

Again, Otto said nothing.

"You will enjoy my dedication of the Serenity Fountain after lunch today," Tuerto said. "My remarks there will make clear what I am trying to say to you."

After five more bulls were killed, Otto and the prime minister and Señor Tuerto's other guests rode in a motorcade to a restaurant near the newly constructed fountain. Otto reluctantly allowed Jess to join the group but insisted that he stay out of their private room.

Halfway through lunch, Jess went into the bathroom to wash his face, and moments later, Otto and Tuerto entered the bathroom.

Jess looked up into the mirror in front of him and met the reflection of Otto's eyes. Otto nodded to Jess and then resumed his conversation with his host as they both stood next to each other at the urinal.

After a moment, Jess turned and slowly walked toward the exit, and then stopped. Without turning around he interrupted the men.

"Señor Tuerto, there used to be countless newspapers and television and radio news outlets in this country," Jess said, shaking his head. "But now, they're all blended into the single voice of *The Trustee*. What a mistake, right?"

"Frank, shut your mouth," Otto said, zipping his pants.

"No, no, Señor Veltraria, allow me to respond," Tuerto said, now washing his hands. He looked at Jess in the mirror who had now turned around to face the two men.

"It wasn't a mistake. I monetized my news business," Tuerto said. "And your comment about one voice is way off. That's the beauty of *The Trustee* newspaper and television and radio outlets – they're made up of everybody's voices. Or should I say, there's a voice for nearly every appetite to listen to. This concept was revolutionary, and I consider myself fortunate to marry my news empire into The Whole Truth Information Trust – a global megaphone that shouts in every direction, in every language and in every rational point of view and political leaning. Why must news outlets of differing ideologies fight their wars by proxy through their reporting? Now we have every viewpoint safely in one place."

"Yes, safely in one place," Jess repeated in a flat tone. "You shot the watchdog."

"See, Señor Veltraria, this is what I'm talking about – a troublemaker," Tuerto said to Otto, who stared at Jess with wide eyes.

Then Tuerto quickly laughed and said to Jess, "I don't have time for your childish conspiracy theories and neither does the world."

Tuerto left the washroom with Otto in tow.

25

After lunch, Jess crossed the street to the plaza that was home to Señor Tuerto's new gift to the world, the Serenity Fountain.

The fountain was more of a large round pool than a fountain with running water. The still liquid was opaque with the bottom of the pool vanishing deep into the ground. Closely spaced black metal rods pushing twenty feet up from the deck of the fountain and topped with spikes surrounded the body of dark water. A thick thirty foot tall stone column in the center of the fountain released a violent flame into the sky. Standing on a long-armed lift extended up to the flame, technicians in purple jumpsuits and black hard hats tested the flame by repeatedly lighting and extinguishing it – all in preparation for Tuerto's ceremonial lighting.

Dignitaries, celebrities and business leaders invited to the dedication of the Serenity Fountain mingled and sat on soft black fold-up chairs. Otto sat next to the prime minister in the front row. Surrounded by his security detail, Señor Tuerto walked around the plaza hugging his guests and shaking hands as he made his way toward the lift that now sat on the deck of the plaza.

Eventually, Tuerto and two technicians mounted the lift. But following a brief exchange, one of the purple men dismounted the lift and another took his place. Then the machine carrying the three men slowly rose in the air and crossed over the spikes toward the center of the fountain. As the lift moved into position next to the unlit column, Tuerto adjusted the microphone that had been set up for his dedication speech.

Without any opening remarks, Tuerto shouted, "Open your eyes!" His voice echoed throughout the plaza and through the city's streets. "Now! Open them now! We haven't a moment to waste. Look around you." He looked down at the people gathered. "Look. Look closely. Who among us is to blame? Who out there is to blame?" The stocky suited man pointed one finger in the direction of his guests and the other toward the street.

"Ladies and gentlemen, we have come to a moment in world history which must first be marked with solemnity – and then with celebration. The sins of so many which have left our global community in pain must be called out in front of all humanity. Our conscience, as individuals and collectively, demand that we shine the torchlight of discovery in every corner of our civilization to identify those people and those organizations who have caused or contributed to the tortured existence from which the world now suffers. It is our task to ask those questions which we are afraid to ask. We avoid the inquiries which make eyes shift, and which make us pause and stutter and hesitate. But the time has come to deny that timidity and to embrace the hard road which we must travel together."

The audience applauded.

"But not all will be with us. Not all *can* be with us. They're the ones traveling on the opposite side of the road, moving in a direction opposite of our own. Swimming hard against the tide of humanity, these people don't care about the drag they create on the rest of us." Tuerto shook his head violently.

"Some kill, some kidnap, some destroy, and some disrupt, but they all frighten – you need only to look on either first page of *The Trustee* to know of the atrocities that these people commit. And they protest in the streets and shout of injustice from the rooftops. These people will do anything and everything to stop the progress and advancement of our society. How can we move forward without addressing this unrest? We will not let them stop us. We will not!"

He was silent for a moment, letting the word "not" echo.

"This beautiful body of water, this smooth, serene stretch of calm liquid symbolizes that ideal which we must pursue on this planet. Let each of us stand at the edge of this deep pool and gaze into its depths so that we may reflect on the pain we have all endured at the hands of those who stand in the way of a destiny of peace and happiness. We all know them, those that complain, those that are discontent, those that are unwilling to step in line and march with the rest of us. Those people, the people that question everything constantly, filling the world with their destructive dissenting noise."

More applause.

"If we are to succeed in building a peaceful, global society, we cannot tolerate every man and woman moving in their own direction. Those that deprive us of that solidarity are the people who are working against us."

Again, he paused allowing his words to settle.

"It's a war and they are the enemies of peace." Tuerto pointed down and said, "They are the people casting their stones into water which should be calm – instead, they only create waves."

The crowd rose to their feet applauding and whistling. Tuerto waved his hands upward directing his guests to increase the applause and cheering.

Then Tuerto was tackled. From behind, one of the technicians lunged forward hitting Tuerto hard. With the purple man's arms wrapped around Tuerto's waist, the two men went right off the lift and plunged into the dark pool below.

The purple man pulled Tuerto under and they both disappeared almost instantly.

The guests ran in all directions, screaming. The prime minister was immediately surrounded by his people who took him away quickly.

Access to the pool in the Serenity Fountain was nearly impossible.

The spaces between the metal rods surrounding the water were too small to permit a person to squeeze through and the rods were too tall and the spikes too sharp to climb over. Tuerto's security team fumbled with the lift trying to get rescuers into the water, but it seemed like ten minutes before the first splash.

Jess found Otto who was being escorted to his car.

"Get lost, Frank," Otto said.

"Otto, don't leave me here!"

"What's wrong?" Otto asked. "Are you afraid your sharp tongue is going to cause you some trouble if you're interrogated tonight?"

"You're going to chide me for saying what no one else will say?" Jess asked.

Suddenly a woman's shriek echoed from the plaza. And then wailing. It was Tuerto's wife.

Otto dropped his head and then looked up at Jess. "Get in, jerk," he said, motioning toward the car.

⊷ 26 ⊶

Café Comercial, in the heart of Madrid, had served thousands hot Café Cortados to Europe's malcontents since the 1880s. The place's dark paneled wood walls, marble floors and leather seats hosted generations of conspirators, all in need of a head-quarters that provided caffeine and cookies. The second floor doubled as a chess room at day and a comedy club at night.

David Clairet and Jess Frank sat, playing chess.

"Don't you need to be rehearsing your set or calming your nerves, David?" Jess asked.

David didn't answer. He looked at the chess board and con-centrated.

"You know, I don't think I've ever seen you in anything but that black three-piece suit," Jess said. "Surely you must be the best dressed stand-up comic in the world."

David looked up at Jess and then returned his eyes to the board.

After a moment, David made his move on the board. "And I don't think I've ever seen you in anything other than that ridicu-lous jacket. I'm surprised they let you into this country with that thing on," David said, now looking up and smiling.

"Your sister teases me mercilessly about this *thing*," Jess said, waiving his right arm around to make the fringe move. "And when we were in Michigan for her launch, she had a lot of fun seeing me in a swimsuit."

"Oh, I can imagine. What a treat to see your twiggy legs connected to a Speedo," David said.

"I didn't go that far," Jess said as he studied his move. "But I do embarrass her in every other way whenever I can."

"Why does she keep you around, Mr. Frank?" David asked.

Jess made his move and said, "I keep her in line."

David laughed. "Really? She's not a wild girl."

Jess shook his head. "No, not like that."

"Then how?" David asked.

"She doesn't know it, but she employs me as her ballast. And her mirror," Jess said.

David sat back and looked down at the chess board. "I know what you mean. With my mother gone, I had that job before I was ten."

"Really? What about your dad?" Jess asked.

David shook his head and said, "Between building his stupid toys that usually didn't work and trying to convince the world that he had nothing to do with my mother's disappearance, he was unavailable in every way."

The two of them looked down at the board in silence for a few minutes. Then Jess said, "That must have been hard for you."

David looked out the window at nothing. Then he sat up straight and said, "Over time, I made the best of my father's neglect. Total freedom. I was a man well before I needed to use a razor. On occasion, my father would try to assert his parental control – and it seemed merely out of obligation – but it was too late. I rejected his authority. And then I rejected all authority."

David picked his king up off the chess board and held it out toward Jess. "Do you know that song by your boss about kings and crowns? It goes, *a farce of a crown, really no more than a clown –* well, that song is my anthem."

Jess sat silent, watching David, and then asked, "Another Café Cortado?"

David put the chess piece back on the board. "No, no more espresso. I'm already fired up enough for tonight. I don't need any more juice."

Jess nodded and asked, "Want to try any new material out on me?"

David rolled his eyes and laughed. "Sure, why not." But then he hesitated for a moment.

"Well? I'm listening." Jess said.

David smiled and leaned toward Jess and said, "I hear that Señor Tuerto was the life of the party last night. But apparently, they couldn't get him out of the pool."

Jess recoiled back and said, "There's something wrong with you. I just spent the first half hour of this game telling you about last night – I saw that man die."

"Oh, I thought you'd get a kick out of a slightly off color joke about the death of a dangerous man."

Jess stared at David but said nothing.

"Take it easy – sorry you had to deal with that last night," David said. "But haven't you ever seen a man die?"

"No."

"Don't be so sensitive, Jess Frank. Death is inevitable. It's all just a matter of how and when."

Jess continued to stare at David.

"Are you staying for my show?"

Jess took a deep breath and slowly said, "Yeah, I guess so. It might be a little painful but I haven't seen you in action since San Francisco."

David laughed. "Oh man, my aunt and uncle hated that show. They think I'm insane. What do you expect from a couple of sweet old winos?" David shook his head and added, "Too bad the old lady is on her way out."

"Königin said that your aunt was sick, but I didn't realize that she was in such bad shape."

"I'm just speculating," David said. "But I think her grape is about to be picked."

Jess slowly shook his head.

The chess game continued in silence for a few minutes.

"Hey, how do you like covering that fraud?" David asked.

"What do you mean?"

"You know, the *Pull My Finger Tour* or whatever the hell that nonsense is," David said.

"Oh, you mean the guy that wrote your anthem?"

"Yes, him," David said.

"I annoy him."

"That's good. He needs to be annoyed," David said. "Tell me, what's the most surprising thing that you've discovered traveling around with him?"

Without hesitating, Jess answered, "His certainty in his near-divine purpose – he's absolutely convinced of it. At first I thought it was funny, even endearing, but then it became just a little scary. But fortunately for everyone involved, I think he's probably a good guy at heart."

David laughed. "No, no – not the man who always speaks the truth, the man who is truth itself – don't tell me they got to you too."

"No, really David, I've spent a lot of time with this guy and–"

"Don't waste your breath," David said. "I know what that guy is and there's nothing you'll say that's going to change my mind."

Jess sat up straight. "That's a hard-headed ignorant man's position, David. You know that."

"No, not at all. I just know what I know and anyone who tries to tell me otherwise is wrong and wasting my time. And theirs," David said.

"Come on, David, now you're just digging your heels in."

"I'm making a point," David said. "Without total conviction, we're delicate flowers getting bent by the wind. And that's very dangerous. Pick a position and stick to it."

"But what if your position is wrong, or partially wrong? And you never allow yourself to hear the voices of those that might be speaking some truth?" Jess asked.

"So be it. Sometimes the truth needs to be sacrificed to achieve an objective. You're way too hung up on the truth, Jess. There are principles much higher than truth."

Jess looked into David's eyes and said, "Searching for truth is the only way out of our confusion."

David shook his head. "No, no, no, Jess – you've got it totally backwards. An endless and futile search for truth gets in the way of getting things done. Look at all of the people shaking their fists to the sky in this world. They're pissed off, they've been shit on and they're sick of it. They demand action, not a philosophical pursuit."

"That's a dangerous approach," Jess said. "Action should be based on a reasoned position, and the foundation for that position can only be built on an accurate understanding of the landscape that we find ourselves in. Pushing headlong with a license to do whatever it takes to achieve an objective, no matter how worthy that objective is, will most certainly lead to atrocities far worse than the problem being addressed."

"Look, Jess, change hurts. You have to look at things from a long term perspective. In order to fix the future it's going to be painful now. Very painful. That's what people can't accept."

"Change and progress at any cost?" Jess said.

"Progress. That's a funny word," David said. "We all have a different notion of progress. See, I think tearing it all down is the only way to make any progress. This life just isn't working – any of it. There's nothing left of this civilization to save."

Jess jerked his head back. "I'm surprised you weren't on top of the Empire State Building with the Crushed, waiving a nice big banner," Jess said.

David pointed at Jess and said, "Don't lump me in with those people. They were amateurs. You don't fight a war without ammunition. They were well-intentioned idiots who quickly learned that this isn't a game."

Jess extended his left palm toward David and said, "Okay, relax." Then he lowered his hand and said in a quiet voice, "The discontented certainly have their choice of team jerseys to wear these days, don't they?"

"Like never before," David said. "But those groups are mostly made up of people that just need a cause, no matter what it is. They're followers marching to a tune of discontentment played by a piper making undeliverable promises."

"People are desperate, so they follow," Jess said.

"Right, and each group claims that they've got the answer," David said. "But it makes no difference. It wouldn't matter if World Fatigue or EarthShake or Light of Freedom or any of the other groups seized power, because it would be temporary – it always has been. The moment the revolutionaries win their revolution, they become the next regime that we need to topple. And rightly so, because the victor always becomes a crooked, bloated bureaucracy whose primary purpose is to perpetuate itself."

"But that cycle is just political and economic evolution playing itself out," Jess said.

"True, but how stupid can we all be, doing the same thing over and over again for thousands of years? I can't bear to watch it. It's one fight after another, only to achieve the same result, over and over again. Isn't it time for the final fight?"

Jess smiled at David. "I hope you're not getting paid by the number of laughs you get tonight."

27

There was no *Trustee* barge for the second water launch.
Tad Corliss was back in London with Dr. Clairet and Jess was still on tour with Otto as his biographer and the *Take My Hand Tour* historian.

Königin looked at the Grand Hotel in the distance, back on the island.

"Looks like they left you with a skeleton crew, Ms. Clairet. But I'm here to keep you safe," a low, calm voice said from behind.

It was Lansing.

Königin turned and smiled. "Well, thank you admiral. But I wish you could help out with the launch – I think I'll be doing this one by myself. It looks like the budget's been cut a bit." She nodded toward the handful of technicians preparing for the launch.

"I think you're right," Lansing said. "Probably all going toward that machine that Corliss and your father are planning to build."

"Yes, I'm sure."

A formation of fighter jets roared overhead. Lansing looked up at the sky after they had passed and said, "Perfect weather today for your launch."

"Absolutely," Königin said, smiling at Lansing. "I didn't expect to see you today. I figured that you had more important people and equipment to protect."

Lansing looked at her for a moment. "I guess who and what's *important* is subjective, isn't it?"

"Yes, of course," she said.

"But even from a purely objective standpoint, Ms. Clairet, you're very important," Lansing said, his smile now faded.

"We're all important in our own way, admiral."

Lansing shook his head. "No, that's not what I mean."

Königin tilted her head, her hair falling against the side of her face.

"We need you, Ms. Clairet," Lansing said.

"Need me? I doubt anyone actually needs me. I mean, I can help a bit with things but I'm sure that people could get along fine without me."

Lansing put his hands on his hips and said, "Not realizing your worth will prevent you from achieving what you're capable of, and you'll cheat a world that is relying on people like you."

"Come on, admiral, don't be so dramatic," Königin said. "It's not that big of a deal. What can I tell you? I'm humble, I don't think too much of myself." She smiled at Lansing, who didn't smile back.

"Be careful, Ms. Clairet. Being humble is one thing, not thinking enough of yourself is another."

Königin felt her face grow hot. She had a sudden urge to punch Lansing in the face.

"Are you all right?" he asked.

Königin looked down and said, "Yes, of course." She could feel his eyes on her. He was so presumptuous, she thought to herself. But she didn't want him to leave to his ship. Her anger evaporated.

"Thanks for your help today," Königin said. "Are you staying at the hotel tonight?"

"No, I'm staying on the *Eagle*," Lansing said, nodding toward a three-masted sailing ship in the distance. "We're moving out first thing tomorrow morning. Why?"

"I was wondering if you brought your swimsuit with you. I'd like to see you do another one of those cannonballs into the pool."

Lansing laughed. "Oh, you saw that, did you?"

"No, but I heard it."

"Sorry, no cannonballs tonight," Lansing said, shrugging his shoulders. "But we can have dinner on the ship. She's an officer training vessel – very special. I'll give you a tour if you promise not to hold it against her that she was built by Nazi Germany and originally named *Horst Wessel*."

"I would never – we can't be blamed for who we're born to," Königin said. "And look what she became after she was liberated."

"Indeed," Lansing said. Then he asked, "Tonight?"

"For sure. I'll swim out to the ship at seven o'clock, okay?"

Lansing laughed and put his hands on Königin's shoulders. "Just show up at the concrete dock at 1800 hours and I'll pick you up."

She smiled at him and said, "It's a date." Then she quickly shook her head and added, "No, I mean we have a plan, it's not a date – you know what I mean."

"Good luck, Königin," Lansing said before he turned toward his transport boat.

Königin watched him walk away. She liked the way that the bottom of his boots firmly connected to whatever he was walking on. It was as if he stepped exactly where he was supposed to step. A young sailor saluted him and then he disappeared down a flight of metal stairs.

Königin felt a tap on her shoulder. "Have you completed your pre-launch inspection?" a coated technician asked.

"No, there's a lot for me to inspect – I could use some help," Königin said.

"I'm sorry, Ms. Clairet, but no one on the crew is senior enough to assist you with the inspection," the technician said. "You'll have to complete it yourself."

Königin crossed her arms and said, "Well, then please let the Kenya team know that we're running late and that we'll have to push the launch back an hour or so."

The technician shook her waxy face. "No, we can't push it back. The launch time can't be changed."

"Who says?" Königin asked.

"Mr. Corliss."

Königin shook her head. She had the technician get Corliss on the phone.

"Mr. Corliss, we need to delay the launch for an hour or so," Königin said. "I need to complete my inspection of the equipment."

"No, absolutely not, Ms. Clairet. We must stay on schedule," Corliss said.

"Why, what's the problem delaying for an hour?"

There was no answer from Corliss. "Hello, Mr. Corliss, are you still there?" Königin asked.

"Yes, I'm here. Look, we can't interfere with Admiral Lansing's tight schedule. He needs to move his fleet out immediately following the launch."

Königin hesitated and then said, "I think it'll be all right with Lansing because they're not pulling out until tomorrow morning."

For the first time, Königin heard Corliss shout. "Listen to me, Königin, that water is getting launched on time, do you hear me? I don't want to be put in the position of having to answer questions about delays from anyone. One hour turns into two hours which turns into two days. I can't afford doubt in anyone's mind. You'd better get off the phone and check your equipment."

"Looks like you've got thirty-five minutes," the technician said. "Better get going."

As Königin tried to work quickly through her checklist she noticed that her jaw hurt – she was grinding her teeth. Words from long ago came back to her. "Figure out what your body's telling you about your heart and mind," her mother had told her. Königin pushed the words away.

Then Königin thought about her phone call with Corliss. She couldn't believe how he had spoken to her – but then told herself that he had his own pressure and that the situation "was what it was" and that she just needed to "deal with it."

Moving hurriedly around the water launcher, Königin rushed through some inspection items and skipped others altogether.

Now underneath the machine, she carefully balanced herself on a narrow metal bar that was part of a large grate. The waves below spat cold water up at her. Königin tried to work quickly, her hands were shaking.

A monotone voice boomed from every speaker on every barge and ship announcing, "Five minutes to launch."

Königin's mind shifted again to Corliss – and then she lost her footing on the narrow piece of metal. She fell straight down, landing hard with the bar right between her legs. One of her boots fell into the water below. The pain from her groin shot up through her body as she bit her lip trying not to make a sound.

Königin slowly lifted herself up and stood slightly hunched.

"We're four minutes from launch, Ms. Clairet. Get out of the way," the waxy faced technician said loudly.

She hobbled in one boot to the far end of the launch barge. There wasn't a chair for her, so Königin sat on the filthy platform and watched as her machine began its low hum. The vibration running through the barge made the pain between her legs throb. She tried to comfort herself with the thought of the water arriving and people rejoicing.

A large countdown clock hit "0" and the first burst of water rocked the barge as it shot into the air. Then the second and third blasts launched. The sound was deafening. Königin covered her ears with her hands. She watched the technician who was in contact with the Kenya team – his job was to confirm that the water had landed properly at its destination.

Königin held her breath as she stared at the man with the old black phone pressed against his face as he awaited confirmation from Africa. After several minutes, he revealed a mild smile as he nodded to the technician firing the launcher – the first burst had arrived. The fifth, sixth and seventh water missiles disappeared behind the clouds. The technician periodically nodded as each installment of water was safely received. Königin began to relax.

Another burst and another nod.

Königin looked out at the *Eagle*, with her tall masts and many sailors sitting high up on the yards watching the launch. She thought they were crazy and brave for perching themselves on the ship's horizontal wooden beams.

But suddenly, the shriek of shredding metal hit Königin. She was back on her feet, instinctively hobbling toward her struggling creation. The water launcher twisted into a Daliesque sculpture, that in no more than a moment, sank into the lake through the opening in the barge. Smoke and a thin mist of water filled the air. The technicians ran about shouting and cutting power.

Königin stared at the empty space where the water launcher had been. The smell of burnt rubber and plastic and metal evoked in her a sense of death.

She looked across the water at Mackinac Island and the hotel on its hill. She thought of the pool and the dining room. She thought of Jess wearing the silly green jacket. The idyllic innocence of it all was gone forever.

Then a sound that was as much of a gasp as it was a scream demanded everyone's attention. Königin turned to see the technician who had been tasked with giving the success nod – he was now covering his mouth with both hands and looking right at Königin. She slowly lowered herself to her knees. She felt like she was falling down a dark hole with no bottom.

28

"Let me ask *you* that same question – what do *you* think happened?" Corliss said.

"All we have are the eyewitness accounts, Mr. Corliss, and they all say the same thing – the machine failed," the reporter said, sitting across from the chairman in his London office.

"Of course it failed, Ms. Wilson, that's apparent. We don't need witnesses to confirm that," Corliss said.

"Then the question is, why did it fail, Mr. Corliss?"

"There's no mystery to that either. The construction was flawed," Corliss said.

The reporter leaned forward in her chair and asked, "Isn't that something that the Association was responsible for, Mr. Corliss?"

Corliss threw himself back into his chair and crossed his arms. "Of course not," he answered. "Others were contracted with to build the machine. We just developed the technology, we didn't build the equipment. We take no responsibility for the failure of the water launcher."

"That seems rather convenient, Mr. Corliss. I don't see how you can distance the Association from this tragedy. Didn't you yourself select the firm that manufactured the machine?"

Corliss leaned forward and pointed his long index finger at the young woman. "How dare you attack the Association for what was not its responsibility. We delegated that responsibility to another party and that party failed – we had nothing to do with what happened."

"All right, then let's move on, Mr. Corliss. I assume given your position with regard to responsibility that you don't intend to compensate the families of the victims?"

"Compensate? With what?" Corliss asked. "Our mission is to help people through technology. Draining our coffers to pay money out to people who we were trying to help doesn't seem quite right, does it? That would just mean that in the end we'll be helping fewer people instead of more, right? Look, I find it quite unfortunate that a couple of dozen people lost their lives in this incident, but you must understand that such an occurrence is just one of the costs of this type of endeavor. It doesn't work out all of the time, but we can't let that stop progress. There are so many things for the Association to accomplish. We can't let an incident – which at the time might seem like a big problem – slow our mission down. I assure you, we'll all see that this was just a small bump in the road on the journey to making the world a much better place."

"Mr. Corliss, before we go there, let's get back to the failure of the machine," the reporter said.

Corliss shook his head. "I just don't know why you would focus only on the negative, Ms. Wilson. Aren't there other aspects–"

She cut him off. "Mr. Corliss, was the machine inspected prior to the launch?"

"Yes, of course it was. We have our protocol and we followed it. Clearly the impending equipment failure wasn't something that could have been detected prior to the launch."

"Were you involved in that inspection, Mr. Corliss?"

"Me, of course not, don't be silly. I'm not an engineer. I wasn't even there at the launch."

"You weren't? Why not?" the reporter asked.

"I was attending to other important Association business. I can't be everywhere, you know."

"I see, but somebody must have been in charge of the launch, right?"

"Oh yes, of course, of course there was someone in charge," Corliss answered.

"Who, Mr. Corliss? Who was in charge that day?"

Corliss sat up straight and smiled. "The best of the best. The creator of the technology herself was in charge – she ran the whole operation. She even insisted on conducting the inspection herself."

The reporter was silent for a moment. "You're referring to Ms. Clairet, correct?"

Corliss nodded. "Yes, of course I am."

"Was she qualified to run the operation, Mr. Corliss?"

"Based on her representations to me, I assumed that she was qualified."

"I see." The reporter said, now looking down at her notes. "What about her mishap at the Pavilion?" she asked.

"What about it, Ms. Wilson?"

"Clearly there's a pattern here. Ms. Clairet seems to have been involved in two failures of the implementation of her technology."

Corliss sat silent for a moment and then said, "Yes, yes, that's true. Of course, in light of recent events, we are reevaluating our relationship with her."

"Oh? What about her being the *best of the best?*"

"Look, we thought she was the best of the best, but perhaps that's not the case," Corliss said, stammering. "She's turned out to be somewhat of a disappointment, I think you'd have to say."

"So, did the water launcher fail due to a construction flaw or because of some kind of fault on Ms. Clairet's part?" Ms. Wilson asked.

Corliss hesitated for a moment and then answered, "Both, I suppose. Yes, both."

"Does that put you in a difficult position, Mr. Corliss? I mean, considering that you brought Ms. Clairet in to work with the Association?"

"No, not at all – we're not responsible for equipment defects or Ms. Clairet's failures."

"But you accept some of the responsibility for the deaths in Kenya, right?" the reporter asked.

Corliss quickly waived his right arm in front of him. "Absolutely not. Let me warn you, Ms. Wilson, about putting words in my mouth. I won't stand for it."

"Mr. Corliss, I'm just trying find out–"

"I would like to know what your agenda is, Ms. Wilson. You clearly are bent on attacking me and the Association and our mission of helping people. What and who are behind your illegitimate questions? I think the real story here is why you and *The Trustee* seem committed to stopping the good work that we do," Corliss said in a firm voice.

The reporter looked at Corliss and said nothing for a moment. "Mr. Corliss, nobody is trying to stop you or the Association. My job is to try to ascertain the truth and report that truth the best that I can, without any agenda whatsoever."

"But Ms. Wilson, if you believed in what we are doing and what we are trying to accomplish, then you wouldn't attack us, rather, you would understand that the *how* and *why* of what happened simply doesn't matter. Yes, it's tragic, people are dead, but bad things happen sometimes. You've got to focus on the big picture, do you understand?"

"Mr. Corliss, I hope you understand that we can't ignore the *how* and *why* – it's my duty as a reporter, and the duty of every reporter, to search for answers, to uncover the truth."

Corliss shook his head. "Let me give you some advice, Ms. Wilson. Maybe you should consider a different line of work. People want news from reporters that care about the issues – reporters who are bold enough to use their influence to make a difference. They want to get their information from people who are strong enough to take a stand on any given situation. And most of all, they want the information that's important to them, not silly details about a witch hunt that makes no difference in the end. Stop trifling with the details of *how* and *why* and start focusing on the exciting stories that will change people's lives. I can't believe that you haven't asked me one question about the ĒMAD."

The reporter took her eyeglasses off and put them on the pad in front of her. "The newspaper that I used to write for was recently absorbed into *The Trustee*, Mr. Corliss. I'm sure they'll be sending another reporter to interview you again once they read the initial draft of my story. You'll get the story that you want."

Corliss smiled and said nothing.

Ms. Wilson continued, "But I won't ignore the facts and I'll never stop asking the questions that every person should be asking. We were supposed to be the guardian of truth – a press free of bias and influence that informs the people with facts and lets them develop their own opinions. We were supposed to keep our eye on the world and provide information to people so that they were empowered to demand integrity and fairness and justice."

"Ah, that's just your perspective," Corliss said. "The way I see it, you're just not keeping up with the evolving taste of the people. Your old school investigative journalism is just a vestige of another time. Some naively noble mission that the people just don't care about anymore. They want to hear about the next best thing. And you happen to be sitting across from the man that may be on his way to developing just that, the Essential Material Acquisition Device. I assure you, there will be a place in *The Trustee* for that story."

Ms. Wilson stood up to leave and said, "I hope that goes better for you than the water launcher did, Mr. Corliss."

29

"What better place to kick-off my tour of the States than red, white and blue New Hampshire? Meadowbrook is such a great little venue. I love intimate settings where I can see people's eyes and we really share the experience," Otto said.

"Sure, I get it, but it's a tiny place – you're leaving a lot of people out," Jess said.

Otto looked up at the ceiling of the limo. "It's amazing. Without fail, you bust my balls about everything that I say and do."

"No, no, Otto, I'm not trying to give you a hard time, I'm just stating a fact. With each show there are several thousand more people camped out in surrounding parking lots watching the performance on those massive television screens. I've never seen so many speaker stacks scattered about. Your voice echoed through entire European cities. And then you choose an 8,000 seat pavilion to start your tour here? I just don't get it. I'm surprised that the town of Gilford is even letting you and your minions come," Jess said.

"I don't think they have much of a choice, Jess. Unless the city elders want to be run out of town." Otto laughed to himself.

The two rode for some time without speaking. Jess wrote in his notebook and Otto hummed one of his songs to himself while looking out the window at the rolling green hills.

The car made its way off the highway and headed toward Meadowbrook.

Otto stopped humming and looked at Jess. "Why do you give me such a hard time about everything I say?"

Jess didn't look up from his notebook as he spoke to Otto. "That's just your perception of what I say to you. I'm really not trying to be difficult – I'm just telling you how I see things. I'm really just being honest with you."

"That may be, but it's annoying," Otto said.

"Of course it's annoying. Most people don't like being challenged. They like the comfort of their self-created reality," Jess said, still writing in his notebook.

"But you're unrelenting, Jess. You never stop."

"That's because everything is so obvious to me and I'm forever frustrated that people complicate reality to the point that it becomes fiction."

Otto sat silent.

"You must be keeping me around for some reason, other than my official duties," Jess said.

"Perhaps," Otto said, smiling at Jess.

The car rode on. Otto hummed "When the Saints Come Marching In."

A few miles out from Meadowbrook, Otto saw a man standing on the side of the small rural road with a sign that read, "OTTO, WHAT ARE YOU WAITING FOR?"

Otto laughed quietly to himself. He saw that Jess had seen the sign too.

A mile further down the road the car came to a stop at a traffic signal. It was a simple four-way intersection, seemingly in the middle of nowhere, but there were a dozen or so people waiting there with their signs. Seeing the long black car approaching, they all became animated and shook their home-made pleas back and forth. A couple of them read the usual "WE LOVE YOU OTTO." A young woman in cutoff shorts shouted "Take my hand" over and over again, echoing the message on her sign. But Otto was most struck by a man in a suit, dressed like a businessman or a lawyer, holding a sign that read "STOP SINGING AND TAKE CARE OF BUSINESS."

Otto looked over at Jess, who was also looking at the man. "He must be forty or fifty, right?" Jess asked.

"Yes, for sure. They're all hurting," Otto answered.

The car pulled away and Otto and Jess turned their heads to watch the group as long as they could.

Meadowbrook Pavilion was a seasonal outdoor amphitheater hiding in lush hills, just a few hundred yards from Sanders Bay on Lake Winnipesaukee. That day, the nearby marina was gridlocked. People stepped from boat to boat to get to the dock. The pavilion was the destination of everyone's pilgrimage.

About a mile from the venue, the car came to a stop in traffic on Lake Shore Road. Cars were parked three deep on both sides of the small road. People filled the street and some sat on the hoods of their cars playing music from the *Take My Hand* album. The limousine driver slid the partition to the side and craned his head around to face Otto. "I'm sorry, Mr. Veltraria, but I've just been told that the road is impassable. I'm afraid you'll to have to walk the rest of the way."

"But I'll never get through this sea of people," Otto said.

"A police detail is being sent to meet you, sir. They're walking up from the pavilion now."

Jess looked at Otto and gave a crooked smile.

"Don't say anything. I know, I did it to myself. Don't say a thing, if you know what's good for you. I don't want to hear it," Otto said.

By this time, the car had been surrounded by people trying to look into the tinted windows.

"Shit. This reminds me of our South America tour years ago. The fans mobbed our tour bus in Rio – I lost a couple of chunks of hair. I'm too old for that now," Otto said, looking out at the people that couldn't see him.

Jess sat back in his seat, smiling. "And to think, Otto, you passed up flying into that cute little airport which is practically next to the stage." As if on cue, the sound of a propeller plane buzzed overhead. "But I admire you, taking the ride from Boston so you could see the countryside." A fan started pounding on the back window. "It *is* beautiful," Jess said.

"Maybe I'll throw you out there to satiate the crowd's lust. A human sacrifice," Otto said.

"I don't think they'd be satisfied with me," Jess said.

A voice on a bullhorn ordered all of the onlookers away from the car as a dozen uniformed police officers surrounded it. Otto opened the door in response to a firm, official knock.

The town's police chief leaned into the limo, smiling at Otto.

"Good afternoon, Mr. Veltraria. It's quite a welcoming committee you've got here," the chief said as he nodded back at Otto's fans, who stood on their toes to see Otto from behind the police line.

Otto smiled back. "That's how I like it."

"Oh, please," Jess said.

Otto turned to Jess and said, "Shut up."

After taking a deep breath, Otto decisively swung his long left leg out of the car and onto the blacktop. The leg was clad in black jeans connected to a fire engine red high-top sneaker. The crowd went crazy.

Otto waited a couple of beats, winked at Jess, and then pulled himself up and out of the limousine by extending his long arm to the top of the open door. The cheers grew louder. Smiling broadly, Otto squared his chest to the crowd and rotated slowly as if he were trying to get an even tan.

"Ready to go, sir?" the chief asked.

"I suppose," Otto said.

The officers formed a protective area that moved in perfect synchronicity with Otto. Jess followed Otto and the chief who walked shoulder to shoulder. A few of the officers walked with their K-9 partners next to them. Without needing the bullhorn, the sea of people parted for Otto and chanted as he walked by. He tried to smile at as many people as possible.

"Do us all a favor and fly into Laconia Airport next year, okay?" the chief said, smiling.

Otto firmly patted the chief's shoulder and smiled back at him. "You've got it. Sorry for the trouble."

After a few moments, Otto asked, "How are things for you here?"

"In what way, Mr. Veltraria?" the chief asked.

"Unrest, dissatisfaction," Otto responded, his smile now gone.

"Everybody's anxious about the state of affairs in the world, but we have a pretty tight community here. Everyone comes together. Our neighbors are our friends. People here are much more about building bridges than burning them."

"You're very lucky," Otto said.

"With all due respect, sir, it's not luck – we've worked hard to create that atmosphere here."

Otto nodded. "What's your secret?"

The chief stopped and faced Otto. The entire security circle halted perfectly in time. "Transparency, understanding, compassion, trust, fairness, balance and discipline," the chief said, without hesitating. "And the citizens are truly in charge here."

Again Otto nodded, and then said, "Not exactly D.C.'s approach, is it?"

The chief shook his head and started walking again. The circle continued on.

"The fact that the chambers of the Capitol Building are bloodier than a boxing ring is shocking," the chief said. "Three fist fights in the House and one in the Senate last week. This is the Congress of the United States that we're talking about!"

"I know. It's disgusting," Otto replied.

"We should throw the whole lot of them out!" the chief shouted.

"No kidding," Otto said, then adding, "On this tour, I've really refrained from adding to the seething divisiveness tearing the world apart. And I've bitten my lip time and time again about those fools in Washington, even though they're some of the worst offenders."

Then a woman's voice emerged from the crowd yelling, "You're just a song and dance man, Otto. No action at all."

The chief laughed and said, "Tough crowd." Then he added, "They're looking for help."

Otto scratched his right cheek with his long fingers but didn't respond.

Ten minutes later, Otto reached his dressing room. He quietly thanked the chief and they parted ways. Jess headed backstage.

Victoria had Otto's dressing room set up just the way he liked it. It wasn't that he insisted on having his comforts there, it was more that Victoria wanted him to be happy and comfortable. She knew how to get him in the right mood for a show.

"Good afternoon, love. How was your trip in?" Victoria asked.

Otto shook his head and said, "You have no idea. I had to walk a couple of miles in. They've turned the road into a parking lot."

"I see," Victoria said as she pulled a small kettle of boiling water off of a portable electric burner.

"But it was fun walking through the crowd," Otto said. "I missed them terribly during my years off. They give me strength and purpose. Oh, and did I tell you – I had a huge police escort. The police chief himself walked me in."

"Sounds lovely," Victoria said, not sounding particularly attentive.

Otto looked around the little dressing room outfitted with his stuff. "You've done well with this little room, Vic."

"We've been in smaller," she said.

He sat in his chair and relaxed his shoulders. Looking into a large mirror on the wall, Otto took a sip of the black tea Victoria had prepared for him. He studied his face. The crow's feet carved into his tan skin looked like directional arrows pointing to his eyes. Then Otto looked down to his flat cheeks and square chin. He touched his face, feeling the day of hair that was showing.

Victoria spoke up. "Shall I take care of that for you, Otto?"

He didn't answer, but moved his eyes back up the mirror until he was staring at himself. He was captured by his own image that seemed to be asking him a question. But he wasn't sure what that question was.

Victoria worked on foaming up a lather in Otto's wooden shaving bowl. He didn't hear her swishing the little brush in circles. But when she pulled the straight razor from his Dobb kit and opened the blade, he saw it glint in the mirror, freeing him from his thoughts.

"We're having a shave, are we?" Otto said, smiling like a child.

"Indeed we are, love. You need to look nice for your people."

Otto leaned his head back obediently.

"Care to listen to some music?" Victoria asked.

"Were you listening to anything before I came in?"

"Just *The Trustee* radio station. I Miss the BBC terribly," she said.

Otto was silent for a moment. "All right then, the news," he said. "And don't get too torn up about the BBC. *The Trustee* isn't bad, you know – their reviews of the tour have been pretty glowing."

Victoria chuckled and switched her little radio on. It was an old crank radio that her father had given her when she graduated high school in Liverpool. She turned the handle several times to power it up. The radio news anchor was reporting on a fight in Congress over the national debt:

Today marked an historic landmark as the national debt of the United States reached 100 trillion dollars. Having defaulted on its Treasury securities obligations last month, the government is unable to sell its paper to continue to fund the operations of the nation. However, the Fund, established by the Guiding Institutions Collaborative, has been providing stop-gap financing to the government. But a fight erupted in the House of Representatives today as the concept of a national debt repayment program was presented by a caucus sponsored by the Guiding Institutions Collaborative, calling themselves the Collaborative Caucus. The National Debt

Contribution Act, as proposed by the Collaborative Caucus, would attach a financial obligation to every living American, beyond the requirement to pay federal income taxes. According to Congressman Rhode Kaye, the leader of the Collaborative Caucus, the obligation would require each American to contribute a certain amount of money toward the repayment of the loans provided by the Fund as well as pay down the accumulated national debt. Upon a citizen's full payment of an amount yet to be determined, a clearance certificate would be issued to that citizen. If passed into law, the Collaborative Caucus's Act would prevent citizens from pursuing higher education, voting, running for public office, and having children until a clearance certificate is obtained. According to Congressman Kaye, these restrictions are merely intended to incentivize people to meet their financial obligations to the country and the Collaborative.

Otto yelled, "Are you kidding me!"

Victoria started on Otto's upper lip with the razor. "Stay still and tighten up," She said.

Slowly, she pulled the blade down over the cleft of his upper lip, leaving his cleanly shaved skin amidst lathered shaving soap. Otto held perfectly still as Victoria then worked on the right side of his upper lip.

The broadcast continued:

The proposal appears to be dividing an already divided House further, as this morning Congressman Samuel Jerez openly jeered members of the Collaborative Caucus as they gave speeches in support of the National Debt Contribution Act.

Now all that was left to shave was Otto's chin and neck. Victoria carefully rinsed the blade in the room's little sink.

"Turn it off, please Vic, I can't listen to it." Otto shook his head and stuck his chin up for Victoria to shave. The radio was now off.

"Most of my friends can't even afford to make the minimum daily payments on their Full-Life Loans these days," Victoria said. "They'll never be able to get one of those certificates."

"Sickening," Otto said quietly.

"Look, love, you're doing your part," Victoria said as she shaved Otto. "Bringing comfort and hope to the people."

Then Victoria was silent as she started the blade down the right side of his neck. In the not too far distance, they heard the impatient rumble of the fans as they waited outside the main gate of Meadowbrook. Otto cracked a small smile when he heard the gleeful sounds of the people that had come to spend the evening with him.

Victoria rinsed the shiny sharp blade again and now put it at the top of Otto's throat, just below his chin. Her hand was steady and she applied just the right amount of pressure as she moved the blade down, perfectly maintaining the correct angle.

Then, without a prelude, the Silence came. In that moment, the raw shock of the sound void filled every space in that little dressing room, in Meadowbrook Pavilion, in the town of Gilford, in the State of New Hampshire, and throughout the United States and throughout every inch of the planet. A sick terror struck in every living creature, immediately followed by a frightened dread that this unknown phenomenon had occurred again. It was over in less than thirty seconds.

Otto was bleeding. The Silence had startled Victoria's steady hand. The blade was so sharp that Otto hadn't even felt the cut. He looked up at her with wide eyes.

"My God, Otto," she yelled as she took the little towel covered in shaving soap and stubble from his shoulder and put it on his throat to stop the bleeding.

"I've cut you, my God, I'm so sorry, Otto," Victoria said, trying to keep herself from crying. She shook her head. "That thing, what is it?" she asked, now crying.

They could hear the people yelling and screaming – their light, joyful expectation now extinguished.

Otto pulled the towel from his throat to see how bad the cut was. A little trickle of blood ran down to his chest. "Vic, just get me a little bandage. It's not deep."

"But don't you think we should call the doctor. You may need a stitch or two."

"Just get me a band-aid, Victoria – it's nothing. I need to get out there, now," Otto said in a square, firm voice.

Otto ran out of the dressing room toward the yells of his crowd. The sound check and other preparations had been halted by the Silence, and the crew looked at each other from behind dazed eyes. The venue was small, but Otto didn't know his way around. He ran down dead-end hallways and found himself at locked doors. "Ah," he yelled out, as if trying to wake himself from a dream.

Finally, he made it to the main entrance, where the upset crowd was surging forward – pushing people up against the closed steel gate.

"Mr. Veltraria, should I open the gate to relieve the pressure on the people in front?" one of the security guards asked.

"Do that and they'll be trampled to death," Otto said.

"I don't think so, sir – it looks like they need some help right now," the guard said.

Otto shook his head. "Think and see a few steps ahead, young man. Few things in life are a surprise."

Otto quickly climbed a short tree next to the main entrance gate and maneuvered himself up onto a little roof above the entrance. Standing above the large "Meadowbrook Pavilion" letters, Otto looked down into the faces of those who had come to see and hear him, and he saw the kind of fear that shakes the humanity out of people. Instantly, he felt petrified himself. He looked down again and suddenly he was afraid of being on the roof, his footing became unsure and he began to sway.

The people at the front of the crushing crowd called out, "Otto" – unaware that he was in trouble. It took only five more seconds before the entire crowd knew it was Otto up there on that little roof. Sounds of despair turned into cheering, and Otto Veltraria quickly regained his footing and stood up straight. He smiled and waved. His fear was gone.

He gently held his right hand up high with his palm facing the crowd. All fell silent.

"Listen. Please listen to me. Stop pushing toward the gate, you're crushing these people up front. Everyone take three steps back. Come on, I'll sing you through it. *One-take-my-hand*," Otto swung his arms back and forth as he sang. "*Two-take-my-hand, three-take-my-hand.*"

Like a giant monster with thousands of legs, the group moved backward slowly. And when it was done with its third step, whistles and applause came out of every pore of the beast.

"Thank you. You see what we can do when we work together?" Everyone cheered. "And this is just the beginning," Otto said, his firm voice carrying to every ear without yelling.

"Look, I don't know what that silence business is all about. I know we were hoping that it would never come again, but it did, and now we're just going to have to deal with it."

People slowly nodded and a low murmur rose up.

"We're going to open the gate now, and I ask that you all walk to your seats and be careful with each other. I promise not to start the show until everyone is settled."

More whistles and cheers. Then Otto lifted his hand again for their attention. "And one more promise, we're going to have a great time together tonight, and we're going to see if we can get some of these mysteries solved. Or at least start asking some of the right questions." His people danced and hugged each other.

Now full of energy, Otto turned around and walked to the edge of the little roof to make his descent down the tree. He looked down at the pavement below and froze. His roadies looked up at him.

Otto kneeled down to steady himself and thought, "How did I get myself stuck up here? How the hell do I get down without breaking my neck?"

"You okay up there, Otto?" one of his roadies asked from below. "Do we need to get you a ladder?" The other roadies laughed, but with a hint of respect for the target of their joke.

"I'm fine, don't be silly," Otto said, peering over the edge of the roof. "Don't you have a show to get ready for?"

Just then, the main gate opened and the people filed through in an orderly fashion, not knowing that their man was stuck on the roof above.

Back in the dressing room, Victoria was listening to *The Trustee* radio station, which she had turned on immediately after the Silence. She had tried to call her parents to check on them but all lines were down. The manicure she got in Gilford earlier in the day had been destroyed by her gnawing teeth.

The door swung open and banged against the cinder block walls of the dressing room. Otto entered quickly and slammed the door shut.

"Love, what happened to you? I know about the blood on your throat, but where'd you pick up that nasty rip in your trousers?"

Otto plopped himself down in the chair that Victoria had shaved him in.

"I don't have the energy to even talk about it, Vic," Otto said as he closed his eyes and hung his head back, his hair nearly touching the floor.

Victoria jumped up and took his hair in her hands, lifting it up, treating each strand with care.

The voice of *The Trustee* filled the room.

According to unnamed sources, it's believed that the Silence was caused by the subversive group known as Inevitable. While the dangerous organization has not yet taken responsibility, anonymous intelligence sources have told *The Trustee* that the Silence is part of Inevitable's campaign to push the world into chaos. This afternoon, the House of Representatives will temporarily suspend its debate of the National Debt Contribution Act so that it can pass a resolution condemning Inevitable and calling for its classification as an enemy of the people.

Otto shook his head and said, "That should be amusing."

"Hold still, Otto, I'm trying to fix this head of hair," Victoria said before making a sound of exasperation. "Maybe you should take a shower, it'll feel nice."

"I don't have time for that, Vic. I need to get out there and get on stage."

A quick rapping at the door was followed by the uninvited entry of Thigpen, Otto's English roadie since the Knew Society days.

"You going on tonight or are we packing it in? The fellas said you was stuck up on the roof. You all right?" Thigpen asked.

Otto rolled his eyes. "I wasn't stuck on the roof."

Thigpen looked Otto up and down. "Yeah, all right. Well, what is it then? Are you coming for a sound check or are we sending your peoples home?"

Otto gently swatted Victoria's hand away from his hair. "No. No one is going home. I'm coming right now. Forget the sound check. We're going to start the show right now."

Standing up quickly, Otto took a last look in the mirror, making some minor adjustments to his hair. "It's going to be the best show ever – they deserve it," Otto said.

Thigpen's demeanor remained the same. "Yeah, well, all right then, Mr. Best Show. Just don't fall off the stage, okay?"

Otto ignored Thigpen and smiled at Victoria. "Come and watch the show, Vic."

As the two men walked toward the stage, Otto asked Thigpen, "Can we get an outside video feed on the big TV screens?"

Thigpen stopped walking and turned to Otto. "Hello, what are you up to?" he asked.

"Just answer me – can we do it?"

"Yeah, no prob. You just tell me what you want," Thigpen said.

Otto took two steps at a time up the stairs to the stage.

The *Take My Hand* show was perfectly timed and staged and left no room for improvisation. Otto's ten backup singers were still in their trailer and his brass and string section were just warming up. The stage lights were idle, recorded rock played in the background as people bought what food was available.

Two huge oriental rugs lay side-by-side on the stage. Otto's dark wood double-keyboard Hammond sat just to the left of center but toward the front of the stage, taking the dominant position. Further left and further back, two electric bass guitars sat in their stands. Toward the back of the stage, in the center, were risers with four levels. The upper two levels were for Otto's singers, a mix of gospel and blues voices. The lower two levels were for Otto's brass and string section. To the right, Shiloh had his drum kit and many other toys to bang on. And to the far right, closer to the edge of the stage, but still not quite as close to the audience as Otto's keyboard, were a line of three electric and two acoustic guitars.

Otto ran out onto the stage looking for any member of his band. Suddenly, shouts rose up from the crowd in front. Otto turned to face the audience, and now a roar began to slowly build as people turned their attention from their conversations to the stage. He was out there alone.

Sitting down behind his keyboard, Otto pulled the microphone toward him and blew into it. Nothing.

"Light it up," Otto yelled to Thigpen who was following Otto with his eyes.

Thigpen motioned to the soundboard and Otto's microphone went hot and his big Leslie speakers began to slowly spin as Otto's instrument came to life.

"The Real Enemy" was always the ninth song in the lineup and Otto was ordinarily backed by the full band on that number. It was the last song on Side 1 of the *Take My Hand* album and the crescendo before the show's intermission. But now Otto began to sing it accompanied by only his keyboard.

People started to run for their seats not wanting to miss a note. Minor mayhem filled the venue.

As Otto sang, and as his long fingers felt their way up and down the old chipped keys, his musicians began to run onto the stage from all directions.

The first to join Otto was Althea. She played her silver trumpet as she walked in her high heels and skin-tight jeans. The sight of her in her black sports bra startled Otto, and then a wave of guilt overcame him as he saw the other partially dressed band members come onto the stage playing. Otto looked at Althea again as he played, now mad at himself for wanting to look at her.

At a two measure rest of her trumpet part, Althea turned and smiled at Otto, and he no longer felt bad about her being only partially dressed, because it was clear that she was totally comfortable with herself as she was. The audience danced and pumped their fists in the air to the music. It wasn't until *The Trustee*'s review of the show the following day that the audience discovered that the band played the first half of the show half-naked because of the unplanned quick start.

The huge screens on both sides of the stage showed video of the band playing, shot by cameramen moving about the stage and positioned on tall scaffold platforms. A dozen screens and twice as many huge stacks of speakers treated the thousands of less fortunate fans outside of the venue.

When "The Real Enemy" finally ended, Althea sat down next to Otto on his piano bench.

"What's the plan?" she asked, her face only inches from his and already slightly wet with sweat.

He smiled at her. "I didn't really think this through."

She laughed and smiled back at him.

"Why don't we play a duet?" Otto said, motioning toward the keyboard.

Althea shook her head and leaned into him. "I don't think you're ready to share center stage, Otto."

Her sweet, earthy scent caught him, and suddenly he was confronted with the realization that he might be attracted to her.

Althea missed nothing – she read his eyes in a millionth of a second. "Should we take it from the top?" she asked.

Otto knew that he had been caught and he forced himself not to look at Althea as she stood up.

"I suppose that makes the most sense," he said, playing with a key on his keyboard as if something was wrong with it.

Althea's crew waited patiently for direction, but Shiloh whistled at Otto and shrugged his shoulders. The crowd began to chant, "Ot-to, Ot-to, Ot-to."

"It's impossible to start moving the numbers around," Althea said. "The show's just too tight for that."

Otto looked up at her and said, "I agree, we'll start back at the top." Then he tilted his head toward the audience and said, "They won't mind if they hear *The Real Enemy* more than once tonight." Althea smiled and nodded at him, and then quickly walked back to her musicians.

Otto turned to Shiloh who was impatiently tapping a drumstick and staring at him. Then Otto's right index finger shot straight up and whirled in a circle. Immediately, the drummer began a count-off, "two, three, four," and then the whole group, some with just one shoe on, others with bare hairy chests, went right into the show's opening song, "I Never Left You."

Otto started out slow and quiet, but he didn't take long to work the number up to speed. Then the horns kicked in, all of them, and Otto's singers clapped and swayed as he played fast and bright to his congregation.

Everyone danced in the aisles and on their seats – there wasn't a still body in the house.

When the song ended, Otto stood up and walked to the center of the stage, microphone in hand. All cameras were on him – he looked like a giant on the large monitors.

"So here we are, making history together," Otto said. The crowd loved that.

He paced the stage.

"We're going to have fun tonight. The only sound that I want you thinking about is the music that comes from this stage. Forget about that weird silence, whatever the hell it is."

The cheer of the crowd had a deep, defiant tone to it.

"We can't live in fear of that thing or who caused it. *The Trustee* is telling us that a group of malcontents caused it – and the government is poised to punish them. But the main difference between the group that created the Silence and our government is that one of them – and guess which one – pretends to act like they're the responsible people in charge."

This time fists went in the air along with cheers.

"My big mouth has been tempered by time, but I can no longer keep it shut." Otto shook his head. "Are we ready for another song?" Otto said as he jogged to his keyboard.

Althea counted off, "five, six, seven, eight" to cue her wailing trombones as they started the next number, "Angry Little Man."

The song had a blues feel to it, with every one of the backup singers pitching in. Snare drums hissed behind bending guitar notes.

"Angry Little Man" wrapped up with a short keyboard solo by Otto. Then Thigpen walked onto the stage and leaned down to speak with Otto. They exchanged a few words as Otto pointed toward one of the screens. Nodding, Thigpen exited the stage at his usual unhurried pace.

Otto took the microphone from its mount dangling just above the top of his Hammond. He walked slowly to the front and center of the stage.

"Are we ready for some more fun?" he asked his audience.

Every form of "yes" was shouted and cheered back to him.

"Well then, here we go," Otto said as he turned toward the screen over his right shoulder.

Suddenly, the images of him and Althea and the rest of the band disappeared from the screens, replaced by a garbled video signal.

Otto waited a few seconds and then said, "Let's go, Thigpen. Just connect the two wires, it's not that hard."

The crowd erupted into shouts and laughter.

Otto was smiling and laughing too. "If you don't get it working, Thigpen, I'm going to make you sing–"

Before Otto could finish his sentence, the screens and speakers carried images and sounds of congressmen and congresswomen shouting incoherently in the House Chamber. Otto's crowd fell silent as they tried to figure out what they were watching.

In the background, behind the arguing legislators, an American flag hung between two marble columns. And in front of the flag, the Speaker of the House of Representatives sat in a large leather chair, passively observing the bickering taking place in front of him.

"We're running out of time – we need to outlaw Inevitable and the rest of these groups immediately," one of the congressmen shouted in the face of his colleague.

"You're hysterical. We have no evidence other than an anonymously sourced story in *The Trustee*," the other shouted back. "Are we just going to ignore the First Amendment?"

"Maybe it's time to rethink the First Amendment – the world is changing before our eyes," the congressman yelled. "We need to stop the chaos at all costs. What good will the First Amendment, the Bill of Rights or even the entire Constitution do for us once our society is in ruin? We need drastic changes. Now!"

"No, no – this is when we need to affirm our commitment to the letter of the Constitution, not abandon it. If you weren't such an unprincipled chickenshit–"

And then, from off-camera, the man was silenced with a punch. And then came another punch, and then another. The live feed from the House of Representatives was now televising a playground brawl.

"It's even worse than I thought it would be," Otto said. "I thought we'd have a few laughs watching these boobs, but this isn't funny at all."

The crowd began to yell different insults at the images on the screens.

Then a congresswoman from the Speaker of the House's own party pulled the Speaker's big chair from behind, flipping the Speaker onto the blue and gold carpet.

More boos and yells emitted from the crowd. Otto saw a fan shove another fan to the ground.

"Cut it, cut it," Otto said as he repeatedly pulled his index finger across his throat to Thigpen, who was offstage. "Come on, quick, Thig, get it off," Otto yelled.

"Sorry people, that was horrible. I was just trying to make the point that this government is confused and incompetent – to say the least," Otto said as he walked across the stage and looked down at his shoes. He looked up at the audience. "I guess I made my point."

Life began to fill the pavilion again and the crowd calmly applauded.

Otto shook his head. "I've kept my mouth shut – but no more. It's time for me to jump in the scrum and push forward. That's what you want from me, and I know it," he shouted. The crowd erupted into cheers. "I know now – this is why I'm here," he said, opening his arms as if to embrace the audience.

Otto ran to his keyboard and played a few notes. Then he stopped playing and said, "I have a little secret to share with you all." The pavilion instantly fell quiet. "You know how there's six songs on Side 1 of the *Take My Hand* album and only four songs on Side 2, with that silent three minute track where Track 5 should be? Well, I'm a little embarrassed to admit this – there's actually supposed to be a fifth song on Side 2 – a final, closing song for the album. But I simply can't bring myself to write it. I haven't been able to. I've been waiting for the right inspiration to hit me." Otto paused, and then sang, "But I think it finally has." The audience lit up loud. "Bear with me," Otto said. "This is going to be a bit rocky – the first verse is going to sound something like this – but this is all I've got so far."

Otto sang alone, gently playing his keyboard, repeating the same verse over and over.

Oh boy, here we go
On a journey to tell them no
Impotent whores and nothing more
Join with me
We'll show those bastards to the door

30

The harsh morning sunlight beamed through the window of Königin's bathroom and woke her from her sleep on the toilet. She was propped up against the wall.

Königin didn't remember the night before. She looked down and saw her underwear around her ankles and her short black boots still on.

She started to remember.

Königin pulled away from the wall and tried to sit up straight. She rubbed her face and then pulled her underwear up.

She forced herself to stand in front of her full length mirror at the end of her gray and pink bathroom. Her face was swollen and her nose and eyes were red. Her hair was tangled and crushed.

She surveyed the bruises on her legs.

The sudden need to vomit gripped Königin. She smashed her knees on the cold tile floor and threw up until there was nothing left to get out.

Königin kicked her boots off and turned the shower on. As the water poured down her face, she tried to remember details, even though she didn't want to know them. The one thing that she was sure of was that she had drank a lot. Königin caught a whiff of liquor from her pores, causing her to dry heave.

She had been at a townhome on the edge of Regent's Park in

northwest London. A mid-level American diplomat threw a party and invited Dr. Clairet, who couldn't attend because he was in the United States. Königin went in his place, even though she was reluctant to go.

It was the first time Königin ventured out since the water launch disaster. It forced her to shower and brush her teeth – activities that she had been taking a break from, along with eating and speaking to people.

The night had started off rather somber. No one was in much of a celebrating mood. If the party hadn't been scheduled a month before, the host, Greg Marvin, would have cancelled it. Not his wife, though. She was half-way through her third gin and tonic by the time Königin arrived, some of which she spilled on Königin at the front door.

As the water ran through Königin's hair, she thought about her walk through the park to the Marvins' house. She shook her head when she remembered that she was miserable then – but that was joy in comparison to how she felt now, sitting on the floor of the shower.

Since Königin moved to London, she had avoided that part of the park where the Memorial Bandstand sat. Jess had told her how the little gazebo that hosted live marching band music had been blown up by the Irish Republican Army years before. She knew that walking past the site toward the party would push her down further, but she didn't care.

In the park, Königin stood still, looking at the octagonal stage capped by an ornate iron roof with a pointed top. It looked like something from the tale of "Cinderella," she thought. But the image of the seven dead Royal Green Jacket band members sent a single quake through her body. Königin was haunted by the idea of innocent people dying, and she always tried to push those thoughts out of her mind when such stories would play over and over again in her head. But today, she punished herself and didn't fight those thoughts.

After her visit to the bandstand, Königin continued through the park on her way to the Marvins' home.

Mrs. Marvin gave Königin a hug at the door, even though they had never met. The woman didn't realize that she had tipped her drink on Königin during the greeting. For a moment, Königin wondered if she had received the hug because Mrs. Marvin pitied her. But that thought was soon erased when the next guest to arrive received the same welcoming gesture, gin and tonic and all. Königin walked into the home, but rather than dry herself off, she chose to ignore her wet blouse.

She looked around from the marble entrance foyer – a few people looked over at her before resuming their conversations. There wasn't a single familiar face.

In the kitchen, there were several bottles of liquor and a few mixers on the counter. On her way to making a drink, Königin was intercepted by a fellow in corduroy pants and a turtleneck sweater.

"Please, let me fix you a drink. No woman should have to make her own cocktail," the man said, his American accent sounding pleasingly familiar to Königin. She smiled and opened her hand toward the bar, welcoming the offer.

"What's your pleasure tonight, miss?" the man asked.

"Bourbon. Give me the Belle Meade," Königin said.

"Let me guess, diet soda too, right?"

"Did I say diet soda?" Königin asked, no longer smiling. Before he could answer, she poured herself a half-full glass of bourbon, neat. She turned around and began to walk away.

"Well, aren't you an obnoxious American," the man called after her.

She turned around to face him. "I'm just not in the mood for any bullshit, all right?"

The man held his hands up, one with a drink in it, in mock-surrender. Königin walked back to him.

She started with his shiny shoes and worked her way up to his thick shiny hair, parted on one side. He looked like a rich guy from New England.

For half an hour they exchanged biographies and figured out who they both knew. His name was Tom, and of course, he knew of Königin.

"This assignment's been interesting," Tom said. "I can't say much, but I've been reassigned from a diplomatic position right into the Collaborative to work on developing the international reach of the organization."

"Hmm, I don't know," Königin said. "Sounds like another bureaucracy."

"Don't be so skeptical, Ms. Clairet. As things get worse around the world, people will welcome the Collaborative's assistance," Tom said. "Anyway, it's been a good way to spend some time over here on the taxpayer's dime. And you'll love my British counterpart, he's been great fun. He'll be here soon – we'll do some shots together," Tom said, smiling. Königin emptied her first drink.

"Have you seen the bandstand in Regent's Park, you know, the one they blew up?" Königin asked Tom as she poured herself another drink.

Before Tom could answer, a deep radio-worthy voice said, "1982. The IRA. What a bloody mess."

"Gilbert, my partner in bad deeds, so glad you're finally here," Tom said. "This is Ms. Königin Clairet – scientist, inventor and bourbon drinker." Tom introduced her as if Gilbert had never heard of her.

Although a little on the short side, Gilbert was built solidly. He wore a white dress shirt with French cuffs rolled up. His cologne gave Königin a headache immediately.

"Pretty nasty stuff, that IRA business. They set off a bomb in Hyde Park that same day," Gilbert said. "Not too far from where you had that nasty fall," he added.

Königin felt like she had walked into a wall. She didn't want to be reminded of that. Gilbert saw her expression change.

"Sorry, dear, shouldn't have brought that up. But you look lovely now and that's all that matters, right?"

"Right," Königin said, quickly choosing to step over the comment and her own thoughts.

She was feeling her first drink take hold.

"I hate the thought of people dying," Königin said. "Every life is a universe, and a universe is destroyed every time someone dies," she said, now staring at nothing.

Tom and Gilbert looked at each other.

"And I've always been able to push those thoughts away – I switch the channel, I turn the page on the newspaper, but I can't now," Königin said.

"Look, dear," Gilbert said, "Let's switch you off this track, okay?"

Königin nodded. "Okay," she said.

"How about some tequila?" Tom asked.

"Sure," Königin answered, nodding. Gilbert fetched three shot glasses and they opened a bottle of tequila that had just been given to the Marvins as a gift.

A round was poured and Tom held his little glass up. "To Ms. Clairet, may she one day launch water again to those thirsty folks in Africa."

Gilbert chuckled. Königin downed the shot without acknowledging Tom's toast.

"Another," Königin said.

Gilbert poured another round, but before he could even try to make a toast, Königin swallowed the drink whole.

"My, my – aren't you loads of fun?" Tom said to Königin, smiling.

Königin shook her head and said, "No more water launches. No more anything. I'm done killing people." Königin leaned against the wall to steady herself.

"Ms. Clairet, please, this is a party. No need to be so heavy. Let's have another drink to lighten up the mood," Tom said, already pouring another round. "A toast," Tom said, lifting his glass. "To Ms. Clairet, who–"

"Oh shut up," Königin said, just before gulping her tequila. Both men laughed.

Like the first subtle turn of a carnival carousel, Königin felt the room slowly start to move.

"Have you ever seen Greg's little den," Tom asked Gilbert. "It's hidden behind a bookshelf in the basement."

Gilbert shook his head. "How perfectly tacky," Gilbert said in his proper English accent. "How American," he added.

"Perhaps, but it's pretty cool. Full bar, pool table, pinball machine," Tom said.

The two men helped Königin down the narrow stairwell to the basement. Gilbert laughed as Tom swung the bookcase to the side for them to enter. Tom closed the bookcase behind them.

"I'm not sure where the light switch is," Tom said as he gently slapped the wall in the den feeling for the switch.

The room was as dark as an unlit dungeon, and even though she was drunk, Königin became immediately aware that she was alone with the two men. She could smell Gilbert, whose cologne had mostly worn off and all that remained was a gentle mix of the scent of his body and the ghost of the cologne.

"You should have found the light switch before you closed the bookshelf, Yankee genius," Gilbert said. Tom slapped the wall one more time and the light went on.

"But that wouldn't have been as much fun, would it?" Tom said, smiling at Königin.

"Okay, who's ready for another shot?" Gilbert asked, holding the bottle up in one hand and the three glasses in the other.

"I guess I'm not done yet," Königin said, now starting to fumble her words a little.

They quickly downed two more rounds of tequila.

Holding onto furniture, she made her way over to the pinball machine. It was a vintage Knew Society themed game. Königin laughed at the cartoon faces of a young Otto Veltraria and Lee Earlman looking at her from the headboard of the machine.

Tom shot pool while Gilbert watched Königin let ball after ball slip between the flippers.

"You're pretty well lousy at this, you know," Gilbert said.

Königin ignored him. She was having trouble standing.

Gilbert moved behind her and put his hands over hers and pressed the flipper buttons with her fingers. Instinctively, she tried to back away, but he didn't move – he was like a brick wall and she only succeeded in pinning herself against him.

Königin felt Gilbert move her hair with his chin, and then she felt his warm, slimy lips on the back of her neck. He crudely kissed her in a few places as he firmly pressed her up against the pinball machine.

Königin could no longer keep her eyes open, or stand – she slumped forward over the top of the pinball machine. Gilbert pressed Königin against the glass with one hand and pulled her skirt up with the other. She tried to stand up and free herself but he had locked her legs in with his. His fingernail scratched her as he pulled her underwear down.

Gilbert held onto her hips as he roughly handled her. He kept her in place – she couldn't move.

Königin went in and out of consciousness, but she knew when Gilbert was done. He backed up, leaving her lying with her face down on the machine.

As soon as Gilbert moved away from her, she felt another body behind her.

"No, no more," Königin said in the loudest voice she could muster.

"Don't be a pain in the ass, I'll make it quick," Tom said. Gilbert laughed.

Königin tried to stand up but Tom grabbed her right arm and bent it behind her back. It hurt, but it hurt much worse when she tried to move.

When Tom was done with her, he pulled Königin's underwear back up and pulled her skirt down, clumsily trying to tidy her.

"Come on, Ms. Clairet, let's get you back upstairs and in a cab. I think you've had too much to drink tonight," Gilbert said. Tom laughed and added, "I'd say so."

Königin then remembered how the party's hostess had given the three of them a knowing, drunken smile when they emerged from the basement. She couldn't remember the ride home.

The phone rang, but Königin didn't move from the floor of her shower to answer it.

A moment later, the phone rang again.

Königin didn't want to talk to anyone, but then it rang again, and she knew that she couldn't escape whatever was waiting on the other end of that phone call.

She put her bathrobe on and slowly walked toward her nightstand, where the phone kept ringing.

She answered. It was her Uncle Sheldon in California. "Königin, I'm sorry child. Aunt Liv is gone."

31

"**H**unger is just a temporary problem now," Corliss said to Ms. Wilson, *The Trustee* reporter. "Or at least it could be, or should be a temporary problem. A shortage of food anywhere is inexcusable. But the Association is on its way to overcoming that global challenge. All we need is the political will – and the funding," Corliss said as he smiled broadly and straightened his necktie. "But we're on our way."

"Mr. Corliss, you're no doubt referring to the ĒMAD project, now that Dr. Clairet has finally committed to work on it under the auspices of the Association – just like his daughter did with her water launcher."

Corliss slowly opened his mouth to answer, but a stream of police cars, complete with sirens and lights, sped past him and Ms. Wilson as they stood on the street corner. Corliss waited a moment for the cars to pass.

"Before we can start to build the ĒMAD, we need a full commitment from the governments of the world and a solid funding commitment from the Guiding Institutions Collaborative – because the resources required to bring it to life will be extensive and exhaustive, but the payoff will be worth every sacrifice made," Corliss said, ignoring the reporter's reference to Königin.

"Yes, Mr. Corliss, I understand, but until the ĒMAD is actually operational and providing food, what's the problem with allowing farms like City Farm to produce food?" Ms. Wilson asked as she nodded toward the old warehouse across the street.

"Ms. Wilson, I caution you against oversimplifying the situation. As you well know, the Collaborative, in concert with our government, is requiring every farm throughout the nation to obtain a Collaborative issued farming permit – and I'm sorry, but City Farm simply doesn't qualify, so it must be shut down. The Collaborative is generously providing financial support to the country and we must respect the Collaborative's requirements, which are quite reasonable. And don't forget, this all for the protection of our citizenry."

"But I would think that feeding people that are hungry right now with food that's right here is reasonable, and if–"

Corliss cut Ms. Wilson off. "I really don't know why *The Trustee* sent you, of all reporters. You just don't seem to understand anything and your priorities are all wrong, Ms. Wilson. Haven't you learned a single thing from our last interview?"

Ms. Wilson ignored Corliss's question and said, "When I heard that the Collaborative had asked you to make an appearance at the shuttering of City Farm and talk to *The Trustee* about it in relation to the ĒMAD, I asked to be put on the assignment. I'm intrigued by the Association's activities – and even though my stories never seem to make print, I'm trying to chronicle the truth while I still can."

Corliss laughed. "You know, Ms. Wilson, you were in fact correct the last time we met – *The Trustee* did send another reporter to interview me after the water launch disaster and she was far more agreeable than you. And what a splendid, supportive article she wrote. But you see, her article was published, unlike yours," Corliss said, smiling and wagging his long index finger at the young woman. "You know, I can't quite figure out why *The Trustee* would bother keeping you on its payroll, Ms. Wilson," Corliss said, chuckling.

The sound of shattering glass traveled across the street from the old brick warehouse. Shouts rose up. Firetrucks surrounded the building and a platoon of firemen prepared their hoses and ladders. There was no fire.

A woman in sweatpants and a tank top ran from across the street and pushed herself between Corliss and Ms. Wilson. "Please help, you can't let this happen. They're going to burn it all down. Please help," the woman shouted, looking at Corliss and Ms. Wilson with wet, wide eyes. "Come, come with me, I'll show you. I know how to get in. I want you to see what they're going to do."

Ms. Wilson began to follow the woman who was heading back toward the building.

Corliss called after them, saying, "Don't interfere. You must let this play out as it should." And then a moment later, he added, "It looks like a dangerous situation."

The two women ignored his words and kept walking quickly. In the confusion of police and people and firefighters, they were able to dodge through the crowd toward the warehouse, unnoticed.

The woman led Ms. Wilson to a rusted steel door behind a dumpster sitting next to the building. When Ms. Wilson struggled to get the door open, the woman shoved the door open effortlessly. They looked back when the door didn't slam shut behind them. It was Corliss, trying to catch up. His steps were tentative – he looked as if he was walking on his toes.

Shouts echoed through the warehouse toward them from the other end of the massive building.

Ten fields worth of crops grew in racks climbing to the ceiling 40 feet above. Fruits, vegetables and flowers packed broad shelving units setup with growing lights and irrigation pipes. Pathways dotted with moveable ladders suspended from above carved through the vertical growing fields.

On the rack nearest to Corliss, hundreds of heads of lettuce were nearly full grown. He was startled by the automatic misters that kicked on, unannounced.

"This is just amazing," Ms. Wilson said, looking around. "The authorities wouldn't let me in when I arrived earlier."

"Thousands of people are eating because of this facility," the woman said.

The group of three walked further into the building, not speaking. The damp smell of the fresh produce was strong.

"This community has been feeding itself. We took matters into our own hands, right here, right in our own backyard, in this abandoned warehouse. This was nothing but a place to buy drugs and a place for the girls to take their customers. But we came together and cleaned them out, cleaned it all out. We scraped together what we could and built this."

Shouts and voices neared. Corliss looked around, quickly, not knowing what to do.

Then, through a bullhorn, a monotone voice gave an order: "By order of the Custodial Enforcement Agency, this building must be vacated immediately. You are not permitted to remain in this building. You must exit this building immediately."

Corliss began to bite his fingernails. Ms. Wilson and the woman ignored the announcement.

After a moment, the order continued, "Protective action will commence in five minutes. You must exit this building immediately."

The woman shook both of her fists in the air, squeezing her eyes shut.

"We must leave immediately and let them do their work. You're interfering here," Corliss said. He was looking around, trying to figure out where the nearest door was.

The clanging of equipment moving into place grew louder.

Corliss looked around, his eyes wide with fear. "Stop!" he shouted. "I'm in here! Don't start yet! I need to get out! Help, help, please help!" he continued shouting.

Ms. Wilson and the woman froze and looked at Corliss without saying a word.

Almost instantly, uniformed Custodial Enforcement Agency officers descended upon them from all directions. Corliss held his hands up as if surrendering.

"Ms. Luke, you know you can't be in here," the officer in charge said to the woman.

"How can you claim to be a servant of the people?" she asked him, shaking her head.

"Ms. Luke, we've been through this. There's nothing I can do," the officer said. "You're operating a farm without the required permit and people could get sick."

"That's absolutely right. I told them not to interfere," Corliss said.

"People could get sick? Really? People could starve. People are going to starve," Ms. Luke shouted.

"I'm not going to have this debate with you," the officer said. "There's a protocol that has to be followed – for everything. Every agency and stakeholder having jurisdiction over this facility and its activities has had its say in this matter."

"Yeah, everybody but me. And the people that need this food," Ms. Luke said.

In unison, all of the officers' radios announced, "We're ready to initiate protective action. Clear the site."

The officer pulled his radio up to his mouth. "Copy that. We're coming out now."

Corliss walked quickly – even breaking into a semi-jog every few steps.

As the group neared a huge opened roll-up door with sunlight streaming in, six technicians protected in silver fireproof suits ran past them into the warehouse. They carried flamethrowers.

Ms. Luke broke away from the group and ran after the technicians. "You can't do this to us," she shouted.

Corliss continued his quick pace toward the door while a few officers ran to retrieve the shouting woman.

The first spit of fire instantly engulfed a wide rack of potatoes. Then, one by one, racks of red peppers, cauliflower, strawberries and garlic were burnt.

"You don't know what you're destroying," Ms. Luke shouted as the officers carried her out.

A hundred yards from the burning warehouse, the officers put the woman on her feet. They all watched in silence as flames ate City Farm. The fire department's trucks were in place, waiting for clearance to start extinguishing the fire. A tall plume of black smoke billowed into the sky.

After a few minutes, Corliss turned to Ms. Luke and said, "You needn't lament the day's events. I assure you, the food will be plentiful once we get our machine going."

Ms. Luke didn't acknowledge Corliss's words, but the side of her face twitched. She kept her eyes fixed on the burning farm. Ms. Wilson wrote quickly in her notebook.

Corliss continued, "When we succeed, your endeavor here will seem quaint and old fashioned – and it will be nice to be taken care of for once."

Ms. Luke turned and looked into Corliss's eyes and said, "We can take care of ourselves if you'll just get out of our way."

———

The next day, both sides of *The Trustee* ran articles about the necessary burning of City Farm for the welfare of the public, but one side took the position that the urban farm should have been destroyed with powerful water cannons, while the other side of the newspaper maintained that burning the farm was indeed the correct approach. Ms. Wilson wrote neither article.

32

Königin sat at the farmhouse table and rested her chin on her folded hands. She stared at the glass of red wine in front of her.

"Königin, what's on your mind?" her Uncle Sheldon asked.

She didn't respond.

The two sat in silence for a few minutes.

"It's so pretty," Königin said.

"What is?" Sheldon asked.

"Your wine. That hue of red is so bright and full of life."

"Yes, it is," he said.

"I hate to say this, because blood shouldn't be considered beautiful, but that's what it looks like," Königin said.

"Don't feel bad, that's how I look at it too. Nothing is wrong with blood. Blood is a gift. It's life giving. But we prefer that silent force of life to stay hidden within us, and not spilled, ever, except when nature requires. The wine is simply homage to that life force," Sheldon said.

Königin didn't respond, but after a long pause she took a measured sip of wine.

"I'm sorry my father couldn't come to Auntie's funeral," Königin said.

"He made the right choice if it wasn't in his heart to come," Sheldon replied.

"It wasn't that he didn't want to come, he just couldn't. He's so tied up right now with trying to get his latest project off the ground."

"Königin, understand this," Sheldon said. "I'm not attacking your father, but I want to explain something to you. He made a choice not to come. And that's okay. But for me, it's very important that you understand that he made a choice. We all make choices. Some are insignificant, and some are not. Too often our mind is clouded with reasons why we can't do something, or reasons why we must do something, but we allow those reasons, those conditions, and those excuses to be factors in our choices. And sometimes that's all right, and sometimes it's not.

"Yeah, that sounds good, but it's not as simple as that, Uncle Sheldon. Dad's project is all-consuming – he couldn't take any time off. So he really didn't have a choice."

"I'm not saying that he made the wrong choice, I'm just telling you that we always have the opportunity to choose, and yes, with that comes the consequences of our choices," Sheldon said. "And we must take responsibility for our choices and their consequences and not hide behind other people or excuses."

Königin sat silent, looking around at the artwork on the walls of her uncle's kitchen. After so many years, she suddenly became aware of the contrast between the stone walls, the wide planked floors, the slowly turning ceiling fan, and the bright little watercolor paintings in their ornate frames.

Out of the silence, Shelden said, "Who am I kidding?" He looked up at the ceiling, his eyes not focused on anything. "I have no right to lecture about choices."

Königin tilted her head.

"I should have tried to do more, Königin."

"Do more?" she asked.

"Yes. We should have gone to the ends of the earth to find experimental treatments. Maybe she would be here with me now."

"Don't blame yourself, Uncle Sheldon – I'm sure there was nothing you could have done."

Sheldon leaned toward Königin. "No, Königin – that's wrong. You can always do something. Your actions may not be effective, but you can always make a choice, you can always take a stand. And at least if you make a choice and act on it, you have the chance to influence events." He shook his head and looked away from Königin. "But I lost my way. They all said she had no chance, so I surrendered."

"Sometimes you just know when you're beat," Königin said softly.

"Learn this from me, Königin – sitting idly by renders you ineffective and weak – and that's how I feel inside right now. I sought and accepted the advice and guidance of others, rather than relying on myself. I've made the biggest mistake of my life. And hers."

Looking down at the table, Königin said nothing.

"And to make it all worse, I've caught myself lying."

"Lying? To who? You don't lie, Uncle Sheldon."

"To myself, Königin – I've been lying to myself. It's how I've been trying to escape facing the fact that I blew it. Telling myself and everyone else that there was nothing that could have been done to save her."

The gush of rustling leaves chattered outside.

"Thank you for letting me burden you with this, Königin. And I'm sorry for it. But I need to confront this. I have some hard work ahead of me. And I have no choice, because lying to yourself will make you rot from the inside out."

Königin hung her head.

Sheldon continued, "If your mother was here, things might have turned out differently. She was powerful, and she derived her power from her absolute certainty in knowing what and who she was and what was important to her. And consequently, she knew what to do in any given situation, without faltering. She had a profound strength."

"Well, I'm not Pearl McCloud – and I don't have that strength," Königin said, without lifting her head.

"I think you do," Sheldon said as he reached across the table and took her hand. "You will find it if you silence every voice in your head other than your own, Königin. Learn to trust yourself. *You* are in charge of *you*, and you know what's best for you."

Königin slowly withdrew her hand from her uncle's. Her stomach began to hurt, and she felt like she was suffocating.

"It just can't be that simple, Uncle Sheldon."

"But it is, Königin."

⊷ 33 ⊷

"Major L'Enfant designed a beautiful capital city for a beautiful country," Althea said.

Otto looked at her bare shoulders as she stood with her back to him, between two marble columns of the Lincoln Memorial, looking out onto the Mall's Reflecting Pool and the Washington Monument behind it. Otto shifted his gaze from her to the Capitol Building in the distance.

"Do you think your grandparents would have ever thought you'd be performing at this sacred place for millions of people, Althea?" Otto asked.

She turned around to him. "You know what, yes, for sure – they would have expected this from me," she said, smiling. "My family has always believed in me. And I always gave them a reason to."

Otto smiled back at her. "You're a fine person. Thanks for all you've done on this tour."

"Thank you for including me," Althea said. "I like where you're taking it all – canceling the small gigs so you can visit with the most people at once. But after this show on the world stage, I'm not sure what's left for you to do."

"One step at a time, Althea," Otto said, letting his eyes stay connected with hers for an extra second.

Althea tilted her head slightly. "Otto, are you looking to get with me?"

"No, no – don't be silly, Althea. Sorry if I sent out a signal I shouldn't have."

"Oh, okay then," she said, shrugging her shoulders but still looking at Otto.

Otto wiped his palms against his jeans. "What do you think of the show's expanded line up?" he asked.

"Pretty good talent, for the most part – I like most of the bands and people you have coming. Wide variety – you've got something for everyone and every age, so that's good for the mission, right? Just don't be surprised when they do things a little differently than you do," Althea said.

"Mission? What mission?" Otto asked.

"Hah, you'd better be kidding, boy," she said. Otto didn't respond.

The two sat down on the top step of the Lincoln Memorial in silence and looked out onto the calm Reflecting Pool, which in a couple of days would be planked over to accommodate the fans coming to see them.

⊶ 34 ⊷

Thousands of busses headed toward Washington, D.C. from all points in the United States. On board, Americans of every background gladly made their pilgrimage to see and hear Otto Veltraria.

Two days before the show, Jess had flown to Indianapolis and boarded one of the buses carrying the hopeful to D.C. He sat next to the bathroom, which leaked the smell of sanitized urine. The location allowed him to casually interview people as they waited their turn to relieve themselves.

"Why? Why bother going?" Jess asked a man in his early twenties who tried the locked door to the bathroom.

"I guess it's something to do, right? I've got nowhere else to be. There's going to be some great music there – and tons of girls," the young man answered.

"That's it? What about the *Take My Hand Tour*? What about Otto Veltraria?" Jess asked.

"Oh, for sure, I'm totally loving that guy. I'm a fan of anybody that busts on *the man* – and he's the best at it."

"Otto's united us against common enemies and it's time to make our voices heard," added a gray haired man as the twenty-something went into the bathroom.

"What kind of person do you think Otto Veltraria is?" Jess asked the man as he waited his turn.

"Guys like us will never meet him, but you can tell from his words that he's a leader," the man answered. "He talks to us and preaches to us through his music and his words. It seems like there's nobody else saying much of anything worthwhile these days, so, you know, his words are that much louder – and more beautiful."

The twentysomething exited and returned to his seat, after he remembered where it was. Gray hair stepped in and closed the door.

Next up was an old lady. She had to steady herself on each seat as she made her way toward the bathroom. Jess stood up when she reached him.

"Sit while you wait," Jess said.

The woman laughed. "Thank you, but I can still stand just fine." Jess smiled at her and sat back down.

"This seems like an awfully big trip for you. Do you think it will be worth it?" Jess asked.

"I think so, but you never know. I've seen many pretty faces, and some not so pretty, and I've been rallied this way and that over the years. But I think Mr. Veltraria is a good man and he's been able to sum up the angst of the country," she said, then adding "or the angst of the world, actually."

The door to the bathroom opened but she let the man behind her go ahead of her. "You know, people don't even know anymore why they're so angry and frustrated," she said to Jess. "I mean, the obvious reasons are out there and there's no mystery about them – the wheels are coming off the wagon and momma can't buy the baby shoes – unless she borrows the money," the woman said.

"But you think there's more?" Jess asked.

"Of course, there's more. Those are just the symptoms. Everybody's so darn mad because we let it all happen. *We're* the problem – a bunch of suckers getting taken every time. We believe what we're told about each other and the world – because *they* insist that we believe. We trust the voice that sounds the most convincing – because *they* implore us to trust that voice. And we indulge our addiction to everything, hoping to satisfy ourselves – but more importantly, hoping to satisfy *them*. But in our hearts, we know the truth – we let them get away with everything they could figure out how to get away with, and we now hate ourselves for it."

"I see, so where does Otto Veltraria come in?" Jess asked.

"Well, he's a consoler," she said, shrugging her shoulders. "Not much more than that. But sometimes you just need to know that others share your feelings, and it's comforting to have a voice that unites you with like-minded people," she said.

"So, do you think that all of the people on this bus share your self-hatred for failing our country and our world?" Jess asked, looking up from his notebook.

The woman staggered back for a moment. She took a breath and leaned into Jess. "I don't think anybody's ready for that kind of soul searching. It's too painful. And it takes effort, and people are lazy. But yes, they share my self-hatred for those failures – they just don't know it, so it bubbles up in the form of garden variety anger and frustration in daily life. If people can begin to admit how badly we've failed, as individuals and as a society, we'll be on our way to redemption."

With that, she stepped in and closed the door without looking again at Jess.

The bus bounced along, and somewhere south of Pittsburgh, a man who looked to be in his early thirties approached the empty bathroom. Jess stopped him.

"I see you're wearing a tour shirt. How much did it cost?" Jess asked.

The man stopped and thought. "I think it was seventy-five bucks. Something like that."

"Don't you think that's insane? For a shirt?" Jess asked.

"Yeah, but it's an official tour shirt," the man said.

"Indeed it is, and it was actually seventy dollars, not seventy-five," Jess said.

The man cocked his head back and asked, "So you knew how much the shirt was? Then why did you ask me?"

"I just wanted to see the expression on your face when you told me how much you paid for the official tour shirt," Jess said.

"Why? Who the hell are you?"

"I'm Jess Frank, Otto's official tour biographer. We're going to include some of these interviews in a book about the tour."

"Yeah, right," the man said laughing as he went into the bathroom.

A couple of minutes later, the man exited without looking at Jess.

"Sir, excuse me, but I have one more question, if you don't mind," Jess said as the man started to make his way back to his seat.

The man slowly turned around to face Jess.

"Don't you think that Otto Veltraria is really just another self-righteous rock star?" Jess asked.

The man slowly approached Jess.

"No, I don't. What I think is that you've got a big mouth that should be kept shut," the man said.

"Really? Why? Otto is always talking about tolerating and respecting the opinions of others. What if that's my opinion? Or the opinion of someone else on this bus?" Jess asked.

"Then that opinion shouldn't be tolerated, or even allowed to leak out of a little weasel like you. You're just trying to attack a good man and I won't allow it," the man said, his fists clenched. "And you have a lot of nerve lying about working for him."

"Do you think Otto Veltraria's here to save you? Do you need to be saved?" Jess asked in a calm tone.

The man grabbed Jess by his suede jacket and lifted him up out of his seat. "I'm not going to listen to this anymore – you've said too much."

Jess stood smiling at the man, not struggling, not even attempting to remove the man's clutched hand from his jacket.

"You goddamn smart-ass, you're off." The man turned his head toward the rest of the passengers who were now silent, watching the altercation.

"We've got a hater here," the man announced.

For a moment, no one said a word. Everyone looked at each other. Then someone shouted "boo." And then "loser" was added in by someone else. And in the span of five seconds, everyone on the bus was booing and shouting at Jess.

The man shoved Jess down the aisle of the bus.

"Let's stone him!" one man yelled. Everyone laughed, but then people started looking at each other again, seeing if anyone took the suggestion seriously.

Jess looked at the sea of faces before him, lining each side of the aisle. They all blended into one angry face.

"Driver, driver, pull over," the man handling Jess shouted to the front of the bus.

The quick deceleration of the bus made Jess fall. He felt his messenger bag hit the back of his head. Almost instantly his entire body was lifted by the other passengers, as if in a mosh pit, and he found himself at the front of the bus, having received scratches, pinches and punches on the way. The open bus door was waiting for him, and several hands threw him out onto the shoulder of the interstate on his ass. The messenger bag flew out of the bus and hit him in the face this time. The door closed and Jess watched as the bus pulled away and blended in with the rest of the eastbound traffic.

➛ 35 ➛

In the House of Representatives, the members were preparing for the afternoon vote on the National Debt Contribution Act. The House was full, as both the Speaker and the Minority Leader had insisted that all of their members be present – and they were. Pressure from *The Trustee* and the White House to strike a long-term deal with the Guiding Institutions Collaborative had grown in intensity as the collective psyche of the nation withered under the circumstances.

The morning session had been unusually civil – consisting of little more than generic soapbox speeches. Phrases like, "We owe it to the American people," and "We must do the right thing," echoed over and over. But members of the Collaborative Caucus repeatedly reminded their fellow House members that the Guiding Institutions Collaborative would be forced to end its funding of the government's operations if the National Debt Contribution Act wasn't passed. "You can't expect the Collaborative's generosity to continue without a commitment by the American people to contribute," Congressman Kaye said to the chamber.

Congressman Jerez slowly made his way from member to member, not attempting to keep his voice down as he lobbied against the bill. "Come on now, don't be stupid about this," Jerez said to a younger member. "You'll wake up with a hangover tomorrow if you vote for this thing. Oh sure, you'll have fun tonight at the Collaborative's boondoggle, but when your eyes open tomorrow morning, you'll remember that they own you and everyone you know. Simply isn't worth it."

"I don't know, Jerez," the young member said. "Kaye makes a very strong argument. We'll never get out of this mess without the Collaborative."

"That fella's a dandy," Jerez said, glaring over at Kaye. "Don't ever trust a man in a light blue suit that's two sizes too small for him."

The young member laughed and said, "No offense, Congressman Jerez, but your square toed boots and that bolo are better suited for a rodeo than the House chamber."

Jerez shook his head and said, "This *is* a rodeo, you idiot."

36

A couple of miles down the street from the "rodeo," dozens of policemen riding loud motorcycles side-by-side led a parade of Washington D.C. police cruisers with their lights and sirens on, nestling Otto's limousine in the middle of the moving fortress. The procession moved up Constitution Avenue toward the Lincoln Memorial.

"Look at all of those buses" Jess said to Otto and Althea, pointing out the window. "I nearly got here on one of them."

Otto laughed and said to Althea, "Jess had to hitchhike from Uniontown, Pennsylvania."

Althea looked at Jess and tilted her head.

"Yep," Otto continued. "I don't know what he said, but I'm sure he shared a little too much truth with his fellow bus riders. He has such a way with people." Althea smiled gently at Jess.

Jess looked out the tinted window at all of the people moving against the backdrop of the square, stone government buildings lining the avenue.

"A chopper's been following us," Althea said.

Jess lowered the window and slightly stuck his head out, looking up. "You're right, it's overhead."

"Police or *Trustee* helicopter?" Otto asked.

"Can't tell," Jess said, his head now hanging out of the car, looking toward the sky.

Otto reached over and pulled Jess back into the car. "Don't stick your head out like that, unless you don't need it anymore," Otto said.

The motorcade drove in the center of the avenue – "non-official" traffic was prohibited because of the show. Hundreds of police on horseback kept the crowd from spilling into the street.

From the helicopter, the birds-eye image of Otto's long black car approaching the Lincoln Memorial filled more than 100 huge screens set up throughout the area. Otto's arrival was witnessed by everyone.

Sauer Belchman, a young deejay with a huge following, had volunteered to emcee the show. Although Otto wasn't familiar with Sauer or his work, he accepted the offer upon the advice and recommendation of others.

"Hey, look people – that bad boy mother-fucker is almost here," Sauer shouted as he pointed at a screen mounted next to the stage. The responding cheers sounded like a jet engine throttling up.

Otto's car drove under a large canopy near the rear of the stage. A camera greeted him as he exited the car, all of which was broadcast to the crowd, along with his wave and a smile. Then the video on the screens returned to Sauer as his skinny body hopped around the stage.

37

Lying on a lumpy motel bed in Wadsworth, Nevada, Königin watched Sauer Belchman on a flickering television. Otto's "people" had managed to assemble the biggest names in the music business. With the Lincoln Memorial as the backdrop, one act followed another, and the audience was treated to a free concert of non-stop entertainment that included a heavy dose of life-affirming messages along with a sprinkling of vague "anti-establishment" sentiment. The two second delay caught most of Belchman's cursing before his words were broadcast to the world.

Königin shifted in the bed.

After a couple of minutes, she shifted again, unable get comfortable. But it wasn't just the bed. She took her shirt off, and then her sweatpants, but still she felt sweaty and stifled. Königin threw her clothes down on the darkened yellow carpet of the dim little room.

Now lying on her side, Königin looked at her mother's crystal Addorra popping out of the top of her open backpack. Uncle Sheldon wouldn't let her leave without taking it. Dr. Clairet had shrugged his shoulders and then nodded when Sheldon asked to take it so many years ago after her mother's disappearance. The dusty little statuette that used to sit on the bookshelf in the family room of her old home wasn't thought of again after it left with Sheldon.

Sticky and uneasy, Königin threw the blanket onto the floor and laid face up on the bed when her uneasiness finally reached the point of being unbearable. She listened to her breathing and began to relax, but then her focus shifted to the sound of Belchman introducing the Rolling Stones. Realizing that the sounds of the concert were adding to her agitation, she turned the television off.

Königin thought about disappearing. Perhaps not literally, but she wasn't sure. She wanted to run, to get away, but she couldn't figure out from what.

After a deep, sustained breath, Königin listened to nothing but the rhythm of her heart beating. As she began to relax again, she thought about the lie that she had told her uncle. He would never let her walk across the country aimlessly, and she knew it, so she had told him that she was going to Seattle to see friends. Instead, Königin had boarded a random bus she hoped would take her somewhere she wanted to be. After shifting around in her seat on the bus for four long hours, Königin got off at Wadsworth, unable to carry on.

Lying perfectly still in her bed, Königin decided that she would continue to head east when she was ready. Maybe she'd leave tomorrow – maybe not. She didn't care about anything, except escaping the feeling of dull helplessness that seemed to be closing in on her.

38

Otto sat in his dressing room, delicately sipping a cup of black tea and watching the show on the television. "Vic, can you believe this coverage? We're global."

"Don't I know it. My mum's watching back home," Victoria said as she fidgeted with Otto's hair.

Otto leaned forward toward the television screen and squinted his eyes. "Vic, what's he saying? Why are they bleeping him out?"

"Who, that Belcher fellow?"

"Yes, Sauer Belchman – what's he saying that needs to be cut out?" Otto asked.

"He's got a nasty mouth, you know. His mum should've washed his mouth out with soap a time or two," Victoria said.

Otto rose from his chair and turned the volume on the television down and the volume up on the closed circuit speaker carrying the show's audio without the delay. He leaned back against the wall of his dressing room and listened.

Belchman was introducing a renowned poet that had been invited to read her work at the show.

"And not only is she one of the world's smartest bitches, her smokin' bod just starts with her tight ass," Belchman said, the crowd roaring in approval.

Otto's eyes grew so wide that his pupils looked lost in the whites of his eyes. He stood up straight and clenched his fists. Victoria put her hands on her mouth and looked at Otto.

"Joni Wynd? He's introducing Nobel Laureate Joni Wynd? My God, who is this pig?" Otto shouted. "I'm going to knock his teeth out."

"No, no, Otto. Calm yourself," Victoria said.

The poet began to recite her words to a now silent audience. Otto slowly sat down and listened. The poem went on for a few minutes, praising Otto's kindness and good deeds in verse. "That was beautiful. She's so sweet," Otto said. Victoria gently rubbed his shoulders.

The crowd showed their love for the poet and her poem with all of their noise.

Then Belchman's whiney voice took over. "Was that totally off the fucking hook or what, my people?" Everyone cheered in agreement.

Without a moment's hesitation, and without looking at Victoria, Otto hopped out of his chair and trotted out the door of his dressing room. As he walked quickly in the direction of the stage, a cameraman tried to keep up with him. The screens were filled with the image of Otto making his way toward the action. The crowd went wild.

As Otto reached the edge of the stage, Belchman turned toward him and lifted his hand for a high-five, shouting, "Let's show our love for this big-balled bastard, he's–"

Otto grabbed Belchman's upper arm and pulled him off the stage as if he was being dragged to the principal's office. The little man was no longer smiling and it was clear that he was in a little pain. The crowd laughed and cheered, certain that they had just witnessed a funny, planned part of the show.

Now backstage, Otto shook his head. "What is wrong with you, Sauer? You can't speak like that at my show, don't you know that?"

"But that's me, Mr. Veltraria. I'm just doing my thing. You know, that's why the people love me, especially the ladies – because I tell them where it's at."

Otto tightened his grip on Belchman's arm and said, "Listen to me, you need to apologize to Ms. Wynd. And then you need to pack your things and leave. I don't want you around the stage – or even near this show."

Sauer Belchman looked deflated. But suddenly his face lit up in anger and he pushed Otto's hand off his arm and looked Otto in the eyes. "Be careful, big man. You might not cuss, but I bet my ass that your pretty words are more dangerous than my street talk."

"Go. Now," Otto said, extending his long arm and pointing toward the dressing rooms.

⟳ 39 ⟲

Otto, Althea and the rest of the band took the stage not long after Belchman was dismissed from his duties. Looking out at the crowd, Otto could see that he had disrupted the flow and energy of the show.

A few minutes earlier, in Althea's dressing room, Otto had recounted the details of Belchman's firing.

Althea looked at Otto's reflection in the mirror as she carefully applied her eyeliner.

"Oh, yeah? So that's what you did?" she asked.

"Yep. I just threw him out. It felt good," Otto said.

"Well, okay," Althea said as she shrugged her shoulders.

"What? You don't think that was the right thing to do?" Otto asked.

"Doesn't matter now. It's done," she said.

Otto crossed his arms, frowned, and stared at Althea in the mirror for a moment. "Enough about that," he said. "Look, I want to play the album from beginning to end, but stay with me – we're going to take a couple of detours."

"What do you have in mind?" Althea asked, applying dark red lipstick.

"Another video feed from the floor of the House. And I need to connect with the people more – I need to get through to them – I need teach and inform them."

"Why not an all-out sermon?" Althea asked flatly.

"No, what are you talking about? That's not even funny. These folks are just looking for some guidance and comforting words – and that's exactly what I'm going to give them."

Althea smiled at Otto but said nothing as they left her dressing room and headed for the stage.

"We've got 2 million people out there and 350 million watching all over the globe. I'm not going to miss this opportunity," Otto said.

Althea nodded. "I get it."

A few minutes later, they played their opening number and the entire crowd sang along with them. It was a bright autumn afternoon and everyone moved to the music. The light, cool air breathed through the huge crowd.

Otto rose from his keyboard and approached the front of the stage with his microphone in hand. The people quieted down.

"Look, I'm going to level with you all. I threw Sauer Belchman out of here. I didn't like his foul mouth," Otto said, shaking his head, which was twenty feet tall in every screen. The crowd exploded into laughter and cheers.

"You know, all that swearing for no good reason, and to refer to Ms. Wynd as a *B-I-T-C-H* – it was just too much for me." The crowd laughed. "So, I'm sorry my people, but I just had to ask him to leave. I'd like to think that we've come a little further than that." The crowd applauded obediently.

Otto returned to his keyboard and said, "This next one is *Angry Little Man* – we can all relate, right?" Whistles and cheers answered Otto. Instantly the music started.

After a few more songs, Otto took center stage again, holding his microphone. "I hope you're all enjoying the food and other necessities available here at the show. Sold by very good companies who really care about people. They give a fair deal – and that's all we can ask for." The crowd quietly listened to Otto. "But, you know, these companies can only do so much – and so many of them have gone under in the last year."

Otto paced the stage calmly. Then he raised his hand slowly and pointed toward the dome of the Capitol Building behind his audience. "And what are *those people* doing to help?" Whistles, boos and shouts answered Otto in a growing rumble. "Tell us, members of Congress, what are *you* doing?" He held his mic out toward the Capitol as if he were expecting an answer to roll over the heads of the two million people between him and the majestic white building on the other end of the National Mall. Otto held his hand up to his ear to listen. "Nothing. I didn't think so," he said. The crowd booed and jeered.

"Let's watch these clowns. We tried this at Meadowbrook and it was a disaster, but we're going to do it again anyway – treat you to a live feed from the floor of your House of Representatives. Let's see who's yammering on the floor right now, who's standing in the way of your future." Otto turned toward the screen nearest to him to watch as the feed connected.

Congressman Kaye was in the process of making his final plea from the rostrum of the House Chamber.

"We're running out of time," he said. "We've exhausted all of our financial resources."

The members of Congress sat in silence.

"Listen to me," Kaye continued. "We desperately need long-term funding from the Collaborative to keep our society functioning. The Collaborative, in its wisdom, established the Fund for that very reason. And in return, each American – if he or she wants a clearance certificate – will pay their fair share of that money back to the Collaborative. It should be viewed as an honor by every American to participate in lifting our nation from this deep depth of debt. The National Debt Contribution Act is the right thing for America, and I'm proud to be a part of the Collaborative Caucus, and by extension, a part of the solution."

Jerez broke the members' silence. "You're just selling a perfumed pile of *mierda de perro*, Mr. Kaye." A handful of the members laughed.

"A what?" Kaye asked.

A congresswoman yelled out, "Dog shit. Jerez says you're selling a perfumed pile of dog shit."

"That's outrageous," Kaye shouted at Jerez.

"Crap. All crap," Jerez shouted back at Kaye. "You're selling a flowered, putrid lie. What you're really talking about is indenturing people – American citizens, making them beholden to the Collaborative. You propose to make Americans pay for rights and liberties that already belong to them! You're willing to subordinate the Constitution and the Bill of Rights to the requirements of an overlord that has contributed to the very condition that it seeks to benefit from. The Collaborative will be our master – and we will be subjugated forever!"

"Stop being so dramatic, Mr. Jerez," Kaye said. "Whether you like it or not, we're already beholden to the Collaborative. And we should all thank the caring and generous patrons that make up the Collaborative. Who do you think will be funding your salary next week?" Kaye said.

"No way, not me, Kaye – they're not paying for me. But I know they're paying you and every member of your Collaborative Caucus."

"There's nothing wrong with that, Mr. Jerez," Kaye said. "It's totally legal – even if you did vote against the bill allowing it. You lost on that one, now live with it. The Collaborative has been generous with the caucus members and our families and your opposition is getting you nothing."

"I want nothing for myself," Jerez said, slowly sitting down while staring at Kaye.

Kaye ignored Jerez and said, "I have a feeling that more of you will be joining the Collaborative Caucus. Let me be clear, a *yea* on the National Debt Contribution Act guarantees automatic membership in the caucus and all the privileges and benefits thereof. And party affiliation is irrelevant – the Collaborative Caucus welcomes our brothers and sisters from both sides of the aisle."

Kaye and Jerez had each spoken without asking for permission. Parliamentary procedure in the House of Representatives had been abandoned.

Jerez quickly stood up again. "Mr. Speaker, this hyena and his *true* constituency have hijacked this legislative body. You must invoke some point of order to restore some sanity here."

Slumping in his chair on the top tier of the rostrum, the Speaker said, "Nothing more I can do, Mr. Jerez. This house is out-of-order."

"Don't quit on us now, Mr. Speaker," Jerez shouted.

The Speaker straightened-up in his chair and looked to his right at a marble pedestal – atop of which sat nothing.

"Eight years ago, the Mace of the House of Representatives disappeared. Stolen," the Speaker said. "That marked the beginning of this chamber's final slide into the business of prostitution."

Jerez shook his head. "It was bad way before then. That was just the half-way mark, Mr. Speaker."

"Perhaps, but the theft and illicit sale of that sacred ceremonial item by a member of the House reflected a growing gross indifference to the respect that this institution demands and deserves," the Speaker said. "Now, this place is for sale piece-by-piece. And in bulk."

"It's not my fault that your fancy bauble was stolen," Kaye said. "I am without sin. I'm working for the American people – trying to find a way out of this tight spot – and I urge all of my colleagues in this chamber to join with me in passing this bill." Kaye cleared his throat and stood on his chair. "Let us acknowledge that as of this day, our old parties of donkey and elephant are dead – replaced by the Collaborative Caucus as the new majority party, and those who refuse to shape and support the future of our nation as the minority."

A mix of cheering, booing and shouting rose up in the House Chamber. The members rose from their seats and began moving about, splintering into a hundred separate conversations and debates.

Otto paced on his stage watching the screens but said nothing. His audience was silent too.

Kaye continued, "And for those of you who know what the right thing to do is but just need one more good reason to join the Collaborative Caucus and help make this bill the law of the land, here it is – you and your families will be exempt from the requirements of the National Debt Contribution Act – no clearance certificate required. This gift to you is made by the Collaborative in recognition of your commitment and sacrifice to this nation."

Jerez's eyes bulged. "I won't let you hold the heads of the American people under water while you take a deep breath," he shouted while pointing at Kaye. "They're already drowning under the burden of their Full-Life Loans and a life that's impossible to pay for – courtesy of those snakes that make up your beloved Collaborative."

"Come on, Mr. Speaker, it's time," Kaye announced, ignoring Jerez. "Call for the yeas and nays on the bill at hand – the most important bill to be considered by this body in a generation – one surely to impact many generations to come."

Jerez lowered his arm and began to walk slowly toward Kaye.

"Please, Mr. Speaker, call for the vote," Kaye yelled as Jerez moved closer. Kaye assumed a rigid boxing stance in anticipation of Jerez's approach.

"Congressman Jerez, a vote on this matter is inevitable," the Speaker said. "Take your seat." Jerez ignored him.

"Yeas and nays are so ordered," the Speaker announced. "With every member present today, we clearly have a quorum."

Breaking from his boxing stance, Kaye ran from Jerez, taking a round-about way to the "Well" at the front of the chamber where he could cast his vote. Jerez's paunchy body chugged after Kaye, with his cragged face and bulbous nose now pulsating from the effort.

Kaye hurriedly fumbled around with a voting card before signing it and casting his vote. The first "yea" was in.

Lunging, Jerez sacked Kaye – the two men hit the floor hard.

Simultaneously, a gasp rose up from the House Chamber and Otto's audience.

The House floor was now filled with a mix of activity – representatives trying to vote in the midst of fights spontaneously breaking out all across the floor. The Speaker slumped in his chair.

The House's Sergeant at Arms, a short man with muscles filling out his old plaid suit, marched around the House Chamber, carefully holding the wooden handle of a toilet plunger out in front of him – it was the replacement of the sacred mace that had been used to restore order in the House when disrupted by unruly members. The original ebony and sterling silver staff-like mace, capped with an eagle with outstretched wings, was gone – and serving in its place was a long, stained dowel.

Otto clasped his hands on the top of his head and just stared at the screen. Then he turned to his audience and said, "Do you believe this? Is this actually happening? Are they actually voting on that bill?"

Shouts and jeers rose up from the crowd.

"I thought that Kaye fellow was just grandstanding," Otto said. "I didn't think that debt contribution law, or whatever the hell it's called, was actually going to make it to a vote. This is just insane."

Otto and his audience watched as votes were cast amid little skirmishes between the representatives.

Then, without even a flicker of warning, the screens went dark and the images from the House were gone. After a few moments, Otto's image filled the screens – and his audience rejoiced.

Thigpen walked onto the stage and approached Otto. "The signal's been cut – both ways," he said calmly to Otto.

"What are you talking about?" Otto asked.

"No more nasty Congress video in and no more lovely Otto going out. Sorry."

"What are you saying, Thigpen? Get if fixed – right now," Otto shouted.

"Not broken, Otto," Thigpen said. "We've been disconnected."

"Disconnected? By whom?" Otto asked.

"By whoever controls the connections, I suppose," Thigpen dismissively answered.

Althea approached Otto and Thigpen, her trumpet still in her hands. "What's up?" she asked.

"Our broadcast has been cut," Otto said, shaking his head.

"Okay," Althea said, nodding. "Let's not forget about the two million people that are right here in front of us." After a moment, Otto nodded in agreement.

Standing at the edge of the stage, Otto calmly said to his audience, "I've had enough. How about you?" A roar erupted in response. "I figured. Let's go – come with me," Otto said as he jumped from the stage to the grass beneath him. He looked back, Althea was staring at him. He smiled at her and jerked his head toward the Capitol Building. A few seconds later, she was next to him, surrounded by their security detail.

The sea of people parted as Otto and Althea marched over the covered up reflecting pool toward the Capitol. Otto walked quickly, only looking straight ahead. Althea grasped his hand tightly.

When they reached the top of the hill on which the Washington Monument sat, Otto could see that the mile of grass between the monument and the Capitol Building was packed with his people. The fifty American flags surrounding the monument waved in the darkening sky. Otto and Althea walked on.

Even though he was surrounded by so many people, Otto was startled by a tap on his shoulder. It was Jess – he had managed to catch up to Otto.

"It passed," Jess said.

"What?" Otto asked.

"It passed. 219 to 216," Jess said.

Althea shook her head. Otto remained silent but increased his pace.

It took another fifteen minutes for Otto, Althea and Jess to reach the back steps of the Capitol Building. By the time they arrived, the Capitol Police had surrounded the building with hundreds of officers wearing helmets and holding shields. The air that had been charged with music an hour earlier was crowded with the sounds of helicopters and bullhorns. The calm air of the new night was stirred by all of the movement.

At the bottom of the steps leading up to the back side of the Capitol, Otto finally came to a stop as he faced a wall of armed police. He turned around and faced the body of people that had followed him and those that remained in the two miles between the stage and where he now stood.

Otto took a deep breath. The people quietly waited for his words.

Before Otto could speak, a man with the arm of his dark suit torn at the shoulder emerged from the back of the Capitol and began to make his way down the steps. It was a member of the House of Representatives. Then another member emerged from the building. She had a bloody lip and her blouse was stained red. And then another. Then dozens walked down the steps toward Otto and his crowd, until more than two hundred congressmen and congresswomen stood on the steps behind the police line.

Through a bullhorn that was handed to him, Otto shouted at the assembled legislators. "We want action – and we want it now." The crowd danced and cheered. "You've abandoned the people," Otto continued. "And if we had our way, you would all be fired – especially for passing that monstrous debt contribution law." The massive crowd exploded into a frenzy of jeers. The mounted police steadied their horses and canisters of tear gas were readied.

Suddenly, Otto felt frozen in place, unable to move. His legs began to tremble. He wished he was back on his stage.

The police held their shields up and drew their batons.

Otto didn't know what to do. The image of a stampede filled his mind.

Then, from the top of the Capitol Building steps, the Sergeant at Arms quickly descended.

"Stand down, stand down," he said to the officers, the order echoing across their radios. He walked through the police line and stood in front of Otto.

"Veltraria, I'm the Sergeant at Arms of the House of Representatives. You'd better not let this thing that you're doing get out any more out of hand. I've got a bunch of bloodied members of Congress up in the House Chamber and I don't want to fight on two fronts at once, you hear me? I will if I have to, but this thing's going to get nasty if–"

Otto took a deep breath, summoned his courage and held his right hand up to the Sergeant at Arms. "Our visit is peaceful, but we want them out," Otto said, now pointing at the members of Congress assembled on the steps. The crowd exploded with the chant, "Fire Them Now! Fire Them Now!" Otto smiled.

As the chant repeated over and over, Otto turned to Althea, who had backed a few feet away from him. She was staring at him, her arms crossed, shaking her head. She mouthed the words, "What are you doing?" Otto turned away and looked back at the Capitol.

From the top of the steps, Congressman Jerez began to slowly make his way down. He went sideways, taking one step at a time.

When he reached the police line, Jerez gently tapped one of the officers on the shoulder who responded by letting him through. Jerez then approached Otto and waited for silence. Otto held his hand up high above his head, and in a few seconds, the last "Fire Them Now" chant died out.

"You're too late, Mr. Veltraria," Jerez said to Otto.

"Too late? Too late for what?" Otto asked.

"Too late to fire us. Every House member on these steps has just resigned – all 216 of us. Members of both old parties, reds and blues alike. None of us will take part in a government that makes indentured servants of its citizens – and we won't be paid with money coerced from those servants."

Althea and Jess looked at Otto, who was speechless. Otto slowly lowered his bullhorn.

Jerez laughed and said, "Sorry to kill your show, Mr. Veltraria. But don't worry, son, there will be other bulls to ride."

Within fifteen minutes, the former members of the House of Representatives were loaded onto busses that had brought Otto's concertgoers to the show earlier that day. The motorcade of busses, led and followed by a dozen armored vehicles, crossed the Potomac River in the shadow of the Lincoln Memorial as it made its way out of Washington D.C.

40

The following article appeared as the lead story on one of the front pages of *The Trustee*:

"NON-CAUCASIANS MAY BE SUPERIOR TO CAUCASIANS"

After conducting extensive research, a team of genetic scientists have announced their position that non-Caucasian people are intellectually, emotionally and physically superior to Caucasian people. The members of the Oslo, Norway, based scientific team, all of whom requested to remain anonymous, based their findings on a highly complex model developed specifically for the purpose of answering age-old questions about racial superiority. In a surprising coincidence of timing, a team of scientists in San Francisco, California, have announced their recent findings that Caucasians are superior to non-Caucasians, however, the Oslo based team has criticized the methods by which the San Francisco based team arrived at its conclusions. In the near future, the esteemed Oslo scientific team will consider publishing its findings.

The following article appeared as the lead story on the other front page of *The Trustee*:

"CAUCASIANS MAY BE SUPERIOR TO NON-CAUCASIANS"

After conducting extensive research, a team of genetic scientists have announced their position that Caucasian people are intellectually, emotionally and physically superior to non-Caucasian people. The members of the San Francisco, California, based scientific team, all of whom requested to remain anonymous, based their findings on a highly complex model developed specifically for the purpose of answering age-old questions about racial superiority. In a surprising coincidence of timing, a team of scientists in Oslo, Norway, have announced their recent findings that non-Caucasians are superior to Caucasians, however, the San Francisco based team has criticized the methods by which the Oslo based team arrived at its conclusions. In the near future, the esteemed San Francisco scientific team will consider publishing its findings.

The following article appeared on the third to last page of both sides of *The Trustee*:

"NATIONAL DEBT CONTRIBUTION ACT PASSES HOUSE AND SENATE"

Today, the bill known as *The National Debt Contribution Act* was passed both in the House of Representatives and the Senate. Congressman Kaye, who spearheaded the effort, announced the victory.

The bill, which was passed by the Senate immediately following passage in the House, celebrates the involvement of each American in the renewal of the nation, conferring upon each citizen an opportunity, and obligation, to contribute to the effort to lift the country from its burden of debt. As put succinctly by Congressman Kaye, the newly installed chairman of the Collaborative Caucus in the House, "In the true spirit of our nation, under this law, our citizens will be incentivized to fulfill their obligations, and thus willingly sacrifice what they must to address those challenges facing us today, and to build a better nation tomorrow." The funds borrowed from the Guiding Institutions Collaborative will be utilized to pay down the nation's debt and restart basic essential government services and programs. Those services and programs ceased to operate when the country lost its ability to borrow money from traditional sources after defaulting on its debt obligations.

The bill, which now sits on the president's desk, also grants the Guiding Institutions Collaborative discretion in creating new initiatives and programs that it deems critical to the recovery and growth of the nation.

Otto Veltraria, who was performing for millions of fans at the time the bill passed, left his perch on the stage in front of the Lincoln Memorial to celebrate the passage of the bill at the steps of the Capitol. Veltraria could not be reached for comment, but eyewitnesses report that he was animated and excited when he visited the Capitol, being greeted by the Sergeant at Arms of the House of Representatives and the Capitol Police.

⊷ 41 ⊷

David Clairet looked at his watch and then at the front door of the restaurant from his booth. He was at the Old Ebbitt Grill, a place where the gears of Washington D.C. turned. This living monument to the Washington machine sat across the street from the United States Treasury Department.

Jess Frank walked in and locked eyes with David.

As Jess slid into the booth, he gently smiled at David, but the smiled wasn't returned.

"So, what's up, Frank?" David asked.

"Where do you want me to start?" Jess answered.

"You know what I mean," David said. "Why are we sitting here? Why did you ask to see me?"

Jess shrugged his shoulders. "No particular reason. But since we're both in town I figured I would check up on you."

"Check up on me? Why are you checking up on me? You should be checking up on my sister. She's a real mess," David said, shaking his head.

"She just needs to figure a few things out," Jess said.

David didn't respond.

The two men sat in silence for a few minutes. Then their coffees were served. A little clinking sound accompanied David's stirring of cream in his cup, his hand was trembling. Jess looked away.

Another couple of minutes passed.

"How many shows are you doing while you're here in town," Jess asked.

"Just two late night sets, tonight and tomorrow night. Last minute gig." David took a sip of coffee, steadying the cup with both hands.

"Well, after the passage of the debt contribution bill and the resulting group resignation by half of the House yesterday, you probably need to rewrite your material, right?" Jess said.

David smiled slightly and nodded his head. "I could go on forever about all of that. It was just precious," David said.

"It was quite a spectacle at the Capitol – I was right there with Otto," Jess said. "But I assure you, he wasn't celebrating anything, despite what *The Trustee* reported."

"What a bunch of fakes," David said, ignoring the comment about Otto. "Who do those congressmen think they are, anyhow? They were all illegitimately elected. I didn't sign on for the whole farce of this democracy, it was just foisted upon me – foisted upon all of us," he said as he motioned his coffee cup at the room around him.

Jess remained silent.

Looking hard at Jess, David raised his eyebrows and said, "And don't even get me started about the Collaborative." Then David fell silent and stared down at the table.

"There are rumors that the Collaborative is considering funding your father's ĒMAD project," Jess said.

David looked up at Jess. "I know. It's a perfect marriage – they'll be very happy together."

Jess laughed.

"My dad's been playing with that thing for years. And now everyone's desperate for it. Maybe the thing will malfunction and give the world what it deserves."

"And what would that be?" Jess asked.

David smiled and said, "The grand finale."

"Meaning what?" Jess asked.

"You know, *bang* – and it's all over," David said, moving his hands to simulate an explosion. "Maybe it's time to start over."

"Oh, that's hopeful, David," Jess said, smiling.

"We've made such a mess of everything, Jess."

"Yes, humanity is in rough shape," Jess said.

"For so long, we've all felt this creeping squeeze, this constant pressure to keep our heads above water. It's made us miserable and scared. With every year we've become more stressed out and angry – and it's because of that squeeze. And now there's nothing left to wring out of us but our freedom."

Jess sat silently while David took a deep gulp of his coffee.

"Where is all the damn money, Jess? The people don't have it. Listen, I'm a free market guy – but when unbridled greed distorts and perverts the market and we all get gouged as a result, I'm not. But at least now there's a singular embodiment of those that are doing that to us."

Jess raised his eyebrows and sipped his coffee.

"The goddamned Guiding Institutions Collaborative," David said. "A multi-headed leviathan growing fatter and more powerful by the day, year after year – and only when conditions became so dire did it become bold enough to coalesce and proclaim its existence and identity as a singly conscious being with a will."

Jess remained silent, looking directly into David's eyes.

David continued, "And after we defaulted on our public debt obligations – I mean – after *they* defaulted on their debt obligations," he said, motioning toward a large window facing the Treasury Department on the other side 15th Street, "everything really fell apart – and fast, right? And what perfect timing, the government defaults at the same time most Americans are defaulting on their own loans. Everyone's fucked, right? Yep – except for the Collaborative, of course. It's all a dream come true for them – but get this, they dreamt up the damned dream."

Jess shifted in the booth but said nothing.

"They've single handedly teed-up the entire world as their borrower – their desperate borrower – and now they're dictating the terms of the loan in the form of illegitimate legislation that we now call the National Debt Contribution Act. The Collaborative has made us weak and themselves powerful – and they used money to do it."

David took a deep breath and another gulp of coffee. Jess didn't try to interrupt him.

"Do you know what all of the members of the Collaborative share in common, Jess?"

"You'll tell me, David."

"Extreme exploitation," David said. "Almost always in a monetary sense."

"What about being a free market guy? Profit is exploitation?" Jess said.

"Nope – profit is fine. In fact, it's much better than fine – it's good. No profit means no business which means no jobs which means no nothing – and that's bad. But here's the thing, those Collaborative fuckers aren't content with just making a lot of money – no, they need an obscenely huge profit and a big fat market value of billions and trillions of dollars, so they jack the prices of everything and then graciously lend us the money to buy all of their overpriced shit! And they do it because they *can* – because they can actually get away with it. They exploit with delight and without a shred of concern for their consumers. The whole thing's a goddam racket. And then they own us – just like they set out to do."

"Sounds about right," Jess said calmly.

"And because they have no sense of humanity or decency, they employ whatever means necessary to run the good guys out of business. They hurt whoever they need to – they just don't care. Their only guiding principle is obtaining as much money and power as possible."

"Sure," Jess said.

"And it's no shock that the rest of the world is in the same crap shape as us. The *dream* is being dreamt everywhere. The willing participants of Europe and Asia and Africa and South America who have same the depraved values as their American counter-parts will join the Collaborative so the same shitty deal can be shoved down the throats of the rest of mankind by their respective so-called governments."

Jess nodded and said, "Indeed. Their top politicians are on their way now to D.C. to learn how it was done."

"How do *you* know about that?" David asked. "That's not been reported yet."

Jess hesitated and then said, "Tad Corliss told Otto. How did *you* know?"

David shrugged his shoulders. "Did Corliss mention when the president is going to sign the bill into law? Is he waiting for his playgroup of international heads of state?"

"No idea," Jess answered.

After sitting in silence for a few minutes, David said to Jess, "Watch this" as he nodded toward two men beginning to raise their voices in a nearby booth.

"I've always believed it," one of the men said to the other. "But finally we have scientific proof that we're better than them in every way. And it feels good to finally say it."

"Oh, please – don't be such a dumb bastard. You actually believe that garbage?"

"Yes, I do – and you're the dumb bastard – it's not garbage, it's the truth. I'm thrilled that *The Trustee* had the courage to run that story."

"You do realize that the other side of the newspaper ran an article about a team of genetic scientists that came to the exact opposite conclusion, right?"

"Yeah, but who reads that side? That side of the paper is for nut-jobs and morons."

David laughed and said to Jess, "And that's the only damn thing that people are talking about today – it's perfect." Then he waved his middle finger high in the air and said, "Keep your eye on the birdie!"

Jess smiled and said, "For such a bitter person, David, I don't get the feeling that you actually hate people."

David took a deep breath and sat up straight in the booth. He put his palms down on the table and said, "I don't hate people – quite the opposite. I care about everyone, all of us, Jess. But I'm so disappointed in us."

42

The Blue Line was shut down for the entire day and people were furious. Those that had jobs were forced to find another way to get to work. Regular service on Washington D.C.'s Metrorail commuter system had already been dramatically reduced due to budget cuts, but this service interruption was for the safety and convenience of only several riders.

The Metro had once been a spotless subway system. For years, its high arched cavernous stations boasted hundreds of embedded platform lights that would flash to inform waiting riders of an incoming train. And although most of the lights were now dead and the trains ran infrequently, the president was still proud of the aging system. The White House arranged for the visiting world leaders to travel to Arlington National Cemetery on their own private subway train.

The group first met for breakfast with the president and Representative Kaye, and then, after leaving Kaye and the president to continue their meeting in the Oval Office, they walked over to the McPherson Square Metro station for the short ride under the Potomac River to the cemetery. On their way to the station and down into the waiting train car, the heads of state were surrounded by translators, *Trustee* reporters and a compact security detail.

The train carried the group away into the dark tunnel, and after cruising through a few stations at nearly full speed, the train emerged from the ground just before the Arlington Cemetery station and slowed to a stop. From there, the dignitaries boarded a small bus and drove through the cemetery on roads named after American heroes, such as "Eisenhower" and "Patton." On their way to the Tomb of the Unknowns, they passed thousands of perfectly arranged small white headstones. As the group proceeded further into the cemetery, the chatter of worldly tongues and their interpreters gradually fell into silence.

Mr. Selfridge, the prime minister of the United Kingdom, was the first to step off the bus. Relying on his burgundy brass-tipped cane, he proceeded slowly and deliberately toward the small plaza where the Unknown soldiers rested. The others followed him, not saying a word.

Admiral Lansing approached the prime minister and saluted him with a white gloved hand – and then followed-up with a firm handshake and a gentle smile. One by one, the admiral extended the same courtesy to the other visitors.

"Welcome," Lansing said, addressing the entire group.

The American president's absence from the group of world leaders would have been more apparent if Admiral Lansing hadn't insisted on representing the nation that day. Lansing stood firmly in his crisp white uniform, complete with many medals.

The admiral led the group to the edge of the plaza where the Changing of the Guard at the Tomb was about to take place. The Tomb overlooked Washington D.C. from a hill across the Potomac River, and it was the final resting place for unidentified soldiers who fought and died in the world wars and the Korean and Vietnam wars.

All of the nations represented that day by their respective heads of state had contributed in one way or another, whether for good or evil, or for some, both, to the legacy to which the visitors were now paying tribute.

Only a few photographers from *The Trustee* were permitted to join the group for the changing of the Sentinels guarding the

Tomb and the quiet wreath laying ceremony that followed. The only sound other than that of the wind softly moving through the cemetery's thousands of trees was the bugler's steady playing of Taps.

"How many more tombs will history require us to build here?" Prime Minister Selfridge said, staring at the Tomb after the wreath laying.

"Only God knows, sir. But we have a say in that," Lansing replied.

The prime minister continued, "This is a dangerous time, is it not, Admiral Lansing? Perhaps the most dangerous time ever."

"It's an age filled with many perils, but we should remember that every generation before us also faced countless dangers," Lansing said.

"Yes, but everything seems so impossible now. So daunting," Selfridge said.

"But the challenges of the past also seemed nearly insurmountable to the people that history enlisted to help."

Selfridge nodded slowly.

Lansing continued, "But never before has our capability as humans been so great. What remains to be seen is whether that capability will be squandered."

"Yes, that's what it's always been about," Selfridge said. "Whether the current generation has the principle, the discipline and the mettle to rise to its full potential to achieve what is necessary to preserve and advance humanity against the forces that threaten it – that's the unknown. Not a day passes now that I'm not reminded of the menace that threatened the world in the first half of the last century – an evil that insidiously and steadily grew under the noses of the people, right in front of their eyes."

"But we know how that story ends," Lansing said. "Victory. Victory as a result of leadership and the realized potential of people. People that united for the ultimate cause – saving humanity. But people don't accomplish these things without direction and a unifying force – somebody must inspire and lead them," Lansing said.

"Yes, of course," Selfridge said. "Churchill and Roosevelt were great men – that's true. But today, we're fighting a different kind of war. Not one with cannons, tanks and planes, but rather a war against the world we have created – one of starvation and despair, hardship and hopelessness. And now, to make it all worse, a fear of some unknown force creating the Silence. I think it's all too much for the people."

Lansing nodded slowly but remained silent.

The president of France, Madame Manion, had been listening to the conversation and she now spoke up. "I would like to add that De Gaulle was also a great leader and should not be forgotten from this conversation," she said.

Lansing and Selfridge nodded. "Yes, absolutely, Madame President," Lansing said. "He was also a great military mind."

"That's right, Admiral Lansing," President Manion said. "And I must agree with you, Admiral, the people have the potential. The men that landed on the beaches of Normandy rose to greatness by the call of strong leaders for an essential and just purpose, and they prevailed. Anything is still possible. I still believe in the power and potential of humanity. It doesn't just simply evaporate over time, lost more and more by each generation. But the people need to be stirred to action."

Selfridge took a deep breath. "Indeed, but remember that the people are sometimes *stirred* by the wrong characters," Selfridge said, motioning as if his finger was stirring a cup of tea. "You know, they are impressionable, and when they're afraid they look for any flashing beacon in the storm – and the opportunists know this. It's often difficult for the people to discern the true leaders from the false leaders, those who act for their own gain or some deviant reason, always at the expense of the world. Just ask the chancellor," he said, nodding toward the German head of state. "He can tell you all about that."

"We won't let that happen again," the Canadian prime minister said, now joining the conversation. "The partnership with the Collaborative will ensure that." Then he nodded his head slowly and said, "I'm grateful we'll have a benefactor to prevent conditions from worsening and devolving into a fertile breeding ground for atrocities borne from economic despair. Our Canadian partners stand at the ready to join the Collaborative and provide financial support to help grow the Fund's endowment."

"It's only sad that the Collaborative can't solve the mystery of the Silence for us," Manion said.

Before anyone could respond, the engine of the bus started and the group was waved in.

"Admiral Lansing, before we return to the train, I'd like to visit the Argonne Cross and pay my respects – do we have time?" President Manion asked.

"Of course, Madame President," Lansing said. "You're all not expected at the White House until dinner."

43

"Just to be clear, he's not coming in with us," Corliss said while bobbing his head toward Jess.

"Agreed," Otto said. "We'll leave him here in the car with Malcom."

"Why, Otto? Shouldn't I chronicle your meeting with the president?" Jess asked.

"No," Otto and Corliss said at the same time.

The four men rode in Otto's limousine up Pennsylvania Avenue toward the White House.

"I don't know how you did it, Corliss, but I admire your tenacity in getting the Collaborative to back the ĒMAD," Otto said.

Corliss smiled and said, "The Collaborative understands that the ĒMAD is just what the world needs right now – and the people will be paying for it with their debt obligation under the National Debt Contribution Act, so why wouldn't they want to build it? It's a no-brainer for the Collaborative, right?"

"Uhh," Jess let out, now covering his eyes.

Otto ignored Jess and said, "Just to be clear, Corliss, I said that I admire your tenacity, not the Collaborative – and certainly not that debt indenture bill. It all makes me sick."

Corliss didn't immediately respond, but then said, "Just keep an open mind, please."

"Why don't you just tell me what the president wants to discuss with me, Corliss. I'd rather turn the car around now and not waste anyone's time."

"Please, Otto, I want the president to speak with you directly. And so does the Collaborative."

"I don't care about what the Collaborative wants."

"Look, this conversation is headed in the wrong direction, Otto – I'm sorry that you're feeling upset. I'm going to zip my mouth shut until we get to the White House, okay?"

Otto crossed his arms and sat back. "Yes, please do."

The four men rode in silence for the remainder of the ride. Jess and Malcom stared at each other, barely blinking.

Fifteen minutes later, Otto and Corliss were sitting at a small table in the president's private dining room near the Oval Office, waiting for the president.

44

As Otto and Corliss waited for the president in silence, Otto couldn't take his eyes off of a painting hanging in the little dining room. In it, a dozen American flags leaned out from stone buildings lining an avenue, blurred by rain and darkened by gray skies. A group of faceless people huddled together and hid under their umbrellas. The image brought a lump to Otto's throat.

The door opened, breaking the silence.

"Mr. Veltraria, so good to meet you," the president said, shaking Otto's hand. "And Mr. Corley, very nice to meet you too."

"It's Corliss, not Corley," Corliss said to the president.

"I'm sorry, but isn't that what I said?"

"No, you said *Corley* with a *Y* – there's no *Y* – it's *Corliss*," he said, emphasizing the end of his name.

"Oh, I see, so sorry Mr. Corliss."

"No problem," Corliss said.

Then the three men sat.

The president folded one leg over the other and took a deep breath. "Let me get right to it," he said. "Tonight, in the presence of the visiting world leaders, I'm going to sign the National Debt Contribution Act into law." The president opened his mouth to continue, but hesitated.

"Go on," Corliss said.

"And the Collaborative wants me to pitch the ĒMAD project to all of them and to basically let them know that their nations may only participate in the Guiding Institutions Collaborative if they're on board with building the ĒMAD."

"I see," Otto said.

"Absolutely makes sense," Corliss said, smiling.

"So what you're really saying is that there will be no money from the Fund for those nations refusing to join the ĒMAD chorus," Otto said.

"Exactly," the president said. "And no money endowing the Fund from the would-be investors of those non-participating nations either. Remember, these countries have oligarch-level rich people, powerful and influential organizations, and companies with big balance sheets – and the opportunistic ones want to be members of the Collaborative as it goes global. They want a piece of the action – they want to put their money in and get a nice return on their investment for the next 1000 years, all while heavily incentivizing their citizenry to pay the debt back to the Collaborative – just like we're doing with the National Debt Contribution Act. It's the biggest public debt refinancing in the history of civilization. But the cost of participation is the ĒMAD – the greatest infrastructure investment the world will ever know. When the heads of their governments show up tonight to discuss and negotiate entry into the Collaborative, they'll learn that constructing and operating the Association's machine is a must."

"As chairman of the Association of Comprehensive Solutions, let me say that we're proud to bring this technology to the world in its hour of need," Corliss said.

The president nodded and said, "I get it Corley, the ĒMAD's your baby." Then the president winked at Otto who smiled back.

Before Corliss could correct the president, Otto said, "It's really Dr. Clairet's baby, Mr. President. He's the mind behind it." Corliss now crossed his arms but said nothing.

The president slowly scratched the stubble on his face and looked at Otto. "Do you think he did it?"

"Did what?" Otto asked.

"You know, killed Pearl McCloud," the president answered.

Corliss's eyes grew wide, and as he opened his mouth to speak, Otto held his palm up to Corliss, who then kept quiet.

"No, Mr. President, I don't," Otto said. "And no one even knows if Pearl McCloud is dead – she simply disappeared."

"She's dead," the president said. "No one disappears for that long. Don't you think she would have wanted to see her kids?"

"That may be so, Mr. President, but her body was never found," Otto said.

"You're missing the operative point here, Mr. Veltraria – the man whose technology we're all banking on was considered guilty by at least half of the world when she disappeared. They hold him responsible for the death of a modern-day saint."

"Well, you don't become a saint until you're dead, so whoever killed her did her the favor of galvanizing her status as a saint in the minds of the world for all time," Corliss said.

Otto let out a snickering sound and said, "Pearl wouldn't have given a damn about that status. How could you say such a stupid thing?"

Corliss sat up straight in his chair to protest but the president held both of his hands up to stop the exchange.

"Listen to me, the world's turning to shit. I've just lost half of the House of Representatives, I have no idea what to do about that fucking Silence that keeps scaring the piss out of everyone, and I now have the Collaborative squeezing my nuts to make sure that I deliver on their demands – so I don't have patience for any bullshit, okay?" the president said loudly.

"Understood, sorry," Otto said. Corliss remained silent and glared at Otto.

The president lowered his hands and sat back in his chair.

"Tell me, Mr. President, what is it that you need from me?" Otto asked.

"The Collaborative needs you as the cheerleader-in-chief, Mr. Veltraria – simple as that."

Otto didn't respond.

"Building the ĒMAD will require world-wide cooperation, and we need a champion of the cause who can help the people understand that their many sacrifices will all be worth it. They need to be excited about the ĒMAD and they need to feel like they're a part of it. Dr. Clairet is too controversial of a figure to be the front man for the project, and as magnetic as Mr. Corliss is, the Collaborative thinks you're perfect for the job."

"I see," Otto said.

"What an honor, Otto. You've reached the zenith of your craft," Corliss said. "Congratulations."

Otto said nothing but looked at the people in the painting hiding under their umbrellas in the rain.

"It's hung there for over a hundred years," the president said, looking at Otto.

"It's either prophetic or just coincidentally sad," Otto said, still looking at the painting.

"What's the hesitation, Mr. Veltraria?" asked the president.

Otto shook his head and spoke slowly. "I don't care for the Collaborative and I find the National Debt Contribution Act repugnant."

"Well, that could be a bit of a problem, couldn't it?" the president said.

"Otto, this will be your biggest gig ever," Corliss said. "You owe it to yourself and your legacy to do this."

Otto ignored Corliss and looked hard into the president's eyes. "Playing along with the Collaborative? Why are you doing this, Mr. President?" Otto asked.

"Now that's a silly question," Corliss said. "The question should be, *why wouldn't the president work with the Collaborative and support the ĒMAD project?*"

The president sat back and sighed. "It isn't a silly question. I do have my concerns and reservations, but there aren't many options, if any, to get out of this situation. Doing nothing may be worse than doing the wrong thing."

"But to be taking orders directly from the Collaborative, Mr. President? Doesn't it delegitimize and sully the office of the presidency?" Otto asked.

"Forgive him, Mr. President, that's the artist in him speaking – you know, the naïve part."

"Shut up, Corliss," Otto said.

"I have to agree with him this time, Mr. Veltraria," the president said. "Not that you're naïve, but don't feign shock over the fact that I have others to answer to. I always have and so have most of my predecessors. Whether it's directly or indirectly taking orders from them, whoever *them* is at any given time, is irrelevant. And now, we don't have the luxury of practicing the art of subtlety – we're simply out of time."

Otto hung his head.

The three men sat in silence for a few moments before Otto looked up at the president. "I won't do it," Otto said quietly.

Corliss rapped his knuckles on the table and yelled, "Selfish, selfish man!"

"I'm warning you," Otto said, now holding his fist up to Corliss.

"Take it easy boys, we're just talking here, okay? Just settle down," the president said.

"Otto, do it for the people you claim to love so much," Corliss hissed.

"What do they get out of all of this?" Otto asked.

"They get the fruits of the ĒMAD, Mr. Veltraria. Everything they lack now they'll have in abundance," the president said.

"Yes? And who will own the ĒMAD?" Otto asked.

"The Collaborative, of course," Corliss answered.

"But it will be built with borrowed money – money that must be repaid by the people under the new law. No clearance certificates releasing them from their indenture until they each repay their share of the debt owed to the Collaborative, correct?"

"It's only right," Corliss said.

"Mr. President, am I wrong?" Otto asked.

The president shook his head slowly. "Look, Otto, things are dire and we need to do something drastic. It's not perfect, but nothing ever is. Those that are willing to join the Collaborative and endow the Fund possess much of the remaining wealth on the planet. I hope that you can appreciate that we're in a hat-in-hand position."

Otto squinted and yelled, "But the people should be getting something more out of this lousy deal."

"You keep forgetting all of those necessities that the ĒMAD will provide to them, Otto," Corliss said.

"For free? All of the fruits of the ĒMAD for free?" Otto asked.

"Oh, come now, Otto, don't be childish. Of course, the people must pay for what the ĒMAD yields," Corliss said. "But I assure you, the Collaborative has committed to keeping prices reasonable. At least for the foreseeable future."

Otto snorted, startling the president.

"Listen, it's all happening with or without you, Mr. Veltraria," the president said before leaning toward Otto and saying, "I want you to know that I hear all of your concerns and I'll absolutely share them with the Collaborative at the right time, but right now, I need to know what it will take to get you on the team."

Otto remained silent and clasped his hands on top of his head.

After a minute, the president said, "Well?"

"If this indenture of the people is going to happen, then at least free them from their suffocating personal debt as part of this massive financing arrangement," Otto said.

Corliss looked at the president but remained silent.

"Details, Mr. Veltraria – I need a proposal," the president said.

Otto sat up straight in his chair and said, "I'll agree to support the ĒMAD provided that once it's operational, the Collaborative will use twenty-five percent of the revenue that the ĒMAD generates to pay down everyone's Full-Life Loans, until they're paid off in full. I want them all to have a fresh start."

The president leaned back in his chair in thought. Then he said, "That seems like an awfully big price tag for your support, Otto – no disrespect intended."

"But look at it this way, Mr. President," Corliss said. "With Otto's idea, the Collaborative will essentially be paying itself, since practically all of the money owed by the people on their Full-Life Loans is actually owed to many of the constituent members of the Collaborative. It's really quite genius."

"Well, that's true," the president said. "But as you can imagine, it's not my decision."

The president quickly stood up. Before exiting the dining room, he explained that he needed to take Otto's proposal to the Collaborative and that he would be back shortly with an answer.

Otto and Corliss sat in silence looking around the little room but were careful to avoid eye contact with each other.

Twenty minutes later, the president entered and sat back down at the table.

"You know what? Kudos to you, Mr. Veltraria – I'm both surprised and impressed," the president said. "You're obviously a skilled negotiator."

Otto leaned toward the president and said, "Tell me – let's have some good news."

"They'll agree to temporarily delay enforcement of their rights against all defaulting Full-Life Loan borrowers and they'll also reduce the interest rate on everyone's Full-Life Loans to zero for the next six months," the president said smiling. "Exceptionally generous gestures – but only if you'll rally the world for the ĒMAD."

Otto's smile quickly disappeared. "That's not even close to what I asked for," he said. "What about paying down the Full-Life Loans, Mr. President?"

"I was told that at this time the Collaborative isn't willing to do that but would be willing to revisit the subject at a later date," the president answered. "But don't dismiss what you've achieved for the people in this process – it's profound."

"Indeed," Corliss said.

Otto stood up and said, "I won't do it. It's just not enough."

The president and Corliss remained seated and looked at each other.

"If you don't cooperate, you've likely given your last show," Corliss said. "Every resource will be committed to building the ĒMAD, so if you're not working toward that goal, then electricity and every other kind of resource cannot and will not be allocated to your performances."

"What?" Otto said, now looking at the president. The president nodded back in agreement. Otto slowly sat back down.

"This is going to be incredibly exciting, Mr. Veltraria," the president said. "You don't want to miss being a part of this."

"And I know that you're not ready to retire, Otto," Corliss said. "You're more famous than you've ever been – and this arrangement is a natural fit. Why disappear into oblivion when you can be the most adored and revered artist of all time lifting the spirit of the world?"

Otto said nothing for a minute. But then he began to gently tap a beat with his foot. "I'll have everything I need for my performances?" he asked.

"Everything," Corliss said.

"And my shows will be broadcast globally?"

"Globally," Corliss said.

The president smiled but said nothing.

Otto took a deep breath and said, "Fine. I'll do it."

The president quickly reached out and shook Otto's hand. Corliss patted Otto on the back and said, "I promise, you'll be fit for sainthood by the time it's all over."

Otto looked at Corliss but said nothing.

45

The return train to the city was waiting at the cemetery's station. Admiral Lansing saw the group off at the platform.

Looking around at the world's leaders sitting on the molded plastic seats of the subway car, Prime Minister Selfridge smiled. Conversation was lively and loud.

The train began its descent underground and the light of the sky gave way to the blackness of the tunnel walls. As the car traveled deeper and deeper it picked up speed.

A few minutes passed as the trip took them beneath the river. The train hurtled and rocked with just a low electric hum behind the chatter.

Then, without even a flicker, the lights went out and the train car was as dark as an abandoned coal mine. The hum quickly faded and the train slammed to a halt. A sudden gasp from the group let out as bodies slammed against each other, oblivious to rank and respect.

Loud voices and strong sharp flashlight beams surrounded the train car. When the car doors were forced open, it was obvious that the dignitaries' security detail was outnumbered. Prime Minister Selfridge gently pushed the muzzle of his bodyguard's rifle down toward the floor, away from the faces and guns staring at them.

"Stand down," the prime minister said quietly. "We don't need a futile gun fight here."

A man appearing to be in his mid-twenties lifted himself onto the train through the open doors. On his hip he wore a holstered stainless steel revolver with a long barrel. He was clean-shaven but his hair was curly and wild.

"Hey, which one of you is in charge?" the man asked. Then, without waiting for an answer, he quickly laughed and said, "No one. That's what I thought."

The group on the train backed up as the man took his place in the center of the car.

"In a moment, you're all going to get off of this train. You'd better move fast because I don't have much time and I have zero patience for any attempts at bravery. We'll be getting you out of this tunnel through an access corridor in the ventilation system. We have vehicles to take you away, and if you cooperate, you may live to see your native countries again – even if just from behind prison bars. But for now, you're detainees of Inevitable."

The prime minister of Japan spoke rapidly in angry tones to the man. His translator said, "The prime minister asks what business you have stopping us here? This action is illegal and violates international law as well as the law of this nation."

The man smiled and shook his head. "Oh my, I really wish I had the time to get into this right now. What fun it would be. Let's just say that we don't see this as a violation of any law. We're just exercising our natural right to protect ourselves from the tyranny of your make-believe governments," he said looking from leader to leader. "You've all done enough damage. The people of the world are suffering and now it's our turn to make things right."

"What does that mean, *make things right*?" the president of France asked.

"I can tell you what is doesn't mean – allowing the status quo to continue," the man said, standing face to face with President Manion.

"Nate, let's get going. We're burning daylight," a voice from the tunnel called into the train.

The man laughed and said, "Burning daylight, how cute, he thinks he's on a movie set. And I guess you now know my name is Nate. Not Nathaniel or Nat, but Nate." He then drew his revolver and pointed it up. "Prime Minister Selfridge, why don't you lead the pack? Those nice people out there will help you off the train." Nate then motioned his revolver toward the group waiting outside of the train.

Just as Selfridge stepped toward the open door of the train car, a series of rapid-fire gunshots lit the dark tunnel – instantly hitting a few members of Inevitable. The remaining members returned fire in a deafening shooting match for survival.

Everyone on the train shrank down low except Nate and Prime Minister Selfridge. Nate leveled the long barrel at the prime minister's face, but before he could pull the trigger, Selfridge jabbed Nate between the eyes with the brass end of his cane. Startled and disoriented, Nate staggered. With one of his glassy black shoes, Prime Minister Selfridge pushed Nate through the open door of the train directly into the exchange of gunfire.

After only a few more seconds of shooting, the echo of gunshots evaporated, and voices of people quickly approaching the train car grew louder.

With his service pistol in his hand, Admiral Lansing leapt onto the train from the dark tunnel. His white dress uniform was now darkened and stained.

"Is everyone all right?" he shouted. Soldiers and policemen surrounded the train car.

Slowly, everyone began to stand up and wipe themselves off. All had survived.

But not Nate – or the other members of Inevitable there that day.

46

The next day, the front page of both sides of *The Trustee* covered the thwarted kidnapping of the world leaders and their subsequent agreement to participate in the Collaborative and cooperate in building the ĒMAD. The layout of the articles and the photos appearing in the two sides of *The Trustee* differed, but the written content was exactly the same.

Nearly every section of the newspaper covered a different aspect of the project, and entire pages were dedicated to Otto, Dr. Clairet and Corliss.

The words "remarkable" and "miracle" and phrases like "game-changing" and "savior technology" appeared throughout the coverage. Negative and doubtful words about the ĒMAD were absent, except for a small section titled "The "Doubters." The Doubters section featured the names and pictures of those who spoke out publicly against the project. Former Representative Jerez and his fellow recently resigned representatives appeared in the section. Their grainy photos were in black-and-white and devoid of smiles.

The two center pages of the newspaper were dedicated to Otto. One side featured a full-page portrait of Otto while the other side contained no less than 200 testimonials of his admirers. Otto looked serious revealing only a hint of a smile. His long hair was tied up and he wore a dark suit with a narrow light gray tie.

On another page, Dr. Clairet's biography accompanied several pictures of him throughout his professional career. There was even a timeline that showed when he invented different things.

Rather than recite the various jobs that Corliss had briefly held over his career, the newspaper focused on the fact that Corliss was a family man and featured pictures of Kim and their child.

An article titled "The World Works Together" explained how the ĒMAD would be brought to life. "The National Debt Contribution Act contains a mechanism granting the Guiding Institutions Collaborative the right to create and fund new programs without the approval of Congress if those programs will contribute to the well-being and welfare of citizens, and the governments of the other nations now participating in the Collaborative have all made similar grants of authority to the Collaborative. As such, the Collaborative has immediately earmarked a significant allocation from the Fund to build the ĒMAD."

The article went on to quote some of the visiting heads of state. "The attack on the train yesterday was a reminder that the situation is dire, and we must take bold action to stabilize the world," the president of Russia said. "Working with the Collaborative and building the ĒMAD is the best option right now. Delay and hesitation may be catastrophic."

The German chancellor told *The Trustee*, "Now we have the technology to meet the world's needs in a holistic way with the ĒMAD. And this is more possible than ever before because the Collaborative has attracted the most successful technology companies to its cause. They're necessary and natural partners because they've spent years improving every part of people's lives – and now they'll lend their collective genius and help endow the Fund to build a technological innovation that will have profound consequences for humanity."

The article concluded by quoting Corliss, who seemed to make at least a cameo in nearly every article. "Solving the world's problems through technology is the goal that I envisioned and set for the Association of Comprehensive Solutions. That day has arrived and the Association is ready to accept and undertake this most important duty. In a few days' time, delegates of each participating nation will be sent to Washington, D.C. to serve on the Association's ĒMAD Governing Committee, and when that committee is convened, we will work together to make the dream of the ĒMAD a reality."

Page Two of *The Trustee* prominently featured an article titled "Seditious Groups Threaten Humanity's Future." The story explained that multiple threats against the project had already been made by various groups, including Inevitable – some of whose members remained at large. "The governments of the participating nations have agreed to form an international military force to protect the ĒMAD during its construction and operation from these groups," the newspaper reported. "Admiral Lansing, the most senior naval officer in the United States Navy, will fulfill the role of Supreme Commander of the force. Yesterday's attack and attempted kidnapping of several of the world's leaders was foiled by Admiral Lansing's heroic actions."

Corliss told *The Trustee*, "Every one of these gangs must be crushed – right down to the very last bad actor. And they're all to be included in the list of Doubters." But Prime Minister Selfridge was quoted as saying, "I don't want to condemn all disgruntled groups outright. There are some that are non-violent and have legitimate concerns, and we must be sensitive to them."

Much deeper in the newspaper, in the lower right corner of a page filled with legal notices, a two-sentence article appeared with no headline. It read, "Although not yet confirmed, it is estimated that when the ĒMAD operates, it will require all of the world's electricity that can be produced through existing conventional means, and perhaps require even more from non-conventional methods as well. In addition to rolling blackouts and rationing of electricity, the citizens of participating nations should expect to contribute to the ĒMAD's electricity demand in other ways, as yet to be determined."

47

The House Chamber of the U.S. House of Representatives was selected as the venue to host the Association's ĒMAD Governing Committee. The remaining 219 members of the House moved their business into Statuary Hall, the lower house's previous home for many years.

Over 120 delegates were sent from around the world to serve on the Committee. Each delegate was jointly appointed by a participating nation's government and Collaborative members.

Running unopposed, Corliss was elected as the Committee Chairman and the Chief Administrator of the Committee. Immediately following the vote, he slowly ascended the few stairs to the chair once occupied by the Speaker of the House. He turned toward the applauding delegates, unbuttoned his jacket, and took his seat.

As soon as the chamber quieted down, one of the delegates stood up at his desk and asked to be recognized.

"Yes, yes of course, Mr. Committeeman, you have the floor," Corliss said with a wide smile and taking care to enunciate every word.

"Chairman Corliss, the Association is an international organization, is it not?"

"Why, yes it is," Corliss answered.

"The Committee is a committee formed of delegates from around the world, is it not?"

"Yes, that's right."

"And the construction of the Essential Material Acquisition Device is an international project which cuts across many countries and international waters and must be authorized by a resolution of this committee, does it not?"

"Yes, absolutely," Corliss answered, his forehead now wrinkled in confusion.

"Then I would like to know why an American flag hangs behind your chair in this chamber selected to conduct international business?"

A low murmur of the delegates filled the silence.

Corliss's smile was now gone. "You must understand, this was the chamber of the House of Representatives for many years, and that flag has hung here always."

"That may be, Mr. Chairman," the committeeman said, "but this is now the chamber where the ĒMAD Governing Committee conducts its business, and I demand that the American flag be removed."

Corliss looked around, not knowing how to answer or what to do.

"Until that flag is removed, I will not sit in this chamber," the committeeman said before turning and beginning to walk up the aisle toward the exit. After a moment, a few more delegates stood up and followed him.

"Wait, stop – don't leave," Corliss shouted as he jumped up. Then he turned around and grabbed the flag with both hands and yanked it from the rod that held it against the wall.

A mix of noises arose from the delegates, not indicating any clear consensus about Corliss's action. He stood holding the rumpled flag in his fists.

A U.S. Marine, part of the military presence guarding the proceedings, approached Corliss and extended her hands to receive the flag. Corliss handed the flag over to the young woman, who was staring him directly in the eyes.

"I had to do it. It had to be done," Corliss said to her in a hushed voice. She didn't respond before she turned away and smoothed the wrinkled areas of the flag as she left the chamber.

Corliss took a deep breath and straightened his suit jacket out as he climbed the few steps back to his chair. The protesting committeeman and those who had followed him sat back down.

A committeewoman stood and asked to be recognized by the chairman.

"Yes, go ahead," Corliss said in a gray tone.

"Mr. Chairman, do you have a draft resolution authorizing the building of the ĒMAD for this committee to consider?" she asked.

Corliss, now somewhat slumped in his chair, looked to the left and then to right, not at anyone or anything in particular, and said, "What, me? You want me to prepare the resolution? Shouldn't somebody else be doing that?"

Once again, a small rustle of voices filled the chamber.

"Not a problem, Mr. Chairman," the committeewoman said. "I'll caucus with those delegates wishing to be involved in preparing the resolution, and we'll endeavor to have a draft for the committee to consider at the opening of tomorrow's session."

Corliss sat up straight and spoke loudly. "Very good, I'll expect it on my desk in the morning." The committeewoman didn't respond as she sat down.

Shortly afterward, Corliss adjourned the session for the day.

48

"How did you find me?" Königin said into the dirty green telephone on the nightstand.

"Apparently, your brother knows people that know things," Jess said on the other end of the line.

"What the hell does that mean?" Königin asked.

"It means that he was able to find out that you're holed-up in a hotel in Nevada."

"Not sure I would call this place a hotel," Königin said. "When did you see David?"

"A couple of days ago," Jess answered. "Not the most pleasant visit. So, what are you doing there, Königin?"

"Nothing."

"Are you okay?" Jess asked.

"I don't know."

"What do you mean you don't know?" Jess asked.

"Will you stop it, please? I just need some time alone," Königin said.

"Okay, well, how's your uncle doing?"

"He's fine," Königin answered flatly.

"How was the funeral?"

"It was as good as could be expected. Of course, my dad didn't show."

"I know – and I know that David didn't either," Jess said.

"Nope. Apparently, my aunt should have died during David's last San Fran tour – maybe he would have come."

Jess let out a little laugh and said, "He does seem to be a busy fellow with all of his gigs around the world."

"Yep, very busy," Königin said.

"He's a tightly wound man, isn't he, Königin?"

"Tell me about it," she answered. "It's like he's carrying all the burdens of humanity on his shoulders – I kind of don't get it."

"What don't you get? I know you're carrying some pretty heavy loads yourself," Jess said.

"Not anymore. I'm done with all of that."

"That's up to you, Königin." She didn't respond.

"Have you been following what's going on?" Jess asked.

Again, Königin didn't respond.

"Are you there? Did you hear me?"

"Yeah, I know what's happening," Königin answered. "The manager of this dump brings me his copy of *The Trustee* when he's done with it."

"He hand-delivers your paper to you? Sounds like a swanky place," Jess said.

"Yeah, right. It's his excuse to talk to me. He creeps me out."

"Enough about your love life, Königin. What's your plan?"

"No plan," Königin answered.

"Then get out of there and meet me in D.C."

"No thanks. Why don't you come out here?"

"No way, I'm in the front row of the most exciting show in the world," Jess said. "I didn't even want to leave Otto's side long enough to call you."

"But you did."

"Look, all kidding aside, I'm worried about you."

"Thanks, but why stop at me? You should be worrying about everyone," Königin said.

"I won't argue with that," Jess said. After a moment, he added, "Are you even a little excited for your dad's ĒMAD project?"

"Whatever."

"Do you think it will work?" Jess asked.

"I have no idea."

"All right, let's switch gears. I bet your dad can get you an exemption from the clearance certificate requirement – are you going to ask him?"

"I hadn't given it any thought," Königin said. "The whole thing infuriates me – pushing the people down further and further – and at a time that more and more of them are going hungry by the day."

"I know, Königin – you don't need to lecture me. But if you change your mind, your dad's working on the ĒMAD in an underground facility near Pittsburgh – go ask him for a job and an exemption."

"No, I'm not interested in either," Königin said. Then she added, "It's good to hear your voice, but I don't want to talk anymore."

"Königin, are you going to be all right?"

"I don't know – and I'm not sure that I care. It feels like nothing matters to me anymore."

"Listen, I can't believe I'm the one saying this to you, but you've worked too hard to just throw your professional reputation away. Every brilliant mind has failures – stop blaming yourself for Africa."

"It's so much more than that, Jess. And as far as my reputation goes – I'm on my way to not giving a shit about what anybody thinks of me."

49

All of the delegates to the ĒMAD Governing Committee stood chatting on the steps of the Capitol Building awaiting Otto's arrival. The president and other world leaders had urged him to attend the historic committee session where the ĒMAD would be "officially" born.

In his lab in western Pennsylvania, Dr. Clairet continued to work on the machine. Otto had visited him the day before but returned to attend the vote on the ĒMAD authorization resolution. Dr. Clairet refused Otto's invitation to join him in Washington, saying, "There's just too much to figure out."

Otto's motorcade arrived at the foot of the front steps of the Capitol. Before Otto could fully emerge from the car, Corliss's hand extended to him. Otto received Corliss's light handshake, but he only saw the side of Corliss's head, which was pointed toward a *Trustee* television camera. Corliss turned Otto toward the camera and posed for a moment. Otto looked to see the crowd of delegates applauding, and then turned back to the camera with a smile and reinforced his handshake with Corliss.

Ascending the broad white steps to the entrance of the Capitol, Otto greeted the delegates with hugs and "high-fives." The images of his celebrated presence were broadcast to the world.

Otto made his way into the round cavernous hall known as the

Rotunda. He first looked at a huge painting on the curved wall – it depicted Thomas Jefferson presenting the Declaration of Independence to the Second Continental Congress. Then a sharp light from above caught his attention and he tilted his head back. Otto's eyes fixed on the fresco painted in the great dome high above. Some of the figures looked familiar, and as he squinted to see them, the movement and sound of the people surrounding him gave way to his focus. Near the center of the dome, sitting in his blue and gold military uniform against a bright yellow background, George Washington looked down at Otto from what appeared to be heaven. Around Washington were many people, painted in pastels of pink, green and brown. One was a woman holding a sword and shield, going into battle, and another woman, draped in red, was looking toward a machine of some sort, an electrical contraption, with Benjamin Franklin looking on. Then Otto looked to a bugler seated next to Washington and he was reminded of Althea – and that she was gone.

"Otto, Otto," Corliss said, nudging him with his elbow. "Come on, let's get this done." Otto looked down from the dome only to find Corliss's nose close to his.

The newly named Chamber of the ĒMAD Governing Committee was filled with jubilant laughs and smiles.

As Otto and Corliss walked down the aisle toward the front of the chamber, Otto leaned into Corliss's ear and said, "How about I sing the National Anthem to start the session?"

Corliss quickly looked at Otto and said, "No, no, we don't need to do that. Let's just get this resolution passed as quickly as possible."

Abruptly, Otto stopped walking. But Corliss kept moving and Otto watched him jaunt up to his chair and flop in it, as if it were a worn recliner in his family room. Looking around the chamber, Otto thought about where to sit. After a moment, he turned around and headed for the stairs to the gallery overlooking the chamber. But before he could reach the staircase, one of the delegates asked, "Mr. Veltraria, where are you going?"

"Upstairs, to watch from the gallery," Otto said.

"But why? You should take one of those seats right down in front," the delegate said.

Otto thought for a moment and then said, "I think I should sit upstairs because I'm a visitor." Then leaning in close to the delegate and smiling, he added, "And I guess I don't feel right about sitting on the floor of the House of Representatives." Otto gently nodded, agreeing with himself. Then his smile faded, and he said, "This is a sacred place, even though it's been profaned by its stewards. I still feel a duty to respect this chamber and what it stands for, and I hope that what we are doing here today will eventually help restore what has been lost."

The delegates discussed and debated the proposed resolution. The proceedings were civil and productive, yielding many modifications to the document.

By the end of the day, the Collaborative had blessed the final version of the resolution authorizing the building of the ĒMAD – and the delegates subsequently passed it by a unanimous vote. The machine was to be built as quickly as possible.

50

The day after the resolution authorizing the construction of the ĒMAD was passed by the Committee, the president hosted a press conference in the Rose Garden to discuss limited aspects of the project.

The small audience sat on white folding chairs arranged neatly on the yellow grass of the lawn. Representative Kaye sat in the front row with some of the Committee delegates. But it was Otto who sat right in front of the president's podium. Jess sat in the last row.

The group applauded as the president and Tad Corliss approached the podium.

Corliss held his hands behind his back as the president introduced him. After a brief round of more applause, Corliss stepped up to the podium. He spoke for forty-five minutes about the Association's accomplishments and the construction of the ĒMAD "that was well under way."

The fringes of Jess's coat danced around as he rapidly took notes in his black spiral notebook.

When Corliss finally finished speaking, he asked for questions. Every *Trustee* reporter raised their hand.

Corliss pointed to a reporter who looked like a doll with flawless clothes and hair.

"Chairman Corliss, would you say that this device will have a positive, uplifting impact on humanity far greater than any other invention in history?" the reporter asked.

"Oh, yes, absolutely. This is what we've been looking for ever since we discovered fire and created the wheel. The ĒMAD is the ultimate realization of humankind's quest to understand and control the universe around us. And most importantly, the ĒMAD is a tool allowing us to harness the power and tap the unlimited resources that the universe has to offer us – but until now, we have not been able to effectively exploit those things."

Jess didn't look up at Corliss, he just continued taking notes.

Corliss called on another *Trustee* reporter – a young person with a welcoming smile.

"Chairman Corliss, what is the raw material that the ĒMAD will produce?"

"It won't produce anything – it will harvest an unending supply of an element-rich hot gas from an adjacent dimension. The gas can be transformed into liquid and solid forms, and when it's mixed with elements from our own world, we'll be able to fabricate every kind of substance and compound, yielding endless amounts of food, water, building materials, textiles, metals of all kind, fuels – you name it, the harvested gas can be used to make it. The ĒMAD will simply open up a hole – a portal into the next dimension, where this primordial substance abounds."

Jess looked up from his notebook and raised his hand.

Corliss ignored Jess, but the president called on him. "Yes, young man – you in the back there."

"Tad, what are the risks associated with this project?" Jess asked.

Corliss stared at Jess and said, "None. There aren't any."

"No danger in opening up a hole into another dimension?" Jess asked.

"Mr. Frank, as you know, Dr. Clairet has been perfecting this concept for quite some time and he knows what he's doing," Corliss said. "It's time to shed any fear and move forward – the people need the ĒMAD right now, it will change everything. For your sake, don't be a Doubter." Jess continued with his inquiry, "Look, Tad, we've established the need for a game-changing turn of events, but do you think your little tear in the fabric of the universe could create a dangerous–"

"Jess, enough," Otto shouted as he stood up and stared at Jess.

"Just one more question," Jess said quickly. "Isn't the ĒMAD just modern-day alchemy?"

Corliss nodded to Malcom who had slowly approached Jess from behind when he began his line of questioning. Reaching underneath Jess's armpits, Malcom pulled Jess out of his chair. Rather than resisting, Jess allowed his feet to drag along the grass as he was hauled away.

Not a single reporter turned to watch Jess's expulsion from the White House grounds.

51

Königin lost track of how many days she remained stalled in her motel room. She finished what food was in the vending machine next to the broken icemaker, but her hunger wasn't enough to push her to leave, so she just stretched out on the bed, thinking. But when the motel manager came to the door of her room and offered her half of a sandwich in exchange for "her company," she stuffed her things into her backpack and left.

As she walked along Interstate 80, Königin thought about how she had yelled at the manager in response to his proposition. She never yelled. She never felt angry enough about anything to yell. But that morning, a spark in her ignited pent up fumes of building rage. "A whore – he thought I was a whore. What blatant disrespect," she thought. The rush of emotion that had taken hold of her felt somewhat foreign, mostly forgotten, but not totally unknown. In those brief moments, she felt the rawness of her feelings in her heart, in her head, and in her fists. The manager ran.

Then an idea crept into Königin's head. "Maybe he was joking. He probably wasn't even serious. Maybe I just totally misunderstood what he said," she thought. Slowly, a calmness took over as she started to believe what she told herself. "Yeah, that's it – I've got it wrong. Who knows what the hell he was saying?" She felt so much better, for a moment.

The wind suddenly swirled around Königin and with it came a ripe stench. For a moment, she couldn't figure out where the smell was coming from. But then she knew.

Königin hadn't washed her clothes since leaving her uncle's place, and she hadn't showered or combed her hair since then either. She looked down at her chipped and broken fingernails. Only a tiny hint of blue polish clung to a few nails.

"I'm so gross," Königin thought. As she walked against the blowing wind, Königin tried to figure out why she had let herself fall into such disrepair. Was it simply a byproduct of despair? No, that wasn't it, she decided. She had despaired many times before but still managed to look good, even if not for the purpose of taking care of herself.

Jabbing into the wind like a wielded knife, a voice asked, "Königin, why do you stink?" Königin was shocked at the sound of her own voice. She laughed, thinking it was funny that she had asked herself a question like that. Or that she had asked herself a question at all. But then she asked herself another question, "What's wrong, Königin?" She didn't laugh this time, but rather, she answered, "Everything." And then another question, "You don't think much of yourself, do you?" The wind slapped her cheeks as she walked in silence for a few minutes before answering. "No, Königin. I have no respect for you." She slowly shook her head and started to cry. "I can't believe how hard I've tried to avoid knowing that," she thought.

Königin stopped walking. She stood up straight, lifted her head to the sky, and yelled, "He wasn't joking. No dignity gets you no respect, Königin." She felt the anger begin to pierce her guts again, the fire was growing in her.

She leaned into the wind and pushed further east.

52

"Nashville? Really? That's the best thing I've heard in a long while," Otto said to Corliss.

"I knew you would be pleased with that. With your involvement in the project, it's a perfect headquarters for the ĒMAD," Corliss said, leaning back in a plush leather chair in the House Speaker's abandoned office in the Capitol Building.

"So, it was a pleasant coincidence that Nashville was the ideal location for the machine's control center?" Otto asked, sitting in a visitor's chair on the other side of the antique wooden desk on which Corliss had propped his shoes.

Corliss looked up at the ceiling. "Well, not exactly, but I implored the engineers to move the control center a couple of hundred miles to make it work."

Otto frowned. "Are you sure that's going to be okay? I mean, I don't want the machine's heart and brains to be built there just so I can have a fun place to gig," Otto said.

"I think you're underestimating your role in all of this, Otto. You are the ĒMAD's promoter – it's booster, and you need a suitable venue for your duties," Corliss said. "It's your job to make sure that the people of the world love the ĒMAD like they love you."

Otto nodded slowly but said nothing. He was now staring at something in the corner of the office.

"Are you listening to me?" Corliss asked.

Keeping his eyes fixed on what he was looking at, Otto slowly stood up and walked over to an upright rectangular chunk of green marble. He reached out and gently touched its smooth cold surface. "This is the mace's pedestal."

"The what?" Corliss asked.

"This is where the mace would sit when the House of Representatives was in session."

"So?" Corliss said.

"So, it sucks that it's empty," Otto said. "And it sucks that it's in here, not in the House Chamber – where it belongs."

"Let's not get into that, Otto. The Committee is using that chamber now."

Otto ignored him and said, "Can you believe they think it was an inside job?"

"What was?"

"The theft of the mace," Otto said, staring at the pedestal and somewhat lost in his thoughts. "I remember reading about it when it happened," he continued. "And the Speaker talked about it the day they passed the National Debt Contribution Act."

Corliss crossed his arms but said nothing.

"A silver and wood scepter – it was beautiful. It was topped with an eagle sitting on a silver globe. The thing must have weighed a ton," Otto said.

"Whatever. Who cares about that thing?"

"I do – and you should too," Otto said, raising his voice a little.

"Why?" Corliss asked, chuckling.

"Because it belonged to the people – and it was a symbol of trust and authority given to a government by free people."

"Your patriotic fervor surprises me," Corliss said. "The government has always been a favorite target of yours."

"Don't confuse my dislike of what our government is with what it could be and should be."

Corliss put his hand up to Otto. "Stop with all of that. Listen to me – in less than a week you'll have the world as your captive audience. You'll fill every screen on the planet and blare through every radio."

Otto's eyes widened. "The show's going to be broadcast on every television channel and radio station?" he asked.

Corliss leaned back in his chair and said, "Well, you *could* say that."

53

The Essential Material Acquisition Device began to grow throughout the world. A thousand steel watchtower-like structures sprouted in the participating nations, all being readied to project an electronic grid into the sky that would resemble a chain-link fence extending beyond the horizon in every direction. The New Hickory Power Plant, on the outskirts of Nashville, would be the fence's gate – the portal to the next dimension – through which the coveted gas would enter this world.

54

An old theater in Nashville was hastily restored for Otto's exclusive use during the building of the ĒMAD. The tired red velvet seats were thin and the years of gum on the floor hadn't been scraped off.

Behind the theater, in the alley, three huge satellite trucks sent Otto's first show around the world.

That morning, the Whole Truth Information Trust had acquired every remaining non-Whole Truth television channel and radio station throughout the world. Within hours, the Trust closed them all, leaving only the Trust's three television channels on the air – which were used to broadcast Otto's live show. And when he wasn't performing, the channels would run documentaries about Otto's career and loops about the Association and its leader, Tad Corliss. Images of people crowding Corliss to shake his hand and pat him on the back were never more than a few minutes apart.

The street in front of the theater had been closed to regular traffic so the celebrities who lined up, one by one, ten by ten, behind Otto and the project could make their entrances and exits in front of the television cameras. The "general public" couldn't get a ticket to the show – Corliss personally oversaw the audience list, citing security concerns.

A few minutes into the show, Otto asked, "People, what do you want?"

Different answers rose up from the crowd.

"Ah, right. You say this and you scream that, but you all need the same thing – and so do I," Otto said, pacing the stage.

Cheers answered him.

"We need a path, a light, a guiding force – and I think we've finally found all of those things," Otto said. "But it's going to take some faith and patience, so hang in there with me, my friends."

Then a shrill voice pierced the audience's calm applause with "Finger the beast, Otto! Name names! Who's to blame?" The crowd roared up in jeers and demands of "Tell us, tell us, Otto!"

Otto shook his head and quickly quieted the crowd down with both hands.

"Look, we've got a moment here. A little window of time and opportunity. Let's seize it," Otto said, rolling his long fingers into a clutched fist. "Let's not focus on blame. Forget the past – let's move forward. The ĒMAD can make good things happen for all of us."

The hall responded with cheers and whistles.

Through the thick security barrier of uniforms positioned in front of the stage, a young girl found a hole and made her way to Otto. He turned to her, startled, but before he could react, she wrapped her thin arms around his legs and pressed her head of long hair against him. The crowd went wild as Otto returned the embrace. He couldn't temper his smile, and he didn't want to.

"It's for her that I do what I do. And it's for all of you," Otto said.

Earlier that day, Corliss had said to a Committee delegate, "I'm feeling generous – I'll get your daughter on stage with Otto, but remember, nothing's free."

Otto took the girl by the hand and sat her next to him on his piano bench. He nodded to his new band leader – and the horns came in softly. His hands slowly moved from the high notes down to the low, dark, heavy notes of the keyboard.

"You've all inspired me – the second verse of my unfinished track just came to me," Otto said, taking a deep breath before beginning to sing.

On a march toward the light
A clear path through the night
That guiding force pulls us through
Pushing, pushing, me and you
On the other side, we'll see who's who

The crowd listened in silence.

"What do you think about adding a second show every night, Otto?" Corliss had asked just before the show. Otto hadn't answered, but he did contemplate the idea. His resurrected eminence was at its zenith.

The little girl's mother stood in the wings. Otto waived goodbye to the child as she was delivered by one of the stagehands.

As he gently played, Otto said to his audience, "You know what I love so much about music? People of every age are touched by this magic that enters our souls – and I've now been at this so long, I have music to offer nearly every generation. Just look around, young and old alike, we're united in this common experience. I'm so thankful to all of you for letting me lead you on this journey, and the best part is, the music sets a pace and keeps the beat as we march forward together. Or better yet, as we *dance* forward together." Everyone liked that and they showed it.

⊷ 55 ⊷

A pickup truck slowed down and pulled onto the shoulder of the highway a short distance in front of Königin. The truck was nearly stripped of its paint by the sun and the windows were darkly tinted. Königin couldn't see the driver or whether there were any passengers.

She quickly looked around, seeing nothing but mountains in the distance and an empty road in both directions. The truck started to back up toward her.

Königin's heart started to pound so hard that her teeth rattled. She knew she should run, but she decided it would be futile, so she just stood still and stared at the truck that had now stopped only a handful of feet from her. Its loud engine skipped a "chug" every couple of seconds.

The passenger door slowly opened and a beat-up brown cowboy boot stepped out. Königin was shocked to feel her body walking toward the truck.

A figure in a jean jacket and cowboy hat slowly rose out of the vehicle and turned toward her. It was man with a wrinkled face – a smiling wrinkled face.

Königin exhaled hard and said, "You scared the shit out of me."

"I didn't do nothing," the man said. "You scared the shit out of you."

Then the driver side door opened and a woman with a gray ponytail neatly tied up through the back of a life-chewed baseball cap quickly approached Königin.

"What are you doing out here, girl?" the woman asked.

"I'm walking."

The woman now stood right in front of Königin. "I see that." Then she smiled and extended her hand. "Sue. It was Suzanne, but that seems too fancy these days," she said, laughing. "Why are you breathing so hard?" she added.

Königin shook her hand and said, "I was scared when you pulled up – I didn't know who was going to get out of that truck."

"Then why didn't you run? Or prepare to fight?" Sue asked.

"I figured it would be useless."

"It's never useless. Never give up – it's your duty," Sue said.

Before Königin could respond, the man said, "I can't believe you're hitchhiking."

Königin shrugged her shoulders. "Well, I am."

He shook his head. "Where you headed?" he asked.

"Actually, nowhere in particular," Königin answered.

"It looks to me like you're headed in that direction," the man said, pointing toward the early sun.

"Yeah, that's true, I am."

"What's out there?" Sue asked.

"I'm not sure."

"Where's your family?" he asked.

"My father's in Pittsburgh right now," Königin said, getting lost in her own thoughts for a moment. "So, I guess that's kind of where I'm headed."

"We're headed north, so I'm not sure we can be of much help," the man said.

Königin looked at them and said, "I'm really not in a hurry to get there. Maybe I won't even end up there."

The man shook his head. "You're a bit lost."

"I'm not leaving her here, Mitchell. She's coming with us. Let's get to Cheyenne and then we'll figure the rest out," Sue said.

"You live in Cheyenne?" Königin asked.

"No, we're headed to Custer – Cheyenne's where we'll turn north," Mitchell answered.

"What's in Custer?" Königin asked.

Sue and Mitchell looked at each other and then Sue said, "We're not really sure, but supposedly there's a stockpile of food being stored in an old mine out there." Then she tapped the tailgate of the truck and said, "We're hoping to load up and be on our way."

Mitchell took his hat off and said, "But we may just run into some trouble instead."

"Mitch, we've been through this – we've got to take the chance," Sue said. He put his hat back on and nodded, not saying anything.

Königin lowered her head and said, "Things are getting pretty bad, aren't they."

"Things have been bad for a long time, but the tide's gone out and now we're seeing all of the trash that folks left on the beach," Sue said.

"I don't think that's exactly how that saying goes, but it's close enough, I guess," Mitchell said.

Then the sun disappeared behind low fast-moving clouds blown by a gust of wind.

"My lord, what is that stench?" Mitchell yelled, shaking his head. "It's worse than a hot garbage dump."

"It's me," Königin said. "Sorry."

"Sue, that's going to be a real problem for me," Mitchell said. "All of us packed in the truck – I'll have to hang my head out the window. Or maybe she can ride in back."

"Don't act like a spoiled child, Mitchell. I'll wet a washcloth and she'll clean herself up," Sue said.

"Thank you, I really appreciate it – but you two go on without me," Königin said. "I'm just fine to walk – I've got some food and water in my backpack."

Sue stopped smiling and stared at Königin.

"What?" Königin asked, feeling as if she was being reprimanded.

"You know *what*," Sue said. "Stop trying to hurt yourself. You're coming with us. And guess what? I know who you are, Ms. Königin Clairet."

"Who?" Mitchell asked.

"I'll explain later," Sue said. "It looks like it's going to pour." Then she stood on one of the back wheels of the truck and pulled some washcloths out of bag and handed them to Königin along with a plastic jug of water.

"Mitchell, dear – please get back in the truck," Sue said.

"You want me to wash-up right here?" Königin asked.

"You're modest, are you? No problem, just do the best you can behind the truck," Sue said, motioning toward the side of the truck facing away from the road. "Mitchell, turn that mirror on your door all the way up to the sky." Mitchell complied.

The gray and black clouds picked up speed and thunder rumbled in the distance.

When Königin was done, she said to Sue, "It helped a little, but my clothes are still pretty funky."

Sue laughed and said, "Nothing a little Chanel Number 5 can't handle" as she pulled a little crystal atomizer from her purse that she had retrieved from the truck. Königin obediently stood up straight and held her arms out to the side as Sue sprayed her.

"I feel even grosser than I did before," Königin said.

"I'm sure you do," Sue answered. "Covering up a mess is always worse than cleaning it proper."

Königin nodded slowly.

"Put your backpack back here," Sue said as she placed the washcloths and water in the bed of the truck.

Königin clung tightly to her bag and said, "I have something really fragile in here. Do you mind if I keep my things on my lap?"

"No, of course not," Sue said as she motioned to Königin to get in the cab of the truck through the driver's door.

The truck's engine hesitated a bit before starting, but then it came to life and idled with its irregular heartbeat. Gravel spit out from under the tires and they set off with Königin swaddled between Sue and Mitchell.

After a minute on the road, Königin's shoulders relaxed, then her entire body. A few seconds later she was asleep.

The sky held its rain back.

⊶ 56 ⊷

"I miss you."

"And I miss you too, Otto. And the band," Althea said.

"Then *please* come back with me, Althea. I need you in Nashville. The show is suffering without you. We have important things to do – and I want to do them together."

Althea didn't answer. Otto reached for her hand across the back of the car, but she gently pushed his hand away.

"Listen, I agreed to get together, but I'm not coming with you," Althea said, looking Otto directly in the eyes.

"Oh, come on, Althea – this is the greatest journey that can be taken right now, who knows where it will lead. How could you miss this?"

"Look, I *am* going to miss it, all the way from Metairie."

"Althea, you're making the biggest mistake of your life. Be a part of this and you'll be immortalized forever. Walk away from this and will you be anyone to remember? Who will you be?" Otto asked.

"Who will I be? Me. I'll be me whether I'm leading your band in Nashville or leading my own band in the Quarter – or playing my trumpet solo for folks – or even just playing for myself. I can't avoid being me, and I'm good with that. Being worshipped by the crowd doesn't do a thing for me. Getting thrown into the pages of history books is okay if it just happens, but when that becomes a man's dream, watch out." Althea said.

Otto shook his head. "That's sad, Althea. You're a wonderful woman with limitless talent and it scares me to think of you living in relative obscurity, you know, compared to where you could be."

"You don't hear me, do you?" Althea said. She leaned toward Otto, her neat red lips only inches from his face. "That's your fear for yourself, Otto Veltraria, not your fear for me."

Otto jerked back. "That's ridiculous, Althea. How dare you," he said in a sudden burst. He turned away from her and looked out the car's window.

After riding in silence for a few minutes, they arrived at the National Archives on Constitution Avenue. Otto had returned to Washington to meet with Representative Kaye, and Althea had remained there after quitting the band.

Otto looked out and up at the white marble building with its thick columns sitting atop a wide flight of white steps.

"What are we doing here?" he asked, his voice normal again. "Isn't this the Archives? Are we going to spend the afternoon researching?" he asked, laughing.

"Nope. Come on." Althea stretched over Otto's legs and lifted herself out of the car onto the sidewalk. She refused help from the security detail.

Althea walked toward the entrance, not waiting for Otto. He quickly caught up.

The machine-gun carrying security people followed the two a few paces behind. Althea leaned into Otto and said, "These boys aren't fooling around. Looks like they've got you buttoned up tight."

Otto nodded. "They're from Corliss's security detail," he said before taking a quick glance back at them. He leaned into her and said in a low voice, "They're not very nice. They never smile."

A moment later they entered the cavernous Rotunda for the Charters of Freedom, a vast marble hall with large historic murals covering the walls.

"Welcome," a guard waiting inside said.

"Thank you for opening up for us today," Althea replied.

"My pleasure, ma'am. It's good to have visitors."

With his hands on his hips, Otto said, "Can you imagine – a government that can't even afford to open its doors to share its national treasures?"

Althea nodded but said nothing.

Otto stood in the middle of the hall in silence. He quietly looked around, not moving from his spot. Then he looked at Althea.

"Why are we here?" he asked.

"I wanted to see this place before I left Washington tonight," Althea said.

"We're sightseeing? That's quaint," Otto said, forcing a smile.

"This is no field trip, Otto. I came to see it while I still could."

"See what, Althea?"

Without answering, she slowly walked toward the broad stone pedestal at the end of the hall, framed on both sides by two green marble columns. She stopped, and standing in a firm beam of light shining from a hanging lamp directly overhead, she clasped her hands behind her back and carefully leaned over that which drew her there.

Otto quietly walked up behind her, his loafers clapping somberly with the cold stone floor. He looked over her shoulder, and there, in front of him, was the Constitution of the United States.

"You're right, Althea, this is no schoolchild's fieldtrip," he said.

Althea remained silent, staring at the document in front of her.

"Look closely, Otto," Althea said, now looking at him, and then nodding downward. "Don't be clumsy. Your precious legacy will be one of support or of destruction of the ideas living in this document," she said, gently tapping the glass with her fingernail.

"Althea, come on, don't be so dramatic. I'm just a music man trying to help out."

"Yes, a man. But we were given a nation of laws, not men, and you don't want to be a part of undoing of that," Althea said.

Otto pulled his head back and smiled. "I never took you for one that would wave the stars and stripes so fervently."

She didn't smile back. "Why? Because I don't have Uncle Sam tattooed on my ass?"

"No, no, because–"

Althea continued, "I come from a long line of people who made the most of their hard-won opportunity. Everything has its price, everywhere, but my family got it done, ignoring the absence of fairness and pushing past hardships, because the more we succeed, the more we right things. And the promise of opportunity and the spirit of fairness and equality that these documents try so hard to give life to go a long way in forgiving the sins of a nation that is still growing up."

Otto shook his head. "That's rather simplistic, Althea. This country has done some pretty bad things throughout its history."

"And it's done many great things too. Every empire has committed its atrocities, and God requires us to repent for them, but time requires us to move forward and makes things better, and holding onto bitterness and blame and self-hatred as a nation weakens us and holds us back from doing that."

"Don't preach to me," Otto said, no longer smiling. "I have respect for the institution of this government, but it's never achieved its potential – and that profoundly disappoints me. We watched those congressmen fight each other in the House Chamber together and we marched to the steps of the Capitol together. But I love what this nation *can* be, and know this, it saddened me to see the Governing Committee take over the House Chamber for its business." Otto put his hand on Althea's shoulder. "But the world is at its breaking point, and we're trying to repair the damage and build a better future – and that's going to require some extreme measures. I'm sorry for that – but what must be done, must be done."

"No, that's wrong," Althea said, pushing Otto's hand off her shoulder. "*What must be done, must be done* are very dangerous words, Otto. Believing that your cause is *necessary* and *just* doesn't give you the right to do whatever you want. No one has that license, no matter who they are or what the cause is."

"Althea, you're being unreasonable. I'm one of the few trying to move the nation forward - the whole world forward."

"That may be," Althea said, "but don't forget that this Constitution is also designed to prevent tyranny."

"Yes, I agree, but why are you talking to me as if I'm the enemy?"

"*Tyranny*, Otto. You know that word. You know that concept. It echoes throughout your music, and I love you for that. But look at the program – and its methods – that you've signed onto. Isn't it all contrary to who you are?"

"No, no – stop," Otto said, holding his hand up to Althea. "I can't question my commitment and my belief in the path I've chosen – it will weaken me."

"If doing that would weaken you, then you have doubts that you're not willing to confront."

"Stop, Althea. Listen to me, I've questioned everything and everyone all of my life, but I can't do that now. The stakes are too high. I must push forward, no matter what. There's no room for introspection and doubt."

"So, you're blindly pushing forward, Otto? Sounds like you've joined the *movement*."

"Althea, please, why are you saying these things? I'm the good guy, remember? Remember me?" Otto said, now trying to smile again.

"Yes, I remember you. Just make sure that you remember you."

Otto shook his head slowly and looked down at the marble floor. Althea walked out to the waiting car.

57

Königin opened her eyes. She didn't know where she was. The cool smell of morning dew and the warm scent of a spent campfire held in the air.

She turned her head to see the woman sleeping next to her. It was Sue.

Königin stretched in her sleeping bag, now remembering how she ended up in the little tent in Medicine Bow National Forest, just west of Cheyenne.

A figure approached the outside of the tent and started to un-zip the flap.

"Good morning ladies, how did everyone sleep?" Mitchell asked, sticking his head into the tent.

"I haven't slept that well in years," Königin said.

"On that hard ground?" Mitchell asked. Sue slowly opened her eyes and smiled at Königin.

"Yes. I know, it doesn't make sense," Königin said, now sitting up.

"We had a nice chat last night. Might have left you peaceful," Sue said in a sleepy voice.

Königin nodded, thinking about the night before. The three of them had carved out their own little campsite in the middle of a clearing in the woods, surrounded by hundreds of pilgrims making their way to Custer for food.

"Maybe," Königin said. "I haven't really talked about my life for so long. And my mom and dad. Thanks for listening."

"You'll get there," Sue said.

"I'll get there? What do you mean?" Königin asked.

"Come on, Königin," Sue said, shaking her head. "You've been tossed around by the waves. You need to figure out how to ride the crest of that wave. And I know you can do it."

Königin sat silent for a moment, and then said, "I don't know why I always feel like the ground is moving beneath me."

"Because you're not grounded. It's that simple," Sue said.

Königin let out a little laugh. "I don't think so, Sue. I think I'm a very grounded person. But life's a bit challenging because I want to be the person that people need me to be – I don't want to let anyone down. And I guess I'm like any other human, I want everyone to like and appreciate me and what I do."

Mitchell came into the tiny tent and sat back on his heels, not saying anything.

"Königin, only one person needs to like and appreciate you – and that's you," Sue said.

Königin let out another short laugh and said, "Believe me Sue, I like myself. I don't think you really know who I am."

"Well, I think I do, Königin," Sue said. "It's you who doesn't know who you are. If you knew who you were, the ground wouldn't ever feel like it's moving beneath you. You'd be planted firmly, no matter what was going on around you."

Königin could feel her face getting warm with anger. "Look, just knowing who you are doesn't mean that you like who you are. I mean, can't you know yourself and hate who and what you are?"

"Yes, for sure," Sue said. "In fact, if you know deep down that you're a hawk but you're too afraid to fly and be that creature, you'll hate yourself for betraying and ignoring who you really are. The trick is to discover your essence, and accept it, and then be a person that reflects that essence through actions and words. And that formula gives you plenty of latitude to grow and change and evolve and become the person you really want to be," Sue said.

"I'm not a hawk, Sue. I'm a woman committed to helping people," Königin said, her voice now growing louder.

Sue sat up in her sleeping bag.

"If you want to help people, Königin, you'd better start by helping yourself. You're no good to anyone if you're broken," Sue said. "And that's probably why you're so intent on fixing everyone else – just so you don't have to work on fixing you."

"Sue," Mitchell said.

"I've helped people, Sue, lots of people," Königin said, staring hard into her eyes. "And don't you remind me of my failures – they drag me down every day."

Sue shook her head slowly and smiled. "They shouldn't. Failure is a key ingredient to success. But I will say, some failures are avoidable, like the ones that you let people push you into just because you don't trust your own opinion."

"What are you talking about?" Königin asked, her lips starting to quiver.

Sue and Mitchell looked at each other.

"I may not like *The Trustee*, but I still read it. And I see that you've got some pretty unsavory bedfellows," Sue said.

"What? Who are you talking about?" Königin asked.

Mitchell looked at Sue with wide eyes but said nothing.

"Let's start with that Corliss fellow, Königin," Sue said.

"You don't know what you're talking about, Sue. He may not be the nicest guy but he's very good at what he does," Königin said.

"Come on, Königin, stop lying to yourself. You know the truth about that man," Sue said.

"You know what, you *don't* know what you're talking about. I think it's terribly presumptuous of you to think that you know about the people in my life."

"I know about you, Königin. And I know that you're a bit of a liar, dear," Sue said.

"Suzanne, enough, leave her alone," Mitchell said, lightly touching Sue's arm.

"A liar? Me? I don't lie. Who do I lie to?"

"Yourself, Königin. You're afraid of everything – so you lie to yourself just so you can get out of bed in the morning. You lie just to survive," Sue said.

Königin's face was burning hot. She shook her head side to side and covered her mouth with her hands.

"Fear, Königin," Sue said. "You use your lies to hide from your fear. You're afraid of failing, so you tell yourself that you're not good enough to carry on, not smart enough to fix your water cannon – but you know that's a lie, just a convenient excuse to let yourself off the hook from doing what you know you should be doing, and you hate yourself for not doing. And you're also afraid of succeeding, because you think you don't deserve success – so you try to subtly sabotage yourself and your endeavors with self-destructive behavior, and then you tell yourself that it's okay because that's all you're really capable of, right? Well, wrong, dead wrong. You are your most dangerous enemy, Königin. You destroy yourself one cut at a time, whether the cut's inflicted by you or you allow someone else to cut you. You punish yourself for not being what you know you really are – a queen, Königin. Your mother knew it and gave you that name for a reason."

"Don't you bring my mom into this, Sue. I don't want to hear about her anymore. That was a long time ago and I've dealt with her death and I practically don't even miss her anymore, so stop talking about her."

"There you go, telling lies again," Sue said, staring back into Königin's eyes. "Just look at that little bag of yours – most of it's taken up by that big crystal Addorra of hers. You've been toting that thing around since you left your uncle's place, right? Just face it, Königin, you've never dealt with her leaving you. And I'm sure that you do remember her and you do want for her, but you're such a coward and you're so damn afraid about how much that truth would hurt that you'll just about sacrifice anything to believe those lies that you just told me."

Königin stood up and pointed at Sue. "You're wrong about me," she shouted. "You're wrong about everything." She grabbed her backpack and jumped past Mitchell out of the tent.

Sue and Mitchell remained silent as they watched her leave.

Königin wandered through the campground, thinking about how nasty Sue was and how much she hated her.

There were hundreds of people waking up and coming out of their tents and campers and cars. Königin weaved around the little kingdoms that the groups of people had established for themselves the night before. Once again, she had nowhere to go, so she wandered.

"Hey, what's your hurry?" a short boy with a big head of messy hair asked Königin as she tried to navigate her way past his little campfire. "You want to be first in line at Custer?" He poked at a few strips of bacon crackling in a black skillet being intensely watched by his two companions.

"Leave me alone," Königin answered, not looking at him.

"Once again, working your magic with the girls, Bennett," one of the boys said, triggering laughter from the other.

Königin turned around to see the boy who had spoken to her stand up slowly and pull his sagging jeans up.

"Pull the bacon off in a minute. Don't let it burn, there may be no more of that. And don't eat my piece," he said.

Turning back, Königin saw him following her far behind – she quickened her pace. Rather than trying to dodge around the tightly packed groups of people on the ground, Königin made her way to the edge of the camping area and walked along a line of tall trees.

After a few minutes, she looked back. The boy was gone. She didn't know if her heart was beating hard from her fear or from the near run she had broken into. As she began to relax, she stepped up onto a tree stump and slowly surveyed the scene in front of her, moving her head as if she was taking a panoramic photograph. The camping area was so overrun with people that Königin couldn't even see the ground.

As the travelers prepared to leave Medicine Bow, the sounds of children running around and old people hacking and music from radios were drowned out as the engines of motorcycles, trucks and cars started. But then, for a moment, a rumble of thunder in the distance was all that could be heard.

Königin didn't want to go with the caravan to Custer, but she knew that no one there was going anywhere else. Standing on her tree stump, she turned around and looked through the line of trees. She wanted to run away from the noise and the reality and the humanity that was behind her. But the sight of the bold mountains in front of her made her feel even more hollow and lost. Königin thought about how she hated those mountains – reaching into the sky so solid and immovable, so sure. They were beautiful, yet so imperfect with their sharp, jagged rocks jutting out. She hopped off the stump, and keeping her eyes fixed high above on Medicine Bow Peak, Königin followed a narrow trail through the trees toward the peak in the distance. The din of the desperate gathering behind her softened as she walked.

The trail ran along a steep embankment above a dead creek bed far below. Königin imagined that the sound of the wind blowing through the trees was actually the sound of the rushing water that had once flowed in the creek.

She pushed deeper into the forest as the sky darkened and the trees waived their branches and leaves against the growing wind. Königin stopped and stood at the edge of the embankment, looking straight up at the low clouds now overhead.

Then a loud voice erupted from close behind. "Hey, looks like you've lost your way."

Königin's heart gave a hard pump and she lost her breath. She twisted around quickly to see the person that she now knew was there – Bennet, the boy who had been following her.

But when Königin locked eyes with the boy, she was surprised to see the look of terror that came across his face. In an instant she understood why, as the weight of her backpack pulled her backwards down the embankment toward the rocky creek bed below. As she tumbled down, boots over hair, the black clouds gave way to dirt which then gave way to clouds, over and over again. The earth kicked her as she went down, the rocks punched and punished her. But even though she knew that her efforts were futile, Königin grasped at clumps of weeds and dead tree branches – she fought for herself, and even as she was hurtling down, something about that felt good.

When she finally reached the bottom of the old waterway, Königin ended up flat on her back, looking up at Medicine Bow Peak – which seemed to be looking down at her. She quickly became aware of the sharp rocks underneath her. And even though every part of her body hurt all at once, she allowed herself to smile at the thought of having survived the fall.

Königin looked up at a low cloud hanging directly above her, and from deep inside of it, big bright droplets of rain began to float down toward her like a sapphire mist coming to cover her. When it reached her, the rain was cool and sweet and she drank it as it fell on her face and ran past her lips. It wasn't until then that Königin realized she was thirsty.

The ground hummed as the rain came down harder. The dirt in Königin's hair and on her face and on her body gradually washed away and joined the mud.

Then the rain stopped abruptly. The cloud had moved away and she could see the rain falling nearby. Königin still didn't move.

"Oh, man, are you kidding me, tell me you're not dead," the boy shouted as he carefully slid down the embankment toward Königin. She stayed still but grasped a sharp rock that was underneath her leg and brought it to her side.

The soaked boy kneeled down next to her and hovered his hands above her body as if to heal her like a shaman.

"What hurts? No, maybe you shouldn't speak," he said, his voice quivering.

"What are you doing?" Königin asked calmly.

Having become immediately conscious of what he was doing, the boy stopped waiving his hands over her.

"What am *I* doing?" the boy asked. "What are *you* doing?"

Königin didn't respond.

"You're that water woman," the boy continued. "You designed that building in London and sent water to the other side of the planet, right?"

Königin stayed quiet.

"Yeah, that's you. I knew it. That's why I tried to catch up with you. I wanted to tell you how amazing that was. I mean, giving the people the water, not that wicked fall. That was pretty bad."

"It was all bad. I killed people in Kenya," Königin said.

"Oh, yeah, I remember that. But you also saved thousands of people," he said.

Her fear of the boy faded and she eased her grip on the rock.

The boy looked around as if to survey the place. "So, tell me Königin Clairet, how did you get down here?"

"I fell. You saw the whole thing."

The boy shook his head. "No, I mean how did you end up here? Or down here, I should say."

Königin closed her eyes and put her hands on her head. "I don't know."

"Really? Are you sure you don't know?"

"Look, give me a break, okay? I nearly just killed myself," Königin said.

"Yeah, I know, I saw it all."

"Ben... Big Ben... Ben," two voices called from the woods.

"Down here, down here," Bennet responded.

"Are you Big Ben?" Königin asked, now starting to laugh a little.

The boy shrugged his shoulders. "I'm Bennett. But my friends have all kinds of nicknames for me."

Königin grabbed her right calf as she slowly sat up. "Ah! That hurts so much!" Blood from scrapes on her face mixed with the rainwater on her cheeks and it looked like she was wearing rouge.

Bennet found a dead branch and snapped it in half for Königin to use as a walking stick. The other two boys made their way down the embankment and walked around gathering Königin's belongings that had fallen out of her backpack.

After a moment, one of them said, "What a bummer."

Königin looked over to see one of the boys holding a chunk of the shattered Addorra.

Bennet looked at Königin with wide eyes. "I'm so sorry, that's terrible." Then he called to his friends and said, "Guys, scour the place, find every piece you can."

Königin sat in silence for a moment.

"You know what, leave it here. Leave every piece of it here. It meant nothing to my mom. And maybe that's because it actually means nothing."

Bennett nodded to the two boys, and in response, they gently placed the pieces of the broken thing with the rocks on the ground.

The three of them helped Königin get up the embankment and back onto the trail, but she walked on her own, using her stick.

By the time they arrived at the boys' campsite, more than half of the people had left for Custer.

The skillet with the remaining piece of bacon sat on the ground next to the ashes of the dead fire.

"That smells amazing," Königin said as they helped her to sit down on a log.

Bennet lifted the skillet and offered the bacon to Königin. "No, no, thanks. I can't take your food," she said.

"Okay, but don't change your mind in two seconds – there will be nothing I can do about it," he said.

Königin's stomach ached with emptiness. She had finished her remaining snacks the night before.

"Here I go," Bennet said, as he slowly picked the little strip of greasy meat out of the skillet. "You sure you're not going to take me up on my offer?"

Königin gnashed her teeth. "Yes, I'm sure."

He laughed and said, "For being so smart, you're pretty stupid." He ripped the bacon in two and put half in her hand. "It's not much, but you'd better take care of yourself and try to stay alive. We all might need you."

In silence, the boys rolled up their sleeping bags and packed their big old sedan, with its four different hubcaps.

Standing next to the open trunk of the car, Bennet turned to Königin. "Are you coming?" "I'll be honest with you, I really don't want to go to Custer."

"Why? You look pretty hungry to me." Bennet said.

"I am, and I understand why everyone is headed there, but it looks like there might be a fight and I don't want any part of that."

"Yeah, that's true, there's probably going to be a bit of nastiness there – must be some serious firepower protecting that food." Bennet said.

"I've been through a lot and I need peace right now," Königin said. "I don't think joining an uprising is going to point me in that direction."

"Sure, I understand, no problem. I bet some park rangers will eventually show up and give you a lift to a bus depot or train so you can get where you're going."

Königin nodded. "I saw them patrolling this morning, they're around," she said. "I'm just not sure where I'm headed."

"Anywhere but the fight, right?" Bennet said.

"Right," Königin answered, looking down at the grass.

"Just don't go searching for answers at the bottom of a dry creek bed, okay?"

Königin laughed. "Okay, I won't."

"Then I guess I'm off to battle," Bennet said, playfully saluting Königin.

"Good luck, and be careful," she said, smiling at him.

"This will be a worthy fight," Bennet said, lowering his hand. "People are hungry and supposedly there's tons of food there. Did you see all the kids that were here?"

"Yes, of course, but hopefully there will be plenty for everyone once the ĒMAD is built. My father's working very hard on it."

"It'll be great if it works, Königin. But we're hungry now and we've been lied to so many times before. I have very little faith anymore. We have to take control of our own destiny."

Königin remained silent. She looked at Bennet's face and saw little wrinkles around his eyes that she hadn't noticed before.

"Can you promise me that the ĒMAD will work?" he asked.

"I – I can't," Königin said.

Bennet smiled. "Thank you for being honest with me."

Königin nodded and smiled back.

"All right then, send me off, your majesty. You will be the first to lead from behind."

"What?" Königin asked.

"Nothing, I'm just being silly and obnoxious. Sorry. Go find some peace and be careful."

Bennet slammed the trunk three times before it stuck shut. Then he started the car and leaned out of the broken driver's side window.

"Hey, quick question. Why no more water launches? Still a lot of parched people out there."

Königin felt her face getting warm again. She gulped and said, "After that horrible failure, I just couldn't do it anymore, I – I guess."

"What a pisser," Bennet said. "We're really in trouble if everyone's just going to give up like that. We need real doers to step up right now."

"Please, don't try to manipulate me, Bennet. Besides, I'm not what you think I am. I'm sorry to disappoint you."

"Don't worry about disappointing me, Königin. Just don't disappoint yourself."

She took a deep breath and shook her head.

Bennet wagged his finger at Königin. "I see you've heard this before," he said, smiling. "And I thought I was so original and wise."

She stood silent.

"Me – I'd rather be dead than not leave my bunker to fight my wars on the front line," Bennet said, no longer smiling. "Any other kind of life is just death with physical demise merely delayed."

The back door of the car flung open with a kick of one of the boys' filthy tennis shoes. Königin and her walking stick got in without saying a word.

58

Four hours later, the car pulled into a gas station. There was a line for the one working pump at the one working gas station in Keystone, South Dakota.

While the boys waited to gas the car, Königin and Bennet went into the station.

The mechanics' area had been converted into a resale shop offering a mixed collection of junk from the past and the liquidated contents of people's homes.

Bennet picked up a dented green combat helmet and put it on.

"What you think?" he asked Königin, adjusting it on his head.

Königin laughed but didn't respond.

"I think I need it. And it fits perfectly," he said.

"Oh, you're serious?" Königin asked.

"Yep."

They each moved in their own direction around the makeshift store, looking at the things that used to be part of others' lives. The broken automobile service lifts were frozen at different heights and now served as racks for hanging clothes and old flags that had lost their meaning.

Using her walking stick, Königin moved through the place carefully. She scanned the offerings with indifference, not paying close attention to anything.

Then her eyes froze on something that she recognized immediately. It was a little device that looked like a lightbulb with four tiny paddles inside of it. The paddles spun around, powered by the sunlight streaming in through the service bay's roll-up door. Königin reached out and gently touched it. She pictured in her mind the day that her mother had given her one – and thought of how she had thrown it away long ago. Königin took a deep breath and fought back the growing lump in her throat. She quickly looked away, but her eyes landed on an old magic set, complete with a top hat, and she felt a pit in her stomach as she remembered how her brother had lost his love for magic tricks after their mother disappeared.

"Check this out," Bennet said. "Time to upgrade your cane, Königin."

"It's a walking stick, Bennet, not a cane," she said, but the words "not a cane" were barely spoken as she stared at the object he was holding.

Bennet placed it in her hands.

"It's *heavy*," Königin said, moving her arms up and down as if determining its weight. It was longer and thicker than a cane and it was made of thin dowels of dark wood, all bound together by criss-crossed strips of filthy metal. A small dented metallic ball sat on top.

"It looks like someone busted something off the top," Königin said, running her hand over a rough patch on the ball-end. Grasping that end in her hand, she put the narrow metal tip of the other end down on the ground. Due to the object's length, her hand resting on the ball-end was considerably higher than her waist. She steadied herself and said, "It's a bit much, but I like it – whatever it is."

"Very cool," Bennet said, nodding. "I don't know what it is either, but I think it's too thick and tall to have been made as an actual cane."

Königin tilted it to the side to look at it again. "You can see that beneath the tarnish is a work of beauty – and it's strong and bold. This is mine. At least for now."

Bennet smiled at Königin.

A round man with a round head and a permanent smile sat at a card table with a little metal box on top of it.

The man took Königin's five dollars without looking at her face for more than a moment. But then he looked up at her again, with a sideways head and squinted eyes.

"What?" Königin asked the man.

"Do you recognize her? The beautiful, world famous hydro-physicist?" Bennet asked the man.

He shook his head. "No, don't know what you're talking about." But he continued to look at Königin.

Then he snapped his fingers and resumed his smile. He pointed up at something hanging on the wall above his head. "Her. You look like her. She was a most wonderful woman," the man said, now giving change to another customer.

Königin hadn't heard a word the man said after her eyes followed his finger to the movie poster hanging high above. There was her mother, posing in her last role, smiling. Königin squeezed the metal ball in her hand.

Staring up at her mother, Königin's muscles tightened. Then she shouted at the poster, "I hate you, mom. You abandoned us. Even if someone did take you, it was your job to make sure that didn't happen. Damn you!"

Everyone in the little store turned to see Königin yelling up at the poster, her cheeks now shining with tears.

Bennet said nothing as he took Königin by the hand and led her outside.

The two sat on a splintery wooden bench that rocked.

"Being a little hard on your mom, don't you think?" Bennet asked.

"I'm mad at her. And I miss her – but I don't want to."

They sat in silence for a few minutes.

"You know what, I give up." Königin said.

"You're giving up? On what? Life?" Bennet asked.

"No, I give up trying to hide from all of the feelings and thoughts that scare me, which is pretty much everything. You know, fuck it, just fuck it. I don't give a shit what happens any-more. I don't have the energy to fight this ongoing battle against the truth."

Bennet nodded but didn't say anything.

"She was right. Every day I create convenient stories so I can live without pain and sadness. It's a habit now – I don't even know that I'm doing it. And I've been doing it for so long that I've forgotten how to be sad. And I've forgotten how to be happy, because I'm afraid of being happy too, because that might go away. I've even forgotten how to be angry and how to be kind. I've never learned to love or to care for anyone because those things are just way too dangerous. Who knows what pain could come from that."

"Or what joy," Bennet said, gently smiling at her.

Königin hung her head down and in a quiet voice said, "Sue was right, I'm a liar."

Then she looked Bennet in the eyes and said, "I couldn't even admit to myself that I was raped. But I was."

"Königin," Bennet said, gasping and shaking his head. He wiped his eyes and whispered, "I'm sorry."

"But never again, Bennet." She sat up straight and in a firm voice she continued, "And it wasn't just then and in that way. I've been taken advantage of and pushed around in so many ways. But that's over." Königin took a deep breath and smiled to the sky above.

The boys blew the car's horn a few short times and yelled how much to pay. Bennet went to see the man with the little metal box.

Königin signaled to the boys that she was going around the side of the station to use the bathroom.

She was pleased to find that the sink worked, and she washed her hands and dried them on her jeans. But when Königin shoved the broken door of the bathroom open, she was startled to see a man waiting there. As she quickly pushed past him, he grabbed her rear end and said, "What's your hurry?"

No one else was on that side of the gas station – they were alone. Königin thought to run, but instead, her body swung around, and in one motion, she struck the man with the narrow end of her thick walking staff. He went down immediately, bleeding from a gash across his face. Then with one hand, she flipped the thing around so that now she held the narrow end. Königin slowly drew the ball-end back over her shoulder and stood over the man. She hesitated in delivering the final blow as her heart yielded to her mind.

"So that's what it feels like to be really pissed off," she said out loud to herself. "I'd better control that one." The man beneath her moaned and nodded.

Five minutes later, Königin was headed to Custer with Bennet and the boys and her newly adopted appendage that she named "Fight."

59

Bennet carefully navigated the narrow winding roads of the Black Hills. Each climb up and descent down revealed swaths of calm green trees and sheer granite rock faces.

Several miles outside of the small town of Custer, thousands of pilgrims set up a community of tents and RVs in Custer State Park, safely away from the epicenter of the growing tension. But Königin and the boys drove right past the park, headed for that singular point from which all activity radiated outward – the Shoemaker deep mine.

Pockets of people congregated on the side of the road and in little clearings that previously served as scenic lookouts. Dozens of military vehicles patrolled the area.

As their car slowly made its way toward the mine, the car in front of them abruptly stopped. Bennet stuck his head out of the window and pulled himself up to see ahead.

"This is it. We're here," he said, turning the car off, right where it sat on the road. Without a word, the four emerged from the car and began to walk in the same direction as the thousands of others headed toward the mine.

Armed soldiers stood on the banks of the moving river of people. The soldiers, who kept their weapons pointed down, helped people who had fallen, and provided medical attention to those who were weak with exhaustion.

Looking ahead, Königin could see two and three-story scaffolding platforms secured by thousands of sandbags. Countless machine guns with helmeted soldiers behind them kept watch over those marching that day.

Finally, Königin and the boys came to a stop, packed in a tight crowd just outside of the now fortified entrance to the mine's main shaft. Königin tried to slow her thumping heart with a couple of deep breaths. She knew that at any moment a spontaneous charge forward would carry her along to an unknown destiny. But she felt at that moment that she was where she should be. Bennet, from underneath his dented helmet, turned toward her and forced a smile.

"Feed us, give us the food," a lone voice yelled from the crowd. A cheer erupted and the entire mass of people vibrated.

The soldiers on the platforms high up looked at each other with concern.

"If you want a fight, we can give you one," another voice snapped, waving a machete in the air. Everyone that had a weapon to rattle in the air did so.

An officer pacing the platform nodded to his soldiers who responded with nodding heads. He then held a bullhorn to his lips and said, "Please, everyone, please go back to where you came from. There's nothing for you here. We don't want anyone to get hurt."

He was answered with a few obscenities and more weapon waving. Suddenly realizing that he was exposed, the officer retreated behind his machine gunners.

The crowd swayed back and forth but Königin pushed down hard on Fight, her staff, to steady herself. She looked over at Bennet – his lips were blue and she could see that he was scared. Königin took his hand and squeezed tightly.

From behind a ridge of the nearest mountain, a large navy helicopter quickly approached. The jeering and cheering of the crowd were drowned out as the dark blue machine flew low, directly overhead. The people were startled but they collectively resisted a stampede.

"Bennet, stay here," Königin said. Before he could try to follow her, she was swallowed up by the crowd that she pushed forward into. She gently maneuvered around people like a ghost, drawing no attention.

After a few minutes, nothing stood between Königin and the tip of a 60 millimeter machine gun. She was at the front gate to the mine area, shoulder to shoulder with the others on the front line of the battle for reserves of food stored deep beneath the surface.

"Let me speak to your commanding officer," Königin said to the young soldier sitting behind the long gun attached to a tripod.

He didn't respond, but a moment later, a soldier with more stripes on the arm of his fatigues stepped in front of her. He was the one who had addressed the crowd from the platform.

"Listen, ma'am, there's nothing we can do for any of you. I'm sorry. Please go home, wherever that is. We really don't want anyone to get hurt."

Königin felt the crowd behind her push forward, and without realizing it, she leaned back into them as if to contain them.

"Whose helicopter is that?" Königin yelled to the soldier, trying to be heard over all the noise. She pointed Fight in the direction of the slowing rotors, but the soldier pushed the end of it toward the ground as if redirecting the barrel of a rifle. "I don't have the time or patience for twenty questions. There's about to be a bloodbath here and you're on the front line. I'd turned around and run the best I could if I were you," he said.

Not more than fifteen feet in front of her, Königin saw a small group of officers quickly approaching.

"Lieutenant," one of the officers called, and the soldier in front of Königin spun around, and upon seeing the man leading the group, he saluted.

Before the saluting soldier could get a word out, Königin shouted, "Lansing. Admiral Lansing."

The admiral instinctively looked in her direction upon hearing his name, but then quickly refocused his attention to the lieutenant to whom he was now speaking.

Now the shouts from the thousands of gathered people were almost constant and Königin could feel the growing heat and sweat building up behind her.

She could see that Lansing's face was tight and his lips pressed together as he surveyed the situation with his hands on his hips. Again, she tried to get his attention. "Admiral, it's me, Königin Clairet."

But the admiral was so focused that he didn't hear or see her, even though she was so close.

"Let's do this already," a voice from the crowd shouted. A roar went up and Königin felt the crowd surge behind her. The officers surrounding Lansing drew their pistols, preparing for the charge that was about to come their way.

Königin turned to the people directly behind her and yelled, "Don't follow me. Stay right here." And then, planting Fight between two sandbags in front of her, she lifted herself up, straddling the massive barrel of the machine gun that was now underneath her. The gunner looked to his commanding officer who already had his sidearm pointed at Königin. She turned and faced the crowd that was now cheering. She dropped Fight and held her hands wide apart, slowly waving them up and down, trying to calm the crowd.

Königin knew that no one there wanted to die, and she gave them a reason, or at least an excuse, not to charge yet.

"Tell everyone to stand-down for five minutes," she instructed the people that she had been standing with. For a moment, they just looked at each other, until she shouted, "Do it now, tell every person next to you and behind you." Quickly her words began to spread through the crowd. The surging and threats began to quiet.

Königin turned around expecting to see a gun pointed at her, but instead, Lansing stood beneath her, offering his hand. She watched the expression on his face change the moment he realized that it was her standing there.

"Königin. Ms. Clairet," he said, withdrawing his hand in reaction. "What are you doing here?"

She reached her hand out for his, her fingers trembling. He extended his hand again and helped her off the sandbags. The officer she first spoke to picked up Fight and handed it to her.

Königin watched Lansing's eyes quickly scan her scrapes and bruises. He shook his head. "How are you involved in this?" he asked, nodding toward the crowd.

She didn't answer his question, but instead asked, "Is there really food in that mine?"

By now, Bennet and the boys had pushed their way to the front of the crowd, watching Königin talk to Lansing.

Lansing crossed his arms. "Look, Ms. Clairet, I'm not going to have this conversation with you standing in front of an angry mob that's about to advance on our position." He pointed toward the small building housing the entrance to the mine shaft.

"Let's sit down, take a breath, and talk about what's going on here. And most importantly, let's get you safe and out of harm's way," Lansing said, already turning away from the crowd.

"I'm not going anywhere, Lansing."

He turned around and looked at her.

"If you think these people are going to wait, you're wrong," she said.

"That may be, but you're in way over your head, Königin. I'm just trying to help you."

"We're all in over our heads right now, Admiral. If you want to help me, then come back over here – right in front of these people. Together let's figure out how this situation ends."

The officers looked at Lansing, waiting for his reaction. He slowly walked back to Königin.

"Is there food in that mine?" she asked again.

He nodded and said, "Yes. A lot."

Bennet started to react, but Königin quickly held her palm toward him – and he shut up.

"Then what's the plan? Keep it from those that need it now and protect and save it for government officials and their well-connected friends for when the world is down to its last scraps?"

Lansing shook his head, laughed, and looked down.

"And to think," Königin continued, "the taxpayers are actually paying for you to keep from their mouths the food that they paid for."

Still looking down, Lansing slowly said, "It's even worse than that, Königin. The food down there now belongs to the Guiding Institutions Collaborative."

She tilted her head slightly and said, "Does it really matter? No. That distinction, if there even is one, is irrelevant to me. They're all just different limbs of the same fiend."

Lansing looked up at Königin and said, "Look, there's still food around – it's not like this stockpile is the last there is and people are totally starving, right? I think this is as much of a political statement as it is a quest for food."

"Political statement, no – but statement of principle, yes," Königin said. "These people – and I'm one of them – are tired of being used and pushed around by those that have power over us. We are pissed off. And as to this obnoxious scheme to store food for the exploiting class – which was news to me – any person having a scintilla of fairness in their heart would be infuriated and repulsed. But listen, Admiral, more than anything this really *is* about food. You get three square meals a day in that uniform, but these people are down to one meal a day or less. So you know what, they are starting to starve."

"The many ironies here are astounding," Lansing said, now starting to raise his voice. "Your father is building a machine – a machine funded by the Collaborative – that will supposedly feed the world, yet here you are involved in an insurgency to steal food – from the Collaborative. Apparently, you have little faith that the ĒMAD will work. If you believed in it, you'd be telling these people to return to their homes and be patient."

"Don't forget, Admiral, I worked for the Association – remember? You forgot to throw that in my face. But I don't care," Königin shouted. "You can remind me of my conflicts and contradictions – I don't care. None of that changes how I feel. But know this, words won't be enough to stop these people today."

Lansing was silent for a moment. Then he approached Königin, speaking to her so closely that she could see nothing but his face.

"This morning, the President of the United States dispatched me here to take care of this mess. All he said to me was, *you take care of it however you want to, I don't want to be involved.*"

Königin nodded slightly, looking into Lansing's eyes.

He continued, "And then I received a phone call from Chairman Corliss. He told me that using force would set a good tone for the future – and he strongly urged me to destroy any insurgency in the most dramatic and humiliating way."

Those words squeezed the air out of Königin lungs, and for a moment, she felt as if cold water was being pumped through her veins. She drew a breath and asked in a whisper, "Who do you answer to, Admiral?"

Lansing moved in even closer toward her. She didn't step back.

"I want to feed these people," Lansing said. "I want to send them on their way with their cars and trucks and motorcycles loaded with food."

Königin smiled and said, "I believe that."

"But I can't just capitulate and set up a buffet. It will lead to chaos and disorder around the country."

"Too late. There's already chaos and disorder," Königin said.

Lansing shook his head. "No, not of the magnitude that I'm talking about. I'm talking about a meltdown of all civility – where the military will be the only hope of controlling and protecting the people. The situation in the country, and the world for that matter, might devolve into that – especially if the Silence comes again – but I don't want to hasten or contribute to that as a result of my caving-in to the demands of a few thousand hungry people."

"So you are ready to have a massacre here because you're worried about setting a dangerous precedent?" Königin said. She watched Lansing's eyes survey the faces in the crowd in front of him. He swallowed and looked down. All at once she felt sorry for him and liked him – but was mad at him too.

"Listen to me," Königin said. "Most people support the ĒMAD project right now, but if you start cutting people down today, then you'll have to secure the nation's support for the project by fear – rather than willing cooperation. If something bad happens here, who knows how *The Trustee* will report it – I guess that depends on what Corliss wants, but if you leave any survivors, the truth will escape. It's all or nothing, Lansing."

Königin looked over Lansing's shoulder and saw the officers watching them.

"Okay, okay," Lansing said in a quiet voice. "But have them all retreat to Custer State Park. There's lots of space there and we'll load them up with food."

Then, before Königin could say anything, a woman's voice rose up from deep in the crowd, hissing through a bullhorn. "Hey, time's just about up." The sentiment was supported with a collective yell.

Königin again mounted the sandbags, this time with the help of Lansing. One of the officers handed her a bullhorn.

"Listen up. Admiral Lansing wants to share some food with us," Königin told the crowd, her voice echoing. The crowd cheered back at her.

"But here's the deal, the food will only be distributed back at the park, so we'll need to make our way there in an orderly fashion. Everyone will be given generous rations, but you must remain peaceful and cooperative."

"Not good enough. We want it all and we want it all now," the woman shouted.

Some people yelled in support of her, but not all.

"What? You're not satisfied? You get food without a drop of blood being spilled. What more could you want?" Königin asked in a calm voice.

"We want it all. And we're not going to Custer Park," the woman shouted.

The cheers now suggested that the woman was on her way to gaining the support of most of the people there.

Königin pointed Fight at the woman and said, "There's a person that shouldn't be listened to. If you follow her, you'll get nothing, except pointless and irreversible violence. Don't let that voice lead you into an unnecessary battle."

The cheering in support of the woman began to die down.

"And besides, what coward leads the charge into battle from behind the backs of a thousand people in front of her," Königin said. "I assure you, with that big mouth, she'll be the first to turn and run."

The crowd erupted into laughter, and when the woman lifted the bullhorn to her mouth to respond, it was slapped down by those around her.

People turned around and began to make their way toward the park, many singing Otto's songs together.

By the time the sun went down, no one was hungry.

After dining with Lansing and his officers, Königin and Bennet and the boys walked through the park.

Dozens of huge tents served as dining halls for the thousands of people now camped out at Custer. The military cooks were joined by civilians helping in the kitchens, and groups of people organized themselves to pitch overnight tents together.

As Königin walked through the camp, she was stopped every several feet by people who wanted to meet her, or thank her, or both. The group around her grew as she walked – nearly everyone that met her ended up following her.

"Taking a victory lap?" Lansing asked as his entourage crossed paths with hers, long after their dinner was over.

"No, I'm looking for some friends of mine," Königin answered, frowning and looking worried.

"Relax," Lansing said, putting his hand on her shoulder. "If they're here, we'll find them."

Königin described Sue and Mitchell and their old truck, and in response, Lansing delegated the task of finding them to a few soldiers in his group. Then Lansing turned back to Königin and asked, "What are your plans?"

At first, Königin almost instinctively answered, "I don't know," but instead, she said, "I'm going to Nashville. There's so much riding on the success of the ĒMAD that I can't imagine not being there."

Lansing nodded and said, "Good."

"What are your plans?" Königin asked Lansing.

"The same as yours. I'm leaving tonight. Need a lift?"

"Nice," Bennet said, smiling. "Königin's bumming a ride on the admiral's blue chopper. Not bad for a busted-up hitchhiker."

"Thanks," Königin said to Lansing, then adding, "Is my dad still in Pittsburgh running tests?"

"No, he's in Nashville now with the rest of the team."

She nodded but didn't respond.

Then a militarized golf cart pulled up, and riding on the back were Sue and Mitchell. Königin move as fast as she could to get to them.

"What happened to you?" Sue asked, pointing at Königin's leg.

"I fell – it's nothing," she said as she hugged both of them.

Königin apologized to Sue for yelling at her, and then said, "Thanks for kicking me in the ass instead of coddling me."

Sue took Königin's free hand and said, "Don't be afraid of anything anymore. Rejecting fear as you did back at the mine will give you the strength that you need for yourself – and for all of us."

"Yes," Königin answered, nodding.

Then Mitchell asked, "Will it work, Königin?"

The people around them fell silent and waited for her answer.

"It might, Mitchell, but I really don't know. I wish I could say *yes* for sure, but I can't, and I don't want to give you false hope, because you – all of you," Königin said to the people surrounding her, "need to be responsible for yourselves."

"You mean like robbing a mine full of government food," the woman who had challenged her earlier yelled.

"I'm just saying that you need to–"

"We can't all be sleeping with the admiral there," the woman said, pointing at Lansing. "If you were anyone else, you would have been shredded by that machine gun."

Bennet ran up to the woman, and with foam flying from his mouth, shouted, "Königin risked her life before the admiral knew it was her!"

"I still think there's something going on between those two," the woman shouted back. "And you can bet she'll be getting a clearance certificate exemption."

Bennet spit at the woman's feet – and Lansing approached her with his hand on his sidearm.

"They're the enemy – get a good look at them," the woman yelled. "They conspired so we didn't get the fight we deserved. We should be storming that mine and killing the enemy. We need war today, not peace."

"Why? Why do we need bloodshed today?" Königin asked.

"Because this is a simple fight of good versus bad – and bad must always be destroyed," the woman proclaimed.

"You're just full of hatred, and the conflict that you stoke is nothing more than a vehicle for your hate," Königin said. "Just turn around and walk away from this woman," Königin said to the group, now raising her voice. "Deny her an audience for her divisive words."

"Now she's telling you what to do," the woman shouted.

Königin pointed Fight at Lansing and Bennet, who were only a foot from the woman. "Don't be sucked in. Don't be seduced. She's feeding on your anger."

Bennet was the first to turn and walk away. Then Sue and Mitchell, followed by Lansing and his officers. And after everyone else turned away, the woman was left standing alone, shouting her words – but no one was listening.

60

Lansing's helicopter was the size of a bus and had two lanky rotors to move it through the dark empty air of the night.

The admiral and Königin sat in broad leather seats facing each other. Her jeans were torn and her boots scuffed and cracked. The day had brought another thin film of dirt to rest on Königin's cheeks. Lansing moved his eyes down to her lap, on which sat her beaten canvas backpack and her oddly thick walking staff. She held them both tightly, even though she had been sleeping since they lifted off from South Dakota. Watching her sleep, Lansing pondered how dangerous she could be to the ĒMAD project.

Without warning, the helicopter jumped and dipped as the wind pushed it around. Königin's eyes shot open.

Lansing could see in her momentary wide stare that she didn't know where she was, but then she rested back in her seat and retightened her grip on her possessions as she closed her eyes again.

"Please, don't fall back to sleep, I've been waiting to speak with you," Lansing said.

"About what?" Königin asked, her eyes still closed.

Lansing wasn't expecting the question. He shrugged his shoulders. "Well, I'm not sure," he said, and after a moment added, "The last time I saw you, we were making plans for dinner."

Königin slowly opened her eyes and smiled. "True. It just took a little longer than expected. Thanks for dinner tonight."

Lansing smiled back. "Sure."

They sat in silence for a few minutes before Lansing forced a question out.

"That water launch incident put you into a tail-spin, didn't it?"

She was slow to answer, but then said, "I've been spiraling for a long time. I thought the failure was the start of my problems, but I've realized that it was more of a symptom than a cause."

"Explain," Lansing said.

Königin sat up. "I knew the setup for the launch wasn't right that day. As you know, they gave me a skeleton crew. Protocols weren't followed. But I was afraid to upset Tad Corliss, so I just told myself that he knew better than me and that everything was going to work out fine."

"So you blame Corliss for the water launch failure?"

"No, it was my fault. At a minimum, it was my fault for not insisting that we abort the launch. I take responsibility for surrendering control of my project to him."

"Königin, your inaction in that situation was understandable. I doubt you could have stopped the launch even if you had tried."

"We'll never know – because I didn't really try," Königin said. "That won't happen again," she added, now looking out the window.

Sitting there, not even filling up the big leather seat with her slight frame, with her dirty face and torn clothes, Königin scared Lansing. He didn't know why, and he didn't know what to say. Then, searching for anything to break the silence, Lansing said, "I wish we were back at that pool on Mackinac Island."

Königin smiled but didn't respond.

"I would do one of my famous cannonballs for you."

"In your little mini-swim trunks?" Königin asked, now laughing.

"Hey, I've got nothing to hide. And apparently you noticed."

Königin nodded slightly and her smile became more subtle. "Yeah, I noticed. I couldn't take my eyes off you."

Lansing swallowed and broke eye contact with Königin.

"Relax, Admiral. We're just having some fun. It's nice to take a break from all of the heaviness of our world."

Lansing nodded.

After a few moments, Königin asked, "Is construction of the ĒMAD on schedule?"

"I think so. But Chairman Corliss only releases information on a need-to-know basis," Lansing answered. Then he picked up a phone next to his seat and gave some orders, which resulted in the helicopter banking suddenly and dropping toward the ground. Königin clutched the sides of her seat at first, but then eased her grip. The windows filled with white light from outside.

Lansing pointed out the window and said, "The ĒMAD. That's going to be one of the main towers – we're near Nashville."

On the ground below were hundreds of people moving about in a construction zone that was lit brighter than daytime itself. Fifty cranes, twenty stories high, lined up and lifted steel beams, connecting one piece to another. Sparks from a hundred different joints all being welded at the same time spit into the sky. A roadway leading to the construction area was jammed with flatbed trucks waiting to unload their materials. The skyline of Nashville sat in the background.

After circling the site a couple of times, the helicopter rolled back to its course and landed a few minutes later on the top of a parking garage in the middle of the city.

"Thanks for the lift," Königin said. "I hope we run into each other soon."

"Yes, I enjoyed the company," Lansing said. And then, as they prepared to step off the chopper, he said, "Don't be reckless, okay? No more straddling machine guns."

Königin laughed. "This from a guy who threw himself into the middle of a firefight to save a group of world leaders under the Potomac River? I'm not sure you're the right man to be giving that advice."

"That was different," Lansing said.

"No, it wasn't. You know what's important to you and you act accordingly, no matter what – that's now one of my guiding principles too."

The two travelers stepped back down to earth and headed toward the beds that were waiting for them.

61

"I hope you're not expecting a tickertape parade, Ms. Clairet," the familiar voice said.

Jess leaned against the hood of a flat-tired car resting in front of a narrow red brick hotel.

The soldiers that dropped Königin off pulled away in their jeep.

She stood in the street, lit in blue from the hotel's dim marquee. Standing with the help of Fight, Königin looked at Jess and smiled.

"Why no parade, Jess? Am I not a national hero?" Königin asked, laughing.

"Hardly, old friend. In fact, a man with my sensibilities shouldn't even be here with you," Jess answered, also laughing.

Königin approached Jess and hugged him.

"How did you know I was here?" she asked.

"You're easy to find. And now it's even easier – there's eyes on you, you know," Jess said.

Königin pressed her eyebrows together. "What are you talking about?"

"National hero? Try *enemy of the people*, Königin," Jess said. "You were crucified in tonight's edition of *The Trustee*."

"For what?"

"Think hard, you'll figure it out," Jess said.

"For helping those people in Custer?" she asked.

"That was only a minor sin, apparently. The real heresy was telling people that there was a chance that the ĒMAD might not work. The chairman will not tolerate Doubters, Königin – and now you are one of them."

"That's crazy. I didn't say it wasn't going to work. It's just that when someone asked me if it was going to work, I told them that I didn't know. I was telling the truth."

"Well, that was your mistake, wasn't it?" Jess said.

"No, it wasn't, and you know it."

"I do. And I think you're great. The three of us should celebrate with a drink, assuming this dump has a bar," Jess said.

"The three of us?"

"Yes. You, me, and that weird staff that you're leaning on," Jess said. Königin laughed and started to tell him about her fall. He looped his arm for Königin to take and the two went inside.

Fight's tip clacked on the shiny white tile floor of the hotel's tight lobby. They pushed their way through heavy crimson drapes that served as the entryway to the bar. The place had the smell of a thousand fires that had burned in the little stone fireplace in the corner of the room. It was a safe cave with a handful of people hiding in the fire's low yellow light.

Jess pulled Königin's chair out for her and put Fight on the bar in front of her.

"Did you go to finishing school since the last time I saw you?" Königin asked.

"No. But I am finished."

Königin laughed and said, "I'm sure."

The bartender turned around from the register and looked down at the beaten-up object on his bar. He had just opened his mouth to protest when he saw the woman sitting behind it. He paused, and then asked her, "What can I get you tonight?"

Königin thought for a moment.

"I know what I'm having," Jess said, but the young fellow didn't look away from Königin.

"Take your time," the bartender said. "This is a well-deserved drink and you should have just what you want."

Königin smiled at him and said, "Thank you. I'll have vodka shaken very cold. But only one. I have to work tomorrow."

"Work? What kind of work do you have tomorrow?" Jess asked.

"I don't know yet," Königin said, not turning away from the bartender. He smiled and started making her drink.

Jess reached into his messenger bag and pulled out *The Trustee* and put it on the bar in front of Königin.

She unfolded the newspaper and quickly turned it over twice, looking for the first page of both sides. Then she stared at the last page of the newspaper where the first page of the opposite side should be.

"Where's the other side of the newspaper?" Königin asked.

"Don't know – I guess they got rid of it," Jess said.

Königin shook her head and turned the paper back over. Then she saw it – a large photograph of herself on the first page. There she was, lying on the ground, bleeding after she fell from the pulpit of the Water Pavilion. The headline read, "This Failure Spreads Her Words of Doubt." Königin looked away.

Jess said nothing.

After a few minutes, Königin picked the newspaper back up and began to read aloud.

There was a quote from her father saying that he was disappointed in Königin's statement made at Custer. Corliss went further, saying, "There are always those that will lie for their own selfish reasons, and it breaks my heart to see that Ms. Clairet is one of those people in this instance. At a time when her contribution is needed the most, she decides to be a destructive voice rather than a productive force. And her participation in a lawless insurgency is further proof that she is not with all of us, but rather against us."

Then a voice from behind her said, "You've got a lot of nerve being in this town, young lady."

Königin turned around to see a man sitting by himself at a table, staring at her.

"We're gathered here from every part of the country, putting everything we've got into this miracle – and you're a Doubter?" the man said. "Chairman Corliss is right. You're not one of us – you're the enemy." He turned away from her and sipped his beer slowly. His brown suit jacket had holes in the elbows and he wore two different kinds of shoes.

Before Königin could respond, the bartender lifted the man out of his chair and began to drag him out of the bar.

"No, stop," Königin said. "Let him stay."

"Really? Are you sure?" the bartender asked.

Königin nodded. The man slowly sat back down.

"I'm not the enemy," Königin said to the man. "All I said was that I wasn't sure it would work, and now, just because I've been honest and I've spoken my mind, I'm demonized because my words don't fit the narrative of others, including my own father. I'm not your enemy. And you're not mine. Those that brand us as enemies to one another do it for the very purpose of driving a wedge between us. And eventually it becomes true, once we forget what we share in common as people."

The man stared at his beer in front of him and then took a sip of it. He didn't respond.

Königin turned back around and pushed her drink away.

"I'm going in tomorrow," she said.

"Going in?" Jess asked.

"To see if I can help."

"Help with the ĒMAD? You want to join the team?" Jess asked.

"Knock it off, Jess. I want to help if I can. I've been absent on this project long enough."

"And you think they want you?" Jess asked.

"Why wouldn't they? It's an *all hands on deck* project," Königin said.

"I guess your dad might be happy to see you, but I wouldn't expect a welcome luncheon from the chairman."

"I can't get hung up on any of that, Jess. I need to do what I can."

"Okay, but just try not to get stoned to death in the town square as you skip in to work."

Königin laughed.

A few minutes later, the man who had scolded Königin stood up and began to approach her. Out of the corner of her eye, Königin could sense that the bartender had reached for something underneath the bar – and was ready. Jess stared at the man but didn't move. Königin's heart fluttered, but without even feeling that her hand had moved, she became aware that she was grasping the narrow end of Fight, ready to swing when the time came.

"You're right," the man said. "You're not my enemy. I'm sorry for yelling at you. I'm just scared to death – everyone is. They're saying this is our last hope." The man's voice was strained and thin. "I get that it's ĒMAD success or bust, but I just can't be reminded of it anymore – I can't even watch Otto's nightly show, even though I know we're supposed to," he said.

"I understand," Königin said. "You're not alone."

The man nodded and gave a hint of a bow before leaving the bar.

"I had you covered, Ms. Clairet," the bartender said.

Königin turned toward him. "Thanks, but I had myself covered," she said, lifting Fight into the air.

"Cool – I heard about that thing," the bartender said.

"You heard about her third leg?" Jess asked.

"For sure. I got a call from my brother who was up in Custer this afternoon. He saw her in action," the bartender said, nodding toward Königin. Then he added, "He said she was inspiring. I'd wager that the whole country knows the real story by now." Then the bartender picked up *The Trustee*, and with a flick of his wrist, he sent the newspaper straight into the fireplace. The calm little flame blew up into a bright hot fire as it consumed its new fuel.

Jess smiled at Königin but said nothing.

Königin stood and said, "I'm going to bed. Jess, if you don't have a room, you can sleep in mine, but I'm not sharing my bed."

Before she pushed her way back through the crimson drapes, Königin turned to the bartender and wished him a good night, and then, waiving Fight in the air, she said, "Remember, I've got you covered."

☞ 62 ☜

Jess suddenly sat up in the bathtub in which he was sleeping. It was 3:30 in the morning. Yelling sirens in the streets of the city forced him up.

The muffled sound of rapidly rolling vehicles came in through the closed window of Königin's room, and when Jess pulled the curtain back, he saw a racing convoy of military trucks rushing somewhere.

He turned to Königin in her bed, but she was still sleeping. The easy look on her face made Jess pause for a moment and watch her. Her sheets rose and fell in steady time.

Jess closed the door to the room behind him quietly. Instead of waiting for the old elevator, he ran down the three flights of stairs to the lobby. No one was behind the front desk so he ran through the crimson curtain and found the bar empty but lit. Then he ran out to the sidewalk and found the bartender watching the armored vehicles.

"Well?" Jess asked.

The bartender didn't turn to face Jess, but he spoke loudly and evenly through the passing noise as if making an announcement at a train station.

"They're looking for the mischief-makers that have descended upon the city," the bartender said. "Some are hiding in the sewers and some in abandoned buildings. Others in plain sight."

Jess looked closely at the vehicles moving past him and said, "That's not Admiral Lansing's military force – who are these soldiers?"

The last of the vehicles wheeled past and the bartender leaned toward Jess. "That's Chairman Corliss's personal security force."

"Are you sure? How do you know that?" Jess asked.

"My friends serve those people food and pour their drinks. Some sell their bodies to them. They're a sloppy bunch," the bartender said.

"Who? Corliss's people?"

The bartender nodded.

"Is Otto one of them?" Jess asked.

"I don't think so. I've been told that he disappears to his hotel room after his show every night."

The bartender turned away from the street and went back into the hotel. Jess followed.

"Which groups are here in town?" Jess asked. "World Fatigue? Inevitable?"

"I don't know," he answered, stretching himself out on a sofa in the lobby.

"You know – you just don't want to tell me," Jess said.

"You're right, I don't want to tell you."

"Are you afraid to tell me?"

The bartender sat up quickly and looked Jess in the eyes. "Don't start with me," he said.

"What's the problem?" Jess asked. "Concerned about Königin's allegiances? Trying to figure out whether she's an agitator today but maybe an associate of Tad Corliss again tomorrow?"

The bartender twirled one of his eyebrows and slowly answered, "Perhaps."

"In light of all that has transpired, your doubt is reasonable," Jess said. "Keep your secrets. I'm not going to politick on her behalf – make up your own mind."

Suddenly the elevator door clumsily banged open. Königin stood in the dim light of the little box, but she didn't exit.

"What's going on, Jess?" she asked, sounding as if she was still asleep.

"Go back to bed, Königin," Jess said. "We just watched Corliss's security detail roaming around the streets looking for troublemakers. Better hide under your sheets and sleep in. I don't think your dad and the chairman are going to let you join the team tomorrow. In fact, I doubt you'll even get near the entrance to the ĒMAD's control center."

"You're wrong," Königin said quietly. "I'll call my dad tomorrow – I'm sure he'll be happy to have me over there to help out." The elevator clanged shut and she was gone.

⟨⟩ 63 ⟨⟩

The next night, just after falling asleep, Königin woke up to a rapid but light knocking on her hotel room door.

As the knocking grew louder and faster, her muscles tensed up and she reached over the side of the bed for Fight. But before she could rise, Jess came out of the bathroom as if it were a second bedroom in an apartment they were sharing. He quickly opened the door and Königin watched his head jerk back in surprise.

"David," Jess said, forcing the name out of his mouth.

"Let me in," David said, pushing past Jess while pulling a small suitcase on wheels.

"David!" Königin shouted, smiling, as she jumped out of bed. She wrapped her arms around him and kissed his cheek. But he reciprocated in such a mechanical way that she pulled away from him.

"What's wrong?" she asked, her smile now gone.

"Nothing. Nothing's wrong," David said, not smiling.

"What are you doing here?" Königin asked.

David shrugged his shoulders and then sat at the edge of the bed. "This town is the center of the universe, isn't it? Why wouldn't I want to be here? With my sister and my dad, no less."

Jess pulled the chair out from under the little desk near the window of the small room and sat on it backwards, facing David.

He rested his arms on the back of the chair, settling in as if to watch a movie.

"You don't have any shows booked here, right? I mean, I can't imagine anyone's spending their precious few dollars on laughs these days." Königin said.

"No, no shows, of course not. And I'm kind of keeping a low profile right now," David said.

"Yeah, a really low profile, I guess," Königin said. "Dad doesn't even know that you're here."

"When did you talk to Dad?"

"Early this morning. I called him over at the ĒMAD control center. I was planning on seeing him but he told me not to come."

"Why not? He wouldn't see you?" David asked.

"Nope. He said that they're down to the last couple of days of work and he can't be interrupted."

"Really? He can't even take five minutes to see his daughter?" David said.

"He sounds pretty stressed out. I'm worried about him," Königin said. "I wanted to help out but he got angry with me and told me to stay away."

"Listen to me, Königin, just steer clear of him and that machine. And why would you want to help the Collaborative build that behemoth?"

"Look, there are a lot of people counting on the success of the ĒMAD, so if I can help, I'm going to."

"I don't even need to ask how you feel about the Collaborative, Königin – we both have Mom's heart – so I'm telling you, stay away from that whole situation."

"David, in my mind, I can separate the ĒMAD from the Collaborative – I have to, for the good of the people."

David looked down and shook his head. Then he looked up at Königin. "When you do talk to Dad again, don't tell him that I'm in town."

"Oh, okay," Königin said, shrugging her shoulders.

As they sat in silence, she thought about how good it was to be with David. She didn't want to fight with him, so she decided not to force the issue about what he was hiding.

But only a few moments later, Königin jumped up and yelled, "Don't bullshit me, David. What's going on? Low profile? Don't want Dad to know you're here? I know your sneaky little act."

Jess sat up straight, his eyes wide open.

"What's wrong with you, Königin?" David asked. "What's your problem, why are you so upset? Your life has really gotten to you. Just relax, you're so uptight. Where's my sweet sister?"

Königin stood still for a moment. Then she walked to the door of her room and opened it.

"Tell me now or you have to leave. I'm sorry," Königin said.

David turned to Jess and asked, "What's wrong with her?"

Jess shook his head. "Nothing. Nothing at all."

"Tell me, David!" Königin shouted, still propping the door open with her hand.

David looked away from her and put his head down. He waited a moment and then let out a little laugh. "It's just a crazy thing," he said. "They think I'm one of the bad guys. You know, a member of one of those subversive groups or seditious groups or whatever the hell they're calling them now – terrorist groups, I think I saw in *The Trustee*."

Königin slowly closed the door and leaned with her back against it.

"Why, David? Why would they think that? That's insane," Königin said.

David shrugged his shoulders. "I don't know, it's got something to do with my act. Certain things I've said – a couple of bad routines. These guys have a lousy sense of humor."

"But you're a comedian. You're supposed to make fun of everyone and everything. Sure, your act's a little edgy in an anti-society sort of way, but that's a big leap to classify you as a bad guy," Königin said.

David laughed. "Right – and look at you – I can't believe they haven't locked you up yet for that bold act in Custer. Nice work, by the way."

"They're stupid," Jess said. "But not that stupid."

David ignored Jess's comment. "It's dangerous for me out there, Königin. I don't want to get swept up in these roundups."

"For sure, David. You need to get out of town right away," she said.

"No, I don't think I should go anywhere right now," David said. "Best to just hunker-down in place."

"You're probably right. Why take any chances?" Königin said. "Just stay here. We'll figure the rest out later."

"Where's he going to sleep?" Jess asked.

"Head to toe," Königin said, nodding toward the bed. "Like when we were kids."

⟸ 64 ⟹

"Königin Clairet and Jess Frank is asking to come backstage," Thigpen shouted to Otto.

Otto nodded quickly. "Yes indeed, tell them to let those two in."

The backstage area was full of moving people preparing for Otto's nightly broadcast.

Otto stared at the stage door, waiting for Königin and Jess.

"Everything okay?" Thigpen asked as he approached Otto. "What do you need?"

"Nothing. I don't need anything. I could do the show with my eyes closed." But after a moment he added, "Although I could use a cup of Victoria's tea."

"So many nights – right in a row," Thigpen said. "We'll be ready for a full-time gig in Vegas when we get past this little situation. Probably could get Victoria back from England for that."

Otto laughed and said, "I don't think so, she's the smart one."

Then Otto saw Königin and Jess showing their backstage passes. He jogged over to greet them.

"Ms. Clairet, how are you? You are quite the hero. I love what you did in Custer. I wish I had your guts," Otto said, shaking her hand. Then Otto turned to Jess and hugged him. "I'm surprised you're still alive you annoying little person."

Jess didn't have time to reciprocate the hug as it took him a moment to overcome the shock.

"You guys are here on a special night," Otto said. "We're celebrating the completion of the ĒMAD. We just received word. The news hasn't been made public yet – I'm going to announce it when we go live."

"So exciting," Königin said.

"Yeah," Jess said, devoid of enthusiasm.

Otto put his hand on Jess's shoulder and said, "I understand if you're still upset about me asking you to give me some space. But you need to know – it wasn't my decision. Corliss needs everyone to focus on one goal right now, and he thought it would be distracting – you know, you following me around and all."

"And recording everything for history," Jess said.

Otto shook his head and said, "Look, you'll have your chance to finish chronicling the tour – but we just need to jump this big hurdle right now. Some of the details will get lost, and that's okay, so long as we achieve our goal."

"I think you've got it backwards, Otto. I think it's all about the details," Jess said.

Königin interrupted. "Mr. Veltraria, have you seen my father? Is he okay?"

"I think he's doing all right. But he's under enormous pressure, of course," Otto said.

"I really want to see him, but he says he's too busy right now."

"He's carrying a huge burden," Otto said. "I mean, we all are, but can you imagine? And especially right now – with the test run tomorrow morning."

"You're testing the machine tomorrow? For the first time?" Königin asked in a high-pitched voice.

But before Otto could answer, he saw several members of Corliss's security force approaching quickly from behind Königin and Jess.

"I think you two are going to be asked to leave. I'm sorry," Otto said.

Königin and Jess turned around to see four people dressed in the now familiar uniforms of Corliss's force.

"You can't be here, let's go," the head man said with his scarred-up face.

"Why can't we be here? We're guests of Mr. Veltraria," Königin said.

Instantly the man pulled a long shiny black club from a ring on his belt. The other two men and the woman in uniform did the same.

Königin instinctively flipped her wrist and grabbed Fight by the narrow end, but before she could draw it back, Jess gently tapped the round end. After hesitating, Königin let Fight slowly slide through her hand until its tip rested on the floor.

"We're leaving," Jess said as he took Königin by the arm.

Otto watched as they quickly walked toward the exit with Corliss's people following them.

"Seen your brother lately, Ms. Clairet?" one of the men shouted at the back of Königin's head. She stopped abruptly but didn't turn around. Jess shoved her forward.

"You'll stay away if you know what's good for you," the woman shouted, just before the door closed behind Königin and Jess.

Otto turned to go to his dressing room but his eyes locked with Corliss's lead man who had ordered Königin and Jess out. The man silently scolded him with a slow shake of his head. Otto felt his throat tightening, but after a moment, he pulled himself free of the man's hard stare and walked away.

◐═◆═ 65 ◆═◑

From inside the back of a van delivering tanks of hydrogen, Königin could see the sun coming up through the windshield. Only the massive outline of the New Hickory Power Plant in the distance stood out against the young red sky in front of her. Königin figured that if she could get near enough to her father so he saw or heard her, she wouldn't be turned away, not even by Corliss.

A few days earlier, Corliss had ordered his growing security detail to replace Lansing's forces at the power plant, the home of the ĒMAD's control center. Refusing to completely retreat from the ĒMAD complex, Lansing dropped his forces back a quarter of a mile from the plant's main entrance.

The van quickly slowed down.

"What's going on here?" the driver said out loud, surveying the scene outside.

Crouching, Königin walked to the front of the van, steadying herself by holding onto the driver's seat. She peered through the windshield. "What are all of these people doing here?" she asked, knowing that neither the driver nor Jess had the answer.

Just outside of the security perimeter created by Lansing's forces, thousands of people were in the process of setting-up camp. The van moved slowly. The soldiers kept the road clear but didn't appear to be interfering with the newly arrived people.

"Get in the back, Ms. Clairet – please," the driver said. "I'll find out what's going on."

Before they started their journey that morning, Königin and Jess decided that they wouldn't dress up in deliverymen uniforms or hide in an empty box, rather, they would just sit in the back of the delivery van and not fear the outcome. "I hate the idea of sneaking around," Königin had said. "It's bad enough that I can't walk through the front door."

The van came to a stop and the driver rolled the window down.

"What's going on here?" he asked a civilian walking alongside the van.

"We're waiting," the man answered.

"For what? The ĒMAD to get started?" the driver asked.

"That too – but we're all here waiting for Königin Clairet."

The driver stopped the van and turned around to look at Königin, who had heard the exchange. He turned back to the man.

"How do you know she's going to be here?" the driver asked.

"She flew here from Custer with Admiral Lansing. If she's not already in the plant, I'm sure she'll be showing up soon. I just want to see her."

"Come on, let's get going," Jess said from the back of the van.

"Good luck," the driver said as he rolled his window up.

They drove past dozens of military vehicles and hundreds of soldiers, but it was Corliss's people that were operating the checkpoint at the entrance to the plant's grounds.

"Okay guys, keep quiet," the driver said as he pulled up to the officer in the little security booth before rolling his window down again.

"Ed? Ed Mann?" The driver asked in a surprise voice.

"Yep. But that's *Security Specialist Mann* to you," the officer said, smiling as he pulled on the badge attached to his uniform.

"I, I thought you were in jail, Eddie?"

"I was. But Chairman Corliss has a knack for spotting talent, you know what I mean?" he said, laughing. "A bunch of the guys from Riverbend Maximum were hand-picked by him to work on his security detail. Pretty cool, huh? Now you can tell everyone that your old high school buddy is a tough guy for the chairman."

"Yeah, wow, that's pretty cool, Ed. Congratulations," the driver said in a breathless voice. "Great to see you. Can I get through now?"

"Yeah, sure, but before you go, you got a few bucks for me?"

"Uh, how much, Eddie? You know, things are tough."

"You got ten?"

The driver opened his wallet and looked in. Eddie tapped his club gently against the side of the van.

"Four bucks. It's all I've got."

Security Specialist Mann stuck his hand through the window and grabbed the cash, folding it over and over so it disappeared into one hand – and then he stuffed it into his shirt pocket.

"Can't let the other snapperheads see. They'll want a piece of the action," Eddie said, laughing again.

"Yeah," the driver said in a quiet voice.

Then Eddie pointed back toward the people setting-up camp and said, "Can't wait to start our *inspections* of *them*. We just need Chairman Corliss to order that admiral to pull his soldiers back a little further. Those military folks are on the wrong side – stay away from them, friend."

Eddie waved the van through the checkpoint with his club, and the van slowly pulled away.

"Look at you – with minions of your own," Jess said to Königin.

She didn't respond.

A few minutes later, the van approached the mouth of a tunnel that ran underneath the building. The huge concrete power plant sat on the bank of the Cumberland River, almost hugging the downstream side of the Old Hickory Dam that towered high above, holding back the waters of Old Hickory Lake.

The tunnel emptied into a vast network of loading docks and staging areas all brightly lit with a blaring green hue. The sound of machinery and truck engines filled the space. The thick mist of exhaust fumes burned Königin's nose.

The van came to a stop at an empty loading dock, and Königin and Jess jumped out of the back of the van and thanked the driver for his help.

They quickly made their way up a narrow flight of metal stairs.

"This place is huge," Jess said. "Are we just going to walk around until we find your dad?"

"That's the plan," Königin answered.

Then a door opening into the stairwell flung open, smacking Jess's elbow.

The woman on the other side of the door, in her yellow lab coat, dryly said, "Sorry."

Jess rubbed his elbow and asked where the executive offices were.

"Up on twelve. Take an elevator from this floor," the woman said, pointing through the door from which she had come. Then she was gone, heading down the stairs.

When Königin stepped through the door, she felt like she had exited the plant and was now outside. But she wasn't. She was inside a vast open space ten stories high.

The vintage turbines of the power plant were each five stories high, painted in shiny black enamel. There were no less than twenty of them. The new machinery of the ĒMAD joined the old machinery in a new purpose.

The building and its apparatus were the heart of the ĒMAD. Instead of creating energy for the region, the turbines now generated energy to power the ĒMAD – and the system also pulled energy from all over the world to fuel the machine.

Königin and Jess looked at each other in silence as they started to walk through the great hall of turbines.

"Where's your credentials?" A guard in a red uniform asked almost immediately.

"Credentials?" Jess asked.

"Your tags, where are they?" The guard asked, tapping his own tag around his neck.

Jess looked at Königin and said, "Run?"

She shook her head and said to Jess, "No, no running." To the guard she said, "I'm Königin Clairet. I'm here to see my father."

Without responding, the man whispered into his headset as he kept his eyes fixed on Königin.

Within seconds, Königin and Jess were met by a dozen more red uniforms. "This way," one of them ordered. Surrounded, they were taken on an elevator to the twelfth floor.

Königin and Jess were put in a long, narrow conference room with old metal chairs that shrieked against the floor when moved. The chipping walls were plastered in a septic green, and low hanging wire fixtures leaked a weak light. The door closed behind them and they were left alone.

Königin walked to the far end of the dinged-up table and slowly sat down in the chair at the head. She rested Fight in front of her on the table. Then Jess pulled a chair out with his boot and sat.

"He must be pissed," Jess said.

"Who?" Königin asked.

"Corliss. That following of yours camped outside the plant must be boiling his water."

Königin ignored his comment and said, "I'm worried about David. I'm sure the hotel's been overrun by people looking for me."

"Well, well – look who thinks a lot of herself all of the sudden," Jess said laughing.

"It's less a function of who I am and much more about people's fear," she said. "They're searching for any light in the darkness. And right now, I am one of those lights."

Jess nodded and said, "True. Your followers have probably turned your room into a shrine by now. I hope David's collecting an entrance fee."

"I'm not kidding, Jess. He has a target on his back. You may need to go back and find him."

Before Jess could answer, the door opened.

Malcolm stood in the doorway, staring at Königin and Jess for a few moments, not saying anything. Then he stood aside and waved in two members of Corliss's security detail who proceeded to pat-down Königin and Jess for weapons.

"Clear," one of them yelled, and then Dr. Clairet rushed in and hugged Königin. Corliss followed slowly behind, not smiling.

"Königin, what's wrong with your leg?" Dr. Clairet asked, subtly pushing Königin away to look at her leg.

"It's nothing, Dad. Just a fall. It's getting better."

"Or maybe Chairman Corliss's goons threw her down a flight of stairs," Jess said, smiling.

"Shut up, Mr. Frank," Corliss said.

Dr. Clairet frowned and said, "Jester Frank, how could you joke about such a thing?"

"Jester?" Corliss said, now smiling. "Jess is short for Jester? That's deliciously perfect." Jess ignored Corliss.

"All right, let's move on," Königin said as she sat back down. Corliss stopped smiling and slowly sat. "Dad, why don't you take a seat," she said.

Königin felt Corliss staring, and when she looked at him, she saw his eyes studying her banged-up oversized staff. He quickly shifted his eyes away.

"You're a hard man to see, Dad," Königin said.

"He's been busy, Ms. Clairet. Not everyone has the luxury of hiking around the country and fueling insurrections," Corliss said.

"I didn't fuel an insurrection, Mr. Corliss," Königin said. "I just helped avoid a needless bloodbath."

"Perhaps," Corliss responded.

Dr. Clairet wasn't even listening. He was looking down at the table and wringing his hands.

"Dad, what's wrong?" Königin asked, surprised by the sound of concern in her own voice.

"Nothing, nothing at all, Königin," he answered, barely looking at her.

"He's nervous. We all are," Corliss said. "There's a great deal at stake."

"What can I do to help?" Kȯnigin asked. "I'll do anything I can."

"How about stop working against us on the public relations front," Corliss said.

"What? Just because I told someone that I couldn't guarantee that the ĒMAD will work you think I'm working against you?"

"That doesn't build confidence in the project," Corliss said. "We need the unwavering, unquestioning commitment of the people. They need to believe that this machine will work and that it will solve their problems and rescue their lives. They've already made sacrifices and they may need to make more – and planting any doubt in their minds works against our objectives."

"But who can say for sure that it will work?" Kȯnigin asked.

"You seem to be missing the point, Ms. Clairet. We won't find out if it works unless the people are all-in on this thing so we can actually get the damned thing running," Corliss said.

"I understand your position, Mr. Corliss, but there should be total transparency about the facts of this project. People should be provided with information so they can develop an independent, informed opinion," Kȯnigin said.

Corliss shook his head. "Wrong," he said. "They want to be led, they want to have questions answered for them, they want somebody else to fix the problem. And that's what we're doing for them."

Kȯnigin didn't respond.

"I must say, Ms. Clairet, you've become very difficult since our earlier association. You've developed a very disagreeable attitude," Corliss said.

Kȯnigin took a deep breath and prepared to lecture Corliss about the water launch failure and her fall at the Water Pavilion, but she stopped. Instead, she said, "Dad, is the ĒMAD going to work?"

"Absolutely, Kȯnigin, no question about it," Dr. Clairet said without looking at her.

"Good," she responded. "The world needs it."

Dr. Clairet looked at her and nodded. His eyes were glassy. He shifted in his seat and asked, "Have you seen David?" Königin watched Corliss's eyes widen.

"No, no I haven't, Dad," she said, shrugging her shoulders.

"I'm very concerned about him," Dr. Clairet said.

"We all are," Corliss said. "If you see him, let us know."

"I think he may be in some trouble, Königin," Dr. Clairet said. "In with the wrong crowd. There's a growing number of people working against us, and Chairman Corliss must neutralize that threat. I don't want David to get hurt in that process."

"Neutralize?" Königin asked.

"Look, Ms. Clairet, I can see by your face and I can hear in your voice that you're going to question me about our security operations," Corliss said. "That topic is off-limits. Just know that all of our detainees are being treated like guests as if at the finest hotel, and they'll all be released at the appropriate time. End of story."

"But Mr. Corliss, don't you think–" Königin started.

"No," Corliss shouted. "We're not discussing this." Then he lowered his voice and said, "We need to get back to work. We're testing the machine tomorrow morning."

"I thought you were testing it today?" Königin said.

"What? Who told you that? How did you know that?" Corliss asked, leaning forward.

"Mr. Veltraria told us last night," Königin answered slowly.

"Did he? Well, apparently that big mouth of his does more than just sing," Corliss said, looking up at the ceiling. Then he took a deep breath and looked at Königin. "He's wrong. We're testing it tomorrow. And I need your cooperation."

Königin nodded. "Tell me, how can I help?"

Corliss stood up and said, "I'm going to instruct *The Trustee* to run a front page story explaining how we've patched up our relationship, and after touring the control center, you're now certain that the ĒMAD will work as planned and that you're joining the chorus of support and urging the people to make whatever sacrifices are necessary to ensure the success of the project."

Jess said nothing but looked at Königin. She didn't return his look, but instead looked directly at Corliss who was waiting for her response.

Königin slowly shook her head and said, "I'm sorry, Mr. Corliss, but that's going just too far. And besides, I haven't toured the control center."

Corliss put his hands on his hips. "If you don't cooperate, I'll just have you arrested."

"Chairman Corliss, please, there's no need to threaten Königin. She'll cooperate," Dr. Clairet said.

"It doesn't sound like it," Corliss said.

"I said I would help, Mr. Corliss. But that doesn't mean I'm giving you a license to use my name as you see fit."

"Oh, please, Ms. Clairet. Don't overestimate the value of your brand. And remember, I can devalue or increase the value of that brand with a few words," Corliss said.

Königin ran her fingers along Fight and wondered if she could bury the globe-like end in his head before she was stopped by someone else in the room.

She put her hands in her pockets and leaned back in her chair and said, "I want to be at the test tomorrow."

"Oh, do you?" Corliss said. "Then I suggest you cooperate. You've all to gain and nothing to lose."

"Fine, but I want your statement to read a little differently," Königin said. "Explain that the well-being of all people is the common ground that you and I share, and my commitment to the people is reaffirmed by the assistance I'll be providing to promote a positive outcome of the ĒMAD project."

"That's beautiful, Königin," Dr. Clairet said.

"Sounds like lawyer-talk to me," Corliss laughed.

"Mr. Corliss, please understand–" Königin said before she was interrupted by Jess. "Save your words, Königin. He's going to release whatever statement he wants."

"How dare you, Mr. Frank. Yet another venomous attack on me," Corliss said. "To have my integrity questioned by you is sickening." Then Corliss turned to Königin and said, "You won't be granted entry to the control room tomorrow if you show up with him."

Before Königin could respond, Jess said, "Don't worry, Mr. Corliss, I don't want to come to your party."

Corliss stood up, and without saying a word, he turned around and walked out of the conference room.

Dr. Clairet stared at the wall, and in a quiet voice said, "Königin, it's so good to have you here."

66

"There's no way he'll still be there," Königin said to Jess as their helicopter flew low over the city toward the hotel.

"I'm sure, but maybe he's left us a clue," Jess said.

The chopper turned slightly on its side and Jess grabbed Königin's leg, squeezing hard. She patted his hand gently. Down below, she could see that all of the streets surrounding the hotel were closed to traffic and people were setting up tents and makeshift living quarters. As they neared the hotel the crowd on the ground became denser, until there was standing room only.

Gingerly, the helicopter landed on the roof of the old building. Ducking, Königin and Jess hopped out, accompanied by four of Lansing's armed soldiers and one of Corliss's men.

The group quickly walked down the narrow stairwell from the roof, led by the muzzle of a machine gun. When they arrived at Königin's floor, three of the soldiers took up positions to protect her entrance into the room. The fourth soldier kicked the door open and quickly entered the room.

Without waiting for the "All clear," Königin entered her room to find it filled with piles of flowers and all kinds of handmade gifts.

Corliss's man clopped into the room and said, "What is all this garbage? Is this why you needed to come back here, Ms. Clairet?

To have your ego stroked by the adulation of miscreants? You're lucky that Lansing offered to waste his soldiers' time for this little excursion." He shook his head and crossed his arms.

Jess stood silently looking at Königin.

"Please, give us a few minutes of privacy," Königin said.

"Nope," said Corliss's man. "I was given explicit instructions not to take my eyes off of you."

"She's not going anywhere," one of Lansing's men said. "We'll wait right outside, Ms. Clairet."

"I'm in charge here," Corliss's man announced. "Chairman Corliss has made it clear that his security detail is senior to all other forces."

"That's not what I've been told by my commanding officer," the soldier answered.

The two men were now arguing in the hallway.

"This ought to be fun," Jess said. "A fight over who is in charge."

Königin gently closed the door, leaving the four soldiers and Corliss's man in the hallway still arguing about who was in charge.

She and Jess quickly searched the room for any sign of David. Nothing. Not even a note.

"I'm sorry, Königin," Jess said.

Königin nodded, not saying anything. She sat at the very edge of the bed that was hidden underneath "thank you" notes and little gifts. After a moment, she opened a small box of chocolates and ate them one after another, offering the last one to Jess.

"No, thanks. I feel like I've eaten the whole box just by watching you," he said, smiling. She laughed.

Suddenly the door to the room flung open and Corliss's man entered triumphantly. "It's settled. I'm in charge. You can't be in here alone," he said to Königin and Jess.

"Okay, no problem," Königin said.

Jess leaned back in the desk chair, crossed his arms and just stared at Corliss's man.

Königin looked at the things that had been left for her and put a few of them in her backpack.

A cheer erupted from the crowd outside. Jess peeked out of the window from behind the curtain and looked down. "They know you're here," he said.

Corliss's man shook his head and let out a mocking sound.

Königin heard the voice of the bartender on the other side of the door. He was arguing with the soldiers. She opened the door to find him trying to hold onto the flowers and gifts filling his arms.

He looked at Königin and asked, "Why would you come back here?"

Königin and Jess looked at each other but didn't answer.

The bartender dumped everything on the bed. He looked hard at Corliss's man, and without turning away from him, he said to Königin, "I hear you've rekindled some old friendships. That's too bad."

"What are you talking about?" Königin asked.

"You and the chairman," the bartender answered. "My buddy who works at *The Trustee*'s Nashville printing press tells me that tonight's headline screams that Königin Clairet has converted to being a believer without doubt. According to him, the front page article says you're now sure it will work and that you want everyone to give whatever is necessary to get the thing working." Then the bartender shook his head slowly and said, "Joining the ĒMAD team is one thing, Ms. Clairet, but this kind of blind loyalty goes far beyond that."

Königin looked at Corliss's man, who simply smiled back at her. Jess crossed his arms and said nothing.

"It's true that I've agreed to help – all the rest is a lie," Königin responded. "But I'm not going to try to convince you or anyone else what's in my heart – you'll know by my actions." Then she nodded toward Corliss's man and said, "And I'm with this creep because I have no choice."

The bartender hesitated for a moment, and then said, "Do what you can." He left the room without making eye contact with any of the soldiers.

Königin walked to the window and saw that Lansing's forces had formed a protective perimeter around the hotel – it was an island in a sea of people.

"Maybe we should just stay here tonight," Königin said to Corliss's man. He laughed and said, "No, that won't work. You two are staying at the plant. That's the safest place to keep you."

Minutes later, the group made their way up the stairwell to the roof. Round, low hanging silver clouds blocked out the sun.

Königin slowly walked toward the idle helicopter, its rotors not yet turning. The chilly wind hit her face and she pulled her collar up. And then she heard a roar of voices climb up the brick walls of the hotel to find her on the roof, and at once she walked toward those voices, obeying the people that called for her.

She walked to the very edge of the roof and looked down. There were thousands of faces, smiling, looking up at her, cheering and whistling. Some waved banners and many chanted together.

Königin kissed the globe-end of Fight and then pointed it toward the people below. They responded by blowing kisses back to her.

As the helicopter lifted off, Königin looked down and tried to see the individual faces making up the crowd. She wanted to see each person.

Then Königin's thoughts turned to her brother, and a sharp fear pierced her stomach. She wondered where he was and whether he was even still alive.

67

Corliss rubbed his hands together as if trying to warm them. Dr. Clairet locked his fingers together tightly and brought them up to his mouth.

Otto tapped-out a tune on his knee.

"Otto, stop that. I'm trying to concentrate," Corliss said.

Otto stopped.

Even though the ĒMAD's main control area moved with activity, it was quiet. Technicians spoke in low voices at their terminals as they communicated with their co-workers stationed in the thousands of towers throughout the world.

The control area was located on the top floor of the plant. It was an open space with a flat ceiling thirty-five feet above. The walls were built of thousands of glass blocks that let in streams of broken, dirty light. The floor was raw concrete, scarred and uneven in many places.

On one side of the rectangular shaped space, the technicians sat at terminals arranged in ten circles, one inside another, so that the smallest circle had only eight technicians working at their screens, chattering into their microphones. Their faces were lit with the orange light of their screens. A column thirty feet tall stood in the middle of the circles – it was covered in red lights that would indicate how much power was coming into the ĒMAD. The higher the lights, the more power was coming in.

On the other side of the control area, a smooth glass room, measuring fourteen by fourteen feet and nine feet high, sat atop a platform surrounded by half a dozen wooden steps leading up to it on all sides. Even its ceiling and door were see-though. This was the "acquiring chamber," the very spot where the gas would be harvested, after which the gas would be stored in a large stainless steel tank connected to the chamber by a series of pipes. Corliss promised the world that acquiring chambers would be built wherever needed.

Ten long wooden benches sat in the middle of the control area, dividing it in half. Five faced the acquiring chamber and five faced the area where the technicians worked at their terminals around the power monitoring column.

Otto, Corliss and Dr. Clairet sat on the bench closest to the technician's area, joined by Representative Kaye. Königin sat alone on the bench closest to the acquiring chamber.

Turning around, Königin asked, "Mr. Corliss, where are the people from the Committee?"

"What people?" Corliss responded without turning around to face her.

"The delegates. I figured they would all want to be here," she said.

Instead of Corliss responding, Kaye turned around and glared at Königin across all of the empty benches. "They weren't invited. And that's not your concern," he said.

Königin sat back and said nothing. She took a deep breath and refused to let her anger muddle her thinking, even though she had started her day contemplating grabbing Corliss's neck with one hand and shoving *The Trustee* in his face with the other – and reminding him of yesterday's conversation about his press release. But she knew that she would be barred from participating if she succumbed to her rage toward that man. And as to Kaye, she didn't care much for him either or the way he spoke to her – but she chose to pick her fights prudently.

"Bringing power online," one of the technicians announced through his microphone, his voice echoing throughout the building.

Instantly the entire plant felt like it was waking from a deep sleep. Königin felt a vibration from the floor travel through Fight to her hand.

From where he sat, Dr. Clairet reached out and gently touched a concrete building column. "The turbines are turning," he said. Then he called out to the technicians and asked, "Are all turbines coming online?"

"Yes, sir. All ramping up to speed," a voice called out from the circles.

On top of the power column, a large display read "00:07:31 to Acquisition" – and it was counting down by the second.

The old plant started pulling in power for the ĒMAD. First, Nashville lost its electricity to the ĒMAD. Then Memphis. And over the next several minutes, millions of people, in one city after another, surrendered their power to the machine.

Königin stood up and slowly walked to the acquiring chamber. She put her boot on the first step and looked in.

"Dear, please move away from there," Dr. Clairet said, turning around from his seat.

The building shuddered.

"Königin, I'm not going to tell you again, move away from there," Dr. Clairet said, raising his voice.

She felt like she was seven years old again and back in her father's home laboratory.

"Königin, get away from there now," Dr. Clairet shouted.

"Ms. Clairet, just do what your father says," Corliss said in a hard voice.

Without turning around, Königin and Fight took a single exaggerated step back from the acquiring chamber.

"Approaching full power," a mechanical voice announced.

The building hummed.

The clock counted down to zeros.

An uneven light, flickering like a fire, immediately filled the chamber.

Otto and Corliss jumped to their feet and turned toward the

acquiring chamber – but they wouldn't move any closer to it. Some of the technicians gasped.

Dr. Clairet, now standing over the shoulder of one of the technicians in the smallest circle, gave instructions. "Standby, opening the portal," the voice now announced. Instantly, the light in the acquiring chamber disappeared, and a blackness in the chamber became darker and darker. It didn't look like black smoke filling the chamber, rather, it looked like the entire volume of the little room was a chunk of deep space, the glass walls of the acquiring chamber were like a window to somewhere else.

"All power committed," the voice dryly stated, and with that, the blackness turned into a deep opacity that Königin had never seen before. It wasn't blackness – it was emptiness, it was vacancy. The temperature of the control area dropped suddenly and Königin shivered.

Then, without warning, the Silence came.

Königin looked to her father and he looked back at her. She yelled for him but no sound would come out of her mouth. The whole world was silent.

But five seconds later, in the middle of everyone's yells, the Silence ended.

"Shutting down – insufficient power to control the size of the portal," the voice reported without emotion. The acquiring chamber flickered with light and then was empty.

Corliss ran up the stairs to the chamber.

"Anything? Did we collect any gas at all?" Corliss shouted as Dr. Clairet checked a gauge on the steel storage tank.

"Nothing," Dr. Clairet quietly said as he lowered himself onto one of the steps of the acquiring chamber's platform.

Königin looked at her father and saw that he was trying to avoid eye contact with her.

As Corliss interrogated Dr. Clairet about the failed test, Otto moved next to Königin and asked, "Ms. Clairet, the Silence – it came back. What is it?"

Königin shook her head. "I don't know."

"Is it related to your father's machine?" he asked.

Königin shrugged, and then after a moment, she said, "It must be. The Silence came when the machine opened the hole." She stared into the acquiring chamber and didn't move.

"What's wrong? Are you concerned?" Otto asked.

Königin didn't answer. She turned around to see Corliss and her father arguing.

"I'll do my part, Clairet. I'll go to the Committee and have them make their citizens crank enough power for the ĒMAD, but you'd better promise me it will work," Corliss yelled.

Dr. Clairet just nodded his head. The technicians all watched in silence.

"And remember, everyone, not a word about the timing of the Silence to anyone," Corliss announced, now standing on top of a swiveling chair while trying to keep his balance. "The official position is that today's test of the ĒMAD had nothing to do with the Silence – totally unrelated, a total coincidence."

Otto and Königin looked at each other but said nothing.

Corliss addressed Otto directly from atop the chair. "You know what you've got to do, Otto. Get on your stage and get the people ready to crank for their lives."

Then Corliss addressed the entire room again, saying "No more tests. The next time that we start the ĒMAD we are going to push it until it delivers!"

68

"Corliss's people are dopes, Königin – but they're vicious dopes." Jess said.

"I have no doubt," she replied.

"No, you don't understand," Jess said, shaking his head. He sat at the edge of his cot in a makeshift bedroom in the power plant.

"Jess, what's going on? Tell me," Königin said.

"While you were at the test this morning I wandered around the plant."

"They let you do that?" she asked.

"They didn't know. Like I said, they're dopes."

"Okay, I get that – so what happened? Did someone threaten you? It certainly wouldn't be the first time," Königin said, trying to playfully smile.

Jess didn't smile back.

"I went up to the roof – I wanted to see if your camping minions had grown. When I got up there, I found a little penthouse that's an old communications room. I doubt anybody's been up there for years – all of the equipment was caked in dust. I'm sure Corliss's idiots don't even know about it."

"Okay, so what's in there?" Königin asked.

"I'm getting to that. Please, just let me tell my story the way I want to tell it," Jess said.

Königin rolled her eyes.

"Mostly television monitors and a bunch of radio equipment."

"Does any of it still work?" Königin asked.

Jess nodded. "I was able to connect to the Whole Truth Information Trust's incoming video feeds – they've tapped into practically every surveillance camera in the world. I was able to look at the streets of San Francisco and the hallways of Parliament in London. I had my choice of thousands of views."

Königin impatiently nodded and said, "That's troubling – but not at all surprising. Is that what you're so upset about?"

Jess shook his head. "There's a whole shortwave radio broadcasting setup in there. I'm sure it's there in case of an emergency – to get information out to the people."

"Yeah, uh-huh, sounds right," Königin said, now motioning with her hands to Jess to speed the story up.

"Just settle down, Königin," Jess said. "I'm not dragging this out to annoy you – it's just that I can't bear to tell you the end of the story."

Königin took a deep breath and said, "I'm sorry, Jess." Then she sat down next to him on the cot.

"I turned the radio's receiver on and tried to find anything that might be on the air. I turned the tuning dial really slowly – and eventually I picked up a faint broadcast. It was a non-*Trustee* newscast – you know, a rogue newscast."

Königin nodded slowly.

"Well, apparently, there was a rogue newspaper being printed in Philadelphia. It was started by a former *Trustee* reporter – Wilson, Wilson. I can't remember her first name," Jess said shaking his head. "Anyhow, their little paper was actually reporting the news – you know, digging around and reporting facts. It sounds like the type of newspaper we always took for granted – no propaganda, no agenda, no taking sides – just old-fashioned impartial journalism."

Königin smiled and nodded. "I would love to get my hands on one of those papers. We need a paper like that to start printing right here in Nashville – we need them everywhere," she said. "The people need facts."

Jess looked down and said, "It's not going to happen, Könignin – at least not anytime soon."

Königin gently rubbed Jess's shoulder. "Go on, Jess."

"Do you remember the thing being exhibited at the Water Pavilion called the Plate, the device that could instantly disintegrate anything?" Jess asked, the pitch of his voice rising.

Königin's hand froze on Jess's shoulder. She didn't respond.

Jess turned and locked eyes with Königin. "They plated everyone involved with that newspaper. And then they plated the printing press itself. All reduced to a handful of ashes."

69

"Quiet, please. Delegates, please, take your seats," Corliss instructed from his podium on the stage of an old symphony hall.

The Committee's Nashville meeting chamber buzzed on at the same volume. The delegates walked up and down the aisles and through the rows, talking and shaking hands with each other.

"Everyone, quiet," Corliss said, his voice growing louder.

Still no response.

Corliss pursed his lips and put his hands on his hips, surveying the crowd, seeking a chance encounter of eyes he could stare into silence. But no one was looking at him, except Malcolm. Corliss waved him up to the podium.

"Get them quiet, now," Corliss said.

Malcolm smiled at Corliss and then quickly put his lips directly on the microphone and yelled, "Shut up, all of you. Shut up."

Immediately the delegates fell silent and felt behind them for their seats as they sat, not taking their eyes off of Malcolm's face.

Malcolm nodded to Corliss and then descended the steps and took an empty seat in the hall's front row.

Corliss surveyed the members of the ĒMAD Governing Committee before him, savoring their immediate submission.

"Now that I finally have your attention, delegates, I bring to you today a matter of most pressing importance. As you know, this morning's test of the Essential Material Acquisition Device revealed that it's not yet fully operational – and that's because the people need to step up a little more and contribute a lot more. Simply put, they're not yet doing their part."

"Chairman Corliss, could you detail the results of the test? Perhaps give us a bit of insight as to what happened?" asked Mr. Tillman, the delegate from Canada. "Oh, and sir, why were we not invited to the test?"

"Please, please, Delegate Tillman, I won't tolerate such interruptions," Corliss said with a reprimanding finger.

"Yes, Chairman Corliss, why could we not attend?" another delegate asked. Now the hall began to fill with a murmur of discussion.

"This is ridiculous, delegates," Corliss said, shaking his head. "That matter is not up for debate or discussion – the Collaborative has made it clear to me that the security and confidentiality of the project cannot be compromised by having anyone other than essential personnel present during operation of the ĒMAD. And I needn't remind you that every nation represented here owes obligations and liabilities to the Collaborative, so their word is final."

"We're non-essential, are we?" Mr. Tillman asked.

"Stop this, please," Corliss said, banging his fist on the podium. "This line of discussion is very disruptive to our process and I ask that you all focus on the primary issue here, which is that in order for the machine to work, we need a lot more power."

A collective moan filled the hall.

"This is going to be a problem, Señor Corliss, a big problem. My people are losing patience and they're tired of living without electricity most of the time," said Mexico's delegate.

Then Ms. Abara of Nigeria stood and cleared her throat. "You've got to be kidding us, Mr. Corliss. You need more power to get your machine to work?"

"Yes, that's right. And the people – the beneficiaries of the machine – must generate that power," Corliss said.

"How much more can you ask of them, Mr. Corliss? Next, you'll be asking for their very life-force, right?" Abara said. The hall fell silent.

Corliss straightened his back and put his hands on his hips and said, "I can't believe this – so now I'm the bad guy. I simply can't believe it. To be attacked like this – it's hurtful." Corliss shook his head and looked down. "After all that this committee has been through, working as partners, showing each other the respect not only to be accorded to all human beings, but especially the respect deserved by all of us here who have done nothing but put aside our own self-interests in sacrifice so that all may live better lives." Corliss covered his eyes with his hands.

"What nonsense," Abara said. "I can't listen to any more of this. Delegates, listen to me–"

"Delegate Abara, you do not have the floor, you must observe our parliamentary procedures before you are allowed to speak," Corliss said.

"I don't need your permission to speak, Corliss – I don't need anyone's permission to speak." She then stood on her seat and started to address the delegates. "How is it that none of us have ever even seen the inside of the New Hickory Power Plant? And now I'm hearing from people that if the machine malfunctions, it could destroy the planet. We need more information, Corliss."

As Delegate Abara continued on, Corliss looked up into the boxes of the symphony hall high above. They were all empty, except the one farthest from the stage. In the darkness of the box, Corliss could see the silhouettes of several people rising from their seats, watching in silence.

"Malcolm," Corliss shouted while pointing at Abara.

A few seconds later, Malcolm grabbed Delegate Abara by her ankles and pulled her legs out from underneath her. She fell, hitting her head on the back of her seat. The other delegates stood and watched as Malcolm and three other members of Corliss's security detail carried her out, bleeding and unconscious.

Corliss again looked up at the box and now saw the dark outlines of the watching people sit back down.

"Sit down," Corliss instructed the delegates. They complied.

"I had Delegate Abara removed as a favor to everyone, and I hope that you can appreciate the necessity of what I just did. And what just happened should remind you all of how important this matter is. We're at a crossroads in the history of humanity, and it's my duty, my charge and my responsibility to shepherd this body of delegates to achieve something for all mankind. For thousands of years, people have yearned to satisfy their most basic needs, but this cruel and unfair world has denied them time and again. And I needn't tell you that today the world finds itself in its deepest despair in want of the most basic essentials of life – to a degree never before seen. But thankfully, the answer to that yearning, the answer to that despair lays right in front of us, within our grasp – and we'll have no one to blame but ourselves if we fail to walk the final yard in the journey to our salvation. Time has run out, our world needs help right now, and if the Silence dares visit us again before we've achieved our goal, the resulting mayhem and anarchy will be uncontrollable."

A civil applause filled the hall.

Emboldened, Corliss continued in a solid voice. "In light of today's developments, and seeing that there may be dissenters among us whose values differ from those of our healthy majority, I think it's important – no, I think it's crucial, that we clearly identify who stands where amongst us. We're at an intersection that calls into question our most fundamental beliefs and we must clearly demark who cares about the future of humanity and who doesn't. I've learned today that I'm just not the same as some other people on this committee – and they're different from me. You could say, we are not alike. But that's all right, because we must foster and cherish tolerance in our new society, and I will be the first to say now that I respect the notions of others which differ from my mine. I understand and accept that people form positions on matters for a variety of reasons, sometimes regardless of the merits underlying those positions. And I understand

and accept that people are confused and scared and often cannot find the courage to stand for what we all know is right. To those people, I extend my hand to them today and say join us so that we may not miss this once in a lifetime – no, once ever opportunity, to rid humanity of misery and install in its place everlasting prosperity and happiness. And to those people who refuse to join us, who refuse to require their countrymen to provide the power necessary to help the ĒMAD succeed, let me say this – you do not have the best interests of humankind as your priority. And that's what separates you from us. We are different." Corliss slowly scanned the delegates, looking many in the eye. "As we proceed in these delicate moments, I know that my conscience will not allow me to idly chat with and sit next to those of my fellow delegates who so profoundly differ from me in the most fundamental ways. To that end, I suggest that we divide this great hall into two seating sections, reserving the back rows for the Doubters that wish to taint this committee, and the front rows for those who have the fortitude, integrity and bravery to fight for humanity. Let each side sit with its brothers and sisters so that we may find peace and strength in the unity of our position and comfort from our unity against our enemies."

The delegates looked around the hall at each other but no one rose from their seats.

"Come now, if you need to move to the back of the hall, please do so immediately," Corliss instructed. Malcolm stood next to Corliss on the stage with his arms crossed, smiling at the delegates.

Not a single delegate stood up.

Corliss nodded and clapped slowly. "Now I'm touched. The unity and love in here is just what we need to get the job done. Thank you, thank you all."

"Finish it," shouted a delegate. "Here, here," said another. Corliss waved his arms in an upward motion calling for more support, which came in the form of shouts, whistles and applause. He smiled broadly and held his clasped hands above his head.

"Very good – let's not waste a minute," Corliss said. "Your people will produce the energy needed by the ĒMAD by simply turning their *cranks*. Plug into an electrical outlet and turn the handle – that's it. Everyone must do it, regardless of age. The people will give life to the machine – this will be their final sacrifice. They'll get what they need and the Guiding Institutions Collaborative will be rewarded and compensated for its generous support."

One by one the delegates stood and applauded.

"And don't miss Otto Veltraria's broadcast tonight," Corliss added. "When he's done singing his sermon, the people will be grateful to turn the crank."

⊶ 70 ⊷

That evening's edition of *The Trustee* was no larger than a postcard, and like a postcard, it had only two sides.

One side carried a single article about the Essential Material Acquisition Device, and the other side had a drawing of a "crank" with detailed instructions on how to use it.

The drawing showed a hand-held gadget with two flat sides and one rounded end and one tapered end, from which a short red power cord hung. A revolving handle protruded from one of the flat sides and the grill of a little speaker broke the even surface of the other side.

All 128 *Trustee* printing plants around the world printed at full capacity. The word "SUCCESS" covered the top third of the postcard in large type.

The story read:

NASHVILLE, TENNESSEE, USA

This morning, the Essential Material Acquisition Device performed perfectly in its trial run. The system achieved its benchmark targets in every category of operation. Dr. Clairet, the magnificent mind behind the society saving technology, told the *Trustee* that more power will allow the ĒMAD to work much more efficiently. Consequently,

Chairman Corliss and the ĒMAD Governing Committee have issued an order requiring the citizens of all participating nations to assist in the production of energy to power the ĒMAD. Each person must continuously turn their crank for three hours tomorrow starting at 08:00 hours, Central Standard Time, exactly one hour before the ĒMAD will officially be brought online for the first time.

Due to the wisdom and forethought of the Association of Comprehensive Solutions, but unbeknownst to the people in an effort to prevent unwarranted concern and anxiety, millions of cranks were manufactured over the past month. As of this afternoon, the distribution of cranks to everyone everywhere was well underway and will continue throughout the night.

At a special meeting of the Committee convened late this morning to approve the order to crank, the delegates unanimously pledged the support of their nations in the required effort to generate more power for the ĒMAD, even going so far as agreeing to impose criminal penalties on those citizens who fail to turn their cranks as instructed. Every person four years of age and older who has one hand capable of turning the handle of the crank must contribute to the effort. Compliance with the order will be monitored through each crank's ability to identify the operator of that crank and all information about that person.

With the occurrence of the Silence this morning stoking more fear of the unexplained phenomenon, and the rapidly increasing scarcity of food and other necessaries around the planet, the need to bring the Essential Material Acquisition Device online immediately is critical. (See the reverse side of this edition of *The Whole Truth Trustee* for detailed instructions on how to plug the crank into an electrical outlet and turn the handle so you too can fulfill your duty to participate in powering the machine.)

When the ĒMAD is started tomorrow, Otto Veltraria will treat the world to a special live broadcast from the very headquarters of the machine. In today's upbeat session of the Committee, Chairman Corliss told the delegates that only Otto would be exempt from turning a crank tomorrow as he'll be mobilizing the people in their final pursuit of mankind's material needs.

Königin Clairet, who boasted that she will be turning two cranks tomorrow morning, was visibly jubilant after today's test of the ĒMAD.

⇌ 71 ⇌

Gin.
 The smell bit Königin's face.

The taste of toothpaste was still fresh in her mouth, but the stench cloud surrounding her father made her want to start her morning ritual all over again.

"Dad, are you crazy? What are you doing?"

"It's a big day, Königin," Dr. Clairet said, holding his coffee mug up in a mock toast.

Königin took the mug from her father and smelled its contents, immediately regretting the deep snort.

"The big ugly machine that we've built is going to swallow up the world today. But who knows, maybe we'll find mom."

Königin ignored her father and said, "Dad, we're less than an hour away from bringing the system online – the people are already cranking. Why would you do this?" Königin asked, holding the mug in front of her father's face.

"Königin, I'm so sorry," Dr. Clairet said, letting himself down onto a chair.

"Dad, what's going on?"

Dr. Clairet looked down at the floor and just shook his head.

Königin crossed her arms and said, "It doesn't work, does it?"

"Well, not really – at least not yet."

Königin slowly sat down next to him.

"Do you just need more time?" she asked.

"I need more everything. Or at least the machine does. It needs more power. It's insatiable. That's always been the problem."

Königin remained silent and looked at her father in his rumpled lab coat.

After a moment, Dr. Clairet said, "We have enough power to get it started, but the problem is that once the machine's alive and going, it takes an enormous amount of power to control it – an impossible amount of power. We just won't be able to control the thing."

"What happens if you can't control it?" Königin asked.

"What happens if you lose control of anything? Bad things happen," Dr. Clairet said.

"If it looks like we're going to lose control of the ĒMAD, can't we just cut the power?"

Dr. Clairet shook his head. "Königin, don't be a child – you should know this – once you breathe life into an enterprise of any kind, there's a point of no return after a certain degree of momentum is achieved. It's no different with the ĒMAD."

"Look, Dad, I think you're a little hysterical. You're exhausted. You're nervous. This is your life's work and there's so much at stake. Please, don't let your fear get in the way of what you need to do."

Königin and Dr. Clairet sat in silence in a quiet narrow hallway away from the action in the control area where the technicians were preparing to start the machine.

Dr. Clairet continued to look down at the floor.

"Königin, I'm telling you, if the machine gets out of control, it will be bad," Dr. Clairet said.

"Dad, you're a scientist, could you be a little bit more specific?"

Dr. Clairet hesitated, and then spoke slowly.

"Without enough power to modulate the size of the portal that the ĒMAD opens into the adjacent dimension, the entire planet could be swallowed up into the ever-expanding gateway, flicked like a marble into a rabbit hole, essentially disappearing to some unknown place and unknown fate."

Königin laughed. "Oh, come on Dad. Now I think you're just being dramatic. That's what happens when you drink a gin and tonic at 8:00 in the morning. There's just no evidence that the machine creates a two-way portal."

At first, Dr. Clairet didn't respond and didn't look up at Königin. But after a moment, he said, "There is."

Dr. Clairet patted the empty seat next to him. "Sit down, Königin." She slowly sat down. Dr. Clairet opened his mouth to speak but nothing came out.

"What?" Königin asked.

Dr. Clairet shook his head without looking at Königin. He wiped away a tear that was starting its way down his cheek.

"What is it, Dad?"

"You know, Königin, I loved your mother very much. And I would never do anything to hurt her, but–"

Königin drew in a deep gasp and breathlessly said, "You sent my mother down the rabbit hole, didn't you?" With her eyes as wide open as could be, she searched her father's face for a reaction.

"Königin," Dr. Clairet said quietly.

"Oh my God, my mother is floating around in some unknown existence that you threw her into!"

"I didn't throw her anywhere, Königin. It was an accident. And who knows, maybe she's still alive."

Königin shook her head. "What is wrong with you? It scares me that we share blood." Then she jumped up and shouted quietly through her teeth, "She's dead, Dad. She's dead to me, she's dead to everyone that knew her. She isn't here. She hasn't been here for more than twenty years."

"Königin, who knows what death is? She may be alive somewhere."

"Stop it, Dad. Don't give me any of your bullshit. You goddamn know what I mean."

"Königin, I swear, it was an accident. I told her to stay out of my lab."

"So you're saying it was *her* fault?"

"No, no, of course not," Dr. Clairet said.

"And that damned machine is causing the Silence. Yesterday I told myself that it was okay, that the Silence was just some harmless but unavoidable side effect of the machine's operation – I fell right back into the habit of lying to myself. I couldn't bring myself to face what the Silence has done to the psyche of the world. And I'm so mad at myself for not speaking up when Corliss ordered us to lie about the Silence." Königin paused and took a deep breath. "Every time that machine starts, the Silence comes, right? Like it did the first time on the day that Mom vanished."

"Yes," Dr. Clairet said quietly.

"It's maddening that I never tied those two occurrences together," Königin said, swallowing hard and trying not to cry.

"I know, for such a smart girl, you would think–"

"Does David know?" Königin asked, interrupting her father.

Dr. Clairet looked down at the floor and didn't answer.

"There's my answer," Königin said. "No wonder he hates you."

The two sat in silence.

"I'm so sorry," Dr. Clairet said. "I know you must be so disappointed in me. I was always afraid of what you'd think of me if you knew the truth, but I'm relieved that you now know. But you must believe me that I would never do anything to hurt you or David or your mother."

Königin looked into Dr. Clairet's eyes. "You know what, Dad, I can't even think about myself right now. How could you give the people of this world such false hope? They're already so down."

"Königin, I really thought I could get it to work. Corliss was giving me everything I needed. He pushed me, you know."

"No, Dad – don't give me that," Königin said. "You'd better accept responsibility for this. No blaming and no excuses – we've all had enough of that already and look at the damage it's done."

Königin shook her head. "The whole world's going to melt down when the people hear that there is no ĒMAD."

"Maybe you can keep the people calm, Königin. You've built quite a following. You're so brave – I never knew. I'm a weakling."

"I know, Dad, you are," Königin said, patting her father's shoulder. "But we'll go to Corliss together and we'll try to make him understand why the ĒMAD can't be started this morning – or perhaps ever. We need to confront this situation head-on and accept the consequences, whatever they may be."

72

Königin and Dr. Clairet sat on a stained little sofa in a window-less office that served as a makeshift holding cell. Königin held her father's hand on her lap.

"The machine is ramping up, I can feel it in the floor," Dr. Clairet said.

Königin didn't respond. She toyed with Fight in her free hand. Dr. Clairet opened his mouth to speak, perhaps to tell her to stop fiddling with it, but he quickly closed his mouth without issuing a reprimand.

"Dad."

"Yes?"

"I saw David. He's in Nashville. Or at least he was."

"Königin, you should have told me right away," Dr. Clairet said, somewhat breathless from the revelation. "How is he? Is he all right?"

"I don't know, Dad. He said that Corliss's people were looking for him."

Dr. Clairet looked down at the floor and shook his head. "He's so sweet in his own way – but so misguided, Königin. He despairs for humanity itself, and he thinks it's his mission to help people at any cost and by any means. I'm afraid he's mixed himself up with some dangerous people in that endeavor."

"Misguided, Dad? Try *unguided* – since he was a kid."

Dr. Clairet ignored her comment. "But you're the real deal, Königin," he said, putting his arm around his daughter's shoulder. "You're more interested in producing results for people, not spectacles. You care, and you focus your abilities on achieving successes that matter. I'm humbled and awed by what you've accomplished. And you did it for you as much as you did it for anyone else, and that's the key – knowing that you're realizing and meeting your potential and knowing what makes you glad to be alive. That was the constant rhythm of thought that your mother beat her soul's drum to. You instinctively know that secret, Königin. Me, I'm just a circus act – and I know that now and I can accept that. But you must never accept less from yourself – you need to fix your machine and send water again, and lead people righteously, and do many other magnificent things for yourself and this world."

Königin nodded slowly. "I hope I have that chance, Dad. But Corliss needs to let us out of here before anything can be achieved – or at least disaster avoided."

Dr. Clairet grasped her shoulders and said, "Listen to me, Königin. I don't know what's going to happen – today, tomorrow, if there is a tomorrow, or even ten years from now, but you figure out what to do and fight like hell to do it, no matter what."

Königin smiled at her at father. "I've already made that commitment to myself, Dad. It's taken me some time, and after too many years, I'm finally welcoming myself home – and that's made me more powerful than I could have ever imagined."

⌬⤙ 73 ⤚⌬

Over the years, Otto had turned down several offers to perform night after night in Las Vegas. He felt that it would "commoditize" him, as he told his friends. But performing at some plastically opulent hotel on the strip would have been better than this, he thought, as he smiled into one of the cameras.

Otto Veltraria was performing from a studio built in a large storage room only a hundred feet from the ĒMAD's control area.

Between songs, Otto would grab his crank from atop his keyboard and crank away, singing little jingles that he made up on the spot.

"We could probably squeeze twenty people in here. Come on, we need an audience," he said to the new stage manager "appointed" by Corliss.

"Sorry, no audience, sir – the chairman's orders." Otto shook his head.

The people of the world had their choice – they could watch Otto on any one of the three Whole Truth Information Trust's television stations.

"We're only fifteen minutes away from bringing the Essential Material Acquisition Device to life," Otto said, forcing a smile. "This is it, everyone, we need to work together and power up our miracle machine. There's something in it for everyone," he sang.

From behind his keyboard, Otto saw Jess quietly enter through an unguarded door nearby. Jess motioned with his head for Otto to come to him.

Immediately, two of Corliss's men descended on Jess. Otto motioned to his bandleader to keep things moving as he jumped up from his piano bench and grabbed Jess's arm and addressed the guards in a hushed voice.

"He's my biographer, let him be."

"Nope. The chairman said that no one is allowed in here without his permission," one of the guards said, shaking his head.

"But this is my show, my stage. Probably the most important act of my life," Otto shouted in a stage whisper.

Jess shook his head and said, "You're wrong, Otto."

"Wrong? What do you mean *wrong*? About what?" Otto asked.

"All of it," Jess said. "The whole thing."

The sound of glass shattering on the other side of the room immediately seized everyone's attention. A stage light on a stand had tipped over and smashed on the concrete floor. The two guards unhanded Jess and ran toward the smoking light. Otto's bass player, who was standing only a foot from the destroyed light, nodded to Otto – and Otto mouthed the words "thank you" to him. He then turned back to Jess.

"What is it now, Jess? And what are you even doing here? I can't imagine why you'd be allowed within 100 miles of Nashville – I figured they would have thrown you out of town by now – or worse."

"They're keeping me here – but forget about that, Otto. Just listen to me before they get me. The machine doesn't work. It won't work. I just saw Königin and her dad telling Corliss that it won't work."

"But that can't be. What about all of this?" Otto said, motioning around and above his head at the building that surrounded him.

"What about it?" Jess asked.

"It has to work – the people – entire nations – the world has put everything into this. This is the solution we've been hoping for," Otto said, breathlessly.

"Hope isn't going to make it work, Otto," Jess said.

"But I have to keep going and believe that it will work," Otto replied.

"Dr. Clairet has stopped lying to himself – so don't you start lying to yourself about this thing, now that you know the truth," Jess said.

"But what about Corliss? I need to talk to Corliss. What's he doing about this?"

"He had Königin and her dad gagged and taken away. And his security detail took away the few technicians that overheard," Jess said.

Otto felt dizzy. He propped himself up on his keyboard. "The people are going to be crushed."

"Indeed, quite literally," Jess said.

"What does that mean?" Otto asked.

"According to Dr. Clairet, the project that you so lovingly sponsored will actually cause the planet to be swallowed whole by some adjacent dimension when the machine gets out of control – which it will."

Otto stared at Jess, not a word coming out of his mouth.

"And you know that crazy silence that's been scaring the daylights out of all of us? Well, that comes when the ĒMAD's portal opens," Jess said.

"Then why is Corliss moving forward?" Otto shouted at Jess.

"He figures that he's screwed if the thing doesn't work, so he might as well roll the dice on the off chance that it will work. Nothing to lose."

"Nothing to lose?" Otto said, now squatting on the floor because he could no longer stand. "How about every human being alive? And my dog?" He shook his head, and after a moment added, "and Althea."

Otto looked up at Jess and said, "You've always known, haven't you?"

"Known what, Otto?"

"That this journey would end badly."

Jess didn't answer.

The two guards looked over at Jess from across the room and began to make their way toward him

"Goodbye, Otto," Jess said as he started to run.

"I thought it was my destiny to help," Otto shouted to Jess.

"It is," Jess shouted back to him before he disappeared through the door.

74

Around the world, millions of people plugged themselves in and turned their cranks furiously.

Like slowly rising mercury in a thermometer, the little red lights on the power column crept upward as energy flowed into the machine.

"We're getting there!" one of the technicians in the ĒMAD control center called out.

75

David's teeth chattered as he slowly waded into Old Hickory Lake from its muddy banks, struggling to hold his little rolling suitcase above his head. His wet tie tugged at his neck and the bank's foliage that provided cover poked his face.

A hundred yards in front of him, across the still body of water, David could see the power plant's smokestacks and its flagless flagpole reaching up from the downstream side of the dam.

"They can't help themselves," David said out loud. "They just can't. And it's not their fault." He was certain that it was up to him to make sure that the ĒMAD didn't chain the legs of the people.

David made it to the edge of the dam and carefully pushed his suitcase onto its narrow lip. Then he slowly lifted himself out of the water and onto the dam, lying next to his suitcase, trying to catch his breath. David shuddered as he looked down the sheer face of the dam to the churning water five hundred feet below, but he smiled when he saw the glowing power plant.

76

Königin and Dr. Clairet quickly looked up as the door of their improvised holding cell flung open.

Representative Kaye entered without saying a word and closed the door behind him.

"You need to let us out of here – right now," Königin said loudly.

"I'm afraid I can't do that, Ms. Clairet," Kaye responded.

"You must stop the ĒMAD immediately, Kaye," Königin said in a firm voice.

"I'm sorry, Ms. Clairet, but you won't be giving out orders today," he said. "And I'm sorry that you won't be witnessing the miracle of your machine, doctor."

"There won't be any miracle – there will only be destruction," Königin said.

"I doubt that," Kaye said, smiling. "In fact, I think you're both liars." His smile quickly faded.

"If you're not going to listen to us, then why are you here? What do you want from us?" Königin asked.

Kaye smiled again and said, "Three things. And I'm quite sure I'll get them all."

Königin and Dr. Clairet looked at each other.

"Number one, but in no particular order of importance, I want your makeshift cane back, Ms. Clairet."

Königin squinted in confusion and leaned toward Kaye as if to hear him better. "What?" she asked.

"Number two, Dr. Clairet, I need you to provide me with the shortwave broadcasting frequency that you had the radios in the cranks tuned to. Apparently, no one seems to know – except you, I'm told. We'll be simulcasting Otto on the cranks – just in case the televisions lose power."

"Wait, back up – what do you mean you want my walking staff *back*?" Königin asked.

Kaye laughed and said, "You will find it interesting to know that what you've been hobbling around on is not a staff or cane at all, Ms. Clairet – it's the missing Mace of the House of Representatives."

Königin drew in a deep breath but said nothing.

"And when I say *back*, I really mean that I need to return it to its rightful owner from whom it was stolen," Kaye said.

She remained speechless.

"But since I have a caring and kind heart, I'm going to let you continue to use it as we accomplish the third thing that I require."

"Representative Kaye, I'm sorry – I had no idea that it was the mace. I'm so sorry. I'm very glad that you'll be returning it to the House," Königin said.

Kaye broke into a short loud laugh, and then said, "No, Ms. Clairet – that thing is the property of my benefactor for whom I confiscated it from the House years ago. It was then stolen from his private collection of goodies. He'll be delighted to have it back."

"You fucker," Königin said quietly.

"Königin, please," Dr. Clairet said.

"And number three?" Königin asked, staring hard at Kaye.

"Ah, number three," he said. "I'm afraid you're really not going to like number three, but at least it won't be too painful. You'll be using your *cane* or *staff*, or whatever you like to call it, on your way to the Plate – it awaits both of you."

Königin slowly stood up and steadied herself with Fight.

"The world thanks you both for your service to humanity, but we can't have a couple of Doubters around," Kaye said.

"Königin, I'm so sorry," Dr. Clairet said, shrunken.

"What's the broadcasting frequency, Dr. Clairet?" Kaye asked curtly.

"Don't tell him, Dad!"

Kaye leaned down and grabbed Dr. Clairet by the collar, shouting, "Now! Give it to me now!"

The old man's body rocked in Kaye's clenched fist.

Königin flipped her wrist and drew Fight back, far behind her head.

While still holding onto Dr. Clairet's collar, Kaye turned toward Königin, drawn into her eyes.

"I'm sorry," she said as she brought the mace down on Kaye's head with one smooth swing. The moment before Königin saw his face covered in blood, she saw that surprised look that bullies get when you stand up to them.

Königin took Dr. Clairet's hand and helped him step over Kaye's body and out of the office that had been their cell.

77

Otto waved the horns down and they fell silent. He shook his head at his drummer and then his bass player. They both stopped playing. Soon the entire band was quiet, giving the little stage to Otto alone as he slowly played somber notes on his keyboard.

"Now I have my final verse," he said, before beginning to sing softly.

So here I am, on the other side
My heart was pure – but perhaps I lied
I thought it was you that I came to save
But in the light I see it now
It was me for whom I braved
All I have is my final bow
I'll wear no crown bestowed by you
That young Lee Earlman really knew
It's me, me, Otto, who must be shown the door
As the world cries to know who's really the whore

The band looked at each other for answers that no one had.

"Ninety percent power achieved," the mechanical voice announced from the control area.

Otto looked up and saw on a monitor in front of him that the red lights had almost reached the top of the power column. He hit the keys harder and harder as he played.

And then Otto's keyboard died – it was silent. No more music.

Otto knew that it was dead, but he kept playing it anyway. It was quiet, except for the sound of his flesh hitting the cold keys. But after a few moments, his fingers stopped moving.

The Whole Truth Information Trust's television channels switched their broadcast to a recording of one of Otto's concerts a few days earlier.

The double doors of the storage room opened and two of Corliss's men entered.

Otto stood up slowly from his piano bench and took a deep breath. Then he slipped his shoes off.

He gently bowed to his band, and then stepped out from behind his keyboard. By the time that one of Corliss's men began to speak, Otto had bolted past both of them, out of his little studio.

78

Königin hid her father in a janitor's closet and instructed him not to leave.

With the help of Fight, she took three steps at a time up the rusted metal staircase to the roof of the building.

A thin slice of blue light creeping out of the partially opened door of the penthouse communications room told Königin that somebody was already in there. She considered turning around, but instead, she kept moving forward. Königin heard switches flipping and saw the escaping light of the room growing brighter. She drew Fight behind her head and nudged the door open with her foot.

"Stop fooling around and get in here," a stern voice said from a dark spot of the small broadcast facility.

Königin exhaled. It was Jess. He stepped into the light of the control console and continued to tinker.

"I think we're too late. Your dad's baby is hitting full power any second," Jess said.

One of the switches Jess had flipped brought a few television screens to life. Now they were watching the ĒMAD's control area from various angles.

"Shit," Königin said as the top of the power column lit up like a game show set piece celebrating a winner. Jess looked at Königin and intertwined her fingers with his.

The Silence came.

They both watched the acquiring chamber through one of the screens. There was no sound at all.

The chamber began to darken, and the space within the glass began to disappear into itself.

Then Otto appeared on the screen, running toward to the acquiring chamber.

Königin shoved her face two inches from the television. From the high angle of the camera aimed at the chamber, she saw the top of Otto's head of flowing gray and black hair as he pulled the glass door open. He hesitated for a brief moment and hung his head. And then Otto entered the chamber. The guards chasing him stopped short of the door and refused to follow him.

The chamber blinked black and white and the Silence ended abruptly. The technicians shouted, "get him out" and "it's losing power."

Masses of black and white and gray strobed rapidly in the acquiring chamber, like a carnival attraction.

Then the chamber was clear. It was empty. Totally empty. Otto was gone.

"No," Königin said to the screen.

The red lights on the column had sunk.

Königin lowered herself into an old office chair at the console. She forced herself to look at Jess.

He stared at the screen that showed technicians running around the control area, playing with the dials and yanking handles.

"So, that's it. Otto Veltraria's grand finale," Jess said as he hung his head and started to clap slowly.

"I'm sorry, Jess," Königin said. Then she added, "Maybe he'll find my mom."

Jess quickly turned to Königin, his eyes wide. "What?" he asked.

"Yeah. My dad just told me," Königin said. "What's in there, Jess?" Königin asked, her voice cracking. "I know it's an opening to another dimension, but is it a passage to another reality? Or is it death? Maybe they're the same thing?"

Jess shrugged his shoulders, but before he could speak, Corliss's voice broke out of one of the televisions. He had taken Otto's place.

"You'd all better be cranking as if your life depends on it, because it does," Corliss shouted from inside of Otto's little studio. "If we don't get the power up for the ĒMAD right now, we're all doomed, all will be lost. Crank as hard as you can. You must join me," Corliss said, cranking his own crank on camera. Corliss and his words were broadcast around the world to every working television screen.

The red lights gradually began to creep up the power column again.

"Otto only wounded it, he didn't kill it," Jess said. "It's coming back."

"Here's the broadcasting frequency for the cranks' radios," Königin said as she held the globe-end of Fight in front of Jess's face – the numbers in black marker were written in Dr. Clairet's perfect handwriting. Jess quickly set the transmitting equipment up. "Get this mic hot," Königin said as she tapped on the old microphone perched in front of her.

"It's ready to go. Are you?" Jess asked.

Königin nodded. "Let's go, no time to waste," she said.

The words "no time to waste" crackled out of every crank on the planet.

"Hello, my name is Königin," Jess whispered playfully as he held his laughter in. She waved her finger at him.

"This is Königin Clairet," she announced. "Please, stop turning your cranks." She paused and then resumed, "Please – stop now! Stop turning your cranks! The ĒMAD doesn't work. It's deadly and it's what's been causing the Silence."

"You'll need to do better than that, Königin," Jess said, laughing.

On the television, Corliss waved his crank in the air and shouted to his security detail, "Find her, she can't be far – she's somewhere here in the plant!"

Then Corliss addressed the camera directly. "Keep turning your cranks if you know what's good for you. Ignore that woman, she's crazy. She's sick. She's dangerous," Corliss shouted.

"So now I'm crazy, sick and dangerous, Mr. Corliss?" Königin said in a tinny voice that came out of the cranks. "You spoke kindly of me yesterday when I lent my support for the ĒMAD project – something I now concede was a mistake for many reasons," she added.

"You're interfering, Königin Clairet. When we find you you'll be punished," Corliss shouted. "And anyone found not cranking will be punished as well," Corliss said as he shook his crank toward the camera.

With each threat from Corliss, the red lights crept toward the top of the power column.

Königin cleared her throat.

"Stop cranking. Stop powering this machine that will only hurt us, not help us," she said.

"She's just noise, don't listen to her," Corliss said. "She's the enemy, she's working against you. *The Whole Truth Trustee* itself witnessed and certified the successful test of the ĒMAD. *The Trustee*, for goodness sake – it staked its reputation on the ĒMAD."

"*The Trustee*," Königin said, laughing. "*The Whole Truth Trustee* lied – the ĒMAD never worked." Königin paused and then continued calmly. "Open your minds and listen, *The Trustee's* function isn't to find and inform us of the truth – no, *The Trustee* is nothing more than an instrument of the Collaborative. It lies – but even worse than that, *The Trustee* keeps us distracted from the truth by dividing us into competing factions on every issue, splitting us over and over again with every new situation. That makes us weak and malleable while the Collaborative's agenda of the day is being carried out. Whether it's the skyrocketing cost of living life or the Full-Life Loans to pay for it all or our new burden of procuring a clearance certificate so we can reclaim our fundamental rights, *The Trustee* helps the Collaborative get away with whatever it wants to as we shift our focus from what's really happening to us."

"She's reprehensible. Disgusting. A monster. We'll all die if you don't keep cranking," Corliss shouted.

"Enough," Königin said firmly. "They constantly lob word grenades at us with the intention of instigating fights amongst us – they want us to hate each other – just think about why there were two sides of *The Trustee*. Once you take a step back from it all, it becomes so clear. But I think deep down you all know this already – just as I did, but I wouldn't let myself see it. We lie to ourselves, we hide from the truth – and I've learned that there's nothing more dangerous than that. I've been doing it my entire life, but no more."

Königin paused. Low pops of static came out of the cranks' little speakers. She continued, "But none of this is new. Humanity will continue to go through this process over and over until we learn the lessons that we already know to be true. But if you keep cranking life into the machine today, I believe we'll deny ourselves the opportunity to perhaps one day get it right. With every turn of that handle, we fuel a blind monster of hope, which has no promise, and we crank out of fear, and we've chosen to believe the lies of others who tell us only what we want to hear, when we know that no promise can be truly made. We feed the machine, we keep it alive all the while it is destined to destroy us, simply because we're desperate and the loudest voice has told us what to do and where and how to attain our deliverance."

Jess nodded to Königin to go on.

"We must actively pursue freedom, but we need to accept that the Collaborative exists to exploit us for its own gain. But we're to blame – the Collaborative will get away with as much as we will let it get away with. We give the Collaborative its power over us through the co-dependent relationship between us and it. It offers us everything and we've taken everything we've been offered – and then we've demanded more and then we've borrowed and stolen to pay for what we think we must have. And because of that addiction we've allowed ourselves to be controlled and taken advantage of. We've allowed this to happen through lies – first, by lying to ourselves. We tell ourselves whatever fiction we need to hear so we don't have to admit that we're being managed by the constituent members of the Collaborative, each lording in their own way, and collectively. Facing that reality may be too scary for all of us, and if we admit that reality, we'll realize that much of this society that we've built is nothing but a house of cards standing on a foundation of illusion. The Collaborative's lies make up that illusion – and our refusal to see that truth allows that illusion to survive."

Königin slowly took a deep breath and shifted in her seat.

"But I'm not saying that we should blow it all up – rather, I'm saying that we first need to be honest about the arrangement with the Collaborative that we have allowed and contributed to – and then, once we face that, we can make conscious decisions about how we want to live and what we want our world to look like. That needs to be a mindful decision, a deliberate decision – not a choice made for us by those who would manipulate us and set us on a cradle-to-grave path that fulfills their economic objectives and their need for power. And we need to see past those issues that purportedly divide us – many of which are nothing more than smoke bombs set-off by the Collaborative's instruments of propaganda. We need to look through the smoke to see how the Collaborative is running our lives in every way. Once we do that, once we accept that truth, we can make decisions about who we give power to and how much power and how *we're* going to control the members of the Collaborative."

"Why isn't she dead yet?" Corliss shouted into the camera. "She's the enemy! The enemy of the Collaborative! The enemy of the government! She must be silenced!"

"Hah," Königin shouted. "Along with *The Trustee*, the other instruments of the Collaborative are our government and every other government working with the Collaborative. Paid-for governments. They don't work for us, they work for the Collaborative. If we survive today, that will be the next battle – do you hear me? Power must reside in us as individuals, then our households, then our neighborhoods, then our cities, then our states, and then, lastly, in our central governments. We should only abdicate our authority and power to each of those entities very sparingly, and no more than absolutely necessary, and when we are failed by any one of them, we must revoke that authority and call the wrong-doers to task in plain sight, because delegating authority always means the potential for abuse of that authority and the trust that is conjoined with it. And if we continue to allow that trust to be broken by the acts of those that act in their own best self-interest when they have taken an oath to work for others, then we have no one to blame but ourselves."

Königin paused, took a deep breath and slowly exhaled. "I have a confession to make – I inadvertently took the first step in purging the wrongdoers from my government. I killed Representative Kaye. It was in physical defense of my father, but Kaye deserved to die for his treasonous crimes of selling-out the American people for the benefit of the Collaborative."

Jess stared at Königin, his eyes wide.

"The National Debt Contribution Act, clearance certificates, the Collaborative Caucus – they're all just devices to exploit and control us for their sponsors' benefit – they deprive us of our freedoms for that very purpose. We cannot allow this scheme to continue."

Then Königin sat back in her chair. "What of Tad Corliss?" she asked. "What offenses has he committed?"

"What about your father's offenses?" Jess uncontrollably blurted out, his words echoing through the cranks.

Without hesitating and without turning from the microphone to face Jess, Königin said, "He's committed many – yes, my father bears a lot of responsibility for what has transpired, but he's no longer an active threat like Tad Corliss is. The man on your television screens imploring you to turn those cranks participated in the mortgaging of our futures and he willingly placed us all in further servitude to the Collaborative so he could build the machine that you're feeding right now."

"I'm the victim here," Corliss shouted. "Wrongly accused, when all I'm trying to do is help. I'm the one doing good here. I'm the one who cares about people, not Königin Clairet. She's selfish. I'm telling you, I know what's best for you. Cranking. That's your solution. The ĒMAD is the answer."

In a calm, steady voice, Königin said, "Otto Veltraria is dead. He died trying to stop the ĒMAD just minutes ago. In his last moments he found the strength to be honest with himself, and his last act was to try to help all of us – by stopping the ĒMAD. Please, face reality and end this mad one-way journey to nothingness. When you decide not to crank, you decide to starve the lie – starve it, and let's join together to reclaim control of our destinies from those who use us in every way and who decide how we will live. Let's stop participating in this relationship with the Collaborative that gives it it's power."

Jess nodded and smiled at Königin. She leaned in closer to the microphone. "But here's the challenge – it's up to us to dismantle the Collaborative without destroying the economic engines that allow and promote freedom and which give the people of this world the best chance to live a good life. And we don't need the members of the Collaborative to pay our way, nor should we want them to, but they need to stop being so damn greedy and controlling – and we need to stop letting them get away with that. As we've seen, we can't look to the governments of this world to help – they're part of the problem itself – and when they do pretend to help, they end up squelching and stifling economic liberties that foster self-determination, and they pick winners and losers through a system of corruption and cronyism – always to our detriment. Know this, we the people must remedy these problems through the decisions that we make about how we live."

After a moment, the red lights on the power column finally stopped climbing. They held steady just a few inches from the top.

"I admit, my credentials to lecture and preach are thin, but I speak from the experience of my own flaws and sins. People died during my second water launch because I allowed myself to be carried along on a current that I really didn't try hard enough to navigate. And it's not enough that my intentions were good – I was weak and unprincipled – and worst of all, I was undisciplined. I see now that throughout my life I have allowed myself to be taken advantage of and used and lied to – but it's no one's fault but mine – because I allowed that. Together, let's stop allowing that. Tad Corliss is lying about the ĒMAD being our savior."

"Her words are lies, not mine," Corliss shouted into the camera, furiously cranking. "She's illegitimate – a fake. She conspired with her father and Otto Veltraria to enslave you all. To kill you all. To subjugate your children. To eat your children! Keep cranking!"

Königin laughed and said, "The more desperate they are, the more outrageous their lies become."

Jess began to flip through the thousands of surveillance camera video feeds coming in from around the world. He stopped at a feed coming in from a camera affixed to a lamppost at Lexington Avenue and 72nd Street in New York City. What drew his attention to that video image was the movement of people starting to stream out of buildings. There was no sound, but Jess and Königin could see that the people were all waving something above their heads with one hand. Königin leaned into the screen to look closer – it was their cranks.

Jess looked at Königin and smiled.

Then, as Jess flipped to other feeds one after another, he and Königin watched people filing out of their homes and their offices in the thousands in Tokyo, London, Cairo, Madrid – everywhere, waiving their unplugged cranks around. She could see that they were chanting something, but she didn't know what.

Königin leaned back and turned to Jess, expecting to see him still smiling. But he wasn't.

"What? What's wrong?" Königin asked. Jess's eyes were fixed on the video image of the power column – the lights weren't dropping.

Jess turned the microphone off and said, "I don't get it, Königin. Why isn't the ĒMAD losing power? The people aren't cranking. At least not enough of them to keep the power up."

Königin slowly shook her head and said. "It must have reached some kind of self-sustaining momentum. I think we're too late."

The two sat in silence for a moment.

Königin took Jess's hand in hers and said, "I don't know what we've accomplished here, Jess. The ĒMAD is still alive."

"It's not about the ĒMAD, Königin. It's about the people powering the machine. Because of your words and your leadership, they're not powering it, not feeding it. Look at them," Jess said.

The video feeds showed millions of people flooding into the streets of every city, waving their cranks.

"No matter what happens, you've freed them. You've helped them face the truth," Jess said.

The thudding of a lone set of boots approaching the open door of the penthouse forced Königin to her feet. Just as she tried to slam the door shut, a black boot jammed the door open five inches.

"Königin, it's me, Lansing. Let me in."

"I'll kill you, Lansing. Or at least I'll try," she shouted as she rammed Fight down on his boot.

"Ah!" he yelled in pain. "Königin, I'm not here to get you," Lansing pleaded. "Something's happening. Corliss's technicians are all deserting. The control room's almost empty. That damned machine is working by itself."

Königin let the door open.

"My dad is down there, Lansing. I've got to save him."

"He'll be all right," Lansing replied. "We found him in the closet – my people already moved him offsite."

Königin then looked at the screen showing the ĒMAD control room. "What are they doing?" she shouted.

Leaning into the screen, Lansing said, "It looks like Corliss's security detail is trying to operate the machine."

Corliss was now in the center of the control room, next to the power column, yelling orders.

The red lights started to slowly climb again.

"No, No!" Königin shouted.

Lansing put his hand to his radio earpiece and said, "Go for Lansing." Listening, he nodded his head a couple of times to himself, and then said to the person on the other end of the radio, "Let them burn."

"Let what burn?" Königin asked.

"*The Trustee*'s printing plants," Lansing answered. "The people are setting fire to them in every city."

Jess took Königin's hand and kissed the top of it.

The three watched as the acquiring chamber began to slowly darken. The top of the power column was nearly lit up.

79

David walked carefully across the narrow dam. His arms shook with exhaustion from carrying the suitcase. He just needed to get to the other side of the dam and make it down the long staircase to the plant below.

With only one shoe, the other one having been surrendered to the thrashing water far below him, he shuffled along as quickly as he could. His blue and black necktie was now tied around his waist and looped through the handle of the suitcase, just in case he dropped it.

Just another couple of hundred feet and he'd be at the top of the staircase. David shivered – he had never felt so wet or tired. He kept his head down and kept moving, trying to ignore the pain and exhaustion that tried to slow him.

The thought of his sister and father crept into David's mind. He stopped abruptly, now frozen on the top of the dam. "Maybe they're both gone, maybe they've deserted the project, maybe they're a thousand miles away," David thought to himself. Then, out loud, David shouted, "Maybe they've opened their eyes to how mad and evil the whole wretched endeavor is and they've run far, far away."

Suddenly, he had the fleeting sensation of a bug buzzing past his ear at a great speed. A pop of wind followed instantly by a single "bang" tickled his sideburn. David looked up.

From the top of one of the ĒMAD's towers constructed next to the plant on the other side of the dam, the muzzle of a rifle barrel pointed at him.

"Oh, shit," David said in a calm voice. He put his head down and quickly resumed his shuffle toward the staircase. "I'm just trying to help the world here," David said quietly. "I don't know – maybe you idiots are better off in chains – it's all you know."

Another decisive pop hissed through the air. The feeling of a screwdriver being driven into his shoulder called David to see his blood pushing its way up through his pierced suit jacket. He felt himself falling, but in his stumble, he was able to direct his fall into the lake next to him rather than off the precipice of the dam face.

David was in the water. And then, almost instantly, he was under the water. The suitcase pulled him down quickly.

As he and his companion sank, David frantically felt around for the suitcase's zipper, only wanting to find the detonator.

David did not use his last seconds of breath to untether himself from what he believed was the mechanism of emancipation.

⚬═⟶⋄ 80 ⋄⟶═⚬

A sudden rumble shook the plant like an underground thunderbolt smacking the building's foundation. The windows of the penthouse rattled.

Königin looked at Jess.

"Get me information, now!" Lansing yelled into his radio.

On the screens, Königin watched as Corliss's people operated the ĒMAD. The red lights were now only half an inch from the top of the power column.

Jess started to laugh. He pointed out the window at the towering dam in front of them.

Königin looked up and quietly said, "Oh no."

A crack appeared in the middle of the dam face – and then the crack quickly shot up to the top of the dam, sending concrete flying upward into the air. Water spewed from the new opening at the top of the dam down onto the plant below.

Königin pulled the microphone close to her mouth and calmly said, "Ignore all of the noise they holler at us, let's think for ourselves, and let's deny them their control over us – it's the only way."

The top of the power column lit up. The Silence came.

The acquiring chamber darkened into a solid black mass. But after a moment, the blackness in the chamber grew, and the glass walls of the chamber were absorbed into the darkness. The opaque void slowly expanded in all directions from where the acquiring chamber had been.

They watched as Corliss's face contorted with terror.

Corliss's people ran, pushing each other, stepping on one another to get out of the control area, away from the growing hole that opened to somewhere unknown. The ĒMAD could not be controlled.

"Run," Königin shouted at the screen that now showed Corliss standing frozen – but her voice was silent.

Königin felt Jess take her right hand, he was shaking. She squeezed his hand tightly.

Then Lansing took her other hand. His grip was firm, and she interlocked her fingers with his.

Looking up from the screens, the three watched the dam shatter. The concrete dam face holding back Old Hickory Lake crumbled into chunks. Unleashed, a wall of water leapt forward toward them. All without a sound.

Königin looked down at the screens and saw the water burst through the brick walls of the turbine room far below them. The whole building vibrated, and then the screens went dark.

"Even though I walk through the valley of the shadow of death, I fear no evil, for you are with me," came out of Jess's mouth, loud and out of tune.

Startled by the sound of his own voice, Jess shut up.

Now the building shook so hard that Königin could feel the whole structure starting to move.

"So we're not going to be swallowed into another dimension, but we *are* going to be swallowed up by that lake," Jess shouted.

"No, we're not, Jess," Königin shouted back. She opened the door to the broadcast room, but the building's roof was gone. Every part of the plant beneath them was underwater and now the water level reached the floor of the little penthouse.

The sound of cracking wood competed with the sharp explosion of each window in the broadcast room as the water squeezed and pulled the walls and floor. Water shot up from the spaces opened between the floorboards, and then the little room was twisted and lifted onto the water like a boat leaving dry-dock for its maiden voyage.

Their quickly disintegrating vessel bumped up against the plant's flagpole that still reached into the sky, attached to the steel frame of the building.

"Come on," Lansing shouted as he reached for Königin's hand.

"*What?*" Königin shouted back, holding tightly onto Jess's hand.

Lansing wrapped his legs and one arm around the flagpole and reached for Königin again.

"Get on, both of you," Lansing yelled over the crushing sound of rushing water. "Hold on to the pole as tight as you can. It's secure. It's our best chance."

But instead of taking Lansing's hand, Königin swung Fight to split the wooden door of the penthouse longways in two. She shook her head. "No, the torrent is too powerful to fight – we'll have to ride it. Come with us," Königin yelled.

"No, Königin, you don't have a chance," Lansing shouted back to her, now hugging the pole with both arms and legs.

With Jess's arms wrapped tightly around Königin's waist from behind, the two straddled the doubled-up pieces of the door as if they were riding a galloping horse.

"We're going to do it our way, Jess!"

Then the water turned them around and around, but Königin wrested control and faced them downstream, moving with the current.

Under and in front of Königin a new river rushed, and she navigated it with all of her strength.

81

Three rifles pointed to the sky and fired together. And again. And then again.

The late day sun cast a dark blue hue on the casket.

Representative Jerez stood and cleared his throat. "I'm not sure where we go from here," he said to the gathered. "But I do know that we need to move forward, instead of backward."

Königin sat in the second row of fold-up chairs arranged next to the gravesite. She looked across the rolling hills of Arlington Cemetery and gazed upon the thousands of grave markers.

Jerez spoke about having known Lansing for many years and being absolutely certain that he was a good man. But then he hesitated.

After a few moments, Jerez said, "I'm not sure how history will judge Admiral Lansing. Was it his fault that by executing his duties he was actively involved in the building of that machine? I simply don't have the answer to that question. But I can tell you that he did what he did because he was following orders, and he thought that he was serving the people and working in their best interest." Then he shook his head and slowly added, "But you know what, sometimes that's just not enough to let a man off the hook – in fact, it never is."

Others took turns speaking kindly of Lansing, some of them recounting his bravery when he rescued the world's leaders under the Potomac River.

Once the ceremony was over, Königin approached Jerez. She extended Fight to him. "Please return this to the House of Representatives – return it to the people."

"I beg your pardon?" Jerez said as he eyed the battered thing without touching it.

"You don't recognize this?" she asked.

Jerez remained silent as he took Fight from Königin's hand. He held it closely as he studied it.

After a moment, he said, "Thank you, Ms. Clairet. With the Governing Committee thrown out now that the ĒMAD insanity is over, the mace will retake its place in the House Chamber."

Königin nodded and said, "The eagle was already missing when it came into my possession. But I'm sorry for the couple of dents I put in the globe."

"I'm sure they were well worth it," Jerez said with just a hint of a smile. Then he added, "I heard you on the crank, and I know you don't think much of what we do here in Washington, but there are those of us that are good public servants. Me and my 215 colleagues will return to Congress to serve the people – each of us taking an oath to reject the influences of the Collaborative, in any form."

"I'm grateful for people like you, Mr. Jerez. You're singularly minded and unconflicted about who and what matters to you – and everything you do is consistent with your conviction. I'm starting to understand that being that way makes life much simpler – to know, in every circumstance, how you feel about something based on what your values and priorities in life are. I think I'm finally knowing what those are for me, and how to be true to them, and it's inspiring to see a leader exemplify that principle. Thank you, Mr. Jerez."

"*You* are that leader, Ms. Clairet," Jerez said. "The people need you. Please, fulfill your destiny. And don't ever let people like Tad Corliss get in your way."

Königin froze at the mention of Corliss. She looked over her shoulder.

"I'm sorry," Jerez said. "I shouldn't even say that name. I'm sorry if I've upset you."

"No, it's fine – it's just unsettling that they haven't found his body yet – or his thug Malcolm's," Königin said. "I'm actually more worried about my dad's safety than my own."

Before Jerez could respond, Jess quickly approached Königin with a man – a man whose face was known to many.

"Königin, meet Lee Earlman," Jess said as Lee gently smiled and surveyed her from top to bottom.

Jerez hugged Königin and then excused himself. She watched as Fight left with him.

"It's wonderful to finally meet you, Königin," Lee said. "You're like your mom – the full package. Wise and kind and beautiful."

She smiled and said, "Jess told me that you dated her before she met my dad."

"So it wasn't exactly like that," Lee said. "We were kindred hearts – it wasn't dating. We saw the world the same way, but I wasn't ready to walk away from it all. But she was. And then she – she found herself needing some stability in her life, and then, you know, married *him*. It all happened so fast."

Königin looked at Jess and then back at Lee.

"She was heavenly," Lee said. "But you already know that." And then, looking past Königin into nothingness, he added, "I loved her – and I still do."

"Me too," Königin said without hesitating.

Then she stood silent for a few moments, looking at Lee. His presence seemed familiar to her, but she had never met him.

"Did you know Admiral Lansing?" Königin asked Lee.

"No."

"Then why did you come today?" she asked.

"To meet you."

Königin didn't immediately respond. She felt a sense of confusion beginning to overtake her. "Oh, thanks – I guess," she said.

"Are you okay?" Jess asked her.

"Yeah, yeah – I'm fine. It's just all been a lot," she said, looking around. "I think I need some alone time." As Königin began to walk away, she turned slightly to Lee, and without looking at him, quietly said, "It was good to meet you." Lee and Jess remained silent as they watched her walk deep into the cemetery among the thousands of grave markers. When she was out of sight, Jess shrugged at Lee.

Königin walked with no destination in mind. In the dim light of the setting sun, she wandered.

In a shadowy tree-filled area, Königin came upon a monument to the victims of a jetliner bombing that had sent a quake through the nation many years earlier. She gently touched the coarse red stone of the memorial. Playing the catastrophic event out in her mind, Königin thought of the innocent families whose lives were changed forever – or destroyed altogether. A feeling of anger welled up inside of her.

Out of the near darkness, and the quiet of the cemetery, a calm voice said, "Ms. Clairet."

Shocked, Königin quickly turned around to find a man standing only a few feet from her.

"I apologize for startling you," he said. "That was not my intention." His bright eyes contrasted with his black windbreaker.

"Who are you?" she asked.

"They call me *Tyburn*. I used to work with your brother," he said.

"You worked with David on the comedy circuit? Have you seen him? Do you know if he's okay?" she asked, nearly crying.

He shook his head and said, "You can be sure that no one thinks I'm funny."

"Okay, whatever – where is he?" she asked quickly.

"I'm pretty sure he's dead, Ms. Clairet. He blew the dam up – and himself with it. I would have heard from him if he'd made it."

Königin's mouth dropped opened. "What? What are you talking about? Why would you say such things? You're lying to me. You must have been sent by the Collaborative."

Tyburn laughed and said, "The Collaborative? No, try *Inevitable*."

"Inevitable? What's inevitable?" Königin asked.

"Are you asking why David named his group Inevitable? Or are you asking what is inevitable?"

Königin stood silent for a moment, putting the pieces together in her mind – admitting things to herself that she didn't want to admit. "I know what Inevitable is," she said. "And I know what it's done."

"Listen to me, I can't stick around here long," he said, looking about. "Bottom line is that you need to join us."

"Join *you?*" Königin asked.

"Yes – you need to join Inevitable."

Königin shook her head. "No. I want no part of what you people are doing."

"Don't be difficult, Ms. Clairet. We have the same foes."

"That may be true, but I want only to help the people – you want to destroy society in total."

"The only way to save the people is to destroy society and start over," Tyburn said.

"You say you want to save the people, but in the process you're willing to hurt people?"

"The world is full of paradoxes, isn't it, Ms. Clairet?"

She shook her head. "You and your group – and apparently David – act under the guise of purported goodness and concern for the people, but really you're just a bunch of angry, miserable people that want to destroy humanity. You can't figure out how to live life, so instead you choose to destroy everyone and everything. Your actions and tactics expose what's truly in your bitter hearts. You have no love for people – only hatred."

Tyburn looked around and said, "While I'd like to continue this spirited philosophical chat, I don't have the time – I need an answer from you. But keep in mind, you have no choice."

"No, I'll never join your group."

"That's the wrong answer," Tyburn said. "You're all about making choices, Ms. Clairet, aren't you? You want to be the master of your destiny, right? Well, this choice is a simple one – you either join Inevitable, or you die right now." Then he started to slowly circle her.

Königin looked around at the empty cemetery around her. "I don't understand, why do you need me in your group?"

"We really don't need you," Tyburn said, laughing a little.

"Then why make me join?" Königin asked, now moving in Tyburn's circular path – her eyes locked on him.

"Look at this as a favor that I and the other members of the group are willing to do for David. Rather than kill his sister, we'll let her join us."

Königin shook her head and shouted, "But why would you need to kill me?"

Tyburn smiled and said, "Let's face it, your voice is going to be way too loud and powerful, Ms. Clairet. It already is. We don't need you drowning out our message or interfering in our endeavors." Then Tyburn stopped moving and looked up at the dark sky and added, "And besides, if you think you'll be able to take down the Collaborative by helping to empower the people, you're wrong." He looked Königin in the face. "The Collaborative is more powerful than ever – in spite of you exposing what it really is. The members of the Collaborative will now just be that much more ruthless – they no longer have anything to conceal."

Königin now stood still and just stared at Tyburn. She said nothing.

Keeping his eyes fixed on her, he reached into the pocket of his jacket and retrieved a short piece of narrow rope. "I'm not doing this to hurt you or punish you – but Inevitable must accomplish its goals at all costs, no matter who gets hurt. Look at your brother, he made the sacrifice. But I'm giving you a choice – a chance to live."

"You and your group claim that you want to free the people from tyranny, but you're willing to suppress my freedom to save everyone else's freedom? You're willing to deprive me of life itself to purportedly save and preserve the lives of others?"

"If that's what it takes, Ms. Clairet."

She stood up straight and said nothing.

"I need your answer – now," he said.

Königin forced a smile and said, "You're a liar who believes his own lies. I'd rather die than betray myself. There's your answer."

Tyburn shook his head. "I'm sorry to hear that." Then, with the rope down at his side, he approached Königin. She didn't move.

Suddenly, he stretched the rope in front of his face and lunged at her. But in a single fluid movement, she dodged him and smashed his face into the stone memorial. He yelled in pain as blood trickled out of his mouth. His eyes were alight with anger and his contorted lips exposed broken teeth. The two slowly moved in a circle again, staring at each other. Then Tyburn advanced fast, holding the two ends of the stretched rope at Königin's neck level. She quickly stuck her left forearm up in front of her, blocking the rope. Then, without hesitating, she drove the heel of her palm up and into his nose with all of her might. He went down immediately, writhing on the ground as he wailed.

Königin stood over him and put her boot on his neck. With her heart pounding, she shouted into the night sky, "This is just the beginning of my fight – not the end!"

Made in the USA
Coppell, TX
19 January 2021